Winds Of Freedom

The Adventures of Flint & Steel

J.P. McMahon

It is not death that a man should fear, but he should fear never beginning to live.
—Marcus Aurelius

Dedicated To:

Everyone who supported me through this process and through the years, you know who you are. A big thanks to my family, especially aunty. I miss you everyday. I wish you could read this. Thank you all for putting up with a writer's crazy.

Chapter
1

Franchesca gazed wistfully out of the coach's window as it rattled through the streets. Today was a day like any other as far as she was concerned, but her mother and father thought otherwise. They insisted that she have a new gown to wear for tomorrow's ball. Her father of course, invited many of his old military comrades; his partners in trade and vineyard owners to his estate in Cannet. Tomorrow was her seventeenth birthday and her parents decided now it was time for her, or more in fact time for them to find a suitable noble to marry. They of course wanted a youth whose father maintained a shining reputation beyond repute and reproach. A boy who had money to his name, a title and lands of his own that he would inherit—or that his noble parents could carve and set aside for him and his blushing bride. Franchesca only wished she could make the choice for herself. Inevitably, she knew what would happen. She would like a boy who her parents didn't approve of because they only wanted to ensure their darling received the very best. Her taste, her opinion was never good enough; never lived up to their expectations. She blinked as she gazed out the polished window pane. The few that stood within the city streets, trees swayed in the gentle breeze. Perhaps I am being selfish Franchesca thought to herself. I have never actually wanted for anything—and they have always looked out for me and done what was best. As this thought crossed her mind, she realized what it was she detested—and that was her parents dismissing the fact that she had a mind of her own—thoughts of her own and wants of her own. Would she always go wanting in that respect? She asked herself. The coach slowed to a stop and Franchesca felt her mother place a hand upon her knee.

"Franchesca darling, we are here." Her mother was a sweet woman, she knew that—or at least she tried to be. However, she also had questions for her mother—questions which always remained unanswered whenever she asked. One question Franchesca asked her only a few days earlier was if her mother was happy with her father. Franchesca wondered did her mother ever have to make sacrifices? Did she go wanting? Did she have desires that she could never fulfill? Did her mother feel like she did? Did she feel like she was used as a pawn, or a piece in games played by her family? Franchesca remembered when she had asked. Her mothers scowl told her she should not ask such questions again; that it was none of her business, and what would she know of such things. We all have our stations in life; she remembered both of her parents saying. We all have our duties, and our responsibilities. The more Franchesca thought about it the more she realized she knew nothing about her parents—nothing that made them feel like people to her. She had grown up hearing of duty; responsibility, money, reputation—but she never heard her father speak of love. She never heard her mother lament to her when her husband went on campaign back in his military days. Franchesca sighed as her door was opened. Standing next to the conveyance ready to give her a helping hand down was the only real friend she had. The man her father hired to watch over her shortly after her birth, Claude. He smiled at her as she placed her soft, smooth hand in his rough and calloused one. Franchesca watched him smile at her; his blonde hair combed neatly lying flat upon his head. Her guardian wore a pistol and a rapier upon his belt, and carried a few scars that showed he was well acquainted with their more violent uses—as well as their ornamental.

"Watch your step Madame." He said as he bowed his head in a respectful fashion. His voice was raspy, but always gentle and full of jest when addressing her. She always imagined his voice was raspy, from a life of shouting orders—or perhaps just a life of shouting in the military. There had been many times when Franchesca had gone to the stables to seek his company. The two joked and laughed together. Claude listened to her when she spoke her frustrations to him. He never judged, and never spoke to her parents about what they spoke of. Yes—Claude was her only friend and confidant in her cloistered sheltered life. He knew she was a girl, of flesh and blood—not some porcelain doll to be out on display and bid upon by suitors as her parents thought. To Claude she was just a person. However, she didn't know what her place was with regard to her parents.

"Thank you Claude." She said returning the smile in kind. Her mother nodded wordlessly as she stepped out and stood behind her daughter. Claude turned back towards the other man on the driver's seat and nodded, making sure that he would stay with the horses until their return. Claude walked the two women to the door of the shop and pushed it open. He stepped in and stood aside, allowing them to enter unobstructed.

"Monsieur Avidno—we have arrived to pick up the gown." Franchesca's mother called out as she entered the shop. True to form her mother and father had gone to great lengths to find the best dressmaker that money could buy. A wiry–looking man with a hooked nose stepped out of a back room and smiled. There was something unnatural about his smile—like a hunter admiring a pelt, or an animal caught in a trap; Franchesca thought to herself. She suppressed a shiver when his eyes passed over her in a coldly apprising manor; as if quickly trying to recall her face, or perhaps her measurements. The later brought a very real feeling of nausea to her already clenched stomach. Unlike other dressmakers who for the sake of modesty, or propriety hired women to take measurements of their female clients—Monsieur Avidno took the measurements of every client himself. He'd taken her measurements himself. He was gifted enough in his craft that most nobles accepted this eccentricity without much protest. Indeed many relished the idea of showing off for him— Franchesca had not. Remembering the nearness of his face and the knotted measuring ropes he used while his critical eye studied her exposed flesh, made her hackles rise. Avidno remained detached—which was a blessing ten times tenfold. Franchesca didn't know how she would feel if he made a remark about her body, or her skin. No doubt as he was taking her measurements and studying her he was already assembling the materials he thought would best complement her figure, complexion and occasion. Today she was going to see if her standing before him in her underclothes was worth it.

"Ah the de Maret family, come at last to receive their wondrous creation." Avidno exclaimed overly dramatically. It's only a dress Franchesca thought to herself. She cast a quick glance over at Claude and noticed him smile. She knew him well enough to detect the sarcasm in the expression. She stifled a laugh as Avidno held up his hand and promised to be right back. Her parents noticed that the man was eccentric; most dressmakers would travel from their shops for a customer as important as her family but not Avidno. The man insisted that they come to his shop retrieve the finished product in person. Franchesca was convinced that if her mother and father hadn't heard of his renown from a multitude of noble lords, and had not heard word that the likes of the royal family sought his services; they would have overlooked the man as a lunatic not worth their time or coin. The dressmaker reappeared a moment later with a long gown made of silk and rich velvets.

"The gold thread for the filigree accenting the garment, comes from the Elvin kingdoms." She listened as he pointed a long spidery finger out noting the pearls which were stitched in a long string stretching from hip to hip. Avidno said they'd come from Dea, as did the delicate silks which made up the bulk of the garment. When her mother asked why he'd not used silk from Chuhuay—a nation famed for its silk, Avidno simply smirked. He explained that he had a supplier in Dea who provided a product of the same quality— indeed better in most cases because it could be offered in more colors, at a fraction of the cost. It was a show of extravagance to be sure, but it was done tastefully. No sooner did Martise de Maret cast eyes upon the gown that she ordered Franchesca to strip off her clothes and try the dress on and stand atop the fitters stool.

Avidno surrounded her with screens to block out prying eyes and to give her some semblance of privacy. The girl sighed to herself as she began stripping off her gown and slid herself into her new luxurious outfit. Now I really am like a doll she thought to herself feeling the sadness stir at the thought. After a few minutes of looking her daughter over and inspecting the dressmakers work— Martise praised, and paid the eccentric dressmaker—inviting him to ball to be held in her daughters honor the next day. Claude held the door open as they left. In Martise's hurry to leave she did not notice the girl walking down the street. She bumped into the passing waif.

"Please miss..." Franchesca's mother stopped speaking when she noticed the girl she'd bumped into was clad in plain clothes and more than a little disheveled. Franchesca's heart sank as she witnessed her mother's cold-hearted rudeness. Without further word her mother stepped into the coach. Evidently seeing the state of the girl, decided her station didn't deserve so much as words spoken by a high and noble lady.

"Apologies, Milady." The girl said sourly. Biting back curses which she surely must wish to lash out with. Franchesca stepped forward and held out a hand offering to help the waif up. She could tell by the red head's accent that she was from Lassin a small town which straddled the border of Eland and Forn. The town's location helped to give its inhabitants a peculiar and distinctive accent.

"I... I am sorry about my mother. Between you and me she is oblivious to—well, most things in this world." Franchesca whispered.

"Please allow me to make it up to you." She said as she turned towards Claude and asked for her coin pouch. She pulled out a few gold coins and held them in her open palm.

"Na, it's alright. Never 'ad anyun apalgize ta me bafore." The girl replied. "Basides—what would a gutterfoot like me do wit' shiny gold coins like dat?" She felt a stab of guilty pain, hearing the girl describe herself in the slur men and women of the upper echelons used to label beggars and the downtrodden. Franchesca reached out and took the other girl's hand gently in hers and pressed the coins into her palm before closing the girl's fingers around them.

"That's for you to decide." She smiled, as their eyes met for a moment. Franchesca gazed at her pleasantly.

"Ta... tanks miss." The girl replied with a slight bow of the head.

"Franchesca, would you leave that urchin to her wanderings; and get in the coach. We'll be late for lunch." Her mother shouted from the coach. Franchesca sighed and frowned.

"I am sorry. I hope those coins find you well." Franchesca replied as she entered the cabin to claim her seat next to her mother.

"Don't mind the misses, she just..." Claude began, as he started reaching into his own purse.

"Need's a good smackin." The girl finished quietly. Claude couldn't help but stifle a laugh. "What's 'er name anyay?"

"That is Madame Martise de Maret, and lady Franchesca." He told her as he pulled a few coins from his own purse out and passed them forward.

"An' 'yer name?" The poor girl asked. Claude bowed his head politely.

"Claude Baume. Chances are you'll see me around these parts quite a bit—don't worry though. Lady Franchesca has learned more from me than her mother." He whispered to the girl with a chuckle.

"My name is Simone—would 'ya tell 'er dat?" She asked as she tucked a stray lock of ruby hair behind her ear. Claude nodded, as he ran his own fingers through his swept-back blonde hair. He handed her a silver coin from his own leather pouch and climbed up into the coach's seat.

"I will see you around Simone." He told her. There was a crack of a drivers whip and the coach lurched into motion. Simone turned and walked away as she listened to it rattle down the cobbled streets. She gazed down at the coins and smiled before putting them into her pocket.

* * *

Franchesca stood with her back to the full-length mirror in her room; scarcely able to recognize herself. Her mother and her maids spent near the entirety of the day primping her in one manner or another. Now that it was done she did not wish to look at herself. It just wasn't her—not that anyone cared. Her long wavy raven hair was resting below her shoulders and put up into an elegant style which made her feel utterly uncomfortable, and was beginning to give her a headache. The maids said it accentuated her delicate oval face, and her soft delicately rounded noble features. Her mother came into her chamber and brushed her cheeks with rouge, and after the hours of primping and fussing she deemed her ready to make her entrance and present herself to the guests and suitor's that had gathered for the ball. She hated make–up, the powders, the rouges; the glossy colored lip wax—she hated it all. It just didn't feel like her. Just like a prized possession to be auctioned off, she thought to herself as she looked at her reflection after they'd finished. Not for the first time she thought of tearing all the hairpins keeping her locks in place and smearing the applied make up. She sighed and waited for her father to come in to tell her when to descend the staircase and meet those who gathered to see her. There was a knock at her chamber door; before she the chance to call out an answer, her father entered the room.

"You look radiant my daughter." Renaud de Maret aquiline features held a genuine smile as he studied her." Are you ready to meet your guests my lovely?" Franchesca allowed a fake smile to cross her face.

"Yes as I will ever be." She answered. She didn't want to in the first place—not like this. Introduce me as a facade—a woman wearing a mask. I'm sure they will be throwing themselves at me, she thought.

"I know it is scary, finding a suitor is always a time of nerves. You know that you can speak to your mother and me if you need advice on the smartest match." If only I could speak to you and have you understand Franchesca thought. She allowed her forced well–practiced smile to linger a moment longer, and nodded.

"Would you do me the honor of allowing me to escort you down the steps my dear?" Franchesca held her arm out to her father. "I love you my little one. You alone are the most precious thing to me." Franchesca smiled. She knew that her father loved her, and she knew she was the most precious thing to him—but in this moment she questioned why. Was she something he could use to expand his wealth—or gain a strong military ally? Perhaps a greater claim to the throne of Forn? Musicians announced that the guest's attention should be directed to the grand central staircase. Strings, horns; and woodwinds began their melodious choir as Franchesca stood upon the landing locked arm and arm with her father. Down below she spotted a crowd of primped and pressed nobles. A zoo of skinned animal shawls and scarves and luxurious fabrics in all colors and shades awaited her. A loud booming voice called out.

"I announce; the lady Franchesca de Maret—daughter of Archduke Renaud de Maret—and Archduchess Martise de Maret." Franchesca could hear the crowd murmuring down below. There were comments on everything, from praising her youthful beauty to the elegance of her dress. She saw the luxurious garments maker Avidno with a glass of wine in his spindly spider-like fingers—his thin mustache waxed to a tight curl. Claude stood waiting at the bottom of the stairs, standing ramrod straight. He managed to lock eyes with her and winked. Franchesca knew that if anyone in the room knew how she felt it was him. Upon reaching the bottom step, Franchesca bowed and curtsied. She stood before them the very picture of a proper lady in waiting. What none suspected was that she was more than happy to keep waiting.

"Welcome, one and all. Please let the celebration continue." She announced—forcing as much sweetness into her tone as she could until she could hardly stand the sound of her own voice. The crowd clapped seemingly all at once. It was like a roar of thunder upon the seas and echoed by the marble of the room to an almost deafening level.

"I look forward to meeting you all." She lied happily giving a polite bow of her head and a formal noblewoman's curtsy. The celebration continued as she stood upon the last stair. One by one a smiling Lordling came before her, bowed graciously and announced himself. So many had come to speak to her that extending her hand was becoming almost a reflex and somewhere around the hundredth kiss placed upon her hand—she could stand to remember any more names—lest something of actual important slip from her skull. She excused herself with all the elegance one could manage when their skin crawled and began walking through the crowds of conversing highborn lords and ladies. Sounds of haughty laughter and gossip pounded against her senses.

"Would you care for a walk in the garden my lady?" Franchesca was so relieved to hear Claude's scratchy voice she almost broke down into tears.

"Please, I fear that if I listen to any more of this pompous caterwauling that I will cease to have the will to live to see my next birthday." Claude chuckled as he allowed her to hook an arm with his.

The silver glow of the moon illuminated the garden with the softness of the caress of silk on skin. Claude walked her over to a stone bench to sit. All was still and silent for a moment allowing her mind to calm. A gentle breeze rustled the leaves and petals upon the fragrant flowers. Franchesca took a deep breath and glanced up at Claude.

"I think you are the only person who understands me in any way, Claude." She told him softly, almost melancholic. He let out a chuckle as he sank down and sat on the bench next to her. He placed his gloved hand upon the hilt of his rapier and adjusted it so he could sit comfortably.

"Well—I did help raise you." He admitted with a smile and a tone of pride and accomplishment in his voice.

"Better than they ever could." She replied as she rubbed her forehead.

"They are just trying to do what is best for you—"

"By the gods, if I had a coin for every time I have heard that I would be richer than my father." She replied sullenly. Claude chuckled, despite her anger. His laugh calmed her—like a fire pit doused with a bucket of water.

"Aye, I know my lady. You are tired of hearing it—and I know they don't act the part all the time, but they are trying." Claude assured her softly.

"You know—sometimes I think about running. I think about sneaking through the halls when everyone is asleep and running away from here— leaving it all behind. But then I ask myself where would I go? How would I survive? I realize then in that moment that I am theirs; they own me." She whispered as she looked up at him teary–eyed. Claude laid a hand on her shoulder and squeezed it to offer some semblance of assurance and comfort.

"They make sure I have the best tutors and the best lessons. They buy the fanciest clothes and jewelry for me—but they lock me away in this palace, without a chance to use any of it." Franchesca said sadly.

"There are worse places to be." Claude replied as he held her in his eyes. "I know you're tired of being locked in this place."

"And that I will go from one gilded cage to another. Once my parents decide on which marriage benefits them the most. After that, I'll be locked away in another little cage with another person telling me what to do and what they want. I'm not a selfish person Claude—I would just like someone to think of me at least once. Why does no one realize I have a mind of my own?" She asked turning to look at him with wide questioning eyes. Claude took in a deep breath.

"You're their child, and they want you to be one forever. All of us know it makes no sense—but that is the way of it. Sometimes things just don't make sense." Claude turned his gaze over at the looming house, seeing the candles flicker in the windows and guests laughing and reveling within.

"Have you had enough air?" He asked gently. She could have said no, and he would have sat with her out in the garden for hours and hours until her parents came looking for her. Franchesca took a shaky breath, savoring the scent of flowers and nodding as she rose from her seat.

"Thank you, Claude; you always listen to me. You always understand." Franchesca told him trying to smile. She tried—but the smile didn't truly manifest.

"You might be of high birth Miss Franchesca—but you have the desire that runs through everyone, from the highest noble to the lowest beggar. You're common minded." Franchesca stared at him with a look of befuddlement.

"You simply want to live your life. You realize money won't be there forever, that we won't be here forever. You don't place such value on possessions and trinkets of gold and silver. You don't believe having gems makes you wealthy—you believe having people who care about you makes you wealthy." He explained as he held out his arm for her to take. His comment about being common minded made her think of the girl she had seen in the streets yesterday. There was a comfortable pleasantness about her—a genuine quality. Not like these pompous, preening peacocks. The lot of them swaggered about the room as if they were the most important thing on two legs.

"I think you're the smartest person I know Claude." She smiled. He grinned back as they walked down the garden path back to the sprawling manor house.

"Ah, there you are my lovely—where did you disappear to?" Her father asked. As he walked over to her—a man of about his age stood behind him and next to him stood what Franchesca could only assume was the man's son.

"I am sorry father; I felt I needed a breath of fresh air, so I asked Claude to accompany me while I sat in the garden." She explained.

"Ah, I see. Franchesca I would like you to meet Lord Gimun Castaine and his son Marcel Castaien. Marcel has made arrangements to travel with the king of Eland on a pilgrimage. He will captain a regiment of soldiers to watch after his Lordship—in an effort to ease tensions between our two nations of course." So it begins again, Franchesca thought as she listened to her father. How she longed for this night to be over.

Chapter
2

Franchesca lay in her canopied bed and gazed up at the roof that hung above her. Her father had the canopy painted in a fashion of the night sky— with constellations picked out in gold and silver and inlaid with semi–precious stones. It was somehow a small freedom for her. She couldn't count the number of times she had laid in her bed and looked up—imagining herself drifting around visiting the stars. Tonight was no different. With a deep sigh, Franchesca closed her eyes and rolled over and waited for sleep to take her. She made a promise to herself that tomorrow she would find a way to experience some sort of freedom from this palace of imprisonment. Perhaps if she begged her father or her mother they would allow Claude to take her beyond the grounds of their estate. She would insist upon it and do all she could to have some level of freedom. Franchesca found herself reflecting upon the events of the night. The countless pompous, arrogant nobles and sons, she had the displeasure of meeting. Haughty conversations of military matters and politics thickened the air of the ballroom. She remembered seeing Claude making stupid faces every so often to amuse her—if only for a moment. It was times like that when she felt that Claude was more of a parent than her own. She didn't remember when sleep claimed her just that it did. When she opened her eyes the next morning, the sun was shining brightly through the window panes of her room. Much like every other morning one of the household servants knocked upon the door and came into her chamber to help her dress and style her hair. Doing as she had done many times before Franchesca told the servant that she would attend to herself, Franchesca didn't know why she bothered; they never listened to her—so, in the end, she always relented. Once dressed, she descended the staircase and made her way towards the dining room. Today, however, she found herself surprised when she pushed open the doors. The room was empty. Franchesca heard heavy boot thumps coming from the other end of the room. Claude pushed open the doors holding her breakfast on a polished silver tray.

"Good morning miss." He smiled as he placed the tray down gently on the table taking a single step back so as not to hover over her.

"What's going on? You haven't..." Franchesca drew her thumb across her delicate pale neck imitating cutting her throat. Claude burst out in laughter as she took up her seat at the table.

"No, child, they had urgent business that required their attention. They left an hour ago—said they wouldn't be back until tomorrow." Claude smirked. He watched as Franchesca's face split into a grin of the purest joy. "They left me to look after you until they return."

"Do you mean it?" Franchesca asked happily practically hanging off the edge of her seat. If she got any more good news, she might leap from the chair.

"As true as the sky is blue." He nodded. "After you have your lessons today, what say we go for a stroll in the city? Does that sound reasonable?" Franchesca threw herself at his chest and wrapped her arms around him, hugging him as tightly as she could. Claude chuckled as he returned her embrace and patted her shoulder.

"Come on now; your instructor will be along within the hour. You have some breakfast and ready yourself. I'll talk to the rest of the house and arrange the workings of the day." He told her as he stood upright, preparing himself to exit the room.

"Thank you, Claude, thank you." Claude winked and nodded.

"Happy birthday miss Franchesca." He told her softly as he left the room. She smiled as she watched him exit through the kitchen door. Her lessons were more tortuous today—they inched along at a painful crawl. It was because she truly could not wait until the lesson was over so for her trip with Claude into the city. She could walk the streets look in the shops, sit and speak with people if she so chose. It was like a dream come true. More than once when Claude was not around Franchesca actually did pinch herself to make doubly sure she was awake. If these damned lessons would just end, it would be the happiest single session of her life.

"Miss Franchesca." Her instructor scolded. "If you would be so kind— please pay attention." Franchesca smiled as she listened to the old badger drone on in his haughty tone of politics and political structures of foreign lands. He recounted how the civil war between Forn, created the nation of Eland—and helped to shape the political structure of their land today. Already today she had been made to recite the major deities of the elves, and several engineering practices invented by the Dwarves that they had shown to men. She felt her stomach tie in a knot of stifled irritation.

"You should pay attention miss Franchesca. After, all you are a distant cousin to the royal family—you might be called to service your land. It would do you well to know its customs and its laws—as well as its allies intimately." Franchesca scowled at the aging man—his head all but bald except for a patch atop his head and a semi–circle of hair that remained.

"It would do you well to remember that you, do indeed address a distant cousin of the royal family as well." She smiled being none too shy about showing her dangerous wit. The tutor went to reply but simply took a deep breath and sighed. Franchesca hated using her wealth, and flashing about the power her family held—but there were times she made exceptions.

"My apologies miss Franchesca." He bowed. "Now let us continue. We only have a few more topics to cover, and I will see you next week." She sighed heavily and nodded, as her torturous lesson continued.

* * *

As the carriage rattled along Franchesca's heart thundered in her chest. She couldn't believe it. She was in the city without her parents. Claude told her she could go with him where ever she desired to go. She didn't mind that he was there; he would not stifle her like her parents. If she spoke, he would not tell her to watch what she spoke of, or say such topics were indecent or unbecoming. More than once during the trip she found herself light headed with excitement. She was practically plastered up against the glass of the coach window. Her breath was fogging it only to fade, and get clouded by her breath once more. Claude chuckled as he watched from his seat. He cleared his throat.

"What did you think of the suitors that came to meet you last night if I might be so bold?" Claude asked as he sighed. Franchesca simply shrugged.

"Be honest." He smirked.

"I hated them." She replied scornfully. "I resent being treated like a farmer's prized pig to be traded to another farmer for his prized bull." She told him seriously clenching and unclenching her fists.

"They could not all be so terrible, surely?" Claude asked with a raised eyebrow. Franchesca shrugged, allowing a slight grin.

"There... was one boy who wasn't so terrible." She recalled a young noble family that was unlike any of the others. They were not of Fornish decent, in point of fact—they traveled from Castella. The boy's father was a soldier of renown and an explorer. However, the family was not a likely match for her—at least in the eyes of her parents. He was outside of Fornish blood, though noble it was unlikely he would rise far in the ranks of the aristocracy of her land. Despite all of this Franchesca found she felt most delighted when talking with him and his father. They joked and laughed, and he seemed even to appreciate her opinions and thoughts—as did his father. More than once Franchesca thought of them that night as she spoke to other preening nobles and their sons. She thought of saying she'd liked the Castellian just to anger her parents. Her father and mother would strongly disapprove since he and his father were both out of Fornish high society. An added bonus sweetening the thought of matching herself to him was that they would take her away to Castella, where she could be free of her parents.

"Well, there was a suitor by the name of Syandro De Madonia." Franchesca replied with the faintest bit of rose pink beginning to color her cheeks as she glanced at the floor.

"Ah—so there is one for you yet?" Claude asked. Franchesca smiled and sighed, keeping her gaze away from his own.

"Not likely. I doubt mother or father will approve. He is foreign, and has only the slimmest razors chance of rising in the Fornish social standings." She replied.

"But what did you think of the boy?" He asked her with a knowing look. She cheeks darkened to a deeper shade of red and shrugged.

"He was the kindest of them all, the only one I truly remember as anything other than a pretentious git. He seemed to care what I had to say—it felt like he respected my opinions. Truthfully—it even felt like his father valued my thoughts." She replied.

"I enjoyed that." Claude smirked as the carriage slowed to a stop.

"Ready?" He asked as he opened the door and exited the vehicle.

"I've been ready for years." She replied as she followed him out. Ever the gentlemen he helped her exit the coach. He nodded up at the driver who smiled down at them.

"I'll be waiting for you." He shouted with a salute, as he reclined slightly in his seat and tipped his cap down over his eyes.

"Well miss Franchesca where would you like to go?" The question made her positively giddy with joy, yet despite all her time longing for this moment, she found herself ill-prepared. She hesitated.

"I... I don't know." She replied, despite her not knowing an effervescent grin was ever present on her face stretching ear to ear. Claude's heart leaped seeing at seeing her joy, and he extended his arm. Franchesca laced her arm with his, and they began walking.

"I know just the place to start." He said as he began guiding her as they walked. After a few minutes of walking, Franchesca could smell something wonderful, and her mouth began to water—and felt her stomach growl. She saw a man ringing a bell standing next to a food cart. No—she studied the figure closer, not a man—a halfling. His type was a rare sight in Forn, and she could hardly keep herself from staring.

"Two if you please, sir." Claude said with a grin as he pulled out a few copper coins and passed them off to the halfling. The man pulled two pieces of pastry from a wooden box and laid them on top of a flat surface on his cart. He used a knife at his waist to cut them lengthwise—then using a two–pronged fork to retrieve two sausages from a makeshift grill he set up. He placed the sausage on the pastry and took a spoon and basted some mustard over top of the sausages before passing them to Claude and Franchesca.

"Thank you again, sir—and here is another for the trouble." Claude said as he gave another copper coin to the halfling. "And thank you for your generosity, kind sir." He smiled as he went back to ringing his bell, shouting his wares.

"I toast to your health and your happiness on your first outing." Claude smiled as he took a bite of his sausage. Franchesca beamed as she did the same. There was a slight audible snap as she bit into it. As the taste of it flowed through her mouth, Franchesca was shocked; it was the best thing she'd ever tasted. She chewed and swallowed quickly and took another bite.

"What is this delightful thing?" She asked as she took another bite hardly finishing what was in her mouth before taking her next mouthful.

"It's from The Empire of Austinea, its called Pikshaff." He told her as she finished the last of her sausage. "It's a sausage made from goose livers, and sheep tongues, as well as a few other organs of the two, stuffed into an intestinal casing." Franchesca stared up at him—her eyes filled with shock, and cheeks bulged with her more recent and unswallowed bite.

"Are you serious?" she asked mouth still full—crumbs of pastry falling from her lips as she spoke. Claude nodded as he took another bite.

"I... I wouldn't have expected something like that to be good in any form. Franchesca expected his revelation to spoil the taste; however, it remained as delicious as it had on her first bite. She'd heard of some things that were difficult to eat when you knew what they were made from.

"That's why I waited until after you finished to tell you what it was." He grinned. "Come on—I know of a few other places you would enjoy seeing." The city amazed her. The twists and turns through the dimly lit alleyways. Franchesca passed by brothels and taverns; she strode down streets that her mother and father would never have taken her down. She doubted that they even knew these places existed. As they walked the cobbles seemed to grow darker and slick with grime. They rounded a corner and Franchesca was amazed at what she saw. Streets packed with taverns and seedy inns. There stood a massive towering building with red curtains in the window and a red lantern hanging from the signpost. She doubted Claude would bring her to this part of the city merely to show her brothels and taverns—but what else could be around this area. They walked halfway down the long street that smelt of cheap stale alcohol. He guided her cautiously around stumbling drunks until they reached their destination. Etched on a weathered piece of wood with its paint fading were the words—Luvilies used Books and Curios.

"I thought a used book might mean more to you because it's not new." Her grin stretched from ear to ear, her guardian knew her better than her parents. They would have thought such a thing below her, and uselessly distasteful. For them, everything had to be the best, and it had to be as new as possible, it was a view Franchesca never possessed. So many of her possessions were brand new and shining—but Franchesca enjoyed having something owned by someone else first. It was broken in, worn—loved. She threw her arms around him and hugged him tightly. The inside of the shop was wonderfully cluttered. Books were stacked without rhyme or reason. Brass statues stood on shelves, or piles of dusty books. A few nails had been pounded into the walls from which hung necklaces or other jewelry such as rings or bracelets. The air smelled faintly of mildewed parchment and dust. It was perhaps the most wonderful smelling room she had set foot in. A hunched–backed man shuffled over and smiled, the few teeth in his mouth were discolored and slowly rotting away. Franchesca strolled around the shop reading the covers and spines of books as she walked through the clutter. Claude made small talk with the aging man while keeping an eye on her. She paused and picked up a book and flipped through its yellowed pages. Blochmenn's Manual of Swordplay and Blade Work—she'd heard of this book before. It was supposedly dictated by the best swordsmen in all of the Empire of Austinea. Her parents thought such things as swordplay, unladylike and too manly—she, on the other hand, was fascinated; besides anything was ladylike if a lady perused or engaged in it. They were of interest to her if for no other reason than it helped her to understand the adventure stories Claude so often told to her. Besides what had her tutor said—someday she might need to serve Forn and the best way to do that was to know of her countries customs and allies—intimately. Certainly, some knowledge of martial skill counted in that regard. One must know how to defend against an enemy, or speak with commanders. She tucked the book under her arm and kept looking around the shop. The Craft and Finer Mechanics of Black Powder Weapons, and its Other Uses. Supposedly the book was written by a man who'd lived with the Dwarves, and studied with them. It was notoriously rare and difficult to come by, and it was said that only a handful of copies existed. A rare book was a prize, not to be passed up—though she suspected it would cost quite a bit. It would be worth it, she just knew it. Franchesca continued studying the stacks while keeping her selections held beneath her arm lovingly. She smiled when she saw another tome labeled Adventures through the great free lands, a memoir of Listriio Dovaun. She approached the elderly man with her selections and noted his surprise. Even Claude seemed surprised by two of her choices. He always told her adventure stories and legends of great heroes in their time together; he imagined that is why she selected at least one book on the subject. The aged man wrapped her books in a large piece of parchment and tied them neatly with twine. He handed them to Claude, who passed him a gold coin, and a small assortment of other smaller coins—with a contented look and a polite nod. As he and Franchesca left the shop, he glanced at her and smiled.

"What would you need books like these for?" He joked. Franchesca shrugged. Relishing the weight of the books in her arms.

"It's not exactly something father and mother insist I have tutoring in— but I find such things interesting. Besides, based on what the tutor said today, it might be handy to have an idea of such things at least. Franchesca explained. Claude's lopsided grin as he squeezed her shoulder seemed to say, I thought so.

Up ahead, she saw a growing commotion as people were pushed aside. Franchesca watched as the girl she'd met only a few days ago ran through the crowd dodging people and squeezing past bustling swaying bodies. A watchman chased after her; his hand held an iron-studded truncheon which he waved angrily as he ran. Behind the watchman, a long of limb lean vulture faced man followed.

"Claude, what do you think is going on?" Franchesca asked. Claude cocked his head and sighed. Without warning, Franchesca bolted towards the girl and the commotion.

"Franchesca!" Claude exclaimed as he ran after her. She reached the scene just as the watchman wrapped a hand around the girl's shoulder, bringing her to an abrupt halt.

"That's her—that's the little thief!" The vulture faced man wheezed and hissed venomously as he doubled over from their pursuit.

"Come on now girl, return what ya stole or I'll give ya a smashing over the head with the old oak." The watchmen warned shaking his cudgel.

"I don' 'ave annythin." Simone replied calmly, holding up her hands. "He tinks because I'm poor I stole sometin when I walked by his damned fruit stall."

"Don't backchat girl, give em his goods, or I'll strip ya bare an give ya a beatin, ere and now." The uniformed man announced as he pointed at her with the truncheon for emphasis.

"I don' 'ave annythin!" Simone protested furiously trying to shrug off the guard's iron grip.

"Liar! Filthy thieving little liar!" The beak-nosed man squawked. As the man in uniform raised his weapon and spun Simone around to strike her, Franchesca could stand by no longer and called out.

"Excuse me—sirs, what is the meaning of this?" She shouted angrily. There was some distance between them and her, but her voice was enough to halt this display of impromptu street justice.

"Mind yer business child." The watchman shouted back without turning. The vulture faced man scowled as he turned to face the girl who dared to interrupt the justice he thought deserved.

"This does not concern you." The shopkeeper with the hooked vulture–like nose growled. His tone dismissive and angry at being interrupted.

"Sirs, you are addressing Miss Franchesca de Maret, daughter of Archduke Renaud de Maret and Archduchess Martise de Maret. You will address her with the utmost respect, or in the name of the Archduke, the both of you will be punished—and severely." Claude announced angrily as he laid his hand on the hilt of his rapier. He stepped up behind Franchesca and glowered at the two men only a short distance away. The watchman gawked saucer–eyed and visibly trembling. The vulture faced man seemed indifferent. With Claude standing behind her evidently, they were both more inclined to listen and speak calmly. Franchesca scowled at them both.

"What is going on?" She asked again far more angrily than she had the first time. The sight of the poor girl being mistreated so tore at her heart. Stoking the flames of her ire was the fact that the uniformed watchmen hadn't released her, nor lowered his weapon.

"This urchin stole from me." The bird–faced man growled as he raised his arms wildly. The image of a bird becoming complete her mind, as his lanky featherless arms took the place of wings—flapping about indignantly.

"What do you presume she stole?" Francesca asked, cocking her head to the side. The bird–faced shopkeeper scowled and refused to answer.

"What do you say she stole?" She asked again as she stepped forward and glared at him.

"A Bushbur apple miss." The watchman answered nervously. If the bird–like man doing the shouting and waving wasn't going to answer the noblewoman, then the watchmen evidently would. It appeared he was not content to be caught in the middle. He had also loosened his grip on Simone.

"A Bushbur apple? You mean a piece of fruit worth less than a brass shilling?" Franchesca exclaimed. "I could walk in the high district market and get five Bushbur apples for the price of a copper penny. Watchman—what is the average cost of such fruit in this section of the city?" There was a moment of silence.

"The lady asked you a question." Claude growled, pulling an inch of steel from the rapier sheathed at his side. With a heavy sigh, the watchman turned to her.

"For good quality, I'd say five for a copper. Bruised and damaged—probably ten for a copper, or five for a brass shilling." Franchesca scowled and shook her head.

"Watchman—you will release her. You, sir—will receive your damned copper penny if it is worth so much to you. Claude, would you please hand me my purse." He dropped her coin purse into her hand and stepped back. Franchesca smirked as she walked past the shopkeeper and strode over to a gutter overflowing with filth. Her smile widened as she dropped the coin she fished out into the filth before she returned to stand beside Claude.

"You may retrieve your payment. Watchman—you are dismissed." The uniformed man quickly saluted and scurried off. The shopkeeper began to walk away, ignoring the coin she dropped.

"Sir—after all of this trouble, you will pick up the coin." Claude gave a gentle tug on his rapier, revealing another inch of steel. The shopkeeper scowled as he bent over and retrieved the coin from the slime of the gutter. She looked on with a satisfactory smirk as she watched him slink away. Franchesca smiled at Simone.

"I... I don' know what ta say. No one's ever stood up fer me bafore." She told her. Franchesca looked her up and down. Her fiery ruby hair was in disarray, and her pale skin was streaked with dirt and filth. "Tanks—I guess ya are notin' like yer mother." Simone smiled as she turned to walk away.

"Wait..." Franchesca called out taking a few steps towards her. "Come with me." It was all she could think to say. It was tactless perhaps, but it just came out of her mouth before she could put the proper words to it. Simone considered her curiously.h

"I... want you to come with me to my home—at least for the night. You can have a meal, and a decent place to sleep and stay warm." That was better Franchesca mused silently as she listened to the words leave her mouth—more polite at any rate, it was an explanation at least. Hopefully, the girl would not think her too strange anyway.

"Wh... why?" Simone asked hesitantly. Franchesca smiled taking another step forward; hands folded politely in front of her.

"Because I'm betting you've never had someone do this for you either." Simone smirked but shrugged. Claude sighed and rubbed his forehead.

"Claude—we will be having a guest over this evening." Claude chuckled as he rubbed his forehead.

"You certainly aim to take full liberties with your parent's absence don't you?" He asked sarcastically. With a sigh, he shrugged and nodded. "Very well, lets us be on our way then." Simone fell into step beside Franchesca.

"Have you ever had Pikshaff?" Franchesca asked stepping in close eyes alight with joy and wonder. Simone snickered, she thought the girl's enthusiasm quite fetching. Simone had the feeling the girl—Franchesca if she remembered her name right, didn't get to speak with anyone her own age very often. Or maybe she did, and she was just a bubbly person who tripped over their own tongue and thoughts quite often.

"When I can afford ta, which ain't often." She replied. Brushing her ruby hair from her face and tucking it behind her ear.

"Claude, can we please get two more before we go back to the estate?" He smirked and placed a hand on Franchesca's shoulder.

"Alright, Miss Franchesca. We can get two more, but let us be on our way." He told them as he guided them back towards the sausage cart and the carriage. As the carriage rolled on, he passed the bundle of books over to Franchesca who grinned back at him.

"Thank you, Claude, for taking me out." Franchesca watched as Simone gazed out the window of the carriage as it worked its way through the city streets back towards the estate. Claude had given her the best gift she'd ever received.

Chapter
3

Simone shoveled food into her mouth as quickly as a gravedigger might work to fill in the grave they dug. Franchesca feared that she might bite her fingers on more than one occasion. She assumed that it had been some time since Simone's last meal. She picked up the glass of wine and took a long drink. Simone placed the glass back down on the table and panted.

"Sorry if I'm bein rude." She said quietly, her cheeks coloring somewhat.

"Think nothing of it. I imagine that you've not had a bit of good food in a long while. When was your last decent meal?" Franchesca replied quietly.

"I don' really know tha last time I 'ad a meal—least not as ya know em ta be." Simone replied as she took another long drink.

"I mostly eat what fruits or vegetables I find—or on rare casion can afford." She went on to explain. "I make due. I 'ave a friend who owns a tavern he lets me stay wit' em when it's not all rented up, an 'ell feed me meals when he's got 'nuf ta spare." Simone added. Franchesca reached out and picked up her own glass and took a sip.

"Can I do anything to help?" Franchesca asked innocently. Simone paused for a moment and looked up from her plate. It was as if she were asked something she had never thought of before—in truth she hadn't.

"I, don' tink so. Yer' not like most of tha high-necks round dese parts are ya?" Simone asked with a smile. Franchesca cocked her head at the phrase. Simone smirked.

"Its what us gutterfoots call some of tha nobles." She went on to explain—further, illustrating the explanation by holding her head up high, keeping her eyes and nose upturned as if in haughty disdain for any who might happen to be below her line of sight. Franchesca giggled as Simone dropped the adopted noble mannerism and returned to her attention to her food. Franchesca smiled and walked over and took a seat closer to her.

"How so?" Franchesca asked curiously.

"Well—most people wit' yer sort of money an' all dose fancy titles don' care if people like me get annythin. Not until a few days ago—I din't even tink a classy high-neck 'as ever given me as much as a brass shillin. Ya invited me inta yer house." Simone said as she stared at Franchesca, before looking about the room. A maid entered the dining room and looked at the two girls in the dining room. She curtsied politely turning her face towards Franchesca.

"With all respect due miss Franchesca—do you think its wise to invite someone the likes of her into the house for the whole night? She might..." Franchesca rose from the table angrily and glared at the woman.

"You mean a person?" Franchesca scowled locking eyes with the maid.

"I meant nothing disrespectful miss..." the woman tried to backtrack— foolish given the fact she had come in and questioned Franchesca's judgment. Doubly foolish given that she did actually mean to be disrespectful, if not to Franchesca than to Simone.

"Thank you for your concern Marrtea you are dismissed." She said with a reprimanding tone to her voice as she pointed at the door. Marrtea bowed politely and quickly left the room. Franchesca walked over to Simone and hugged her gently.

"I am sorry. You deserve none of this, to be treated like a common thief and worse." Simone shrugged as she rose from the table.

"I'm used ta it. When yer a gutterfoot like me evryone's got somethin 'ta say an' a nose to look down on ya. Seems dat even tha nobles of dis place ferget dat someun, somere 'as a low opinion of em to." She looked around the large marble dining room and chuckled.

"What do ya do fer fun round dese parts nyway?" Simone asked as she walked over to a small decorative table—the dark wood was inlaid with golden flowers and crafted silver birds. She looked back over at Franchesca after a long moment of silence. Franchesca allowed herself to slump into her chair.

"I don't believe you would call what I do around these halls fun. I feel like a prisoner here." She sighed as she moved her dress so that she could seat herself comfortably.

"My parents have grand plans for me; I'm to be a good little doll and dance to their tune and do as they wish me to do. As such I mostly do a lot of reading about subjects which do not interest me at all; I also do various hobbies that a good and proper lady should do. I do needlepoint, arranging flowers—waiting for my brains to leak from my ears from boredom. You know the things that happen within the walls of a prison?"

Simone chuckled. "If dis is prison, den who do I 'ave ta rip off ta grab a seat in a cell 'ere?" She made Franchesca grin.

"I perhaps sound ungrateful, it's just—I don't feel human here. I am well aware my parents love me, but they do not understand what it is like to be thought of as a piece of property. It seems that is all I am to them at times." Franchesca explained sadly.

"I only got a chance to go into the city today because my parents are away." She looked up at Simone. "That is also how I knew I would be able to invite you over to do something special for you." She went on to say. Simone allowed a lopsided grin to creep upon her face—beginning to tap her chin as she looked at Franchesca.

"Den what ya say ta me 'an you makin a bit of fun ourselves?" Simone asked with a grin that split her dirt-smeared face. Franchesca's face lit up with a smile, and nodded. Let's go den—I'm guessin ya 'ave an upstairs." Franchesca nodded as she showed Simone the way, leading Simone to her room. She threw open the door and recognized Simone's face as it began to glow with joy—as she beheld the splendor of the room beyond. Franchesca always thought of it as a simple room, her room. To Simone, a waif from the streets, her room must seem to be a palace itself.

"Look, dere's a balcony come wit' me." Simone looked over the edge and raised her eyebrows with a reckless smirk. "Look at dat stone dere, an tha red flower painted on it?" Franchesca nodded. "We'll let's find out who can spit it in tha center of tha flower. Like darts wit' out tha pointy bits." Franchesca looked at Simone as if she had just grown a second head.

"I... I don't know how to..." Franchesca began,

"Ta spit?" Simone asked with a chuckle. "Jus' watch me, it's easy." Franchesca listened as Simone drew in a deep breath and made a horrible sound by snorting forcefully and then as if she were blowing a cavalry horn she spat a wad of phlegm and mucous over the edge of the balcony. There was a splattering sound as the gob of sputum landed on the hard stone.

"I was close." Simone smiled. "Come on—it's yer turn ta try, I'll help ya." Simone encouraged. Franchesca laughed as she stepped forward and stood next to Simone. The girl talked her through step by step describing what she needed to do. On Franchesca's turn—she gave her best effort, but it was obvious that it was her first attempt. The spit caught on her chin and landed on her dress. Franchesca grunted in frustration while Simone laughed. It was not the laugh of someone mocking her for a failure; the sound was the laugh of a friend. "Come on, try again." She smiled. Franchesca tried once more, and a time after that. She was about ready to quit, but Simone insisted that she have one more attempt. After a moment's hesitation, Franchesca tried once more. This time, her wad of expectorant cleared the balcony edge and landed in the grass below the decorative stone.

"I did it!" Franchesca exclaimed proudly and more than a little surprised. She snickered, and Simone laughed with her. The two went on spitting over the edge of the balcony trying to hit their target. They laughed and joked—as they made up stories in between bouts of spitting. Claude heard their laughter from in the hallway and strode over to the doorway of Franchesca's room. He leaned against the doorframe and listened as she laughed, watching as Franchesca enjoyed herself. More importantly—he listened as she laughed with a friend. The first true and honest friend she'd ever made.

"All right you two," Claude said after watching them for a handful of moments with an easy grin on his face.

"If you keep on in such a way you'll make a river down upon the lawn. I can see it now, spit mire they'll call it." The girls giggled. "It would probably be wise to get some rest, Miss Franchesca, since you don't have any lessons tomorrow you can spend more time in the city." Claude smiled. "Miss Simone—would you like me to show you to your room?"

"It is alright Claude; I'll show her." Franchesca replied eagerly. She led Simone down the hall and showed her to her the guest chambers.

"What did he mean when he said ya did't 'ave any lessons tomorrow?" Simone asked. Franchesca looked at her curiously.

"I... have tutors that come to teach me history, customs, geography—well lots of things really. Why?" Franchesca replied. Simone shrugged.

"Jus' curious, only lessons tought ta me are usually tought by watchmen. Don't tink a whack on tha back is a lesson." She sighed.

"You've... never had a lesson? Not in reading, writing... or... Simone chuckled at Franchesa's shock. Franchesca sighed; she forgot that not everyone received lessons of the quality she was fortunate enough to receive.

"Have you never been taught anything?"

"Well, nutin from books. I learned how ta pickpockets, escape routes—not really book tings." Simone explained. "Dey don' teach folk like me anythin we don' need ta learn." "Would you like me to teach you?" Franchesca asked, eyes bright and beaming. She thought that everyone should be given the opportunity to learn—it was fair enough if they didn't want to but they should at least have the option.

"Ya'd do dat fer me?" Simone asked in disbelief as she took a step forward.

"Of course, you're my friend." Franchesca said with a grin as she placed a hand on Simone's shoulder. She felt as if something within her grew. A weight fell from her back and for the first time she was able to breathe.

"I'd like dat—friend." Simone smiled back as she walked forward and embraced Franchesca. She continued walking Simone to her bedchamber laughing and joking the all the way.

"Would you like to have a bath before bed, or in the morning when you wake?" Franchesca inquired as she walked over to the bed and pulled out a corner of the blankets. Simone's bare feet sounded off the wooden floor with a gentle thump as she walked over and sat down.

"If it's all tha same—I tink I might do dat in tha mornin." She smiled. "If dat doen't offend ya, miss?" Simone replied stretching her shoulders out.

"Of course not, and don't call me that. My name is Franchesca." She told her gently. Simone nodded. "I'll see you in the morning." Franchesca told her as she rose from the bed. Simone pulled her legs up and stretched out on the bed.

"Franchesca" Simone called out before she left the room. Simone examined Franchesca as she turned and smiled back at her. "Do... do—ya pity me? Is dat why yer doin all dis?" She asked quietly. Franchesca shook her head.

"No, not at all—I... I can't really describe it. When I saw what my mother did... I mean I'm not like her in the least. I'm not even truly like my father. And maybe that's why. Aside from Claude, you're the only person I feel I have a connection to. I don't want to be a prim and proper little doll–like my parents wish me to be. I want to be..."

"Free." Simone answered with a smile. A slow grin crossed Franchesca's face, and she nodded in agreement.

"Ye... yes free. There is... well, you might think I sound a bit mad for saying this. There is just something about you that makes me feel alive. Perhaps it is the nature of your spirit, but when I first ran into you, I did that kindness for no other reason than a desire, a need and a want to do it. Now that I'm in your company there is a freedom that comes with it—I can't explain it." She answered. Simone smiled and nodded her understanding. It was a relief that she wasn't a simple charity case. She'd been pitied before, and the gifts of fruit or bread that had been passed to her from pitying hands the looks in their eyes made the food taste sour and stale. Everything here was different. It was light, sweet and revitalizing.

"Thank you for everything Franchesca." Simone told her softly, breaking her thick Lassin accent. Franchesca dipped a small curtsy and bow of her head as she strode out of the room. Franchesca walked back to her and stepped on to the balcony. She looked up at the shining silver of the moon, hardly taking note of its red twin—and closed her eyes. A single tear rolled down her soft pale face as she gave a whispered prayer of thanks to the Heavenly Lady for the day she enjoyed. She thanked her for Claude, as she always made a point to— and now Franchesca was given another soul to thank the Heavenly Matron for. "Dearest Lady—I thank you for your gifts this day." She whispered as she pressed her head to the cold stone of the balcony. She lay prostrate for a few moments listening to the trees rustle in the cool breeze. When she finally went to bed, she the most profound, peaceful contentment she could ever remember feeling before settle upon her. All was quiet until she heard the hooting of a lone owl. Franchesca smiled and drifted off to sleep. For the first time, she did not gaze up at the painted stars and the fine lines of gold and silver. For the first time she was happy being right where she was, and being with the people who surrounded her.

* * *

Simone reclined in the warm waters that filled the tub. Usually, when she was able to take baths, it was in a river—and rarely was that ever warm. There had only been a handful of times when she was able to pay to take a bath in a bathhouse. This was altogether entirely more pleasant because it was privet. She dipped the cloth into the water and wrung the fabric out before leaning her head back and placing the soft square cotton cloth over her face. After a moment she dipped the cloth in once more and rubbed her face. The water sloshed as she scrubbed at her pale skin. Simone smiled as the warm water caressed her skin; the delicate floral scents wafting up from the soap, bubbles tingled against her flesh and nose. There was a soft knock on the door, in a relaxed voice she answered. "Come in." Franchesca opened the door holding an arm full of towels.

"I brought these for you, for when you're finished." Franchesca told her with a nod towards the folded towels.

"I'm almost done nyway." Simone replied as she let herself slip under the water for a moment, allowing her hair to become thoroughly wet. She held herself under for a few seconds before coming back up with a short gasp to catch her breath. She breathed heavily as she moved her red hair from her face. She squeezed handfuls, to rid her ruby locks of excess water before standing up. Franchesca backed away quickly. Her heart thundered behind her ribs.

"Oh—I didn't expect... I wasn't expecting you to finish so quickly." Franchesca said as she looked around nervously. Simone looked down at her naked form.

"Are ya nervous?" Simone asked with a chuckle and a crooked grin upon her heart–shaped face. Franchesca observed that despite a life lived on the streets the girl's teeth seemed to be very well taken care of. For a moment she wondered how Simone managed that—before propriety asserted itself once more. That wasn't all she'd observed. Simone was as lean as a back alley cat. She couldn't exactly count her ribs—but Franchesca suspected that if she laid a hand on her chest, she could feel them easily enough. She was willowy, but her height was average—perhaps a little shorter. Such was to be expected when a body wasn't fed on a regular basis, after all. Now that her skin was clean, there was a gentle luster and softness to it. Franchesca wondered what her skin would feel like beneath her fingers—like silk she imagined. By the Heavenly Lady's holy light where from her mind did that thought come from?

"No—it's... its not that I just—I did not know you were not worried about your modesty." She replied as she glanced back at Simone. Franchesca watched as Simone shrugged. By the Heavenly Lady, why didn't she turn away? For a moment she wondered if she actually desired to turn her gaze.

"Dey're jus' tits—it's not like ya 'avent seen 'em bafore. Ya see 'em evry time ya look down." Franchesca giggled nervously as she handed Simone a towel. There was truth in that. There was something about her—all of her. Franchesca felt her eyes drawn to Simone's aforementioned breasts where they lingered a moment longer than they should have. They were small, but there was enough of a swell there that Franchesca reasoned would fill her dainty hand if she placed it over one. She felt her eyes wandering down her frame. Just a bit lower was a flat, taut stomach. Franchesca blinked and swallowed.

"I don't believe I have ever met anyone like you, Simone." Franchesca told her. She tried to gain control of her thundering heart, hoping that its pace would slow and more importantly, that Simone wouldn't notice how she was beginning to stare without being able to remove her gaze. Simone held her gaze for a moment before wrapping herself in the offered towel. Though Franchesca hoped against it—Simone had noticed. She noticed Franchesca's heart thundering in its prison. Franchesca's eyes eagerly combed Simone's form, as points below her waist disappeared beneath the soft cotton of the towel.

Simone smiled and nodded after what felt like an eternal moment of silence.

"I'll take dat as a complament." Simone replied with a lopsided grin brought on by biting her lip. Franchesca giggled and felt her cheeks begin to color, and warm, a strange feeling of disappointment settled over her upon seeing her friends freshly towel wrapped figure. She blinked for a moment in bewilderment and wondered why and where such feelings had come from.

"As well you should." Franchesca assured enthusiastically with a wide–eyed grin. By the Heavenly Lady; why did she say that?" Would you like to have a lesson before we go out into the city again?" Franchesca asked quickly trying to change the subject and cover her awkwardness. She wasn't used to having strangers stand wet and naked in front of her. Even though Simone was her friend, she doubted this was the sort of things friends did with one another.

"I don' know where ya would start." Simone replied. A broad smile crossed her face, and she nodded. "I would like dat though." Franchesca grinned. "I'll get dressed."

"I'll meet you in the library. It's just up the stairs and three doors down and to the left." Franchesca said. She hurried up the stairs; her heart beat like a drum within her chest as she opened the door to the library. Why she asked herself? Why did this seem to affect her so much? Franchesca giggled nervously; perhaps it was the sheer shock. Simone was certainly not like many other women she had been in the presence of. Perhaps that was a good thing. Perhaps that was the reason she felt taken over by such a sight. Franchesca shook such thoughts and wonders from her head. Now was not the time to dwell. She walked over to the bookcases and began scanning the shelves. Simone was right—where should she start? Franchesca rubbed her forehead, tucking a length of her wavy raven hair behind her ear. Simone didn't know how to read. Franchesca sighed—she supposed the most logical place to start was teaching her the alphabet of their land. In her studies Franchesca learned a few different languages, Franchesca supposed that she could teach Simone those later if she wished. She laid out a piece of parchment and gathered a quill and ink. She set the desk up neatly and gazed at her work with delight. She heard Simone's bare footfalls ascending the steps and grinned, feeling a tingle run down her spine when she walked into the room. "Let's get started." Franchesca smiled as she pulled out a chair for Simone.

* * *

The carriage rattled and shook as it wound through the streets. Franchesca had mixed feelings about returning to the city today. Though it meant freedom, it also brought on a sense of loneliness and heartbreak. She wouldn't be able to return home with Simone. Franchesca vowed to herself that she would find a way to get Simone into her home and have her stay. Perhaps she could persuade her father to bring her on as a maid—or maybe she could watch the horses in the stables. The thoughts made Franchesca sick, Simone didn't deserve that. She deserved to be treated as a guest because she was her friend. Maybe she could have her brought on to be one of her personal attendants; she never did like the women her father and mother selected for her anyway. They were always so old and smug. If she did such a thing though, she would be taking away from Simone what she admired, and what she hoped to have. Would Simone even wish such a thing? Maybe she preferred her life with its wondrous unpredictability. What should she do? She just wanted her friend close to her. If she could persuade her parents to bring her on as an attendant, Franchesca would see that Simone did as little work as possible.

"What does your father do?" Franchesca asked softly. "That is if you don't mind my asking." She added meekly. Simone let out a sigh.

"I do my best ta avoid seeing him. Tried his hand at bein a merchant—dat did't go so well. Though he doen't see it dat way. He fancies himself a noble, he hardly 'as 'nough coin to keep round what he's got, an' ta get drunk. Suppose if ya need someone killed, he's tha one ta ask though." Simone scoffed. It was a lie—but she told it enough times that she'd almost convinced herself that it was the truth.

"Do... you have a home to go to?" Franchesca inquired. Simone simply let her shoulders hunch before shaking her head.

"I don' tink so. He travels round a lot makin camps 'ere an' dere, or holdin up in some abandon buildings. He spends a lot of his time in tha district closest to tha docks. Probably smuggling counterfeit brandy, an' dwarf ale. I can always see if my friend's tavern's got a free room fer me ta stay in." Franchesca decided now would be the best opportunity to ask her boldest question.

"Si... Simone, if I could get you a position in my home—would you stay with me?" Claude looked at her wide-eyed. Simone's expression softened, she allowed herself a smile and a sigh.

"Yer a sweet ting." She told her quietly. "Ya know as well as I do dat yer mother an' father wouldn't give a gutterfoot like me a second look."

"That's not what I asked. If I persuaded them, would you come? Would you want to... I mean?" Franchesca replied. Simone leaned forward and touched her face gently.

"Yer a good person Franchesca—an' it's a kind offer. But yers is a world I would never fit inta. Basides, what would happen if I told ya, yes, an' ya saw yer parents shoutin deir order ta me evryday? I know ya care bout me, I know I'm yer friend an' I know if it was all up to ya I would live in yer house quick as a blink." Simone smiled.

"I don't want you to go." Franchesca said sadly as tears welled up in her stormy blue eyes. Simone reached out gently and wiped them from her cheeks and smiled.

"I know ya don'. But I ain't goin no where. I'll be here when ya make it back down." Simone told her softly. Suddenly an idea struck her.

"Claude... I have a favor to ask of you." Franchesca whispered. Claude raised a curious eyebrow as he looked at her.

"What is it?" Though he had a feeling, he knew where the conversation was headed, and he didn't have it in his heart to refuse her. Besides, it would not be a terrible thing to accommodate.

"If... if Simone wishes might she come to your cabin on the estate?" Franchesca asked, her eyes wide and watery. Claude sighed but allowed a roguish grin to tug at the corners of his mouth. As he thought, Franchesca's request wasn't unreasonable—not terribly. By all the gods when the girl got an idea in her head, she found some way of seeing it accomplished. A trait her parents didn't seem to truly appreciate.

"Aye—if she wishes. I suppose your father won't have much to say about that." Franchesca looked over at Simone and had the same look a child might have when they've found a way to get the maid to give them cookies, using a loophole in their parent's instructions.

"At... anytime you wish, please come back." Simone smiled as she reached out and grabbed Franchesca's hand tightly.

"I will, I promise." She replied softly as she hugged Franchesca. The coach rolled to a stop, and Franchesca swallowed the lump in her throat as Claude opened the door. Franchesca looked at Claude before gazing at the ground.

"How about we all get some Pikshaff?" Franchesca asked. Claude pinched the bridge of his nose stifling a laugh, while Simone let out a giggle.

"Alright miss Franchesca, let's have a bite to eat. I think if you could manage such a feat, you would have that Halfling live on the estate so that you could get some street food whenever you wanted." Claude joked. A few hours passed with Franchesca enjoying the last of Simone's company. She didn't know when she would see her again—and it broke her heart. As the hours passed Franchesca was acutely aware of a heaviness growing within her chest. By the gods, it required an immense amount of will to keep from collapsing into a sobbing heap on the cobbles. When the time came to say their farewells and even with all of the assurances that she would see her again, Franchesca couldn't help but weep. Simone wiped the tears from her friend's face and hugged her tightly. People stopped and watched as a shabbily dressed street dweller embraced a girl in fine fabrics and ornate looking clothes as if it was their first time seeing such a spectacle. It made Franchesca seethe with anger. Simone hugged her briefly, kissed her cheek gently.

"I'll see ya again soon, I promise." She said reassuringly—sharing a conspiratorial wink Franchesca smiled even as tears rolled down her cheeks and nodded. She looked on with a breaking heart, as Simone shuffled through the crowds that had gathered. They were ogling the strange sight of a noble girl weeping as a nameless little guttershite walked away from her presence. Franchesca could hear cruel whispers about what they just witnessed. Some of the crowd murmured her name and whispered questions to one another.

"Let's take you home Miss Franchesca—your mother and father will be home soon." Claude said as he placed a hand upon her shoulder. He squeezed it in a consoling manner as Franchesca nodded.

"Yes... please, Claude. I can't stand to be around these wretches a moment longer." She hissed sadly as she looked at those gathered. Once Claude stepped into the coach and closed the door, she collapsed onto his lap and wept. She cried harder than she ever had before. Franchesca felt his strong hands stroke her back and shoulders firmly and mustering all the gentleness he had within his heart. He didn't tell her that everything would be alright, because he knew at that moment those words would offer no comfort. Claude himself was very aware of the tear rolling down his own cheek, as he looked upon the girl it had been his duty to watch over for so long weep in such a way. That sight broke his heart. Though Claude would never admit it, more often than not he hated Franchesca's parents for what they were doing to their daughter. The restrictions they put on her and locking her away in a gilded cage—parading her around for others to look at.

Her parents had acquaintances, and contacts—business partners; her father even maintained contact with old comrades from his days of military service. Franchesca had nothing aside from what they allowed her to have, and it always infuriated him. So often Claude felt that he indeed was her father with the way she confided in him. The young woman was more like him than her parents, an observation that they seemed completely oblivious to. They thought they were doing what was best for her, keeping her safe and giving her the best of everything—in truth they were killing her spirit. Claude would have done anything to make them realize the damage they were doing to their daughter. He had tried speaking to them before, but every time he was met with the same response, such concerns were none of his business. He always found that strange since Renaud and Martise de Maret and had hired him to protect Franchesca. Claude rested a gentle hand on her head and stroked her hair as she sobbed.

"I am so sorry Miss Franchesca." He whispered as he continued stroking her hair gently. "I really am."

Chapter
4

Franchesca's parents returned home, and for the next few days, life returned to its soulless mind–numbing claustrophobic oppression. She listened as they recounted their business; she assumed they wanted her to learn about it as a lesson of sorts. Diplomacy and all of the other tedium she could associate with her parent's lessons in what it meant to be of noble birth. One thing which had surprised her was the invitation of Syandro De Madonia and his father back to the estate. Renaud de Maret went on to explain that there was the distinct possibility that Syandro's father would be planning an expedition to the Tomblands of the sand–swept east. Naturally, of course, her father wanted to attach his name and a small portion of his coin to the daring endeavor. Franchesca thought to herself; it could work in my favor. After all, it showed that the De Madonia family was ambitious; if Syandro's father returned, he would indeed be a wealthy man, if not in gold and treasures he would make it up with investors and contributors for his next grand adventure. Perhaps such a feat would make his star rise, even within the rigid social and noble ladders of Forn. Maybe, just maybe Franchesca could indeed wed the man she thought most deserving; or at least did not make her skin crawl with revulsion. In truth, she did find Syandro quite handsome. He was also one of the handfuls of suitors who were around her own age. It disturbed her greatly to think of some of the older men her father and mother might arrange her to be wed to. She listened to her father drone mindlessly on about her future and well being. He smiled at her.

"Perhaps this might be the beginning of a prosperous endeavor. Maybe so prosperous, he can see your star rise my darling." Her father told her with a warm smile. The remark made Franchesca's eyebrows climb in suspicion.

"We noticed you seemed to enjoy your time with Syandro at the gathering. If all goes well in this endeavor, I would go so far as to say that it's a sign gifted by the Heavenly Lady of good fortune and favor." Renaud winked as he tented his fingers in thought, a self–satisfied sneer growing on his face. Franchesca returned his smile with one of her own. As had always been the case there was a condition of plot and invisible webs woven around her. Her parents even went so far as to use her as bait. Franchesca decided she would play along; perhaps it would go well. Maybe she could grasp on to some grain of happiness and marry the man she felt could be right for her. She looked blankly at the plate of food before her, stabbing it absentmindedly.

"Are you alright darling, you've hardly touched your dinner?" Her mother asked gently.

"I'm fine; I am not exceptionally hungry this evening." Franchesca replied. She closed her eyes and took a deep breath. Despite the prospect of courting Syandro her insides felt heavy. Her heart slowed to crawl. "If I might trouble you, mother and father; might I be excused? I think I should like to turn in for the night." She explained.

"Well of course darling." Her mother told her quietly. Franchesca left the room slowly and walked upstairs her jaw clenched, and her head hung. She pushed open the door of her chambers and locked it behind her. Her eyes fixed upon the balcony door, with a slow stride she walked towards it and opened it. She stepped out into the cool night air and looked down. Franchesca managed a smile as she saw the decorative stone in the garden path down beneath her balcony. She spat and listened as the gob of saliva hit the rock below. Franchesca giggled softly to herself before gazing down once more. She sank to the ground and curled her legs beneath her, and leaned against the stone of the balcony ledge. She missed Simone terribly so. It had only been a few hours since their parting, but Franchesca found herself wondering what Simone might be doing now? Where would she be? The thoughts hurt, more than she believed a thought could hurt. They felt like physical blows. She worried about her. Was she going to be cold tonight? Would some harm befall her out in the dark streets? Franchesca whispered silent prayers to the Lady, asking that she watch over Simone and keep her safe. She also whispered prayers for the success of Syandro's father's expedition. Surely Syandro would allow her to bring Simone into their home; surely he would allow her to be treated as an equal. That thought brought some comfort to her, it managed to entice a smile to crawl across her face, and for a moment she felt hopeful. But it was only for a moment. She closed the doors to the balcony and walked over to her bed. She lay atop the covers and gazed up at the stars made of gold and semi–precious stones. She once again found herself wondering what it would be like to be anywhere else, but this time she wondered what it would be like with Syandro and Simone. Franchesca closed her eyes as tears welled up within them. She pressed her pillow to her face as she wept. After countless tears were shed, she fell into a deep sleep.

* * *

"So Miss Franchesca if I might be so bold." Syandro began. His Castillian accent was thick upon every word as he spoke. Franchesca found that she didn't mind, it was a soft accent, quite seductive. Gentle almost musical and quite pleasant to listen to.

"What is it you do to entertain yourself?" He asked politely. Franchesca shrugged. She obviously could not tell him what she and Simone had done to amuse themselves that night. It was doubtful any noble wanted to hear such things; it was scandalously improper of a high lady.

"Mostly I read. If not that then I focus on my lessons." She replied. Syandro smiled.

"Truly? So you don't practice fencing? I only ask because more than once I have seen you glance at my blade. The night of the party I noticed you watching your bodyguard's blade as well. I thought you might practice. You seem eager to." Franchesca was shocked. She didn't think she was so open about the wanderings of her eyes. Moreover, she didn't believe she'd gazed that long. Then, as if reading her mind, Syandro continued.

"I have been taught to observe; I am expected to be a warrior and be capable of defending myself as well as my lady at all times, as well as be prepared to run a noble house of fair Castella." He reminded with a lopsided smile that was far too handsome for his own good. "Therefore, I see much." He winked.

"My apologies if you found it rude." Franchesca replied hastily. Syandro laughed as he stepped in front of her. By the Heavenly Lady, he was an observant one, handsome as well. How long had her eyes lingered? Only a few seconds at most; though she'd thought that when her eyes took Simone's slender petite form as well, yet Simone had noticed. Perhaps her glance was more of a stare. Syandro had noticed too. Franchesca was sure of it. A brilliant white toothed winning smile came easily to his strong features.

"Let us not pretend we are two nobles at court. Let us be ourselves; plain and simple, honest. I will be Syandro; I would like you to be Franchesca." He told her as he paused for a moment and looked at her with striking hazel eyes, tiny slivers of amber ringed by the deepest green flecks.

"I... I don't understand." She replied.

"I don't want you to be the girl you think your parents wish you to be. I want you to be the girl you wish yourself to be. If fate would have us wed, I would like to know the real you. I want you to take off your mask so that I might glimpse the real face of Franchesca de Maret. Not the mask your parents have spent so long crafting for you so that it might be in place because they believe the real you might say something or do something improper." Syandro smiled. Franchesca grinned and bobbed her head enthusiastically.

"Ok, Syandro." She began. "I have gazed at the hilt of your blade I admit. I have a fascination with swords and weaponry. I know it's not very ladylike." She mocked. "Does that frighten you?"

"Quite the contrary." Syandro replied. "In Castella women are as free to wield a sword as any man; even the nobles, in fact, they are encouraged. I notice here in Forn, very few women wield a blade, though many chose to wield their tongues as weapons instead." He smirked. Franchesca couldn't disagree. She could also see the subtle point of what he was saying. Wit was one thing, but having wit and not knowing how to defend yourself could work to your detriment. "May I be so bold?" He asked as he took a deep breath.

"I see you are different from many of the women in your country. You have passion, and you have wit." Syandro reached out and touched her face gently. "I would be quite honored if we were to be married." He smiled. Syandro slid his hand down her arm to her hand and brought it up to his lips and kissed them gently. Franchesca beamed a wide grin her face reddening at the flattery. "Perhaps I can invite you to our estate in Forn, and within the courtyard, I can teach you the basics of blade work." He whispered. Franchesca felt a joyous grin pull at the corners of her mouth.

"That would be, wonderful." Syandro nodded, and the two shared a conspiratorial look as he arched his eyebrows.

"I shall see what I can arrange." He assured. "Would you like to continue on our walk, Franchesca?" It was nice to be asked if she wished to continue their walk. She felt as if she could say no if she desired such a thing.

"I think I would like that." She linked her arm with his, and they continued their walk through the garden. Storm clouds darkened the sky in the distance ready to unburden their weight at any moment. Syandro noticed a change come over Franchesca. If he was able to see within her mind, he might see that she thought he cut a striking figure in his uniform. How she admired the cut of his golden piped uniform and the way it showed off his lean and muscular frame. If he could read her mind, he would know how she thought the dark crimson fabric of the uniform complemented his sun kissed olive skin and how she wanted to feel the brass buttons stopping an inch beneath his armpit. Syandro truly was handsome, and his smile was infectious. Franchesca turned her attention from him once more and to the rain clouds. The thundering in her heart which had begun when she looked at him had slowed. Simone. Franchesca's mind thought of her friend.

"If you are worried about the rain we can go back to the house. Perhaps sit in the parlor and take some wine?" Syandro began.

49

"No, it's not that. I... I just have a friend I worry about when it rains. Well, in truth, I worry about them quite a bit." Syandro snickered.

"Surely your friend is in fine spirits, perhaps sitting by the fire." It was possible Franchesca thought. Simone could be in a tavern sitting by their fireplace keeping warm and out of the coming storm. Of course, she could also very realistically be outside, roaming the streets and back alleys. Syandro didn't know this, of course, so she held her temper in check. Sometimes she supposed ignorance brought bliss, but not when you cared for someone. I hope you're at your friend's tavern Franchesca thought.

"Perhaps, yes." Franchesca replied quietly despite her doubts. She sighed and rose from the garden bench.

"Why don't we go back to the house? It might be nice to sit before the fire and converse for a bit." Syandro bowed as he laced his arm with hers and they walked back to the house.

"I have heard your father speak very highly of the wine that comes from his vineyard. Is it as good as he says?" Syandro laughed. There was no real way to answer that, Franchesca thought.

"I truly don't know; it's all the wine I have ever known. He has only imported or purchased three other barrels of drink. He claims to be saving them for a special occasion." Franchesca replied.

"Perhaps your wedding." He said with a roguish upturn at the corners of his mouth. She shrugged and agreed that it could perhaps be that occasion, but she wondered. After a few hours of sitting and more pleasant conversations, Syandro and his father had taken their leave. Renaud de Maret had given Syandro's father two bottles of wine in addition to a small lockbox filled with gold and silver coins to aid in financing his expedition. It was the most generous Franchesca had ever seen her father. Perhaps he was changing. But was unlikely, Franchesca told herself with a sneer. Impressions counted for a lot; her father was probably doing nothing more than showing off that he could afford such generosity. It was a way of showing the De Madonia family their place, in the most subtle way possible. Franchesca had gone and secluded herself within her room after Syandro had left. She sat at a desk and began reading the books that she had bought. There was a heavy–handed knock on her bedroom door which startled her. She looked up from the page she was reading and closed it. Franchesca walked to the door and opened it and found Claude standing outside in the hallway.

"I apologize for disturbing you so late Miss Franchesca." Claude told her quietly.

"It is no trouble, Claude, I was just reading. Unfortunately, when you knocked I had reached a frightening part." She replied as she invited him to come in. Claude shook his head.

"No, I should be getting back. I wanted to let you know that I have a guest if you would like to come visit them." He smiled as she looked up at him wide–eyed in disbelief.

"She... she's here? She came?" Claude nodded but held his finger before his lips. Franchesca made to run past him, but Claude motioned for her to stop.

"I will come to get you after your parents retire for the night. Keep the door unlocked and be ready." He told her. Franchesca nodded quickly. "Don't worry; she's fine. She just wanted you to know she'd come." Franchesca bobbed her head enthusiastically.

"Tell her I can't wait to see her." She told him in her happiest whisper. Claude placed a hand on her shoulder.

"Remember to be ready. When your parents retire, I will come and get you. I will take you to my cabin, and you can speak to her for a while." Claude told her. Franchesca's heart thundered in her chest as she watched him walk away. She was so excited to see Simone again. Walking over to her bed she sat down, her limbs trembling with uncontained excitement. She thanked the Heavenly Lady as she looked out of the window and waited eagerly to see Claude open the door once more.

* * *

The wait felt like an eternity. Franchesca tried to read so time would pass quicker, but found that her mind raced. Questions raced through her mind. What had happened since they parted ways? Franchesca then found herself wondering if there was any food she might be able to give to Simone, something more than bread and cheese. Were there any left over's of the roasted goose they had offered to Syandro and his father had? Before she knew it, Franchesa found herself pacing to and fro. Finally, the moment happened. Claude opened the door and stepped in keeping his finger pressed to his lips. Franchesca strode over quickly to him, and he led her through the house.

"Hold on." Franchesca whispered as she took the candle from Claude's hand and looked about the kitchen. Luckily, there were some leftovers. She grabbed a hunk of bread and cheese, but she was also able to grab a portion of roasted goose and a few pieces of fruit. Franchesca placed them in a basket and threw a small square of fabric over them before returning to Claude.

"Lead the way." She whispered with a grin. Claude led her hurriedly to his cabin. It was a small structure across the property. Though it was small, her father had it built well. He insisted on it. It was used as a way of payment to Claude after agreeing to be her bodyguard. The rain fell in a steady downpour and by the time Franchesca arrived at Claude's cabin she was thoroughly soaked. Once Claude opened the door, and Franchesca laid eyes on Simone she rushed forward. Embracing Simone tightly, she began to cry as she hugged her.

"What's dat about?" Simone smiled as she held on to Franchesca tightly.

"I've missed you terribly." Franchesca replied.

"Oh, I'm sorry." Franchesca said after a moment of sudden realization. She stepped back and noticed that she had soaked Simone's clothes with her own.

"It's fine." Simone smiled. "Claude 'as been lettin me sit by tha fire."

"Speaking of, it would be good for you to do so as well Franchesca. The last thing you need is to catch a chill from sitting in your wet clothes." Claude reminded as he hung his cloak on a carved wooden hook by the door.

"Come on." Simone said as she pulled Franchesca over to the fire. The two sat in front of the crackling flames and Franchesca set down the basket of food she had brought for Simone between them.

"I didn't know what you have had to eat the past few days, so I wanted to do something for you. I know it's not much, but..." Simone smiled at her as Franchesca pulled back the coarse fabric. Simone reached in gently and sat cross–legged by the fire. She pulled apart pieces of bread and popped them into her mouth slowly.

"How... have you been?" Franchesca asked. Simone paused and gave the question some thought before shrugging.

"I've been doin alright. No worse dan any other time." She laughed. "I've been keeping round tha docks; dere's been a few empty storehouses I've managed ta hunker down in." Simone told her. Franchesca felt her heart wrench sadly.

"I wish I could do something more for you. This... this is hardly enough." Simone waved her hand at the food showing her what she'd done already.

"Dis is more dan most would ever tink of doin. I'm grateful to ya, an' Claude." Simone walked over to a chair and sat down.

"It's not much, but you're free to stay here if you like." Claude reminded. "You might have to lay low, but between Franchesca and me we can see that you get fed and keep dry and warm." Simone nodded.

"Tanks ta tha both of ya." Simone told them as she pulled off a piece of roasted meat and ate it.

"So what 'ave ya been up ta yerself? Yer mother an father pullin at yer nerves?" Simone asked with an arching of her eyebrow. Franchesca sighed but nodded.

"They are still putting plans forward to make sure I marry who they would like me to. They want me to have someone powerful, but not too powerful. So that joining to our family might increase our power more than theirs. They think it would make whatever family I become married to indebted to them."

53

Franchesca grumbled as she held out her hands towards the fire to ward off a chill.

"The only bright spark within that situation is that the man I seem to prefer is from a very bold family. His father is planning an expedition to dangerous, uncertain territory. With enough luck, it will buy some favor in my father's eyes, and I won't be forced into a wedding in which the groom makes my skin crawl." Franchesca continued looking away from the fire; she watched as Simone looked down at the basket and slowly picked up another bit of food.

"Ave ya ever jus' tought of tellin yer parents how ya feel?" She asked, awkwardly avoiding Franchesca's gaze and eating slowly. Simone gazed sidelong at the flickering flames as they crackled in the hearth.

"They never listen." Franchesca replied with a shrug. "Claude has heard me tell them a great many things. He has heard me make small requests, or even just ask questions. They never take the time." Claude, nodded as she gazed back at him.

"Maybe ya should tell 'em, who ya want an' dat what dey want doen't matter. After, all its yer future." Simone added as she looked blankly at the fire taking another bite of food. Franchesca thought about what she had said. Maybe it was time for her to say no. Perhaps this was all a test. A way to make her stand up and assert herself. Could it be that's what her mother and father had been waiting for all along? It was worth a try. Franchesca stared at Simone; she could tell something was not right. Simone seemed different. Distant, almost closed off.

"Are you alright Simone?" she asked. Simone blinked and allowed a smile that didn't quite reach her eyes to cross her eyes, she nodded quickly; unsure of what else to do.

"I'm alright. I tink I'm jus tired. It's been a long few days." Simone brushed it off. Franchesca looked at her stained and ragged clothes and her dirt striped skin.

"Are you going to be here tomorrow? If you would like, I can give you another lesson." Franchesca asked. Simone just bobbed her head before running her fingers through her bright ruby red hair. Franchesca rose from where she was seated and nodded happily down at Simone.

"I should be heading back. I don't want my parents to come searching for me. Or check on me to find out I'm not there." Franchesca smirked.

"I will see you tomorrow, and I'll make sure to give you a lesson." Simone nodded as she watched Franchesca exit Claude's small cabin. Franchesca felt her feet kick up loose droplets from the sodden grass; there were a few times she had to step around a large patch of slick mud. She imagined what she and Simone would have done if they could. Franchesca could easily imagine Simone scooping up a hand full of the slippery mud and smearing it over her clothes or her face. The thought made Franchesca smirk slightly, as she rushed into the house. She silently crept through the dark, empty kitchen. As quiet as a mouse she crept back into her room and stripped off her wet clothes. She threw the gown over a chair to let it dry. It didn't matter much even if she were discovered at this point. Now that she was within the walls of her room she could easily say she went out on the balcony to look at the moon and whisper a prayer to the Heavenly Lady. Franchesca slipped on her nightgown, the fabric felt warm and soft against her skin, bringing her a sense of simple comfort. She pulled the corner of the covers and slid into bed. She could feel the strength of her heartbeat; she could all but hear the blood surging through her veins. Its crimson flow echoed like thunder in her ears. There was a feeling of such exhilaration that Franchesca could hardly stand it. She closed her eyes and took a deep breath. Suddenly she knew. It was because her friend was so close again. Her arms brought the blanket up, and she hid her face beneath them to hide the broad smile that crossed from ear to ear upon her face. She drifted off to sleep with a contented sigh.

Claude looked over at Simone, thought to speak; to move towards her, and hesitated. He knew Franchesca well enough to know when to speak and when to listen. He knew her well enough to know her moods and what upset her. This situation required a bit more care.

"I get the feeling you're not as alright as Franchesca thought you were." He put into words quietly. Simone shrugged and let out a nervous laugh; as she cast a sidelong glance to the ground once more.

"I'm not bad; jus' ave stuff on my mind is all." Simone acknowledged. "I'll be fine. It's most likely nothin anyay." She said. "Yeah, I'll be alright." Simone assured with a voice and a look that only gave muted voice to the torment she felt within. Claude fixed her with a look that made her aware that he could tell something was bothering her, but within that look was also the understanding of her wanting to keep it private.

"Well if you say so. Just know, Franchesca isn't the only one you can talk to." He said with a reassuring grin. Simone bobbed her head in understanding. "Come on; I've got another bed in the back. You can have it for as long as you wish to stay. No reason you should be sleeping on the floor." Claude told her. Simone pushed herself to her feet and followed after him.

"You should get some sleep; I would imagine Miss Franchesca will be in as soon as she can to see you." Claude told her gently. "If you need anything, just let me know, and I'll see about getting whatever it is." He grinned as he bowed. Simone allowed herself a laugh even though she didn't much feel like it.

"Ya know I'm not one of yer fancy high-neck ladies in lace. In fact, I tink ya outrank me." Simone reminded with a smile.

"You're still a lady and Miss Franchesca's guest." Claude said with a wink.

"That means you outrank me. Sleep well, Simone." Claude told her as he turned and walked down the short hallway to his room. Simone looked at the bed and sighed. She crossed the room and laid her head on the soft pillow. It was much different than sleeping in a pile of hay and straw, and much more comfortable than sleeping on canvas bags of grain or sand. Simone wrapped the soft woven blankets around her and sighed contently. It's not so bad, she thought to herself.

Chapter
5

Franchesca pointed to one of the words she had written on the parchment as she showed it to Simone. It was a simple exercise that her tutors used many years ago.

"Cat." Simone answered. Franchesca smiled and nodded as she moved her slender finger to another word at random. "Pie" Simone nodded with a smile of her own. Franchesca then pointed to three random words in a row asking Simone to repeat them in the order she pointed out." Dog, Boy, Girl."

"You're really making very good progress." Franchesca told her cheerfully as she put the parchment down. "You'll be reading and writing in no time at all." Franchesca added merrily.

"Ya tink so?" Simone asked. Franchesca reassured her as she rubbed Simone's shoulder. The two sat in silence for a moment at Claude's table. "Are yer mother an' father draggin ya off somere taday?" Simone asked. Franchesca nodded as she sank into a chair.

"My father wanted to observe the quality of the ship that Syandro's father has swooned over. Apparently, it cost a great deal, and according to him was worth every bit of coin. My father doesn't truly believe the vessel is really what masseur De Madonia claims it to be—but if it is, he would like to set eyes on it. He has said if by chance the ship is as grand as Cyrillio De Madonia makes it out to be that he would like one commissioned to add to his merchant fleet." Franchesca huffed as she placed her head into her hands and leaned against the table.

"They thought it a good idea for that reason; my beloved mother and father also want to observe how Syandro interacts with his father on this occasion. I think my father wants to make sure that he sees that his father puts him to work. After all—hard work is what leads to fortune—and money is of great importance to my father." Franchesca scoffed. Simone snorted as she sat across from her and looked her in the eyes.

"Ave ya ever tought 'bout gettin away from 'ere?" Simone asked. "Ya know, just... runnin?" Franchesca nodded slowly before a blissful expression crossed her lips.

"I did—a lot. Then I met you. I realized then that I didn't want to run anywhere that you weren't." Franchesca explained.

Simone laughed. "Yer, a right romantic." She told her. Simone leaned in close and gestured for Franchesca to do the same.

"Ave ya tought 'bout sneakin out? I mean in ta tha city." Franchesca looked around the room nervously. Her heart was again thundering in her chest.

"I... I," she stuttered as she shifted her eyes around, unable to focus on one spot for too long.

"Relax, it's only me." Simone assured laying a calming hand on Franchesca's shoulder. She glanced about then back to Simone once more.

"I have. I mean, I thought about sneaking into the city to see you. To—go and have... fun. I mean, you've seen what little there is for me to do here. I thought I might go and try what you do—what other people do for fun." Franchesca confessed glancing to the floor fighting off the color in her cheeks.

Simone nodded. "Would ya like ta, still?" She asked arching an inquisitive eyebrow.

"Are you asking me to sneak out?" Franchesca asked wide-eyed, feeling her throat go suddenly dry.

"Aye—look I'll leave in a little while an' I'll get ta tha docks. I can ask 'round bout dat fancy ship, belongin ta tha man wit' dat fancy Castellian name—an' I can wait for ya round dere. I'm sure you'll see me. When ya do, I'll nod an' you'll know where ta meet me again tanight."

"Can I ask Claude to come?" Franchesca asked timidly. She didn't want Simone to think she didn't want to spend time alone with her—that she didn't trust her, but she was nervous about traveling all that way—at night no less.

"I 'ave a feelin 'ell be talin ya nyway." Simone smirked with a sly wink. "Ya might even find a new pair of clothes in yer room later. Won't be nearly as fancy as what ya wear round 'ere tough." Simone explained.

"You already asked him?" Franchesca whispered. Simone nodded appearing very pleased with herself. "I... I don't know. I'm not sure what to think about this. I don't know what to say..."

"Say you'll come." Simone pleaded softly. With the way her emerald eyes peered into her own—Franchesca could only nod. She would do it. She would sneak out into the city and meet Simone. How was she going to get out of the house that was a question? And how was she going to get there? Suddenly Franchesca thought that she might have made a mistake.

* * *

"Ah the de Maret family." Syandro exclaimed happily as he strode down the boarding ramp of the ship to meet them. He bowed politely to Franchesca and her parents before extending his hand and giving her father a firm handshake, followed by a gentle kiss on the top of her mother's hand.

"If I might be so bold as to do the same to your daughter?" Syandro asked with a polite bow. Renaud de Maret gave his permission and carefully studied Syandro as he placed a gentle kiss on the top of Franchesca's hand. "Come; let me be the first to welcome you aboard my father's proudest ship. Syandro exclaimed.

"It was christened the Sea Rose." Franchesca stopped and gaped in awe at the magnificent vessel. Gold embellishments glistened in beautiful carvings which were etched upon the doors of the captain's quarters. The stairs of the quarterdeck were painted a vibrant red and the handrails a purple with gold and silver filigree. The rails of the ship were painted the same deep red that the stairs were painted. The sails were a royal purple—and the rose upon the sail was picked out in gold thread.

"Is she not beautiful?" Syandro asked with a smile as he grabbed a taut length of line and stood upon the rails. One hand rested upon the gold and ivory pommel of his blade. Franchesca noticed that the blade he carried today was different from the sword he carried at his visit to the manor house. It hung at his side; the blade was shorter and broader. No doubt it made it more efficient for use aboard the ship should the need present itself.

"Masseur and madam, my father awaits your presence in his quarters—shall I show you to them?" Syandro asked with a grin.

"Lead the way." Renaud smirked as he extended his arm. Franchesca followed and gazed on with awe as her eyes took in the opulent captain's chamber. Velvet pillows of red and gold lay upon couches and divans of luxurious foreign fabrics. A polished silver tray sat atop a thick wooden table. Settled upon a spotless, polished silver tray stood a bottle of wine and three delicate looking glasses ready to be filled. The ships quarters appeared as if it had an accommodation for every luxury one could ask for—at least while pitching up and down and swaying upon the sea.

"Father, your guests have arrived." Syandro announced proudly giving a bow of his head and sweeping his arm to his stomach.

"Ah, so they have. So what do you think of my ship? Grand is it not?" Syandro's father asked as he laughed happily. He was a jolly man; with a slight paunch to him which spoke of his well-lived life. Franchesca also observed a few paled scars upon his olive skin that hinted at his military experience.

"My boy, would you go make sure that the crew finishes bringing the cargo aboard? I don't need them to waste their time gambling—there's much to do, and I'd like to set off before the end of the week."

"Of course father." Syandro bowed respectfully. "Miss Franchesca, would you care to accompany me?" Syandro asked with a polite smile. Franchesca noted the slight rigidity that passed over her father and mother. Now it was their turn to be put into a position where being polite meant it was time for them to do something they were uncomfortable with. A show of force and of wit and will from the part of Syandro's father. It was clear to see why he had risen in the social ranks of Forn. He knew when to bite his tongue and when to play his wit. It appeared he maintained quite an excellent knack for keeping people off balance. Franchesca nodded with a smirk all her own—which had nothing to do with being in the presence of Syandro. She relished her parent's discomfort and the true test of their generosity.

"I would enjoy accompanying you." She replied as she walked with Syandro out of the cabin. Syandro's heavy soled boots thumped against the deck wood. He glanced over his shoulder and smiled after they walked some paces away.

"My father knows that your parents are testing me as well as him. In truth, he enjoys the game." Syandro chuckled easily.

"I enjoy watching your father best them. All too often people simply collapse under the will and coin of my parents." Franchesca replied as she allowed her gaze to flit around trying to find Simone.

"My father has no real need of money. We have more than enough. We have lands in Castella, and lands here. In truth, he cares nothing for his social standing here." Syandro conspiratorial smirk and a mischievous twinkle in his eye. "Except of course he enjoys the social gatherings his position affords him—if for nothing else than to make nobles dreadfully uncomfortable." Franchesca laughed.

"Then why is he here?" She asked as she stopped and gazed up at him. He held up his lean muscled arms as if showing her the world around them and grinned.

"It's for the adventure." Syandro explained with enthusiastic joy. "Life is an adventure—my father has taught me. Money dwindles, influence waxes and wanes like the moons; but adventures no one can take from you. Adventure's... they only end when your life does—and then you have new adventures—or so we are told eh?" Syandro chuckled. Adventures—Franchesca thought to herself. Syandro made it sound even more enchanting than she thought possible. Though she read books and listened to stories of questing hero's, their expeditions; and their magnificence—she'd never felt the passion. Now standing before Syandro, aboard admittedly the grandest ship, she had ever seen—the passion of it gripped her. She grasped its importance, and she was sure of the desire. All at once she became keenly aware of the what was missing

61

from her life. Adventure. The wild, spontaneous nature and unpredictable whims of following the road to an unknown destination—or lack thereof. Doing something just because it could be done. Or trying to do something to see if you could; and if not, being able to say you tried.

"I must say I find you quite fascinating Syandro." And incredibly handsome she mused within the safety of her head—allowing her eyes take in his broad muscled shoulders. Franchesca's eyes met his with a twinkle and a grin of their own. Then out of the corner of her eye, she saw her—Simone. She gazed at her for a long moment and gazed on as Simone grinned recklessly. Simone took out a short bit of charcoal and began scratching something on the side of a red brick wall.

"Is something wrong?" Syandro asked. As he turned his attention out to the crowd trying to find what had so distracted her, his hand reflexively straying to the hilt of his blade.

"No. It's nothing at all." Franchesca replied with a smirk. She looked on as Simone ducked behind a building and ran off back deeper into the city. It's about time for me to have an adventure of my own, Franchesca thought.

* * *

Franchesca slipped out of her room, her heart racing faster and faster with every footstep. She held a well-worn pair of boots as she walked, not wanting to put them on for fear of the noise they would make against the floor timbers. She was doing it; she was actually doing it. She was sneaking out. Franchesca gave serious consideration to holding her breath as she walked—thinking in the deep stillness that perhaps she was breathing louder than normal. It certainly seemed that way to her. It's my nerves; she told herself as she crept along. She slunk down the stairs as quickly as she could manage before grasping the cold handle of the door. Once outside Franchesca quickly sat down and tugged her boots on. The night air was brisk against her skin. She stopped to think for a moment; it was brisk to her—how many times had Simone been forced to sleep or trudge around in such chilly weather? Franchesca tied her wavy hair back into a simple ponytail and took a deep breath, the cool air flowing into her lungs filled them with the chill of the night. It was two miles to the city and a good walk to the docks where Simone had made a mark asking Franchesca to meet her. Simone had placed a large black "S" on the red brick wall of a tavern that lay only a few paces from where the Sea Rose docked. Franchesca closed her eyes and relished the sensation and the rush of excitement. I best be on my way then she told herself as she started off sneaking through the grounds of the estate. Slipping through the countryside was easy enough. It was a cloudless night and the light of the twin moons shown down on the open countryside offering pale and gentle red tinged silver light. The two–mile trek to the city felt like an eternal struggle. Her body ached with anticipation, and her heart pounded feverishly within. The exhilarating feeling of being out roaming the country at this hour was intoxicating; true it was frightening as well. There was always the concern of being accosted by bandits and brigands, but it was nice to worry. How often did people think that she wondered? Never the less, she did utter a quick prayer to the Heavenly Lady asking that as she followed the path of the gypsy and the shieldmaiden she be given quick feet and a stout heart. Franchesca beamed at being out in the crisp night air free from the ever watchful criticizing gaze of her parents was indescribably freeing. Franchesca relished in the scent of the wildflowers, and the country grass. Even the ache that crept into her thighs and feet from her long trek was something that brought a tremendous amount of satisfaction to her. One did not truly enjoy such things traveling within a coach. Perhaps they enjoyed them, but they did not appreciate them. She smiled; in that small moment, Franchesca envied the coachman. They were able to ride outside and gaze at the world around them. They could feel the wind, and they smelled the world around them with the added speed and power of horses before them. Her parents were rich; but who was truly wealthy? I am, Franchesca thought to herself as she strode through a wild bush. Then she regarded the thick stone walls and gate mountings of the city before a satisfied expression came to her delicate features. Two lanterns hung from hooks on both of the large pillars that the iron gate was bolted to. She strode through the gates and gave a polite, yet inconspicuous nod to the two guards, who simply returned her nod with one of their own. Her eyes widened at the sight and size of the open oak doors on the other side. The thick iron bars were a decent defense to be sure—but the heavy iron-banded oak doors beyond were an extra layer, should the city fall under attack. From what little Franchesca had studied of famous battles and Khaos invasions, it would be far too easy to mount a team of twisted beasts to yokes and pull the barred gate free of their mountings to gain entry to the city. She hoped there was no cause for those monstrously thick oak doors to shut while she was there; if that happened, she would never get home. Of course, if that did happen, she would have far worse problems than her parents discovering she'd snuck away. The leather soles of Franchesca's boots thudded against the paving stones. The bustling sounds of life echoed all around in every direction. Merchants were still out shouting about their goods. Food vendors cooked for small crowds that gathered around them. Carts creaked, carriages clattered and rattled as they passed by. Street performers danced, played, or juggled trying to impress those revelers still out and about in an attempt to earn some extra coin. Franchesca stopped in the middle of the street for a moment and closed her eyes. She took a deep breath; savoring the coolness of the night air, and the mingled aroma's of the city that she stood in. The countryside where her parent's estate resided along with a few others was as quiet as a basilica graveyard at this hour. Here within the city walls, it might as well be midday. When she opened her eyes, she turned and headed off in the direction of the docks.

After many long minutes walking towards the dock and sidestepping swaying drunks, Franchesca reached the Sea Rose. She studied the charcoal scrawled "S" Simone had made and waited. There was a sharp whistle, and Franchesca turned and noticed Simone leaning against a building; half cloaked in the shadow it offered. Franchesca ran over to her and threw her arms around her and hugged fiercely laughing all the while. Simone did the same.

"Come on. Let's get ya yer first proper drink." Simone smiled. Franchesca tilted her head up towards the carved sign of the tavern. The Rusty Harpoon looked like a building her father would only set foot in if he were to spread oil and pitch on the interior to burn it to the ground. Her father didn't believe in taverns—he did, however, support more than a few wine parlors within the city. They were a civilized thing in her father's eyes. Places where gentlemen met and discussed business transactions and arranged shipments or weddings to each other's children. Renaud de Maret claimed that taverns were where the uncivilized lower class met. It was a place for farmers to blow their pittance, or shore men to sleep after ordering around. What Franchesca observed within was a world different from what her father asserted. They were people, and they smiled. There were soldiers, and shore men—sailors and even well-dressed nobles. Franchesca watched as they celebrated; she could not rightly guess what they were so joyous about—but they all seemed to be celebrating something. Some were clearly drunk—their limbs flailing about like untied rope caught in a stiff wind. Others who walked past her and Simone, simply strode over to friends and shook hands or embraced and began laughing or making jokes—without the familiar swaying of limbs or slurring of speech which marked them as drunks. Some were crude, others she didn't understand—which probably meant they were extremely crude, and it was better she didn't understand. Merry music played as violins lutes and flutes created a happy melody. Patrons stomped their feet, clapped and banged their glasses crafted of horn against the wooden tables. Each seemed to lend their voice to the song, though it seemed everyone sung a different song at heart; somehow it all seemed to fit together in perfect harmony. As Simone and she walked into the tavern Calldunish squeeze pipes began to play—everyone appeared to stop what they were doing, and all began to sing the same song regardless of what they'd been doing moments ago.

"Oi Simone!" A happy voice called out from behind the bar. Franchesca regarded the barman as he held his arms open in a welcoming gesture.

"Oi Fabrice!" Simone smiled as she led Franchesca over to a bald man with a collection of scars on his face and more than a few on his bald pate. The man behind the bar was thick of limb; belly, and beard.

"I ain't seen you round these parts in a few days—thought ya had forgotten bout yer old friend Fabrice." He smiled as he filled a tankard to its brim and placed it on the bar for her. "Is this the girl ya been talkin on an on about?" Fabrice asked as he filled another tankard.

"Aye; Fabrice, meet Franchesca de Maret. The nobleman's daughter with a heart of gold rather dan pockets of it." Simone grinned as she hoisted her tankard.

"Welcome, ta the Rusty Harpoon miss, any friend of Simone's drinks fer free; an is always welcome." Fabrice placed the tankard down on the bar and smiled.

"Scuse me—I think I hear someone that needs a good head smackin." Franchesca listened as Fabrice shouted towards a crowd as he rolled up his sleeves—continuing a stream of obscenities in such a combination that Franchesca was stunned by the originality more than the actual swearing itself. She observed the large man smack a rowdy patron in the back of the head before scolding him.

"So, what do ya tink?" Simone asked taking a drink from her tankard.

"I've never felt more at home." Franchesca replied as she took a drink from her own. The contents of which were so strong that it reddened her cheeks and caused her to cough slightly. Simone laughed.

"How do you know Fabrice so well?" Franchesca inquired as she took another sip, doing her best to become accustomed to the strength of the brew in her cup.

The lie came swiftly, comfortably and before giving it a second thought, it was out of her mouth. She didn't want to lie to Franchesca, but she did. It was second nature.

"He was tha only decent man my father ever made contact with. He's more family ta me dan ma own father." The truth was she'd wandered past Fabrice's tavern on a freezing night and been half delirious. After her torn and bloody feet had failed her Simone had fallen through the door of his tavern. He'd taken one look before taking her upstairs and putting her to bed—Fabrice had even paid a churgeon to come and give her a once over. There had been nothing more wrong with her, other than her half–frozen feet. That tale was too personal and too sad to tell. Aside from that, it would raise more questions about the history between her father and herself—questions she didn't want to answer—about a man she didn't want to think about. Simone told her a practiced pleasant and comfortable story—the one she used most often. Simone gazed back over her shoulder at Fabrice and took a deep breath. She owed him more than she could ever repay. Franchesca glanced around the room watching as people danced drunkenly around tables and chairs. Darts were thrown wide of their targets, and men began contests of arm wrestling. For every display of loud, abrasive behavior Franchesca could see men who tucked themselves away in quiet corners and wrote on long strips of parchment or read thick books whose titles she could not make out clearly from her seat.

Simone tapped her on the shoulder, and she followed the tilt of her head as she nodded towards someone who had just come in the door. His length of coal black hair was combed neatly.

"Ain't dat tha lad yer father saw dis afternoon?" Simone asked, pointing towards the door. Franchesca's heart froze within her chest. Sure enough, Syandro De Madonia along with two ragged clothed men walked into the tavern. Syandro turned, and his eyes met Franchesca's. She turned away hurriedly, attempting to hide her face behind her hand.

What was she going to do? Was Syandro going to tell her father or his father? Maybe he would use this as leverage in the petty noble games that they were being made to play a part in. Franchesca was so lost in her thoughts that she didn't hear Syandro's thick–soled boots until he was two steps away.

"I must say—this is a most pleasant surprise." Syandro said with a smile as he bowed politely.

"Please, Syandro; don't tell my father..." Franchesca began to plea before Syandro started to chuckle holding up his hand to reassure her.

"I have no intention of speaking a word to anyone Franchesca." Syandro smiled. Her eyes widened in delight as he waived the idea off as if it were an offensive smell, or bothersome insect.

"It seems to me that you are finally beginning your own adventure." Franchesca smiled broadly as she bobbed her head eagerly.

"I would like you to meet my friend, Simone" Franchesca told him happily as she introduced them.

"Syandro De Madonia—son of Cyrillio De Madonia, of Castella." Syandro replied with a confident smirk as he extended his hand towards Simone.

"Simone." She replied simply. Her eyes raked him up and down as if sizing him up for some confrontational purpose. Simone nodded her head to the blade at his waist.

"Ya ever use dat ting? Or is it more fer show?" She asked as she took a drink from her tankard.

"If I was not pursuing a marriage with Franchesca I must say I would try to pursue one with you. You seem to have a bit of Castellian spirit within you." Syandro grinned as he allowed his eyes to roam up and down her form appraisingly, in a less than subtle manner. Simone smiled slyly as she tipped the rest of her tankard into her mouth and swallowed it.

"I 'ave a feelin ya wouldn't get very far wit' tha likes'a me." Simone replied with a knowing grin before she winked at him.

"I don't know if I should be insulted or if I should have once viewed it as a challenge. However, we will never know." Syandro smiled back with a bow of the head. "To answer your question, however, yes I have used this." He was going to explain further when Fabrice interrupted the impromptu meeting with a shout.

"Oi—there ya are. I was expecting ya an hour ago." Fabrice announced loudly as he walked over to Syandro. Simone noted him curiously. "Them barrels of rum and ale ain't gonna fetch themselves ta yer father's boat."

"Three kegs of rum, and eight of ale correct?" Syandro asked.

"Aye, my looks might have left me, but my brains work better than ever." Fabrice replied as he scratched the chin that lay beneath his thick gray beard. "Must be because I ain't gotta worry bout pleasen any little lady folk." Fabrice chuckled.

"Like ya ad one ta start with." Simone shot back with a chuckle. Fabrice laughed with the ease which came when friends jibed and ribbed one another as he poured her another tankard.

"Somethin wrong with the brew miss? Yer cup is still full; cryin out ta be drunk, it is." Fabrice nodded towards Franchesca.

"Oh, it's fine. I... I've just never had anything so strong before." Franchesca replied with a bashful glance up at him. She hoped she wasn't being rude. By the gods the brew was strong. She wondered if he made it himself, or if it was merely another piece of life she'd been missing out on. Fabrice winked as he beckoned her closer.

"The best way ta get yerself used ta it is ta drink it fast as ya can." He whispered with another conspiratorial and mischievous twinkle in his eye. "Ya want one while yer men take the kegs and load em ta the ship?" Fabrice asked, turning his attention to Syandro.

"Yes, if you would be so kind." Syandro nodded as he pulled up a stool and sat next to Franchesca. Taking Fabrice's advice, Franchesca lifted the cup and drained it as quickly as she could manage. It was as if she'd swallowed a branch from a thicket—there was a flare in her cheeks which stung as if she had sat in the sun for hours. She coughed and shook her head, before chuckling.

"I think he gave me a bit of bad advice." Franchesca began with a slight slur, as she cleared her throat of the burn; blood rushing to color her cheeks from embarrassment from her slurring. It was only one drink by the light of the Heavenly Lady; she felt so embarrassed. Simone chuckled and nodded as Fabrice poured out another measure and gave a tankard to Franchesca and Syandro.

Franchesca grasped the handle and brought them mug to her lips and took a long sip. The fluid burned less this time; maybe Fabrice was right after all. Her arms had the feeling of weightless sheets, and her muscles seemed to lose their rigidity. Franchcesca stared over Simone's shoulder and noticed two men sitting at a table.

It appeared to her like one simply laid his palm flatly against the table top while another danced a knife between his fingertips. The display ended abruptly when she realized the knife nicked one of the men's fingers—he cried out in pain. Simone turned her head and followed Franchesca's gaze. Simone peered over her shoulder upon hearing the commotion. Franchesca noticed her roll her eyes.

"Armatures—no idea how ta handle a knife." Simone said with a snort. Franchesca watched as the man cradled his bleeding hand wrapping a handkerchief from his pocket to staunch the blood.

"You know what they were doing?" She asked curiously.

"Do ya wan' ta try?" Simone asked as with a sly smile as she set her mug down on the bar. Franchesca nodded—perhaps a little quicker than she meant to. It seemed to be getting harder to control her muscles.

"What... do you do?" Franchesca asked as Simone led her over to the same table. Simone held out her hand—silently demanding the knife.

"Jus' sit down, an' put yer hand flat on tha table wit' yer fingers relaxed." Franchesca placed her hand on the table as Simone had instructed. Franchesca felt her heart pounding in her chest—just as it had when she'd seen Simone after her bath. By the Heavenly Lady why did that spring to mind, what was going on? Not that she felt she should complain, still she was nervous. She felt alarmed that the first place, her mind fled to when confronted with such a situation was the sight of her friend's exposed curves. Franchesca blinked rapidly feeling her mouth go dry.

"Do ya trust me?" Simone asked staring into her eyes intently.

"Yes—I... trust you—Simone." She stuttered and slurred slightly with a smile. Syandro stood by the table, eyes darting from Simone to Franchesca worriedly. Simone turned the knife over in her hand inspecting it feeling the weight, checking the balance. Without warning, she slammed it in between Franchesca's ring finger and middle finger. Franchesca was suddenly feeling herself becoming more and more sober with every dying second. Her mind focused now on the sharp steel in–between her fingers and the swift movement which put it there.

"Jus' look at me." Simone whispered as she guided Franchesca's gaze up away from the hand she had laid on the table. The knife was pried free, and suddenly Frnachesca's ears were picking up a slow, steady rhythm of steel thumping against wood. Franchesca fixed her eyes to Simone's. There was an unspoken bond between them, and Franchesca thought that as long as she stared into Simone's eyes, nothing would happen. Her ears picked up the growing frequency of the thumps, and the complex rhythm Simone created.

She felt the air and the cold steel of the knife blade pass between her fingers. First, she felt the thump of the blade an inch away from her thumb on the outside. Then the blade came down between her pinky and ring finger; then it thumped inside her thumb. The game continued without a definite rhythm or pattern. Sometimes Simone repeated the same spot twice—other times she chose another spot—yet the speed and ferocity of Simone's stabbing grew quicker and quicker as the thrusts became more and more unpredictable.

"Simone—I..." Franchesca watched as Simone pulled the knife back high over her head and struck it down with mighty force right where she'd started. Franchesca kept her eyes locked with Simone's. Her heart leaped excitedly within her; she was sure if the organ possessed legs it would be swaying and rocking. Franchesca glanced down and noticed there wasn't a single scratch on the flesh of her hand or any one of her fingers.

"How... how did you?" Franchesca tried to ask. Simone simply smiled and leaned back in her chair.

"I'm jus' dat good." She said as she pulled the knife free form the table and studied it appraisingly. "Ya wanna try?" Simone asked offering Franchesca the handle. Franchesca quickly shook her head.

"No! I can't—I don't want to hurt you..." Franchesca said fearfully. Simone just smiled at her. There was a gentleness there, and understanding that even Franchesca found hard to understand.

"Den ya won't." Simone replied as she pressed the handle of the knife into Franchesca's palm. Simone laid her hand down on the table, fingers splayed in a relaxed manner. Franchesca gawped at Simone's hand and began to tremble.

"Hey—jus' look at me." Simone told her gently. Franchesca gazed into Simone's eyes and took a deep breath. Suddenly there was a thump. It was not the mighty and powerful thump Simone opened with, but more of a gentle and cautious one. Then there was another—and another—and still another. Before Franchesca was aware of what had come over her, she found herself reacting and the knife was thudding against the table between Simone's fingers. It was slow; painfully slow if one were to compare it to the speed of which Simone had displayed moments ago, nor was it as varied in pattern, but by the gods she did it. Franchesca looked up into Simone's eyes and watched as she grinned back at her. With a final thud, Franchesca released the knife handle. She averted her gaze to the scarred table—terrified she had in fact wounded her friend, but neither one had noticed. She was sure that when she glanced down, there would be a crimson puddle spreading around a fleshy island that was once an attached finger. No such sight greeted her.

"I told ya dat ya wouldn't hurt me." Simone said. Franchesca rose hastily from the table her knees shaky, and her legs weak. Simone regarded Franchesca as she walked over to the bar and sat down. Syandro sank into the seat Franchesca had been sitting in across from Simone and smirked.

"Care to test yourself against me?" Syandro asked with a sly smile. Simone stood and shook her head.

"Nah—I don' trust ya like I do her." Simone replied with a smile of her own, as she walked over towards Franchesca. She had no reason to distrust Syandro, but she did. She had no reason not to trust him either, Simone reminded herself. There was just a sense she had around him, something which put her on edge. Maybe it was because she'd just met him. Was it because of how he spoke about her? Was it that he saw her as a challenge for refusing his advances? He saw her as some sort of prize to try and win—if he weren't trying to win Franchesca's heart. The nerve. As if all women should be flattered to receive his attention. She'd met men like him before. She hated them too. If Franchesca married him, if she spent time with him would there be time for her? Would she still want to be in her company? Maybe it was the way he looked at Franchesca.

Simone couldn't help but notice his eyes weighed her like a wolf eyeing a sheep. That is if a wolf had a particular fondness for exceptionally well–sculpted tits and ass—without truly noticing how charming her smile was. He drank her form in; not her—not all of her. Not only that, but he wasn't exactly subtle in hiding his observations of other women around him either, Simone herself was included in those passing observations. He was looking through eyes that desired conquest of the flesh—not the joining of hearts. Perhaps he would change; maybe it was just her feeling insecure and jealous. Or maybe it was her feeling something else entirely; she told herself as she walked over to the bar searching out Franchesca. Simone found her at the bar and smiled.

"What's on yer mind?" She asked as she sat down on the stool next to her and met her eyes.

"How were you so sure nothing would happen?" Franchesca asked. Simone simply smirked and shrugged.

"I don' know really. I... jus' guessed. I can be clever dat way." Simone whispered as she picked up her drink and took a sip before looking at Franchesca.

"I've played bafore—ta be honest. Ya learn a ting or two on da streets. Ya knick a bastards hand in a game it doen't go so well, so ya better learn an fast" Simone explained.

"Come on—we should probaly get ya back home." Simone told her gently as she placed a hand on her shoulder. Franchesca's heart began to pound like a blacksmith's hammer on an anvil, though as always she didn't know why. Franchesca could feel eyes on her as they walked towards the door. She glanced over her shoulder and noticed Syandro studying them as they made their exit. Franchesca grinned at him, but she noticed that his smile back seemed different. It appeared strained and false.

A mask, Franchesca told herself silently. The two walked through the winding city streets giggling and joking like the best friends they were. Franchesca felt so complete when she was with Simone. She didn't rightly grasp how... or why, but Simone seemed to understand her, better than she thought anyone understood her. The two of them trekked their way through the countryside back towards Franchesca's home.

Simone accompanied Franchesca back on the long walk to her parent's estate. She was content to be in her company, even if she did feel the heaviness within her chest from listening to her speak of Syandro. She also wanted to be there should Franchesca need help—it was late, and Franchesca was still young and ignorant with regards to the ways of the dangers of the world. Being a noble prepared you for some things, and hindered you in others. Simone lived on the streets; she'd learned a fair bit of fighting, and if she needed to, she could defend herself and Franchesca. Of course, if the worst happened she could sacrifice herself in more ways than one so Franchesca might get away—she wouldn't lose a friend not again. The conversation drifted to more jovial things which distracted Simone from the ache in her lower back. She was thankful that Fabrice had enough food that he could give her something to eat. Simone had no doubt that Franchesca would have given her whatever she could grab from her home once they arrived, but she didn't want to take advantage of her generosity.

"Are you going to stay in Claude's cabin tonight?" Franchesca asked. As they closed the distance to the grounds of the estate. Simone shrugged.

"I might; I don' really want ta make my way back ta tha city so late." She explained as they approached the low stone walls. Franchesca nodded happily.

"I'll come see you later tonight." She smiled. The two parted ways once they arrived upon the grounds of the estate, and Simone slipped discreetly towards Claude's cabin. Franchesca snuck back into the house and dashed up to her room as quietly as she could grinning all the while. She walked out to the balcony and looked up into the night sky. She found herself reflecting on her experience in the city. The fun she had and the taste of freedom that always seemed to accompany her when she was with Simone. Before she knew it, Franchesca found herself smiling up at the night sky.

Not just tonight; but every time she was with her. Suddenly she found herself delving deeper into her thoughts. Franchesca's heart froze in the middle of its rhythm. She felt her pulse quicken, her thoughts of Simone seemed to race and flood her mind. The memories of Simone's hand upon her shoulder, or the feeling of gentle warmth which suffused its way through her when they embraced. Gods how that warmth lingered; it kindled something within her. How could one person, make her feel that way? How could one person make her feel so free? How did Simone make her feel such joy? Why is it I am filled with a fear I have never known, she asked herself? It was not a fear of Simone; it was a fear of being without her.

Fear of saying something, or doing something that would drive her away. Half the time she wondered if she giggled too much. Franchesca didn't want Simone to think her a fool—though perhaps she was. Sometimes she felt foolish. If Simone knew where her mind went to when she'd been afraid she most certainly would have thought Franchesca a strange. That thought alone worried her. She feared not seeing her or embracing her. Simone was her friend, like Claude, she loved them both—no. Franchesca stopped and thought to herself as she slid down and sat against the stone balcony rail. It all made sense, at least to her. Gods was it true—did she? Could she; was it possible? Franchesca thought of her walks with Syandro, of all the time she had spent with him. She enjoyed his company. She found him handsome; very handsome if she were honest. He was charming and sweet—but there was some disconnect between them. It was true he wasn't like the other nobles she'd met—nor was his father. Franchesca enjoyed conversing with him, enjoyed spending time with him—but though she admired his physical form, and his company was enjoyable, but something within her didn't stir—despite his best efforts and hers. She'd been more infatuated with his sword and conversation than his physical form. Was she trying to force a connection between them? As she sat upon the stone of the balcony, she entertained the thought of marrying him. Franchesca didn't deny they could find some sort of happiness if they were to marry—but they would never truly bond completely. They would never truly understand one another. Franchesca cared for him deeply, but she did not love him—not enough to marry him as she'd once thought. The only time she'd felt completed, the only time she'd ever felt anyone truly understood her, was when she was with Simone.

By the Heavenly Lady's silver radiant grace was is true? Franchesca asked herself over and over—she rolled the questions around in her mind; she examined herself and all she thought she had known to be true. It was so hard to believe. To her profound shock, she found things she had never truly asked or taken stock of before this very moment. Franchesca recalled gazing upon Simone when she rose from the tub. She had been too embarrassed, too shocked to admit it then but she enjoyed what she saw—enjoyed it immensely. It made her heart gallop like a heard of stampeding horses; the sight sent an electric tingle in her spine—fingers, in her toes. Franchesca's pulse raced even now as she remembered where else a keen hunger had announced its desire to be filled. She swallowed—she tried to make sense of it in her head. Could it be? The more Franchesca seemed to think about it the more her pulse hammered. She roused to her feet quickly and ran out of her room, hurrying down the stairs, her pulse raced almost as quickly as her legs. She had to know—needed to know. Before Franchesca was fully aware of it before she could fully think of the possible consequences she was running through the grassy field that lay between the manor and Claude's cabin. What if she was wrong, and she made a huge idiot of herself? What if Simone didn't feel the same way? Those thoughts were trampled underfoot as she ran leaving them behind. As she ran through the grounds of her parent's estate, caring nothing for sneaking or quietness now that she was out of the house. The grass was soft and cool underfoot. She hadn't even bothered to pause to slip her boots back on or her slippers.

All she could think about was reaching Claude's cabin to see her. She had to see her. She had to know—and she would, shortly. Franchesca would know once she laid eyes on Simone, then she would know. Franchesca opened the door quickly, trying to keep it from clattering against the wall—which she managed, with some degree of success. She didn't even know if Claude was home, she didn't know if she cared. Did he know? What would he think? Simone came rushing out of the hallway and gazed at Franchesca eyes wide as saucers with worry.

"What... what is it?" Simone asked in a panic, as she stared at Franchesca silhouetted in the doorway. As Franchesca looked at her standing in a pale ribbon of moonlight her mind raced. She was a girl—a woman. Did it matter? Syandro was a man—should that matter? Why should one matter more than the other? Did one honestly matter more than the other? Or did the heart not want what it wanted? Right now all that she could see, all that she could think of was her. Simone's flaming ruby hair was bright even in the darkness. Her own heart drummed beneath her ribs. As Franchesca's eyes feasted upon her— she knew. She knew then and there. With the silver light cascading around her Franchesca walked over toward Simone and placed her hands on Simone's face. Almost as if the two shared the same mind, and the very same thoughts; they kissed. They each fought to pull one another closer. Each battled for purchase with each other's clothing grasping, tugging, and releasing frantically. Their hearts pounded against one another as they grasped each other, each trying desperately to pull the other closer. Franchesca felt a smile grow upon Simone's lips as they kissed.

"I was wonderin if you'd ever notice." She gasped as she kissed Franchesca again.

"I want to be with you." Franchesca said as she fought for breath lost within the passion of the moment. "I... I realized that tonight. I—want you, Simone." She continued. Simone panted as she leaned in and placed her lips on

Franchesca's. Since Franchesca hadn't bothered to change, Simone's hands drifted down to the bottom of the simple linen tunic. She was grateful for that, she wanted to feel her touch—and the simple clothes she was dressed in would make it so much easier than having to undo numerous ties and buttons. Franchesca closed her eyes and shuddered as Simone slipped her hands beneath, and up to the simple wrapping she'd used to secure her breasts. Her skin was so soft before Franchesca could think any further Simone lifted the tunic over her head and left it in a pile on the floor. Her heart thundered like a storm; though Franchesca felt more than a little self–conscious. Simone might have been thought of as thin, perhaps underfed, but by the gods of men, she was beautiful. Lean and having a body begging to be touched—which no doubt came because she had to run, jump and lift herself over obstacles to get away from the city watch. Franchesca had led a life of leisure. She believed her body was overly soft—it wasn't as though her parents had her do much of anything in the way of physical activity. For that reason, she felt her body suffered—and for that reason, she felt more than a little modest. No; Franchesca admitted to herself as her blood raced, embarrassed. As the linen lay puddled upon the floor, she put her arms up reflexively. Simone took a step forward and caressed her face.

"Ya don' need ta hide." She assured, running her hands down Franchesca's arms. "I tought ya were beautiful tha first time I laid eyes on ya. I... I wish I 'ad the courage ta tell ya when ya let me sleep over—when ya saw me in tha bath." Simone confessed as her pale cheeks reddened slightly.

"Ya don' 'ave ta hide." Simone whispered continuing to run her hands down her arms and when they reached her wrists—Franchesca allowed them to fall away; she turned her head slightly and blushed. She stepped closer and embraced her. Simone thought she was beautiful—had always thought she was beautiful.

She grasped hold of Franchesca's hand and led her away to the bedroom Claude had allowed her to use. Franchesca halted in her steps for a moment. Simone turned and looked at her wide–eyed—each of their hearts pounding like a smiths hammer. Was it a joke, a cruel joke? She'd never force Franchesca—but where had the hesitation come from? She'd seemed so eager only moments ago.

"I don't know how—I mean... I've never been with... with anyone." Franchesca stuttered nervously. Her blood pounded, and pulse raced within her ears. As part of her tutelage on being a proper lady of a noble house, Franchesca had received some lessons about a woman's duties in the bedchamber with regards to her future noble husband. Somehow she doubted those books and teachings would be of much help here and now. Franchesca's eyes drank Simone in; as a soul lost in the desert gulps down water. Her breath coming more and more rapidly. Her nerves aflame as Simone's eyes combed the bare flesh of her torso moving steadily up to meet her eyes.

"I don't know what to do." Franchesca repeated nervously as she met Simone's gaze. Simone stepped forward and pulled her close, causing a gasp to escape Franchesca's lips. Simone's hands slid to Franchesca's waist, and as she leaned in and as her face drew closer to Francesca's own she felt the heat of her breath upon her neck.

"I have... an' I do know what ta do." Simone tucked her thumbs in between Franchesca's hips and her wool pants, and Franchesca felt her knees shudder, and her eyes begin to roll. They continued to the small bedroom. As Simone tugged Franchesca's trousers down and laid her back upon the bed, Simone gazed upon her with more longing, more desire than she'd ever seen in another person's eyes before. After a deepening kiss, she was aware of her body responding on its own. As Franchesca's body reacted enthusiastically, instinctually, she felt it safe to say with no small degree of certainty that Simone did indeed know what to do.

Chapter
6

The two spent hours entwined with one another; sharing the warmth of one another's flesh.

"Why didn't you tell me?" Franchesca asked as she ran her hand over Simone's smooth skin; letting it roam gently over her unclothed body. Simone shrugged with an amused grin; she took a deep breath.

"It's not like I did't tink 'bout it. I tought 'bout tellin ya earlier—but den ya started talkin bout dat Syandro fellow. Ya seemed happy, an' I wasn' gonna ruin dat."

Franchesca smiled. "I like Syandro... but since meeting you, I realize I couldn't love him the way I love you. I enjoy his company—but I feel I need your company... I want you. You just, you stir something inside he doesn't." Franchesca thought for a moment. Perhaps she was being foolish. They were both young after all, did they know anything of love? She reminded herself, her parents were ready to marry her off. Well, she told herself—if I'm being foolish—if we're being foolish what better time than when we're young?

"You make me happy Simone; happier than I ever pictured myself with him." Franchesca admitted. Maybe it was best she took some of Syandro's advice with regards to this, and just enjoy the adventure—travel the road and see where it led.

"I just want to be with you." She told Simone softly as she pulled her unclothed form closer. Simone laced her fingers with Franchesca's and kissed them gently. "I'm going to do everything I can to make sure I get what I want for a change." Franchesca told her in a quiet whisper.

"An' if yer parents decide otherwise?" Simone asked, relishing the feel of her lover's silky skin against her own. It was a question neither wanted to think about, but that didn't mean they shouldn't think about it. That it was such a probability, made it all the more reason to plan for it.

"Then I run, and leave this place behind." Franchesca replied as she squeezed Simone's hand. Franchesca decided, no one was going to ruin her happiness. She had stood for the will and whims of her parents for too long. She had been their pawn in their schemes as much perhaps more so than a daughter to them. From now on Franchesca was going to make her own decisions; she was going to live her life. If her parents refused to allow her to grasp onto any happiness, why should she stay? She didn't care about money or fancy possessions. Those things meant nothing to her. Besides there were a hundred other ways if not more, one was able to make a name for themselves in the world.

"But what 'bout all ya would be loosin?" Simone asked. Franchesca smiled sweetly caressing her silky skin, allowing her fingers to play in pools of her crimson hair.

"They are just things. They mean nothing if I can't be happy—and the only way I could ever be happy is with you. I would rather leave everything behind and have nothing to my name with you than to have these things without you." Franchesca told her softly.

"Really?" Simone asked as she rolled over and peered into Franchesca's eyes. She nodded.

"As long as we are together, that's what I care about." Franchesca replied. She sat up, letting the pale light of the twins moons shine over her naked form as she reached up and unfastened the clasp of her silver pendant. The shining pendant depicted a woman's silhouette with a crown of eight stars with her swanlike neck resting in the crook of a crescent moon as she gazed down.

"I want you to have this." She told Simone gently. She fastened the chain around Simone's slender neck and smiled as the pendant rested on her chest.

"It's a pendant of the Heavenly Lady. I think it suits you." She smiled as she kissed the pendant which now rested on Simone's naked chest.

"I want to give it to you as a sign of my love and to ask her favor as she watches over us. And I want you to have it as a gift." Franchesca added with a gentle smile. Simone reached up and touched the pendant gingerly. As if afraid she'd break it, or tarnish it. No one had ever given her a gift before—certainly nothing so fancy anyway.

"I, actally 'ave sometin fer ya too." Simone told her as she rose from the bed and walked over to her trousers, unashamed of her nakedness and dug through the pocket. She held her fist tight as she walked over to the bed and pressed the contents into Franchesca's palm—closing her fingers about it firmly. Franchesca looked down; there in her palm were the two gold coins that she'd given Simone on the day they first met. She looked up at Simone in shock.

"Dey... balong to ya—in tha same way I do." Simone told her gently.

"You, never spent them?" Franchesca asked as she traced the outer edge of the coin working her way around and in feeling the embossed image beneath her fingers.Simone shook her head.

"Dey were tha most impotant tings to me. Bafore you—no one 'ad given me annythin least not like dis. I kept em ta remind me of you, an' yer kindness. Jus so I could ramember someone cared. Sometimes I would jus hold em an' look at em bafore fallin asleep. Jus' so I could tink of you." Simone told her. Franchesca smiled as they kissed again. No—I'll not be denied my happiness, she thought to herself. Not ever again.

* * *

It had been some days since her night with Simone. Despite all, she told herself she'd become lost once more—allowing herself to be stuffed into a box of her parents devising. She awoke in the morning after leaving Simone, to the news that her father and mother had set up a meeting with another noble and his son. It was, if she was being polite in her recounting of events—a dreadfully boring day. Once again forced to spend time in the company of people who numbed her mind. She could allow her mind to wander freely and truly miss nothing—as long as she allowed a pleasant grin to remain upon her face and continued to nod every so often. In the many moments of silence, her mind went back to that wonderful night past—to the pools of moonlight puddled on Simone's pale skin. The soft whispers and the scent of sweat as pleasure thundered through them like a herd of wild horses. Despite all her bluster and fury after their passion—Franchesca had fallen back into her old, meek and demure ways. She drifted along with the flow of her parents' desires and put her own aside more often than she truly liked to admit. Still; her first encounter did teach her something—and had sharpened her nails somewhat. It taught her to be bold. In one of the lapsed moments of conversation, she told the youth, whose name she couldn't be bothered to remember; that he was a dreadfully boring pompous buffoon. It showed great restraint on her part as well—because Franchesca wanted nothing more than to launch into a tirade which would have no doubt ended with him curled on the ground in tears. She wanted to call him an overbearing self–righteous ass; after his comment about the poorer citizens of the city—so the fact she'd not used profanity, nor spat on him or resorted to violence, was a great personal victory. It didn't matter to her that the youth's father withdrew the marriage proposal. Nor did it matter to her that her father and mother scolded her with a vigor she'd never before seen the likes of during the carriage ride home. Franchesca smirked once their tirade had reached its end. She imagined Simone's grin once she had the chance to recount the story, but Franchesca's smirk wavered.

How long would it be before she got the chance to tell Simone the story? She folded her hands in her lap and closed her eyes taking a deep breath. Not for the first time she thought of just baring it all to her parents and letting the cards fall as they would. What would happen? A vision flashed in front of her as the carriage rattled along. Her father yelling and screaming—raising a hand to her; the first time—the only time he would ever think of striking Franchesca. Her mother; grabbing a fist full of hair and holding her before a mirror—shouting something, as she forced Franchesca to look at herself as they screamed at her. Would this be the occasion? By the Heavenly Lady's light could she tell them? What if Claude paid the price? What if her parents removed Claude from their service—then who would Franchesca speak to? Who would look out for Simone and how would they meet in secret? Simone said there would be a time, a moment to tell them; and when it came to be ready. With such a thought in the forefront of her mind, the days of her life passed before her one after another in a dreadfully slow crawl. Franchesca strode into the sitting parlor where her parents were receiving visitors. It was some distant cousin—or so she had been told. It'd been a little over a week since her night with Simone. As Franchesca had done so often before, she confided in Claude. She told him everything from her feelings for Simone, to how she felt about Syandro. At one point she thought of marrying the man— by far the finest catch of the suitors who came to the announcement party. However, after her night with Simone the feelings she once thought she held for Syandro—she realized were a pale shadow of her feelings for Simone. Throughout the conversation, he listened. He offered neither criticism nor advice until she asked. Franchesca didn't ask what she should do about her feelings; she asked him when he thought she should tell her mother and father. She'd to ask him if perhaps she should say nothing and do just as she'd told Simone and run. Claude assured her, that though her parents wouldn't understand, and though they would likely disapprove; they were still her parents, and they did love her.

"They deserve to know how you feel. I've told you before, they may not say or do the right things to show they care every time—but they do love you, Franchesca. Give them a chance, to get it right before you decide."

"I will not bow to their wishes anymore." She told him adamantly. Claude bowed his head and smiled.

"That is up to you. But they deserve to know what is in your heart—just as much as Simone does." Claude smiled. Franchesca remembered hugging him and crying on his shoulder yet again. She didn't know how many times he had comforted her, or how many time's she'd cried on his shoulder. Somehow, no matter how sad or hurt she felt—Claude's embrace and presence always seemed to offer her some peace. Franchesca had made a decision. She'd chosen this day to tell them; and to lay her heart bare with them, come Khaos hells or high waters. Then, as things so often did, an unexpected obstacle revealed itself. She hated being made to make pleasantries—especially to those she was hardly familiar with. She bowed politely when she entered the room, making sure to use her best curtsy. Franchesca felt nervous enough given what she'd decided to do later when she was alone with her mother and father. She didn't need them to yell at her because she didn't give her most polite curtsy. She knew she was already going to receive some sort of tongue lashing from her parents after she spoke her piece, Franchesca did not need to give them time to warm up.

"So—I hear that fellow whose voyage you decided to so boldly back, has set sail." Her cousin Quentin observed pompously." You always did find the most new and exciting ways of throwing money away, cousin." He added. Franchesca had met him only once before when she was younger. She knew from that short meeting that she hated him.

"A Castellian bravo—could you imagine if he were to chart the Tomblands of fallen Apsu? The riches—the pride that would lay at his feet. Why he could almost receive anything, he wishes from her highness."

"I am assuming you have a point, Quentin?" Her father asked with a sigh as he took a sip from his wine glass.

"Will you do the same for me, good cousin?" Franchesca almost choked. She watched as her father looked over at her mother. "Think of what such a thing could do for our family. The prestige it could add to our name."

"I think all of Forn knows our name well enough. I think we are in high enough regard, that risking more of my coin would be foolish. Especially if such an expedition, was captained by you, Quentin. You might be related to my wife, but make no mistake—I hold no respect for you." Renaud told him in a relaxed dignified fashion.

"Your words are scathing cousin. You risk your coin on a damned Castellian, but not your own kin—tell me why?" Quentin asked as he reclined in his seat and put his boots upon the tea table in front of him.

"I have no faith in you. You are nothing more than a petulant child. I gave money to the Castellian not only to fund his voyage—but to make him especially aware of my standing. If his son wishes to wed Franchesca, I want him to know who is truly the most powerful in the union of the family's."

Renaud replied smoothly as he looked down at Quentin's boots on the fine wood of his table; scoffing slightly. "If you seek glory—ask for your coin elsewhere, it might change my mind if I knew you had other backers." He added as he rose from his chair. Quentin's eyes crawled over Franchesca, looking her up and down as snake watches a mouse.

"I am hurt by your lack of faith cousin..." Quentin replied placing a hand on his chest, allowing a serpents self–serving sneer to grace his sharp predatory hawkish features.

"He is not alone in his lack of faith." Martise de Maret replied softly. "He is right—ask others in the family—or any of your gambling friends. Now I am afraid the subject is closed. You are welcome to stay the night as our guest. But other than a meal, a bed and a roof—you will receive no other aid from us." Franchesca's mother warned. Quentin merely bowed his head as he stood from his chair.

"Very well, cousins." He paused and looked at Franchesca and smiled. It was a cruel smile. "Though—I have just remembered. I think it was a week ago—perhaps a little more..." Franchesca's heart sank. He had seen her in the Rusty Harpoon.

"I believe I saw your lovely daughter in a tavern by the docks. The Rusty Harpoon—it's called." He remarked calmly.

"That is impossible. Franchesca was here asleep." Renaud replied scornfully, fighting the urge to rise from his chair. Struggling to keep the color of rage from his face at the accusation he believed baseless and utterly false.

"You know—I thought that myself, but when I arrived here I asked one of your housekeepers. She said there had been a number of times in the past week, where young Franchesca was not in her chambers. She said she searched the house for her—but she was nowhere to be found." Franchesca's stomach burned with anger. If she found out who spoke to Quentin, she would throw them from the house personally.

"Now... suppose that other potential courtiers were to hear of such a thing? Sure, it is fine if she was to marry the Castellian—but I think all of us know your pride would never allow such a thing." Quentin said calmly gazing at them as a wolf eyes a wounded deer in the forest.

"Even if she were in such a place, other nobles attend such places. After all—you just admitted that you do." Martise replied. Franchesca could see her father had already put the pieces together, though her mother had not.

"Oh, true—I admit I frequent such places. But how many other suitors do? How many other suitors have your... ridged sense of refinement? You must take such things into consideration. Give me coin, and I'll keep my lips sealed tighter than the palace gates. The choice is yours, dear cousins." Quentin yawned and smiled as he cracked his neck. Franchesca's fists were balled tightly—ready to strike him,—how she restrained herself, not even she knew. "I'll let you think on such things until the morning when I must be off." Quentin told them as he walked towards the door.

"I should kill you in your sleep." Franchesca hissed in a whisper as he made to pass by her. Quentin smiled and winked.

"It's just business—nothing more; and nothing less." He replied quietly with a self–satisfied sneer as he passed her. Franchesca could only imagine how he received the scar on his cheek. He probably tried to extort coin form the wrong person. Perhaps it was a gambling debt the unkempt scavenger tried to duck.

"You can't truly believe him?" Franchesca asked as she strode further into the room. Martise looked at her daughter, as did her father.

"Tell us the truth girl—were you there?" Should she tell them? Perhaps the truth would be the best way to make sure she got what she wanted. Or she could lie, and they could call Quentin's bluff—if he proved it true she'd get what she wanted. After all, if no one wanted to marry her, then what would her parents suggest? Knowing them, they probably already had an alternate plan of action.

"Yes—I was there." She admitted as she gazed down at the floor releasing a sigh. Renaud let out a long sigh as he rubbed his head. Martise walked over and closed the doors. The polished doors made a loud crack as they were slammed shut.

"Why on the throne would you go to such a place? What sense deserted you, child?" Her mother asked.

"I am not a child!" Franchesca replied hotly, as she stepped towards her mother. "You plan on marrying me off, and you still refuse to see that I have my own thoughts and desires. You... refuse to allow me to live my life." She continued.

"Why were you there—and what were you doing?" Renaud asked angrily as he sank back into his seat. He had a look in his eyes that screamed of wanting to break something—wanting to scream and shout.

"I just wanted to go and see what it was like. I saw it when we went to visit the Sea Rose." Before she could say anything else, her mother cut in once more.

"Did you go to meet someone? And how about being missing from your room on the other nights?" She asked angrily; fighting the urge to pace—perhaps fighting the urge to rise and strike her, she couldn't tell which.

"I went to see Claude in his cabin on the grounds, and no—I wasn't meeting anyone—at least certainly not anyone you would care about. Not any of the men you've been trying to marry me off too if that's what you're worried about." Franchesca replied angrily.

"Only a friend I met in the city." Her parents looked curiously at one another. There was a long, tense moment of silence before her father sighed again.

"Damn that leach." Renaud hissed as he slammed a fist on his desk, before promptly placing a hand upon his chin in an effort to keep himself from descending any further into his rage.

"You're not going to pay him, are you? So I was in a tavern, what does that matter?" She asked glancing between them.

"To find someone worthy of courting. You're our daughter; we don't want you associating with those who cavort in taverns. You are a distant member of the royal family we want to find you a worthwhile match..." her mother began.

"What does it matter, Quentin, admitted he spends time in such places." Franchesca interrupted; looking at both of them in a shocked manner.

"That's exactly the point. You've seen Quentin—would you truly want to marry someone like him? If he admits to being there, what others—or worse, could congregate there." Her father explained calmly.

"How could you do this Franchesca?" Martise scolded. Franchesca looked at her and scowled as she shook her head.

"You still insist on treating me like a prized horse—as if you want to breed me to a stud of your choosing..." Martise's hand shot out lighting quick and slapped Franchesca's face. The blow stung fiercely, but Franchesca didn't flinch; didn't react. She would not give her mother the satisfaction.

"How dare you!" Martise hissed. "How dare you use such language, and say such things. Have you no respect for yourself; for us—for your family name, or its reputation? Have we not given you everything?" Her mother hissed as she circled her daughter.

"It has nothing to do with you! It has nothing to do with our family name or our reputation! This is about me! It's about me being happy. It's about me making my own decisions, feeling content with my own choices. It's about me doing what is best for me. By the Heavenly Lady, I am tired of living my life for you, mother—and you." She proclaimed as she pointed at her father.

"You lock me away from the world, yet make sure I am educated on all the things I will never get to see or use. How should I feel?" Franchesca asked as tears rolled down her cheeks. "You say you love me, but all you truly care about is coin and reputation. All you've ever see from me is how I can bring you both more of each. I'm just a game piece to the both of you." She bore her soul, every thought she'd believed for so long spilled out in a rush like a river overflowing its banks.

"Very well." Her mother began angrily. "What do you want? What is it we are overlooking?" Franchesca's heart pounded anxiously within the walls of her chest. She'd meant to tell them—and that moment was upon her. Though given all that had just unfolded—the time was hardly ideal.

"I—don't want to marry Syandro..." she began her mouth going dry and heart pounding with such force she could practically feel it in her throat. Heavenly Lady, please don't have me slosh up now.

"We wouldn't let you—not unless his father returned from the Tomblands..." Renaud began. Franchesca held up her hand. It was the first time in her life she ever interrupted her father, and it only made her heart race even quicker than before. Gods above she was nervous.

"I don't want to marry Syandro—or any of the suitors you've chosen. I despise them all; each one of them makes my flesh crawl." Martise stood in front of her and cocked her head.

"What are you getting to Franchesca?" Martise asked suspiciously. Franchesca's heart froze in the middle of its last beat as she gazed at both of her parents.

"I've met someone else. Someone I do, love. Someone, who I've chosen to give my heart to." Her parents watched her closely. Renaud rose from his seat and placed his palms on his desk looming over it like a giant, ready to uproot it in a fit of fury. They hung on her every word, like hungry beasts waiting to tear her apart. They would trounce upon her happiness—just as they had done so many times before; she was aware it would happen before it happened. Still—it did not matter, she was holding to her word. If they would not accept her wishes, then she would run away. I'm not going to be their pawn anymore; I'm going to be me. Franchesca told herself.

"Her name is Simone." Her mother's eyes went wide with disbelief. Her father sank heavily back into his chair as if his knees simply disappeared and ceased to exist. The atmosphere of the room became heavy and thick with tension. It was as if Franchesca could sense both of their hearts beating in the stillness.

"Her—her name?" Martise asked hesitantly. Franchesca nodded slowly. Her eyes were steady and fixed—locked with her mothers unflinchingly.

"Get out of my sight girl. Get to your chambers and don't come out until we have sent for you." Franchesca simply smiled at her mother and father. Not a happy or timid smile, but one of satisfaction. There was something very liberating about being proven right once again. Her smile was self–assured and cocky; she inclined her head sarcastically and without saying a word obeyed her mother—for the very last time.

* * *

Franchesca paced through her room, tapping her chin thoughtfully. What was she to do first? Despite the situation, she found herself laughing. Franchesca sat on her bed and lay back stretching her back and shoulders. In the time since she first spent that night of bliss with Simone, she found herself recalling; other times between then and now that she snuck into Claude's cabin. The two would become lost in joy and passion for hours on end. The thought of those nights gave her goosebumps. It also made her realize how much Claude cared for her. After all, he allowed them to meet, and he never spoke a word to anyone. He allowed her to be free—for that was what she felt. By the Lady she felt free, and unburdened since she'd spoken to her parents; it felt wonderful. She felt light, and more like herself now than she ever remembered feeling before. Something rankled her however now that she thought about the conversation with Quentin. Franchesca scowled. Someone had seen her. Some¬one had said something—and she had a suspicion of who it was. Despite that—there was nothing she could do, and nothing she could say because she held no proof. Not yet anyway. She recalled a night when she snuck out to the stables—where she took the gold coin's she'd given Simone when they first met—the very coins which Simone gave back to her their first night together. That night she took a farrier's hammer; along with an iron nail and punched a hole through each of the coins, to turn them into necklaces—one for each of them. That night she felt eyes on her. She'd sensed eyes on her before. Eyes—which were watching the two of them, since Simone's very first visit. If only Franchesca could prove, it was her. Damn—Marrtea and her pettiness. With a sigh, Franchesca began thinking once more about the best means of escape. She listened to a tapping at the glass pane which was set into the wood of her balcony doors. She glanced over and felt her blood surge quickly through her veins. It was Simone. Franchesca ran over and threw open the doors and wrapped her arms around her.

"How did you get up here?" Franchesca asked excitedly.

"Jus a quick climb, it was easy 'nough." Simone replied happily as she leaned in and kissed Franchesca.

"We have to get ready to leave." Franchesca replied hastily. Simone nodded, though she closed her eyes and could not meet Franchesca's gaze.

"What's wrong?" Franchesca asked gently. She looked into Simone's emerald eyes—hoping that there was no more bad news. She had enough ill news already today.

"I... jus feel bad 'bout ya leavin all dis." Simone replied, as she held up her arms and gestured encompassing the room. "Ya 'ave everythin 'ere, nd I'm takin ya away from it all." Franchesa smiled as she looked at Simone.

"It looks pretty enough. I know it must look like I have everything—but I would rather spend a thousand lifetimes without a coin to my name and be with you; than I would, one lifetime here surrounded by all of this without you. I meant what I said that night. I'm leaving this place—and I'm doing it gladly." Franchesca assured as she embraced Simone. As Franchesca pulled away, an idea came to her. She ran over to her wardrobe and looked at her dresses. Franchesca turned to Simone and smiled.

"I've got an idea." Franchesca grabbed a black dress and held it up. She gripped it in the middle and began to rip it. Simone nodded as she pulled a slim knife she kept tucked into the waist band of her trousers. She tossed Simone a handful of dresses and watched as she used the knife to cut them into ropes. Franchesca walked over, and grabbed the last three books she bought, when out in the city with Claude. She also grabbed a small pouch filled with coins and placed them on the stack of books, and then proceeded to create a makeshift satchel to carry her them.

"Start tying bed sheets and the clothes together. We'll climb down." She whispered. Simone nodded tucking the blade back into its hiding place, as

Franchesca began hastily changing into the simple linen shirt, and trousers she'd worn the night she'd snuck away into the city. She slid her boots on and smiled at Simone. At that moment Franchesca heard the sound of footsteps in the hallway—along with raised voices. Franchesca peered over at Simone and held her finger to her lips; as she threw a long knotted line of sheets, and taffeta dresses over the side of the balcony rail.

"What do you intend to do?" She caught her mother asking through the barrier of the closed door.

"I'm going to speak with her. I want her to leave this foolishness behind. She is a de Maret, perhaps seeing her name upon the deeds of inheritance; as well as a written record of our standing claim to the throne of Forn, will be enough evidence for her to drop this juvenile foolishness. She must know if she ever wishes to sit upon the throne she must keep up her appearances. I am aware it is not pleasant or maybe even fair—but she must." Renaud answered. His tone was level, but it still bore the edge of irritation and anger. The sound of a man not used to dealing with his own daughter.

"You heard the girl Renaud—does it sound like she can be reasoned with? She gets her stubborn pigheadedness from you." Martise replied hotly. They will be in for quite the surprise when they open the door Franchesca thought as she hurried about the room.

"As well as her sharp tongue and wit I imagine—but her temper, she gets from you." Renaud shot back. Franchesca listened as his hand grasped the doorknob of her chamber. As the hinges squeaked and the door creaked, her father stepped into the room. His eyes narrowed angrily at the scene before him.

"You disrespectful little..." Renaud stifled his tongue as his boots thumped against the timbers. He waved a pair of documents in front of him.

"Have you any idea what you are doing? Do you know what you are ruining?"

"You say ruining—I say casting off chains." Franchesca retorted as she stepped forward. "I'll not be your doll anymore!" Franchesca hissed. Her father shoved Franchesca aside and stepped towards Simone, leveling a thick accusatory finger.

"This is your fault! You gutter trolling whore; do you realize what you've done? Do you know the name you have destroyed? Can you comprehend the planning you have laid to waste? You have ruined her, you have ruined her life!" Renaud hissed as he stepped forward. He raised his hand and was ready to strike Simone. As his hand began its descent, something caught it. His hate-filled eyes looked on in disbelief as Franchesca grabbed his wrist. She shoved his arm away—and kicked him in the stomach. The kick was harder than she meant to deliver and it dropped her father to the ground, but she didn't care.

"If you try to touch her ever again—if you try to bring her harm... I will kill you." Franchesca looked up and noticed her mother standing wide-eyed in the doorway. She picked up the papers her father had carried and knelt down and looked at him. She placed a knee on his elbow and grabbed his hand. She ripped the signet ring from his finger and smiled as she held it up in front of his eyes.

"I am your daughter—even if from this day forward you release all claim to me, and wish I never existed... I promise you; I will not be forgotten." She rose and scowled at her mother, as she stuffed the papers and the ring, into her makeshift satchel. Simone ran towards the balcony and began her climb down. Franchesca walked out to the balcony and looked back at her mother, who had rushed to the aid of Renaud.

"Perhaps if you cared less about your station and titles, it wouldn't have come to this." Franchesca told them quietly.

"We gave you everything!" Her mother howled tears rolling down her cheek as she glanced from her husband to her daughter. Her confliction was evident in her expression. Who should she favor—who's reason did she attempt to appeal to.

"Except the freedom to be myself. What you deem everything—is truly nothing, without that." Franchesca replied as she began her descent. She found Simone waiting for her down below and smiled as she dropped the last few feet. The two began their run across the estate. Franchesca glanced over her shoulder and looked as her parents stood upon, what was once her balcony. The pang of guilt and regret settled in her gut. A realization that events had come to this. Despite the sorrow—she knew it was indeed the only way. Her parents would never accept her for who she was—or who she wished to be. They never would accept her dreams and her ambitions. She listened as the sound of horses hooves thundered across the grass. That meant that a call of alarm had gone up, but how? Her parents surely couldn't raise it that quickly. Perhaps a bit of her father's military fitness still lingered in his aging frame. He certainly picked a marvelous time to prove he's still as fit as ever Franchesca thought. It didn't matter—she and Simone ran towards the road off in the distance.

"Don' look back." Simone panted, as she ran and jumped a narrow gap in the ground. Franchesca followed her lead and jumped over the opening, and they continued through the woods that would take them to the road. Franchesca panted as she slowed. She wished she was more fit. Adrenaline was the only thing keeping her going, the mad desire to get away and be free of her parents and be with Simone. Her life of leisure was telling; however—the worn dirt road was only a few feet away, she felt winded, and her muscles burned with ache. The two of them walked on to the horse trampled cart traveled earth of the road and grinned. Only then as their breathing slowed did they hear the sound of horses. No not horses, a horse. Not a loud rumbling gallop more the soft, gentle clattering of a horse striding towards them. It still made Franchesca's heart sink. Franchesca's heart lamented at the thought of running once more—but it would not let her down. She and Simone turned. Sliding out of his saddle, making his way towards them, was Claude. Immediately Franchesca's eyes filled with tears. Claude strode over and wrapped his arms around her and held her tightly.

"Are you going to take me back?" Franchesca asked sadly. Her parents would be that cruel. They would send the one man who loved her as a father himself to retrieve her—to cut her happiness to ribbons before it even had a chance to be fully birthed. It would be easier that way no doubt. Claude shook his head as he kissed her forehead, fighting off the tears threatening to pour from his eyes like a rainstorm.

"I'll say I never saw you. But it would break my heart if I didn't have a chance to say goodbye." He told them gently as he walked over and embraced Simone. "You look after her, you hear?" He asked as he peered into her emerald eyes. Simone nodded—eyes heavy with sorrow. "You too, look after her." Claude told Franchesca as he placed a hand on her cheek and wiped away a tear.

"Now you two run, they'll not be far behind." He told them gently, as he gave Franchesca one last parting embrace. Franchesca returned the embrace of the man who'd been more of a father to her than her real father. She hugged him tighter than she'd ever done before. It was painful letting him go; because this would be the last time, she would ever be able to feel his arms around her. In her life, Claude had always been the only constant comfort and companion, she ever truly had. The two once again ran as fast as they could. Franchesca's chest heaved with sorrow, and her heart felt weighted by the loss of her close friend and confidant. Though she gained Simone, parting with Claude was a sorrow she was ill prepared to face. After a time of cutting through the brush and scrub of the woods—and hiding at the sound of every hoof beat they heard, Franchesca and Simone finally reached the city. Simone gazed at her and slipped her hand into Franchesca's. She laced her fingers and squeezed reassuringly.

"I'm glad you're here with me." Franchesca told her, albeit weighted with sadness. Simone understood and smiled.

"I'm glad too. We better find a place ta lay low." Franchesca smiled and nodded at Simone's suggestion.

"Let's go to the Rusty Harpoon." She replied happily. Franchesca knew there was a great chance; her father's watchmen would be there to look for her. But she also knew there was a chance her father would dangle a bribe in front of Quentin's greedy, money craving eyes, to go and retrieve her. Franchesca smiled at that thought. If Quentin did show his face, she would have the chance to kill him—just as she wanted. With her heart full of thoughts of revenge and the happiness she felt being with Simone, the two made their way towards the tavern. The hours passed by, as Simone and Franchesca sat at a corner table; watching the door—waiting for Quentin or some member of her father's bodyguard, to show themselves. The hours spent watching was wasted, since no one came looking for her.

"Come on; let's find a place ta sleep." Simone whispered to Franchesca as she planted a gentle kiss on her neck. Franchesca agreed—it'd been a long day; and she would have liked to have found a place to lie down, hours ago. It was only her desire to see Quentin pay for what he had done to her that kept her at the Rusty Harpoon. The two of them walked the streets by the docks. Simone paid careful attention to the comings and goings of workers, at various warehouses. Finally—after a half hour of walking, Simone found a warehouse that was quiet enough for the two of them to sneak in. They climbed up to a hayloft and smiled. "Well, this is it—ever so humble." Simone chuckled as she sank into the hay. Franchesca lay next to her and giggled.

"At least I'm with you." Franchesca leaned in and kissed her and smirked. So many times she gazed up at the canopy hanging above her bed and wondered where she would be later in her life. She imagined freedom and being on her own. Her imagination was a pale substitute now that she was actually experiencing it. The two embraced closely and before either knew it, they were both asleep. Each secure and warm within one another's arms.

Chapter 7

During the daylight hours, the docks were a busy place. Crews of longshoremen loaded and unloaded shipments from foreign lands—and ships of strange foreign designs docked in the quay. Franchesca sat in the window of the hayloft that was used to store feed for the horses that would pull carts laden with freshly unloaded cargo from warehouses further into the city. She and Simone slept in the hayloft of the warehouse the night before after having found the loft empty and as suitable a place as any to rest and stay hidden. She surveyed the scenes unfolding before her and smiled. The smell of the sea intermingled with the scents of a variety of foods offered by the vendors which patrolled the docks with carts looking to feed the menagerie of workers. A clear and sunny sky shown overhead and the air stirred fresher off the waters of the harbor. Franchesca felt like she was truly breathing for the first time. Too long had she breathed in stale parlor air, within an opulent glorified cage of her parents crafting. She heard the groan of the wooden ladder behind her and looked over her shoulder as Simone climbed up. She handed Franchesca a chunk of bread and smiled. She glanced down at the bread and took in the scents wafting from the food vendors below once more. She wished they could slip down and have a warmer meal—a real meal. Despite this setback, she still felt more liberated than she ever recalled feeling within the company of her parents.

"Not much—but it'll hold us fer a little." Simone nodded as she tore a piece from her own loaf chunk. Franchesca bobbed her head and tore away at the bread.

"What do ya want ta do taday?" Simone asked as she ate another piece. Franchesca shrugged. She thought about being free for a long time—wondered what it would be like without her parents around, and wondered about how it would feel walking the world on her own. Though she longed for that moment—she never took the time to think about what she might like to do, once she was actually free to walk about the streets of the city.

She was poorly prepared to answer such a question—which only made her feel foolish. Worse still, it made her feel stupid in front of Simone. She didn't know—but she bet Simone would be able to answer in the blink of an eye. She'd been out on her own for a number of years. Franchesca tried to cover over her embarrassment and her ill-prepared nature with quick thinking. Franchesca never had to think of what she might like to do—what was there to do when one suddenly found themselves without coin to their name. Truth be told—after the events of a few nights ago, all she wanted to do was spend time with Simone. She managed to take a small purse of coins when she fled, and they needed to make that money last for as long as possible. The scent of the food from the carts wafted into her nostrils yet again, and her mouth began to water. Franchesca pushed the thought aside with effort and gave Simone's question some serious thought.

"If you like, I can give you another lesson." Franchesca said—trying to hide the reddening of her cheeks. She didn't know why she always blushed when she spoke. Perhaps always took it a bit farther than the truth, but by the Heavenly Lady, she certainly was keenly aware of the heat in her cheeks more often now than she'd ever remembered before meeting her. Simone thought it a pleasant enough idea and agreed. She settled down crossing her legs and sat across from Franchesca, as she eagerly awaited the lesson to begin. Franchesca began to teach what she was capable of to Simone. She might not have been a professional tutor, but Simone genuinely wanted to learn. Franchesca wanted to help and would do whatever she was capable to make sure Simone got as much of an education she was capable of providing on her own. It was a minuscule offering anyway—at least her love would be able to read as she wanted. After a half hour or so, Franchesca took out another one of the books she hastily grabbed as she fled. She might have called it packing once—but that was not an apt description. It was too hasty; too chaotic, to be called packing. Fleeing was rushed a spur of the moment thing. Packing usually involved some kind of organization and thought a well thought out plan. Her only plan had been to snatch up the books she'd bought with Claude on their outing. Other than those and the clothes she had on her back Franchesca had nothing. She sat against a wall next to Simone, and the two began to read. When Simone had trouble, Franchesca would help. She reminded Simone of the sounds the letters made rather than tell her the words outright. Franchesca would also remind her of marks upon the letters which indicated the sound being drawn out or shortened. Sometimes Franchesca reminded Simone of how the sounds of letters changed when they were next to one another, in certain cases. Before long Simone was reading sentences by herself.

"You're doing very well. I think you've just about got the hang of it." Franchesca smiled as she hugged Simone. After reading a few more pages, they reached a natural stopping point. They decided to walk the city streets after Franchesca slipped her books into her makeshift pack and slung it over her shoulder. Simone showed Franchesca a few other sights—both pleasant and unpleasant, just so that Franchesca would know what areas to avoid. Simone pointed to one area and told Franchesca—one night while she was out, she had seen a dead body within that particular alleyway. After a walk they turned a corner, it was then Simone mentioned that the shopkeeper in that particular establishment; sometimes gave her a few brass shillings, if his day was a profitable one. Simone even said that she delivered messages for him, on a few occasions and he paid her. The vast scope almost seemed to overwhelm Franchesca, but it exhilarated her at the same time. She and Simone were making their own way. They were in charge of themselves. Every day no matter how hungry she became, Franchesca woke up with a smile. Simone didn't try to control her; didn't have any real expectations, or burden her with tiresome mind–numbing tasks. In fact, any tasks that needed doing were performed together.

They searched for new places to sleep, sometimes splitting up and arranging to meet up at a predetermined location. They hunted for coins that had fallen from purses or pockets and had gone unclaimed by the other poor folk. Times did grow trying for them as the days passed into weeks, and it wasn't long before she and Simone used what little coin Franchesca had been able to bring with her. When their money ran out, Simone enlisted Franchesca's help in providing a distraction to merchants, while she went about lifting a few coins from their purses or pockets—or stealing a bit of food from the stalls. Apples and other fruit were the easiest things to take without anyone noticing; still, they knew that they wouldn't be able to survive on such things alone. When they found the coin, they bought bread or cheese—but such luxuries were few and far between. Franchesca found it hard to believe; there was indeed, something she missed about living under her parents' roof. She missed sitting at the dining table and eating full meals. Gravy over perfectly roasted meat and potatoes or turnips—things such as food sounded more appealing to her now than a roof over her head. Franchesca sighed as she walked with Simone. She reminisced about heavy meals when Simone had probably eaten very few full heavy meals in her life. The only one Franchesca knew of with absolute certainty, being the one she provided to her when she brought her into the house while her parents were out. Such reminders always put a sense of perspective on things for Franchesca.

"I'm sorry we couldn't get more. I wish I could give ya more food." Simone told her with a quiet sadness, which Franchesca could tell came with wounded pride. Simone was good at picking pockets and cutting purses. But the two of them encountered a streak of ill luck. Franchesca shook her head as she lay back next to Simone in the currently empty space they occupied.

"Don't worry about it. As long as I'm with you, that's what I care about." Franchesca reminded.

"After all—didn't I tell you this before we left?" She smiled as she ran her fingers through Simone's bright red hair lovingly. The two of them begged and stole where they could—but even Simone admitted, there seemed to be fewer coins in fewer pockets lately. Perhaps it was just around the docks and the poor quarter; but if they were to go into the noble district and crafters quarter, they would stick out like a four-armed marauder. Franchesca knew that the locals, fortunate enough to live in those districts; would watch them closer than they minded their own children—worse than that, she and Simone would become scapegoats for whatever ills and problems were holding the quarters at that moment. Simone turned to Franchesca and sighed as her stomach rumbled. She leaned over and kissed her lightly. It had been a long and hot day.

"We can try again tomorrow." Franchesca nodded as they drifted off to sleep in each other's arms, keeping each other warm in the cool night breeze. Tomorrow would be better, Franchesca thought as her eyes fluttered closed. Yes—there was tomorrow.

* * *

Simone and Franchesca walked the streets. Franchesca managed to flee with a pair of boots when she left home. She and Simone had been sharing them; one wore them one day and the other on the next. Today Simone wore them while Franchesca walked along the cobbles—the flesh of her bare feet smacking and scuffing with every step. They were in dangerous territory. They had decided to walk right along the border of where the poorer district met, the richer district. It had been Franchesca's idea; she thought there might be more coins within those neighborhoods. That they might be far enough out of the wealthier lords and ladies way, that they would avoid suspicion. These were the areas where people, who fancied themselves upper class on the cusp of nobility, lived. In truth, they were only moderately wealthy—but made a point of putting on a grand show for the little folk, as they liked to call those more impoverished than they were. Despite their displays, the streets contained beggars, cutpurses, and muggers—just like the poorer districts. The day wasn't as hot as it had been yesterday—which Franchesca was thankful for especially when she walked. When she'd asked Simone if she would like the boots yesterday, due to the heat—Simone shook her head and saying her feet were used to it, having rarely seen shoes at all. Still, Franchesca felt terrible. She and Simone looked at one another as they approached a cart laden with apples and other fruits. Simone gave a slight nod as they steered towards it. She taught

Franchesca the best way she found to take a piece of fruit without the merchant's knowing. You walked by with your arms relaxed—as if you were going to walk by and as you passed the very last corner of the stall, you let your fingers pull a piece into your palm and keep walking calm and steady. Simone told her—by the time the merchants have decided you're not a threat; so they don't need to worry about you, you're mostly past their stall. Since you've passed their cart they don't focus on you—instead, they turn their attention to someone else, or even somewhere else. It'd been sound advice—which had seen them fed on numerous occasions. The two of them walked towards the cart; passing the merchant and as they reached the back, they each pulled a piece of fruit into their palms and began to walk away. But, just as they went to pass an alleyway—hands reached out and grabbed them. Before either Simone or Franchesca were able to manage a shout or utter a sound, palms were clamped tight over their mouths. They began to struggle, kick and squirm—but were pulled against ridged, thickly muscled bodies; which dragged them down the dark alleyway, with little enough trouble it proved freighting. They were shoved through a blackened doorway into an even darker room. The floor swiftly rose up to meet them, as they fell to the ground. Simone and Franchesca made to rise—to bolt for the still open portal, but a squat heavy man stepped into the doorway and then proceeded to stride through with confident ease, latching the door behind him.

Franchesca's mind raced. What was happening? Were these old enemies of Simone's? Perhaps they had run a fowl of someone unknowingly. The two of them had pilfered goods from stands and carts after all—not to mention more than a little pickpocketing and purse cutting. Had someone noticed and followed them? The streets were a dangerous place for street urchins. They were even more dangerous for two urchins who happened to be young women. Franchesca wondered what fate awaited them. She wondered at the fates of other young street urchins who might have been in the same situation. How many other's had been dragged off the streets—pulled into gods only knew where? Were they going to be killed, her stomach sank—or worse. The streets were a dangerous place, especially with no one to speak up for you. Or when no one cared.

A slow, mocking clap filled the silent blackness of the room. In a moment, the darkness of the room began to fade as their vision began to adjust. It was still too dark to make out any real detail, other than the most basic outlines of the men. One was squat and broad–shouldered. He was the man from the streets—who had precious little trouble dragging them in here. He couldn't have done it on his own. There was no way he would be able to keep them both from screaming out and struggling. That meant there was another man beyond the door—waiting to close it after they were released. Simone held that bit of information in her memory for later use—hoping as she consigned it to her memories that there would indeed be a later. It would be a shame to observe only to have someone make some statement out of hand and kill them. A torch in a simple iron ring sconce crackled to life on the side of the room followed shortly after by an oil lamp which stood on a now partially illuminated desk. The room was still dim, and shadows hung about it like cobwebs, and whoever was there stayed hidden in them. Franchesca had seen rooms like this before. It looked to be a simple room—perhaps a ledger office of a small shop. Her father had an office like this—and she'd been forced to endure enough of his business trips in her younger years to see the back rooms of many shops. This was a place where people with a head for numbers, would look over tallies and totals and shift coin around for shipments and other expenses. There was no money in the room now, she noted. A lanky figure stepped forward from behind the desk—still keeping him cloaked in shadow and hiding his face. He stepped out—slowly, into the light provided by the torches and grinned with all the warmth of a viper. Franchesca and Simone were both well acquainted with this man. It was the merchant—with the vulture–like face—¬who'd accused Simone of stealing from him. A predatory sneer was prominent upon his avian features.

"So the little bitch is without her bodyguard—and from the looks of you without her coin." The man grinned, rubbing spindly hands together. His hands reminded Franchesca too much of a spider for comfort. The slow way he rubbed them together did not help the comparison. He paced about placing his hands behind his back, like a general surveying his troops.

"You thought the two of you could steal from me? Thought you could humiliate me, and get away with it?" His smile showed a great many teeth—far too many to be comforting. Like one of the ocean sharks grinning as it caught its meal. More disconcerting was that a number of his teeth were not as white as they could be. Up to that point, he kept his hands clasped behind his back—now he let them fall to rest easily at his sides. He held a simple cudgel that appeared as if it saw much use—and it appeared that vulture face thought blood was wood varnish, given the cudgels current color. Franchesca turned and noticed that the squat, broad-shouldered man likewise, held a simple, blunt beating instrument. Franchesca was quite aware of Simone's desire to grab for her short knife—like a separate palpable pulse. She always kept it with her, tucked away under her shirt and held against her waist by the simple length of rope she used to secure her trousers about her hips. Franchesca didn't want to leave bodies—she didn't want to kill, but didn't know what to do. What were her options? By the Heavenly Lady's silver light what was going to happen to them?

"Me and Lefty get em after you're done with em, right?" The bruiser from behind asked. Even though neither was turned to face him; each was keenly aware of his smile slithering across their backs like a slug coated in foul slime.

"I like's the look of the black haired one. Though the redhead isn't without charms of her own." It took considerable effort for Franchesca to restrain herself and not let out a shiver. Or vomit, at the sound of his appreciation of her and Simone.

"By all means—make them suffer. Humiliate them, degrade them. Share them with your friends—with your damned dogs; I don't care what you do— so long as they suffer and learn a lesson." The lanky vulture faced bastard said as he glared at them. Gods they meant to beat them—then rape them. Ice shot through Franchesca's veins and fear gnawed at her guts.

105

"You little bitches will be thrown in the gutter to fish out whatever damned coins you can sift out of the shit, sound familiar?" The man with the beakish nose asked with a satisfied sneer.

"Bend over a fence an get fucked." Simone shot back. Franchesca admired her bravado but wondered if there was anything they could actually do. She wished she could tell them something equally impressive and bombastic—but that would only make the situation worse—worse than it already was—and it was bad enough already.

"Don't worry—you'll get fucked enough for the both of us." Vulture face grinned as he stepped forward. Simone took a step back and pulled out her knife. Vulture face paused and gazed wide-eyed over his prominent beak-like nose at the steel in her hand—hoping it was dull. Before Franchesca was aware of what was happening; the scene around them erupted into chaos and motion. Rather than charge forward and bury the knife in bird face's, chest or eye; Simone turned and ducked an incoming blow from the basher behind them. Franchesca stumbled backward clumsily, narrowly avoiding being struck by the bruiser's cudgel. She was useless in a situation like this—she was simply trying to do her best to stay out of the way. Simone lashed out with the knife and scored a deep slice across the squat man's bulging arm. He leaped back with a hiss and scowl—but Simone pressed forward. She charged and flung herself at him. He grinned as he caught her seemingly out of the air and held her against him. Franchesca pieced together that was where things went very wrong—very wrong for him.

Simone squirmed and kicked; she got enough of a knee into the squat man's round gut, that he loosened his grip on her, just enough that Franchesca cringed at what happened next. Simone thrust into the man's crotch with the knife, and he howled releasing her immediately. She twisted and yanked the blade out and plunged it in again, and again until a crimson bloom spread across his trousers.

Franchesca felt the vulture faced merchant grab, and yank back a fist full of her hair. He jerked her head back hard; until she was turned and forced her neck back to gaze up at him. If he pulled her neck back any farther, she worried he'd break it—or her back. He jabbed his cudgel into her stomach, and the air rushed from her lungs in a burst. Franchesca gasped, his eyes bulging with hate and fury as he turned her around by her hair to face him fully. He pulled her up until she stood without being bent over like a crab.

"Call the bitch off." He hissed shaking her head by the hair. Franchesca still couldn't breathe, but she'd be damned if she listened to that bastard. Out of fear–fueled instinct, she lashed out and caught him in the stones with her foot. She wasn't able to kick as hard as she might have liked; since she wasn't wearing the boots she'd been wearing the day before—but his grip loosened immediately. She stumbled back and tried to catch her breath. As she worked to fill her lungs, she gazed up and saw him wincing. She reached up and snatched the cudgel from his hand. It was easier than she thought. Of course, he was preoccupied with the blinding pain she just unleashed between his legs. Franchesca gripped the cudgel and struck him across the head. The blow caught him on the side of the jaw as he tried to turn away. He stumbled back, his hand flying up to his jaw. Simone was beside her now, her knife coated in blood. He scowled up at them, eyes watering from the pain flooding through him like a river, overflowing its banks. She watched as Simone calmly strode forward and pressed the knife to his neck.

"Ere's how its gonna be. Yer gonna walk us out by dat door over there." Simone pointed towards the other door; which led to the front of the shop. "Yer gonna do it an' yer not gonna make a bleedin sound—cos if ya do I'll take yer log an stones off like I did his. Yer gonna fergit dis—yer gonna fergit us if ya don't," Simone paused a long moment and leaned in closer; pressing the knife tight against his throat, "I'll find ya—an' I'll take my time with ya." She whispered. She made a small cut on the man's neck to punctuate her point and met his gaze.

"Savvy?" Simone asked with the sort of calm anger that should always frighten one when they heard the question directed at them. Franchesca hadn't noticed in the heat of the moment, but it looked as if the bruiser clipped her with a fist across the eye; for one was beginning to blacken and swell slightly. Not surprising given the situation. When a man gets stabbed, repeatedly; in the crotch, there is bound to be some wild flailing Franchesca thought. Simone grabbed the scrawny bird–like man behind his collar and began to bring him up; she spun him with a shove and pressed her knife against his back. Slowly he led them to the front of the shop. Franchesca snatched up a small purse of coins from the counter and gave it a jingle. They would eat tonight; perhaps better than they had in a long while.

"I won't forget this—I won't forget you." He hissed as he laid a hand on the door. He wanted to look behind him and glower at them, but Simone's knife placed against his back kept him from doing so.

"Ramember, what I told ya." Simone replied from behind him as she wiped her knife across his clothing, to clean it. He scowled and shoved the door open to the bustling streets beyond. Franchesca and Simone strode out, leaving him further humiliated—robbed of a purse, and with a dead body in the back room that would be very hard to explain should anyone happen in on him. Franchesca knew they wouldn't be rid of him. He was an enemy now, and he would do anything he could to see them suffer. They would need to be careful. Or would they, Franchesca wondered as she watched passing guardsmen. She dropped the cudgel into the street; ignoring it, and hurried toward him as Simone secreted away her knife once again. Franchesca continued towards him feigning panic the closer she drew.

"Sir—good you're a member of the watch. I've seen something—heard something from that shop over there." Franchesca said as she tugged on the man's tunic and pointed towards the building they just exited.

"Terrible noises sir sounded... it sounded awful." Franchesca pleaded. "I thought I heard a man cry out in pain; I wanted to run in and help—but I'm so slight, I didn't know if I could; then I saw you passing by." Franchesca continued.

"You heard it too miss?" The watchmen asked pointedly as he looked to Simone, taking a step forward.

"Aye, sir." Simone agreed, catching on to Franchesca's plan quickly, and fighting off a smirk." When we was passin by tha alley, we heard tha cries an when we tried ta go take a closer look—a bruiser told us not ta go any further. Told us it was a just an argument; didn't concern us—an' ta turn right 'round."

"Alright, I'll take a look; you two be on your way now—go on, and here's a silver for the tip." He said as he pressed a small coin into Franchesca's palm. The two bowed their heads and thanked him quickly before they walked off into the crowds; disappearing into the city. After a long walk, Franchesca turned to Simone and grinned.

"What do you feel like eating?" Franchesca asked as she jingled the purse of coins she snatched up on her way out of the office. Simone beamed.

"Sometin hot." She chuckled as slung an arm around Franchesca's shoulders holding up the silver the watchmen had given them. Later that evening, the two made their way back to the Rusty Harpoon where they could afford to spend the night; and have a decent meal. They could afford it because, Fabrice, did his best to take care of Simone. At first, he refused to take their coin; but they both insisted. Their bed was comfortable, even though the mattress was stuffed with straw rather than feathers. Their meal, which consisted of a bowl of rabbit stew cooked in goose broth; came with a side of fresh yeasty bread, a slice of onion pie, and spiced peas with garlic. They allowed themselves further luxury when they ordered their drinks by ordering not only ale but two cups of spiced wine. The food was better than it had any right to be; given that they were in one of the poorer sections of the city. Most places this side of the city were happy to pass off boiled water with bark as soup. Whoever Fabrice employed to cook the meals at the Rusty Harpoon, knew their way around a kitchen. Franchesca didn't remember the last meal— the last proper meal anyway, she'd eaten outside of her parent's estate. With their stomachs full and contented they had gone up to their shared room. Sharing the room saved coin, and something she and Simone didn't mind in the least. The two lay back on the bed. It was a little lumpier than Franchesca's old mattress had been—but by the Heavenly Lady's tender mercy, it felt luxurious. Simone curled up close to Franchesca and smiled at her. It was a cool night, and they left the shutters open so that they might enjoy the breeze. Franchesca asked Simone if her eye was alright and the girl just smiled. She dipped a scrap bit of cloth Fabrice gave them, into a bowl of cool water and gently pressed it to Simone's eye.

"Hurts a bit—but I've ad worse." Simone assured as Franchesca touched and cleaned it gingerly. Franchesca asked where she learned to fight—where she learned to blackmail. Simone assured her that you tended to learn those things when you lived on the street—because if you didn't, you wouldn't live long. The truth was close to that. She learned much of that on the streets. Unfortunately, she learned much more from her father, but she couldn't tell Franchesca that; could she? Maybe she could—someday, but it wasn't today. Her relationship with her father was a puzzle cube—her feelings about him were just as knotted. She wasn't ready to talk about her father with Franchesca—wasn't prepared to talk about her past. Just wasn't ready to tell Franchesca the truth, not the whole truth anyway. I hope it doen't make me a bad sort she thought to herself. Simone assured her that she'd taken more than a few lumps, and beatings—and had ran off or hidden more than once, more than twice. The two shared a laugh.

"If ya don't learn dat stuff quick, yer life on tha streets is gonna be a shortun. I've never liked it though, not really. Jus' fight when I hav ta—cause I hav ta." Franchesca nodded as Simone pulled in closer to her and laid her head on her shoulder.

"I... 'ave an idea, don' know if ya would agree wit it or not—but it's worth a listen to." Simone began. Franchesca nodded as she turned her head to look into Simone's eyes. "How bout we stow away on one of dem merchant ships. Travel somewhere... else." She whispered. Her accent shifted slightly. Franchesca shrugged; with a smile on her face, and began to think it over.

"It can't possibly be any worse. Perhaps we can get a fresh start. After all—I have my father's ring and papers as well as the leftover coins from today. Perhaps we can use those to acquire something—if nothing more than a few meals." Franchesca nodded. Her heart fluttered with excitement. She was going to see the world; she didn't rightly know where in the world she would be seeing next, but the very prospect of setting foot in an entirely new land was exhilarating. She laced her fingers with Simone's and squeezed them softly.

"Let's do it, let's set off together—we'll see the world; you and me." Franchesca said with a beaming smile. Simone nodded, and the two of them began to think about where they would travel and what might await them; talking long into the night of what they thought lay before them.

* * *

Simone and Franchesca sat in the corner as they routinely did. Fabrice provided them with free drinks and even sat to join them, using the time to say farewell to Simone. As they drank and laughed, Franchesca watched as Syandro walked into the tavern. It was different than last time. He was alone—except for the cold steel of the blade sheathed at his side. He noticed Simone and Franchesca and strode over, dipping to an elaborate low bow before taking a seat.

"Greetings to you all." He said cheerfully. Fabrice passed Syandro a cup, and he poured a measure of the alcohol that was being shared between them. "I hear you have abandoned your parents; as well as their estate." Syandro smirked.

"How did you hear that?" Franchesca asked curiously as she took a drink. Syandro chuckled as he set his cup down and slouched in his chair.

"Word travels fast in some circles; the nobility is one of those circles. Your father sent riders to my father's estate, hoping that you would be found there." Simone looked at Syandro carefully; studying him as she always did.

"He has sent word of your flight to any and everyone he believes might aid in finding you." Syandro continued, taking another small sip from the measure of Elandian brandy; Fabrice poured him.

"You're not going to tell him where I am are you?" Franchesca asked worriedly. Syandro scoffed and waved his hand as he drained the rest of the drink in his glass. He breathed between his teeth as he attempted to recover from the strength and the momentary burning of the liquid as it coursed down his throat. Fabrice sighed inwardly; none knew how to drink a proper brandy. He swished his glass back and fourth swirling the amber liquid within and took a sip—all the while feeling foolish for setting out good brandy, for the youths gathered around the table.

"Of course not." Syandro replied eventually as he cleared his throat and poured another measure—not waiting for Fabrice to do so. Admittedly he'd gone searching for her in the city a few times, hoping perhaps to run into her. It did hurt that she wouldn't seek him out for a casual meeting. But what could he do—he supposed it was the safest course of action. If her father looked for her, he would no doubt be watching the De Madonia estate closely—that included watching him just as closely. If only the pompous ass could see how smart his daughter actually was, Syandro thought to himself studying the brandy in the glass.

"I admire you in fact—striking out on your own and making a name for yourself." Syandro smiled. It appeared not all news traveled quickly within the noble circles. Perhaps her parents were keeping the reasons for her flight a secret. They must have agreed to pay Quentin a princely sum as well. Maybe they decided to finance his voyage and other investments if he agreed to keep his mouth shut about Franchesca. The thought made Franchesca smile. She turned to Simone and Fabrice and cleared her throat.

"Would you... both mind if I spoke to Syandro alone for a moment?" She asked hesitantly. Fabrice agreed as he drained the rest of his drink and set the glass down on the table. There was a dull thud as he placed the vessel down and stood up. Simone put on her best—most practice false smile slowly nodding as she rose from the table.

"I'll only be a moment." Franchesca assured Simone nodded as she and Fabrice walked towards the bar; leaving Franchesca and Syandro to themselves. The thought of her being alone with him, made Simone's skin crawl. She didn't know really know why. Just the sight of them made her hackles rise. Maybe it was because, at one point, Franchesca considered marrying him—and thought him a likely candidate for her heart and affections. Simone wished she had her drink with her still. She would just have to trust them both. She trusted Franchesca—but something about Syandro still sat wrong with her. Perhaps it was because she still remembered him gazing at her like a prize to be won. The appraising glances he gave to other women in Franchesca's presence. Maybe it was just that he didn't know about her and Franchesca. Simone found herself sighing—hoping that he could let go and be happy for them both after Franchesca told him.

"What did you wish to talk about?" He asked as he took a drink from his refilled cup—swirling the contents gently just as Fabrice had done moments ago.

"About... us." Franchesca began hesitantly. If Syandro was alarmed or on edge, he gave no sign. If that was a good thing, Franchesca couldn't be sure. "I... don't rightly know how to say this—but I don't think I can marry you. I... don't believe I can." She whispered. Syandro simply smirked and let out a nervous laugh.

"I would not expect you to make any such decision at this point in time. You still taste your freedom, still exploring yourself. You need to truly find your desires..." Franchesca held up a hand to cut him off, silencing any more of his speech. Syandro was sweet and truly had a way with words. She didn't doubt if she allowed him to continue he would launch into some grand thesis—or quote great swathes of poetry of people truly finding what they wanted in life when they are allowed to experience life unchained. He was sweet, and he meant well—but he didn't have the whole picture. She knew why she'd left home, but he didn't.

"I... mean, I don't believe I can marry you because—I'm in love with Simone." Franchesa whispered. She put as much gentleness into her tone as she could; hoping not to upset him. She didn't want to break his heart. In the short time they spent together, she felt his attachment to her grow. She knew that he cared deeply for her—and she'd never liked hurting people. After all, there had been a time where she thought she would marry him as well. Syandro smiled as he took a drink and set his glass down smoothly. He shrugged after a moment.

"Then I wish you the best. Truthfully, I do." He replied with a grin. The expression came easy, in war you never allowed your opponent to see what you felt—and love was ever a battlefield. The woman he desired had rejected him, that did indeed make this war. Still, he supposed one could be civil in war. He didn't want to drive her further away after all.

"Are... are you not upset?" Franchesca asked, somewhat surprised. She'd all but agreed to marry him—or at least she felt she had led him to believe so and here he was saying it was okay that she broke things off. She was happy at his understanding of it, of course—but there was still something surprising about the simple shrug and good will. Not entirely unpleasant, she thought; still somewhat surprising, however. Syandro shook his head.

"No, of course not." He lied. His insides felt as if they were encased in metal and he was being dragged down to the center of the earth with every passing breath.

"Your friendship is what I care most about, Franchesca. I find you fascinating—and the greatest of company. You are witty and inquisitive and filled with a tenacity that I think would put all of Castella to shame—most of Castella anyway." Syandro replied with chuckle. He hated the sound of his own voice. He hated that he was not fighting or raging against this—indignity. No woman had ever spurned his affections or attention before. The women of Castella found him charming and desirable—as did the women he spoke to in Forn. He saw how their faces blushed and they turned into fawning dullards—who spoke of their dresses and fished for compliments. Why was she different? It was fascinating—but how it infuriated him. Franchesca smiled as she listened to him speak. His heavy accent, though delightfully pleasing to the ear, meant that sometimes she needed to listen carefully. He took another sip from his cup; his pride dealt a terrible blow with her rejection. Still, he thought, perhaps there was a chance. Maybe if he could spend more time in her company—Franchesca might grow to forget Simone—perhaps she would even tire of her. In Syandro's experience with noble women, even the ones who wished to go against their parents—tired easily. They needed newness—they needed to drift and do as they pleased. Syandro had seen it time after time— heard rambling story after rambling story from his father. His father shared tales of his roguish youth and his beddings. Most made Syandro chuckle, but all of them only proved to him that women came and went as they pleased. Eventually, they all chose what they felt best suited them. Syandro's father once confided in him that women—in many ways were like men. They were ambitious; they had their appetites—their passions. Syandro set his cup down on the table and smiled—yes; there was a chance. Until his time came, he would merely play his role. After all, no women had been able to resist his charm so far. He was fawned over by Duchess' in the Empire of Austinea; women of Castella and Forn. He had never gone wanting for their affections— and it took very little to impress them; he found himself in their bedchambers easily enough, if he so chose to peruse them. On a few occasions, he had. This time would be no different; Syandro knew how to get what he wanted. He only needed to wait. She would see—he, was in her best interest. Franchesca would see that he could care for her far better, far more completely than Simone. After all, Simone had nothing to her name. Syandro held titles; lands, property—and, coin, the things one needs to continue to live.

"Thank you for your understanding." Franchesca replied softly. "I hope to see you again soon. Tomorrow Simone and I are planning on stowing away on a merchant ship." Syandro's heart pounded. If he wasn't careful, his plans would be dashed like an egg upon the cobbles; before he had time to set them. After the shock of the statement wore off, his mind began to assemble a plan that would address the current turn of events.

"Why don't you stow away on a ship I am traveling on." It would give Syandro a chance to extend his stay in her company—as well as keep her safe. Sailors were a rough bunch, even if they sailed under a flag of so–called civilized country or household. Though it burned his guts to do it; Syandro knew he would also have to make sure no harm befell Simone. At first, he'd thought of paying for their passage, but gave a mental shrug. No—this would be a good experience for Franchesca. If she wanted to experience life as a pauper and a waif he would help facilitate that—he would just help keep her as safe as he could manage while doing so—that would be his only concession. He was still interested in her after all; still cared for her—still intended on marrying her in the end. Franchesca desired an adventure so he'd help to provide one. Besides she'd just broken her—well not engagement precisely why should he pay for her passage? More to the point, why should he pay for the passage of the other woman competing for Franchesca's affections as well? That was like giving a knife to a man you knew wished to kill you, stripping naked and turning your back to him. Foolish indeed—no he'd stow them away, and on their own heads be it. It was true enough about sailors. Their reputation was a hard one—their life was a hard one. They would enjoy the soft curves of a woman when they could.

"I can see to your protection, at least in some regard. I can hide you both easily enough. Since my father gave me the duty to see the ship and its cargo back to Castella—I will have more sway on the ship. I can keep you safe, and hidden. You don't know what they do to stowaways. If they are men or boys, they're beaten and pressed into service. If they are women... it is not nearly as pleasant as a beating." Syandro explained. The thought made Franchesca cringe and shudder. "I can arrange a way for you both to be brought on board, in secret. Once you're there, I can slip you both food and drink." He continued tapping his strong chin—already piecing out the details within his head.

His idea had merit. It would indeed be easier—and though there was still danger in the folds of his plan, it was far safer. Franchesca wasn't even sure how she and Simone would sneak aboard a ship. She wished she had enough coin to simply buy passage aboard. But wishing wasn't the same as having, and if she and Simone wished to have a chance at a new life; they would need to conserve what little coin they had. Part of her wished she could simply ask Syandro to pay for their passage—but she wouldn't feel right about asking for such a favor.

After all, she'd just broken any hopes of a potential engagement. It would seem cruel to ask him to pay for their passage.

"When are you setting off?" Franchesca asked leaning in and placing her arm on the table as Syandro smiled at her.

"Tomorrow." He replied simply as he poured himself another drink. Franchesca stiffly nodded in agreement.

"I will arrange a crate. I will try to make it as comfortable as possible." Syandro said, as he downed the contents of the glass and placed it back on the table with a dull thump. He stood and smiled down at her." Meet me by a ship named the Gilded Merchant. It will have royal blue sails with a gold scale and two eyes within the arms. I will see you there before sunrise." Syandro bowed his head as he walked away. Franchesca walked over to the bar and leaned against it. Simone watched Syandro leave before looking at Franchesca.

"What'd he ave ta say?" Simone asked. Their eyes met as she took a deep breath. They'd been over there talking for a long time. The language of Syandro's body went rigid for a moment. She guessed that was the moment all was laid bare to him.

"He's getting us out. We're stowing away on a ship he's been ordered to see back to Castella. He's going to see we are hidden and looked after as best he can manage without letting anyone know we're aboard." Franchesca replied.

"Do ya trust him?" Simone asked raising an eyebrow. Franchesca looked at her curiously. She had never been asked that before—not about Syandro anyway. "Do ya trust him?" Simone asked again.

"Yes... of course I do." Simone merely nodded as she took a drink and placed her cup down.

"Alright, den. Guess we best be on our way." Simone replied as she stood back from the bar and smiled at Fabrice.

"Be thinkin of ya both." He grinned as he bowed politely. "Stay safe ma'ladies—and one day soon ya come back and see old Fabrice." He told them with a chuckle as he embraced each one. As Simone walked towards the door, an uneasy feeling wormed in her stomach. What was Syandro playing at?

Perhaps her feelings had no merit, she thought. Still—something felt strange when he was around. Maybe it was her own jealousy, knowing that for a time, Franchesca had been attracted to him. Surely that fear was unwarranted after all the two of them had shared. Simone glanced over at Franchesca who was smirking, a wide grin from ear to ear as she squeezed her hand cheerfully. Simone smiled—we'll have to see, Simone told herself. Still, I'll ave my eyes on him she told herself relishing the feeling of Franchesca's hand squeezing hers.

Chapter
8

Franchesca wiped a bead of sweat from her brow and sighed. Her muscles ached and protested as they cramped, longing to be stretched. Her lower back burned with the longing to move—to twist and stretch with repositioning. Perhaps leaving Forn by stowing away on a ship wasn't the best of ideas. Now that she'd done so, she cursed herself a fool; for not thinking of simply roaming through the countryside—using the coin they'd managed bring with them on their passage. Why didn't she think of finding a band of gypsies? Then she could travel, eat her fill; or at least better than a scrap of bread and salted pork. Most importantly, she would not be sealed in a cramped box; sweating out every drop of water she managed to drink. She tilted her neck to the side feeling it crack. Her heart froze in her chest. Had anyone else heard it? Would they be found out? Another perk of traveling with gypsy's, she wouldn't have to worry about being found as a stowaway. Despite the circumstances, Franchesca tried to look on the bright side. At least she was leaving Forn—like she had always wished to. At least she was with Simone, which made things tolerable. Still, she longed to see the sky and feel the fresh air wash over her skin again. Of course, having a meal would be a wonderful thing to have as well. If she saw salted pork again, she feared she would vomit. Of course, there would have been a risk to traveling with gypsies now that she thought about it. She had plenty of time to think in here. It was entirely possible to have paid for passage, but the moment word of a reward from her parents got out, they would turn her over and pocket both payments, then she would've been truly screwed. In truth, the cramped box was their only real option, and they both knew it.

The Gilded Merchant swayed back and forth on the rolling seas. The first day—or so she thought—Franchesca had lost track of such things like day and night; being stuck in the dark crate in the bowels of a dimly lit cargo hold. The ship had been jostled and shaken in a severe storm the first day of their voyage—she believed; if it proved to actually be the day. They couldn't hear anything down in the hold, and the jostling and shaking of the ship very well could have been nothing more than choppy seas. Her and Simone had their heads slammed against the wooden box, more than once. She looked up through one of the air holes Syandro had drilled in the crate and sighed. When Franchesca slept, she heard the sound of the nails being pounded into the crate to seal her and Simone in. Her ears rang with the silence—and her stomach lurched with every thump or thud. When timbers creaked, it was a startling sound—given the sheer volume and weight the silent blackness imposed. This is the thing nightmares are made from, she mused miserably. The silence, darkness, and fear of being discovered; doing something that you know you should not be.

"Chesca?" Simone whispered softly as a mouse's scurry.

"Yes?" Franchesca replied. Hoping to the Heavenly Lady, it was not as loud as she heard it to be. Simone's pet name for her stirred her heart—made her long to be free doubly so she might stroke her hair, her face. Simone had used it the night before they left and it made her cheeks color. She'd never had anyone give her such an affectionate name before. Her parents true, but most parents possessed such titles for their children. Besides they were meaningless anyway, she thought. The sound of Simone's voice brought her back to herself, but she held on to the name she'd been given—stroking it as lovingly within her heart as she would Simone's skin once they got out of this box.

"In Forn—dere is only one god right?" She asked voice labored and panting. It was strange that she would bring up the topic of religion. Franchesca never heard her speak of such things before. Of course, we have a lot of time now, and not a lot to do don't we, she thought feeling a cramp knot itself tightly in her lower back.

"Well—goddess but yes—at least that the royals of our land acknowledge. Only one native to Forn, but other beliefs have made their way to the land as well. Ragnar, and Shya; from the Empire of Austinea, for example. Why do you ask?" She explained quietly, attempting to work the knots of her muscles out.

"I tought somewhere—I 'eard dat dere was eight." Simone replied. "Not sure whichun I should be axin ta speed dis trip up so we can get out of dis damned crate." Simone let out a rasping chuckle. She did her best but, Franchesca was able to tell she was miserable—perhaps because she was as well.

"There is one goddess, but she has eight aspects—or personalities." Franchesca whispered. "Would you like me to teach you; what I know at least? I'm not a leader of a basilica—but I can tell you what I know. It would pass the time." Franchesca whispered.

"I'd like dat." Simone replied softly. By the shifting in the box, Franchesca assumed Simone was trying to adjust herself into a more comfortable position. Comfort being what it was given the confines; perhaps was a little generous. A less miserable position was more accurate, Franchesca mused.

"Well, first is the Doting Mother or just the Mother for short. She represents healing and hope—life and protection. Second is the Gypsy which represents youth and joy and adventure. Third is the Shield Maiden; she represents strength and warriors. Then The Aged One or the Hag; she represents wisdom that comes with age—from living. Fifth is the Seamstress she represents crafting and creativeness—the desire to express one's artistry. Then The Bride which represents love—and marriage; as I'm sure you can imagine. Seventh is The Fishwife; representing prosperity and good fortune. The eighth and last is The Wanderer or The Guest. The most misunderstood, and feared." Franchesca was silent a moment. "That aspect represents death." She whispered.

"Essentially each of the eight aspects represents a time in a woman's life, and also a man's. We grow from children to young women, older still. We go from youthful women, then old women—or youthful men to old men; maturing all the while. We love, we suffer loss—we fight and work for our desires. We learn, and we prosper. But we are all still one person; that's what the aspects are meant to show." Franchesca explained.

"So, it's meant ta show how life changes; but even though it changes its still tha same? Or how yer still tha same; even if life changes, even if you change a bit." Simone asked.

"Essentially, yes." Franchesca replied. She heard her love release a quiet but thoughtful sound.

"I guess dat explains a bit. My father did't believe in annythin; 'cept, of course, coin an' profit." Simone whispered. "I don't know who's got the truth of it, but if it's—"

"The Heavenly Lady." Franchesca finished her lovers' sentence, with a small smile as sweat trickled down her forehead.

"Right—if it's her, I hope she gets us out of 'ere soon." Simone giggled quietly.

"Who do ya tink I should pray to; ta get out of a hot, cramped box?" Simone asked. She was grinning, and it made Franchesca smile as well. Just then—the two of them made out the sound of heavy boots thumping loudly against the timbers. The noise was drawing closer and closer—and Franchesca could feel a presence outside the crate. A sudden knock on the wood, followed by a whisper; eased the tension. It was Syandro. Franchesca enjoyed a wave of relief as it rushed over her, putting a salve on her raw nerves.

"Some food, and water." Syandro whispered as he stuck two hunks of bread through one of the air holes. "Ready for water?" He asked.

"Yes." Franchesca whispered as she stuck a finger out of one of the air holes—letting Syandro know where her mouth would be. He uncorked the canteen and placed it into the hole and tipped it up. Franchesca drank as long as she found herself able. She pulled away with a gasp for air and smiled for some relief. Her mouth had been as dry as a desert for hours before Syandro's arrival.

"Ready, Simone?" Syandro asked. He'd been doing his duty, but he hadn't enjoyed it. Of course, he knew neither one of them were enjoying their time trapped within their crate, so he supposed the scales of the universe evened out

122

a bit. Simone wasn't a bad sort; he did kind of like her, might actually like to get to know her—after she broke away from Franchesca.

"Aye." Simone replied just as the mouth of the canteen was placed by her mouth. The water was cool and refreshing—and perhaps it was a trick of her mind, but after a few gulps, she felt cooler even within the baking confines of their crate.

"How much longer?" Franchesca asked as Simone gulped down mouthfuls of water. Castella was only a week away at most Syandro assured—it felt as though they'd been in here for at least two. Though they drank and were fed— it was such a minuscule amount so that they wouldn't need to void themselves. They couldn't, after all, pry open the box and nail it shut whenever they needed to use the privy. Franchesca never thought she would miss something so mundane; or gross as the need to relieve herself. While she—they, appreciated what he'd done, and what he was risking in helping them; they were at their wit's end. At least she was, though it wasn't much of a leap to assume the same for Simone as well.

"The storm the first night blew us off course—we should arrive tomorrow." He explained in a hushed tone. Suddenly the air was split apart by the ringing of the ships large brass bell. All fell silent for a few terrifying heartbeats—there was the shout of alarm that could make one's blood run cold.

"Pirates!" voices shouted from above. Though the words were muffled by the layers of timber of the decks hanging over their heads—it was an easy enough word to recognize.

"Damn." Syandro hissed, not caring if he were heard. The air was split apart by booming thunder and the barking of heavy iron cannons.

"Syandro what do we do?" Franchesca asked—but Syandro didn't reply. Another boom of cannon fire—then Franchesca listened fitfully to a whole stampede of boots thumping away. He was going to leave them. Was this where her life ended? Trapped in a box stowing away aboard ship, which came under attack by pirates? Or would it end when the pirates sank the ship?

Would she and Simone be discovered when the pirates boarded the vessel and broke open the cargo crates? What would happen to them? Franchesca thought she might have an idea. Then she heard the sound of heavy boots thumping on the floor of the cargo hold once again. With a thump against the crate, Syandro pushed on a crowbar. The wood of the box began to crack and splinter. The iron nails began to squeak and groan as he worked the lid off.

"You will stand a better chance if you are out of the crate." Syandro said as he pried the lid off with one final push. He reached his hand down and helped Franchesca rise to her feet, allowing her to stretch for a moment before helping her step out from her wooden prison. Franchesca turned to help Simone as Syandro had done for her.

"Find somewhere and hide. If it sounds like the worst has happened, I would jump overboard, if none have found you." Syandro told them. After delivering his alarming outline of possible scenarios, Syandro turned and bolted up the stairs of the hold.

"What should we do?" Franchesca asked as she glanced at Simone. She bit her lower¬–lip timidly, unsure of what possible answer she might fear more. She'd wanted an adventure; she certainly had one now. Gods above, next time she would need to be a bit more specific; apparently, they listened—and looked for loopholes.

"Ya know how ta fight?" Simone asked. Franchesca shook her head. Claude had taught her a few fencing moves, parries and thrusts; but hardly enough to be used against men whose business was killing, and who's hobbies included maiming.

"Ya may 'ave ta learn." Simone replied. "I don' tink we got much choice. We can stay in 'ere like trapped rats an' wait for em ta find us—or we can go up deir an' start stabbin an' slicin. Basides ya know if tha ship stands an' drives em off, we're still likely found out nyway." Simone added. The ship was rocked violently, and the air was filled with the cacophonous sound of splintering wood and the screams of dying and wounded men.

"Now is as good a time as any." Franchesca replied as she and Simone set off towards the stairs.

"Stay close ta me. I know my way round a blade; an' I know my way round a fight." Simone told her, as they stormed up the stairs. She paused halfway up the stairs and looked back at her.

"I love you Chesca." She said leaving her accent behind peering deep into her eyes, for the first time in what felt far too long. Franchesca grinned and reached out and squeezed her hand. She planted a small kiss on Simone's hand, before pulling her in for a deep kiss for the first time in days.

"Gods above, I've waited a long time to do that." Franchesca replied. "I love you." With a kiss and their love reaffirmed they ran up the steps.

* * *

"What news captain?" Syandro shouted as he darted across the deck. The ship was rocked viciously, as cannonballs struck its hull and flew across the deck. The hit changing the cannonball's trajectory. Syandro noticed a sailor disappear in a spray of crimson, and another have his leg savagely ripped free by the speeding iron. The cannon's of the Gilded Merchant thundered their reply to the shots fired against them. The captain handed Syandro his spyglass and pointed.

"Closing fast, flying a sable flag; red stitching depicting a harpoon through an eye. It looks large enough to take us." The captain whispered.

"Have you heard of this pirate before?" Syandro asked as he studied the incoming ship. So much for a quiet sail back to Castella he thought.

"Aye." The captain replied with a curt nod; he was a heavily built man by the name of Jullian; with a thick salt and pepper beard. "He goes by the name of Rolf the Black. They say he is on the upward swing in pirate circles."

"That means he's new, and without a fleet." Syandro mused as he lowered the spyglass continuing to glance about.

"Some say he sails for Konrad Kursz." Captain Jullian replied as the air was torn apart by the slapping thunder of cannon fire. Rumors say that's why he's on the upward swing. Patronage from a madman and terror of the seas will do that for a fellow." He reminded.

"Never the less." Syandro began. It mean's he doesn't have a fleet, and if he is by chance under the gaze of Kursz, it mean's he'll go to foolish length's to impress him. Raise the white flag, get them in close."

"He'll not have surrender; he takes no quarter." Jullian announced taking a deep breath.

"Does any pirate? Raise the white flag, draw them in close. When they are near, give them a broadside volley from our guns. Then tell the men to take the fight to them." Syandro said as he handed the captain the spyglass. "Tell the men we make the first blow, and we give no quarter." Syandro told him as he laid a hand on the pommel of the blade that hung at his waist.

* * *

The lookout smirked as he lowered the spyglass. "White flag goin up sir."

"Of course it is. Sails ta full—we sack that fat merchant lout as soon as we are in range. Ready a boarding party, and make sure their blades are sharp." Rolf hissed as he scratched his bald head and flashed an ale–soaked smile. He dumped the rest of his mug mead on the deck before turning to his crew.

"An offering to Stromboze! Ready yer selves you flea–bitten curs, we got a merchant ship ta loot!" Rolf roared as he drew his blade and waved it above his head. The crew erupted into a wild cheer. It will be a nice crimson offering to the pirate god. They drew sabers and hatchets and clanked them together in celebration of the blood that would be spilled. Knives were pulled from sheaths, and hooks were taken up in grimy hands; along with cudgels and bucklers. The seas were no place for the faint of heart or for ships without any defenses. Konrad will be pleased; Rolf thought as he looked at his blade. It had been pitted and notched with its frequency of use. I'll get a second ship for this; Rolf smirked as he strolled along the side rail. His powder–blackened fingers drummed against the wood of the rail, as he sneered. He glanced down at his discolored fingers, before tightening his fist.

"Grapples ready you dogs! Pull that fat, gold–laden whore in fer a steely kiss! ' Rolf roared. As the grapples were thrown and Rolf's crew began to pull their prize closer—aided by the waves of the sea; a shout came from the vessel, which Rolf hadn't expected to hear. As his ears registered what was shouted, he was deafened by the thunderclap of cannons. His ship rocked and shook violently—the tides had turned. Rolf's surprise turned to rage as his body trembled violently.

"What are ya waitin for lads?! Kill em and don't stop till they're all dead!" Rolf shouted as he grabbed hold of a rope and leaped towards the Gilded Merchant. His crew roared behind him as they sprung into action, jumping to the ship to begin the slaughter.

"Run em through, and slit their throats!" Rolf billowed, as he plunged his blade through his first victim. The sound of steel against steel and screams of the wounded and dying flooded his ears. The scent of blood traveled through his nose, the air was so full of it—Rolf tasted it in the back of his mouth. His arm absorbed the impact, as he raked his blade across another sailor's weapon. He was in his element.

"Tell me, lad, you ready ta die?" Rolf asked as he kicked the youth in the groin and brought his saber down, cleaving into the young man's sternum. Rolf kicked the boy off the blade and howled wildly.

"Stromboze welcome's ya!" Rolf spat as he plunged his blade into another sailors throat.

"Get up there and get the flags lads! I've got a captain ta kill!" Rolf shouted as he waved his blade above his head in wild circles. The pirate captain killed any who got in his way. He stepped over dying men; parried blades aimed at him and removed any limbs that obstructed his path. Then he saw what he was looking for. Standing at the ship's wheel, blade in hand; slashing and thrusting with all the expertise of a trained swordsman, was the ship's captain. Alright ya, little worm let's test yer skills, Rolf thought to himself as he strode calmly up the steps.

* * *

Simone opened the door slowly and peered out into the scene of chaos unfolding atop the ship's deck. Her muscles still ached from being cramped in the box, but she couldn't let that stop her. She closed the door quickly after she watched a pirate shove a crewmember off the Gilded Merchant. After she heard the man scream, Simone opened the door once again. It appeared as if it was clear. She threw open the door and stepped out. She glanced around quickly and snatched up the dead crewmember's blade. She waved behind in a silent signal for Franchesca to follow. Simone snatched up another blade quickly; she didn't have to look far. The upper deck was a raging storm of death and blood—weapons were strewn an arm's length from one another in nearly every direction. Simone handed Franchesca the cutlass and smiled.

"Remember, stay close to me." She told her. Franchesca gripped the handle of the blade tightly. It was as if she'd just swallowed an entire field full of butterflies, and her limbs trembled as if she were stuck out in the snow, completely naked. Her mind was cleared when a screaming brute charged towards the two of them. He swung wildly; Simone rolled out of the way and brought her blade down on the back of the man's legs. Panicked—Franchesca thrust her sword forward, finding herself shocked at the lack of resistance, as it slipped into the man's chest. The weapon was sharp—very sharp. She had just ended a life, she thought to herself. Her hands were trembling with nerves and excitement, with panic—by the Heavenly Lady; she'd just killed a man. Her stomach threatened to erupt and splatter its meager contents on the deck. Thankfully there was little enough in it that, the feeling died. Franchesca had no doubt that if her stomach purged what it was holding she indeed never would eat salt-pork again. Still, she had taken a life; there was a thrill, a rush that came with such a realization. She had defended herself and helped Simone. She knew she should not be excited—but there was indeed something thrilling about preserving one's own life when another sought to end it. Franchesca ripped the blade free from its fleshy sheath and looked at the thick crimson that covered it. Lady forgive me, and Shield Maiden stand with me;

grant me strength and courage, Franchesca prayed silently as she followed Simone.

"Where do we go from here?" Franchesca asked. Simone pointed towards the ship's wheel with her blade.

"If we can kill dat one dere, I think we can sail tha rest of tha way out of tha box. We would probaly also strike a little fear in tha boys. Not one of em would lay a hand on us." Simone smiled. "Or call it bad luck dat we came aboard." She continued.

"That's a grand plan, but it's a very big if." Franchesca replied; looking on in wide–eyed astonishment, at the burly pirate captain; as he swung wildly at the sailors still offering resistance between him and the ship's captain. She should listen to Simone about such things. No doubt she knew better, at least as much as anyone could know—certainly knew her way around a brawl in any event. With a sigh, Franchesca relented. "I love you." She told her. Simone smiled and nodded.

"I love you too." Simone replied as they ran towards the ship's quarterdeck.

* * *

Rolf the Black struck down the last sailor between him and the Gilded Merchant's captain. "Ya 'ave two choices. Ya can die on yer feet, and it'll be slow and painful. Or ya can die on yer knees begging fer yer life—and I'll make it nice an quick." Rolf growled as he sneered at Jullian. The captain smiled as he scratched at his face beneath his thick beard.

"Or you could fight me." A voice called out from behind him. It was a youthful looking boy, perhaps in his twenties with black hair slicked back and tied back in a nobleman's dignified style. Rolf watched as the youth pulled his blade free of the throat it was embedded in. Rolf spat and chuckled.

"I'll kill the both of ya; never hurts ta make an offering ta Marienndet when ya can afford ta. What's yer name, boy? Ya must have sizable cannon and shot, in those britches; ta pick a fight with the likes of me." Rolf sneered turning his back on captain Jullian.

"I've seen pirates before; you're nothing special." Syandro replied as he stepped over the dead man. Holding his blade in a relaxed manner, his hands and arms lose. He'd dueled before; this was nothing new to him.

"Ye go ta Stromboze nameless then." Rolf replied calmly as he lunged and swung his blade towards Syandro's stomach. The fight continued one blow after another. Rolf lashing out with his steel as quick as he could manage, yet somehow his opponent's blade was always there to block and parry. Somehow the tide had turned, and Rolf found himself on the defensive. The youth's sword wove in and out, without rhyme or reason—yet they were always smart strikes and thrusts. There was a hot wave of pain as his opponents blade cut across his forearm. Rolf reached around with his blackened hand and pulled free a long knife—grinning as he batted away Syandro's blade with his sword and lunged with the knife. Syandro stepped back just in time and brought his blade around to block the blade of the knife. Captain Jullian lunged forward and swung down at Rolf's blackened hand, hoping to sever it. But the pirate captain had a sixth sense about him—born from a hundred fights and a thousand taproom brawls. Rolf kicked him in his stomach, doubling him over. As he went to strike the man's bearded head from his shoulders, Syandro's blade intervened. Rolf lashed out with his knife and managed a cut across Syandro's wrist. With a hiss of pain, Syandro was then kicked in the stomach and stumbled backward.

"First I'll be killin yer captain, and then I'll rip the skin from yer bones and hang ya from the mast. I'll tan yer hide and use it as a flag." Rolf growled, as he turned towards the Jullian, who was still on his knees; trying to suck air into his lungs.

"Look's like it'll be quick after all." Rolf hissed as he raised his blade once again. Suddenly a girl launched herself at him. Her ruby red hair flying behind her as her leap carried her through the air her blade poised to strike. Rolf stepped back and swung his knife, batting aside her sharpened steel. She landed with a thump; and rolled behind him to struck out again. He parried once more and glanced back; hearing another battle cry, as another girl launched herself off the deck at Rolf's back. Rolf growled as he brought his knife up to receive the blow from her blade. He kicked the girl in the stomach as she landed and then swung around to block the red–headed girl's next strike.

"I should cut yer fingers off, and give ya ta the crew!" Rolf billowed as he stomped towards her. "Bet they'd have fun with the likes of you."

"Too bad ya won' get tha chance." Simone replied as she lashed out with the blade of her cutlass once again. As he blocked it, she rolled on the deck and plucked up another knife, from a fallen sailor.

"Yer a crafty little rat—I'll give ya that." Rolf nodded as he raked his knife across his sword blade. Syandro leaped at him once more, and the dance of whirling steel began once more. Rolf stumbled as Syandro landed a cut on his thigh. Soon the quarter–deck was a storm of steel and curses. Seeing their captain fighting not one but two opponents; four members of Rolf's crew rushed towards the quarterdeck, and the melee grew. Franchesca batted aside an overhead strike aimed to split her skull—before thrusting into her opponent's gut. She twisted the blade free and aimed a strike at Rolf's back. As the blade descended, he stepped forward—and out of her rage. All her blow managed to do was tear at the ratty patchwork coat he wore over his shoulders.

"Will ya not just surrender?" Rolf shouted as he swung his blade at Syandro's neck, which was met with a parry.

"Why, we're winning?" Syandro replied happily. Rolf kicked him in the stomach. Simone lunged and thrust one of her blades into his thigh. Rolf hissed with anger as he punched Simone in the face. White stars exploded in front of her eyes, as she felt her jaw rattle from the blow. Rolf stabbed Jullian through the shoulder. There was a thunderclap and a shower of blood. All fell silent as the smoke cleared from the barrel of a pistol, Franchesca picked up from a fallen pirate. Rolf turned his eyes wide and stunned as his legs slowly collapsed underneath him. Rolf the Black crumpled to the ground with a gaping hole in the front of his skull. Franchesca held the pistol her arm outstretched and level—steely resolve and pride, flowing through her veins, keeping her muscles still and intimidating. As the smoke wafted over Franchesca, she turned and looked at the remaining pirates. A smile crossed her face; confident and imposing.

"You have until I reach the count of five—any still on the deck after that, you will be run through." Franchesca watched as a pirate began to smirk. Before he could say a word, she lashed out with the blade in her other hand and removed his head from his shoulders. "One." Franchesca began firmly. There was a mad rush as the pirates clamored over one another to dive overboard or to leap back to their floundering ship. Gods, had she done that? Had she actually looked so imposing; so commanding? She felt queasy from the knowledge and sight of the lives she had taken—but seeing Simone was a soothing tonic for her nerves and roiling stomach. Franchesca walked over to her and helped her to her feet with a smile. Syandro looked up at Franchesca and Simone as he bit down a curse. Franchesca smirked as she walked over to him and helped him to his feet. Syandro quickly grinned back at her as he sheathed his blade.

"Nicely done." He bowed—swallowing his pride. He wished he would have been the one to fell, Rolf. It would have been an excellent showing of skill; a notable and noble feat that would have impressed Franchesca. Sadly, however—despite his best efforts, it was ripped away from him at the last moment—by the very woman he was trying to impress. Despite the setback, he found it refreshing; and quite intoxicating. There was something he enjoyed immensely, about women that could fight; and hold their own in the thick of brawls and battles. Jullian held a meaty hand over his wounded shoulder and scowled at Simone and Franchesca.

"I don't take kindly to stowaways." He growled. He spat on the deck and scowled at the both of them. "Still—it appears, I owe you a great deal of thanks. That leaves the question of what to do with you."

"Sir, I am the one that arranged their passage. Syandro told him. I vouch for them." He explained with a bow. Jullian stared at Syandro for a moment in astonishment.

"Well then—you will fall under the protection of Syandro, and the two of you will be pulling your weight aboard the ship until we make port. You do well enough; you may even get paid." Jullian looked around the deck; seeing the dead and dying, their lifeblood soaking into the timbers. "Looks like a few wages will go unclaimed." Jullian grunted. Gather the dead, give em their rights. Let's get underway. You two, get down there and help."

"Yes, sir." Simone replied as she and Franchesca descended the steps of the quarterdeck, and began helping the ship's crew gather the dead. Simone and Franchesca began grabbing hold of the ankles and writs of fallen pirates dragging them to the sides of the ship; where they began the task of pushing them overboard. A few of the crewmen looked at them suspiciously. Others looked at them with a desire that was all too easy to be aware of. When Simone caught their gazes, she merely smiled and drew her thumb across her throat, for emphasis she would point to the bloody body of a fallen pirate. Most men let their thoughts fade after such a display; others it seemed were willing to question her resolve. That changed when she came across the body of a pirate who hadn't yet died. She knelt down and picked up a knife and dragged it across the dying man's throat. After such a demonstration any who harbored thoughts of her being an easy mark for abuse or victimization; shrank away, keeping as far from her as they could manage. Syandro stood atop the quarterdeck watching as the two went about their assigned duties. For a moment he wondered what would happen once they reached Castella. Would Franchesca simply melt away into the sprawling cities, or would she and Simone wander through the sunny countryside? He tapped his chin, deep in thought. His mind was miles away before the touch of the captain's hand pulled him from his concentration. His father told him, many foolish mistakes were planned too far ahead; focus as much as you can on the present moment. Jullian looked at Syandro before nodding.

"I want you to find the carpenter, find out how long it will take to repair this damage. It's going to take a fair bit of coin to fix all of what those bastards have done. What we can do ourselves, we will, after we limp into the harbor of Castella the rest can be fixed." Jullian told him. Syandro bowed politely.

"I would have the chirurgeon see to your wounds." Syandro told him, he would need to do the same for the wound upon his wrist. His pride wouldn't allow him to show any such concern over an injury where Franchesca might overhear. Captain Jullian waved Syandro away and laid a hand on the ship's wheel, before barking out a stream of orders; calling for full sail's and another crew member to take the position in the crow's-nest. Syandro walked away, heading down below deck to find the ship's carpenter tapping his chin thoughtfully. Perhaps there was a way after all. Once in Castella; there would be some business, which might blow the winds of fortune in his favor. For the next three days during their travels; the carpenter and his apprentices did their best to patch up the ship. The damage had been more extensive than previously thought; with one rudder being terribly damaged. That repair saw the ship stranded in the same place for two days; until the carpenter could manage to patch up the worst. A repair he wasn't fully confident in but said in his best estimation, would see them to port so that it could get fixed properly. Scraps of wood were used, along with tar to patch the holes blown in the ship by the cannon fire; to keep the sea wind and spray out from the inside of the ship. It wasn't the best repair that could be done, but under the circumstances; it was the best the carpenter could provide. One of the cannon balls fired, by Rolf the Black's ship; had fired through the storage hold containing the repair materials—destroying most of it. What had been salvaged was only small bits and pieces, the largest of which were used to fix the rudder. As a result, below deck became a cold; sea leaking mess. Despite the discomfort, Franchesca found it somewhat liberating and exciting. There was an element of danger, and discomfort; which she'd never experienced before. Despite the danger, Franchesca felt safer with Simone around. Having Syandro around had also proven to be a blessing, she would make sure to thank him for all he had done—in some way. She admired him and cherished his friendship. It was a remarkable thing for him to offer to hide them aboard; it was another thing entirely, to accept responsibility and the consequences when confessing to smuggling them aboard. Perhaps his status aboard the ship meant that he wouldn't be punished; he hadn't so far and three days had come and gone. Most of the crew resorted to gambling during the time it took for the ship's repairs to be completed. Some who wanted to hold on to the few coins in their pockets simply lounged about and slept as long as possible in their free time. Others passed the time by drinking; dipping into stores of ale and strong Castellian rum. The remainders, arm wrestled or played the knife game, she and Simone had played at the Rusty Harpoon; Franchesca heard more than one cry of pain, and a shriek or two of agony when things went very wrong, signaling that a finger or palm was pierced with sharpened steel. Simone chuckled at the displays and finally demanded she be given a turn. A few crewmen scoffed and mocked her. Their mocking fell silent when everyone that sat across from her walked away unscathed; except for their bowels and bladders feeling looser. During the evening of the third day, their destination was finally in sight. It had taken much longer than Syandro had expected, between the repairs and sailing. The carpenter had said it would be best to sail at half sail; so as not to strain the repairs he had needed to make with what scraps were available. The great harbor of Castella was an impressive sight. Syandro gazed upon it, with Franchesca and Simone at his side. In the center of the harbor there stood two massive sturdy, yet ornately carved columns of iron; which stood atop long two long pathways. Atop those vast columns, stood, two colossal statues; cast in bronze. Their presence was awe–inspiring and frightening. One of the figures was a beautiful woman in a flowing classical gown with a strap over one shoulder, the other bare. A toga if Franchesca remembered the name of the garment correctly. One hand was held open in a gesture which seemed welcoming; the other hand had its fingers entwined with that of the male statue's a few paces away. The male's other hand rested at his side, his palm atop the pommel of a broad blade leaning against his leg. The statues were coated heavily with verdigris from their long exposure to the elements. The man's form was clad in an armored breastplate but wore long flowing toga over his armor as well.

"The Giants of Castella." Syandro said softly, his voice beaming with pride. "They have stood watch over the great harbor for thousands of years." Syandro told them as he bowed his head politely. He fell silent for a moment, and Franchesca could see him mouthing a silent prayer.

"Who are they?" Franchesca asked. "I've learned very little about this place." She confessed as she gazed up at the colossal statues and their grand pillars.

"They depict Emaziai and Caszall. They were wife and husband, and it is said that they were fierce warriors and lovers. They gave birth to the first peoples of this land and helped guide them to found the kingdom before you. They gave to the people of this land a portion of their passion. And it has persisted in every generation since the founding." Syandro smiled as he took a deep breath of the sea air. Bells chimed at the approach of the ship. Franchesca noticed that within the large towers that the giants stood upon, there were burning lanterns, hanging over the windows. She guessed that such a thing was used to keep the ships from running aground or crashing into the massive pillars, in the dark of the night. Even along the wide paths that lead to the pillars which helped to create the massive harbor, lanterns were hung from long poles showing the safest path into the harbor. The ship was guided through the waters, by signalmen. The harbor Syandro explained was also known as the sea gate, due to the fact it was as defaceable as any city gate. As Franchesca peered over the side of the ship, she could make out stone walls, even pillars of metal. She could see thick chains with spikes and gouging studs beneath the churning clear blue, green waters. Syandro explained that the chains and metal pillars were connected to a crank over onshore and when threats appeared the defenses could be raised to keep ships out of the harbor from landing troops or getting within cannon range. The steel pillars would break hulls; the chains would gnaw and gouge the wood, it was like a metal spiders web. Workers threw grappling hooks, as the crew worked the sails.

Once the sails were furled, so the ship's speed wouldn't be overwhelming; the dockworkers tugged their lines, bringing the ship in as close as they could. Once that was done, they tied the ship to dock and brought over a ramp. "Now we await the dockmaster." Syandro told them quietly. Franchesca looked out and watched as a man stormed towards the ship, a long red and silver filigreed silk cloak, flowing behind him. A gold–hilted blade hung at his side; its pommel a collection of sapphires and rubies. That must be the dock master, Franchesca thought to herself. Judging by Syandro's scowl, however, she thought perhaps he might be someone unpleasant. She gave a mental shrug, people in positions of authority often were unpleasant.

"You're late." The man shouted as a second encased in heavy plate, wearing a morion helmet atop his head; carrying a halberd, hustled behind him. His boots polished to a glossy sheen.

"We were attacked; there was damage done to the ship which needed repairing. For two days we were dead in the water." Captain Jullian replied as the man stormed aboard the ship.

"Attacked by whom?" The man asked as he rested his ring–laden hand on his bejeweled pommel. Franchesca glanced at Simone and could tell she was thinking the same thing as she was. What an ass he was, both doubted the man knew how to use that sword, and it was mostly for ornamentation.

"Rolf the Black." Syandro interrupted, as he walked over to the richly dressed stranger. The man let out a sigh and waved his hand.

"I don't care; I want my cargo. I've customers waiting." Franchesca snorted at his reply. If he didn't care why did he waste his time and the captains by asking. Gods save us from self–important idiots in positions of authority, she thought as she began coiling up the thick rope just as the crew had shown her.

"You know we cannot release it without the dock master's order." Jullian replied. "If you want it, see if your money and title can rouse him from his slumber and get him down here." Captain Jullian added as he descended the steps of the quarterdeck. The richly dressed man produced a rolled up piece of parchment and handed it to the captain.

"I have already taken the liberty of securing that order." He nodded towards the parchment. The richly dressed figure said haughtily waving his hand dismissively.

"Syandro, get the men to unload his damned cargo. I'd like this worm to crawl away from my ship as quickly as possible." Syandro sighed and nodded. With a shouted order, a group of sailors walked below deck and later resurfaced with three large crates. Two seemed to be filled with wines and brandy's; the last crate was sealed, but it appeared as if the two carrying it were straining beneath its weight.

"What do ya tink is in dere?" Simone whispered in Franchesca's ear. Franchesca shrugged, she didn't know. Whatever it was, it must have been quite a hefty prize, to make two well–muscled sailors, strain so.

"I trust your father has kept his word." The man said as he looked Syandro dead in the eye.

"I am here, as is your parcel. Besides, my father's voyage is well underway, what would you do if he had shorted you?" Syandro asked with a smile.

"I see his son standing before me..." the reply only made Syandro chuckle and his smile grow wider.

"I am still not worried." He mocked, as he looked the man up and down. The man ordered the two sailors to place the box at his feet.

"Let us be sure." The man said as he nodded to the heavily armored man behind him. The spear point of his halberd pried up the lid of the crate, the nails issuing a squeak as he pumped the haft up and down to loosen the lid. The well–dressed man knelt down and picked up a bundled parcel and examined it. He removed the paper it was wrapped in and grinned as he laid eyes on the book. "Your father did indeed come through." The richly dressed stranger smiled as he returned the book to its crate, and stomped the lid back down to seal it. He turned and gave a high pitched whistle and waved his hand. A few dock workers walked the ramp and took up the packages. "Thus concludes our business venture; young De Madonia. Let us hope we never have to deal again." The man sneered as he walked behind those carrying his cargo.

"He seemed pleasant." Simone muttered watching the man depart his lackey in toe. She looked on as the dockworkers loaded up the crate into a cart. Syandro sighed as he turned.

"He was an old associate of my fathers. Long ago, he did my father a service and told him someday he might need a favor in return. Shortly before we left for Forn, he decided to ask that favor be fulfilled."

"Is that what your father asked you to make sure arrived?" Franchesca asked. Syandro nodded." Do you know what it was?" Syandro shook his head and shrugged.

"It looked like nothing more than books to me." he replied as he watched the man get into a black coach and drive off.

"Though, my father did warn me to be cautious." Syandro said as he smirked." I suppose the only way to find out, is to wait and see if he comes calling. Now, captain—it seems our business is concluded."

"Aye—yours and my business; but mine with these two isn't. They are going to help unload the cargo—that's if they wish to be paid." Captain Jullian smiled turning his sternest glare on them." That's to be their lesson in stowing away." He explained as he studied them.

"What will you pay them..." Syandro began. He was going to argue against it. It was to be his first great act. He would use his golden tongue and get Franchesca and Simone out of this bit of trouble. It would be the first thing to show her how great he truly was, bend the captain to his will and walk away. But he never got the chance to finish his thought.

"I would actually like to." Franchesca replied with a shrug. She thought it was only right to work. After all, she had stowed away, besides she didn't mind a little hard work. She'd been spared from it all of her life. It might be nice to jump into this life with both feet as they said.

"Me too." Simone replied. Syandro bowed. He thought them fools, but what could he do? They had arrived in Castella, and he did have business to attend to. He also desired a drink; a good drink. Proper Castellian spirits to refresh and relax him after the voyage and his sojourn in Forn. He regretted that it would mean leaving Franchesca—regretted more so that it would mean leaving Franchesca and Simone in each other's company. He wanted to show her around, to awe her and guide her through the bustling streets of Marcilona; the city of his birth. He could wait. He could help them—but the idea of such labor was a distasteful one. Syandro thought about it and decided that he needed a drink more. He needed to think about what he could do to catch Franchesca's attention. He needed the break.

"When you are finished, look for me in the Green Eyed Cat." Syandro told them." When you arrive, I will buy you a drink; but until then." He bowed and dismissed himself, walking down the boarding plank fury rising within his guts.

"Alright—you lot, get ta work!" The captain bellowed. Simone and Franchesca set off down the stairs leading to the cargo holds, their night had only just begun.

Chapter
9

Syandro sat in a dark corner of the tavern. Pipe smoke created a gray haze, as patrons drank themselves into a stupor. He thought for a moment about how to lay out the foundation of his plan. It began forming before his eyes—he actually see his thoughts and visions, in the smoke drifting within the tap room. One by one, every idea; every plan, drifted further and further away; fading to impossibility. He might as well try to grab the smoke. There was something in every idea that was flawed. When you are unsure of your next move, wait to see what your opponent does next; his father would tell him. Syandro had always been impatient; sometimes the trait served him well. Other times it only led to more confusion. This was one of those occasions. He hoped perhaps once in Castella, Franchesca might like to stay at least for a little while; long enough to give him time to prepare so that he could align his plans. So she might come to see him as he saw her. Surely this tryst with Simone must only be a phase. As Syandro surveyed people in the tavern, as they swayed and drank, stumbled; he smirked. Slowly an idea came to mind. He recalled a talk in Franchesca's garden when he'd visited her parent's estate; in Forn, to court her, where she confessed she would like to learn to use a blade. That would give him the time he sought; it would allow him to test his opponent before making his move. That is the course of action; he told himself. If I keep showing her the respect she desires while staying by her side, she will grow to care for me as more than a friend. If I give her what she desires, I become that much closer. Once drawn close, then all shall be made clear to her, Syandro nodded with a smile. He sipped from the glass of ale in front of him. Finally, he discovered a way to buy himself time. He thought as he drained the glass that he'd also found a way to resolve yet another problem. He smiled at the two of them as they walked through the doors of the tavern. Syandro couldn't tell how long he'd sat waiting for them. His legs and ass had grown numb and heavy, as did everything else below his waist. Even his small toe felt as if it were weighted down like a bursar's purse. After many hours, accompanied by the dying light of day; Franchesca hurried over to the table and sat down, a smile beaming upon her beautiful slender face. Even with the dirt and grime that daubed her skin from the journey, and the hard work she had just done at the docks, she was beautiful.

"Guess what?!" She exclaimed. Before he took another breath to answer, indeed before he was truly aware of what was happening; or forming a guess, she decided to answer for herself. Evidently, a handful of seconds was simply too long to wait for him to string a thought together. She was eager, and she was happy. Positively beaming even, which only brought a grin to his face temporarily making him forget about the tingling numbness in his lower extremities.

"We were offered jobs at the docks. Captain Jullian liked the way we worked, and that we got on with the crew—so he's given us regular work." Franchesca told him excitedly, as she dropped the makeshift bag she had brought with her.

"Wonderful news indeed." Syandro nodded as he took a sip from his glass. It appeared they intended on staying in Castella in; Marcilona for some time after all. Wonderful news indeed, at least he wouldn't have to try and persuade her to stay; or worse, try and convince Simone to stay.

"Does that mean that you will be staying in Castella's wonderful city of Marcilona for a while?" He asked raising an eyebrow. He wanted to make sure, besides it was polite conversation. Franchesca nodded enthusiastically; her smile bright as the noonday sun.

"Tell me, Franchesca, would you still like to learn how to use a sword?" Syandro inquired, curiously. "If so—I would be happy to teach you, teach both of you. That is at least I could impart all that I have learned; and we can practice together, just as you said back in Forn. It may prove a handy bit of knowledge to have; especially in an environment such as the docks." He explained. Franchesca looked over at Simone, who merely shrugged.

"I could also teach you enough Castel to make conversation. After all—if you are going to stay here for an extended period, it would be most beneficial to you if you learned enough to converse; and be aware of what is going on." Syandro said pleasantly.

"I would like that; I would like that very much." Franchesca admitted with a grin, tucking a stray lock of wavy raven hair behind her ear. Syandro keenly felt Simone's icy glare upon him. She was studying him. It made him uneasy—if it was a discomfort he found he was unable to say. His experience in fights warned him to be ready, and watch her as carefully as she watched him. Gods, was she sizing him up? The thought of it brought a lopsided, wolfish grin to his lips.

"Tell me, do you both have a place to stay?" Syandro asked. Franchesca looked back at Simone, who shook her head.

"My father has a small office close to the docks; he used to conduct business and arrange his shipments and imports there. Since he is obviously out on an expedition; you are free to use it. It has a few rooms and a small yard that he used to hold supplies and shipments. I can come and meet you to practice, within the coming days. There is also a bathing chamber. The tub is small, and the bathing chamber is smaller still. Sometimes he would conduct business late, or after he arrived back in town—he would stop there and wash before coming home." Syandro told them as he looked around and pulled a key from a pouch that hung on his belt.

"I should imagine that the two of you are rather exhausted and would enjoy some rest and a wash yourselves. I can arrange some food to be brought to you if you like." Syandro said. Franchesca nodded as she and Syandro rose from their seats.

"Come, I will take you to the office." He told them. His legs remained numb as he stood. Perhaps it was from sitting for so long; or more likely it was from having few tankards of ale, mead, and rum in wait of their arrival, but his head felt fuzzy upon standing.

"Follow me." He said with a shake of his head and a stomp of his leg to force feeling and for blood to begin circling once more. They stepped out of the tavern and into the city streets—Syandro lurching to and fro slightly as feeling slowly returned to his legs, and worked to regain the equilibrium he'd lost due to his sleeping legs and the pleasant feelings alcohol had provided. He led them back towards the docks. The night air was crisp, and the scent of the sea drifted through the air; as they moved closer towards the docks and the harbor. After a few twists and turns, they arrived at a modest looking building. Syandro unlocked the door and showed them in. The interior was dusty, and a few cobwebs hung from the ceiling and candlesticks.

"The rooms are upstairs." Syandro pointed as he lit a candle. "I will take my leave and let you both rest; as well as, arrange for a bit of food to be brought over." He bowed politely.

"Sleep well." Syandro smiled as he closed the door behind him.

* * *

True to his word Syandro arranged a delivery of soup made with fresh mussels, peppers, garlic; and, a spicy Castellian pork sausage called Churtzzie. Accompanying the soup was a loaf of freshly baked bread and a jar of butter, Synadro knowing they must have been tired of dried, salted meat; and stale bread. He also arranged a bottle of wine; and roasted pheasant complete with grilled vegetables. They ate every morsel of food, attacking it with vigor and that neither was aware they possessed. Both knew they were hungry—neither realized just how hungry they were until they smelled the aroma. Hadn't realized how empty their stomachs felt until the first notes of flavor–filled their mouths from their first bite. It was hot and fresh, not preserved and dried; or stale, as they'd become far too used to. Which made all the difference to their previously complaining stomachs. After the two attacked the food with a gusto which belied their slight frames, they went upstairs so they might lie in bed, and embrace each other in ease and comfort for the first time in weeks. Simone let her fingertips drift over Franchesca's exposed skin, causing her to shudder with a chill of excitement.

"What do ya make of Syandro?" Simone asked as she pulled her unclothed body closer to Franchesca's own.

"He's a good man, a good friend." Franchesca replied quietly; relishing the tingle her lovers touch sent through her.

"Do ya trust him?" Simone asked. "I know I asked already—but sometin sits funny wit me." Simone replied. "Tha way he looks at ya..." Simone hated this about herself. She hated that even though she was locked within Franchesca's arms, her mind traveled down the road where Franchesca let her go. Her arms no longer encircled her, and once again she was left alone with nothing. Of course, she'd seen the way Syandro carved her up like a spitted pig. There was the possibility that he would kill her and take Franchesca from her. Simone didn't know which was worse. Gods she hated being paranoid.

"He's only a friend." Franchesca assured, lacing her fingers with Simone's. "I already told him that nothing would happen between him and me, and he still agreed to hide us; to let us stay here, and let's not forget the food either." Simone sighed as she kissed Franchesca's neck.

"I sapose yer right. I—jus worry bacause ya both come from a world I could never be a part of. I guess I jus worry, 'bout ya leaven ta go back ta dat world wit him." Simone confessed quietly embracing Franchesca tightly.

"You're not going to lose me—not ever." Franchesca told her as she turned and embraced Simone tightly. "While it's true we came from the same world; I happily gave that up to be with you. If asked to do it again, I would decide the same. Syandro is a good man, and indeed handsome... but I don't love him. I don't find in him the same beauty I find in you." Franchesca told her, as she rolled over and looked into Simone's sparkling emerald eyes.

"I love Syandro the same way I love Claude. Much would not have been possible without him—or it would have been made far more difficult. Syandro is like a brother; or a cousin. Much as Claude was like a true father, or uncle." Franchesca assured. Simone smiled and nodded. With her mind at rest, the two drifted off to sleep in each other's arms, waiting for the arrival of a new day; when work at the docks would begin. Franchesca placed her makeshift satchel beneath the bed in the office. Its belonging's too important to her to risk getting ruined at the docks. She pulled Simone close and enjoyed the warmth of her skin against her own.

"I love you." Franchesca whispered as she ran her fingers through Simone's bright red locks. Not for the first time did she reflect on how lucky she was.

"I love ya back." Simone replied with a warm grin as she laid her head on Franchesca's chest.

The days seemed to roll into weeks and weeks into months. However, the blur seemed far more jovial and less rushed, than the life she left behind. There was something about the laboring which Franchesca found freeing and rewarding, something outside of actually being paid. It fanned a flame; a feeling of accomplishment within her and a joy that she completed jobs with her own two hands, and that she was part of a team. It didn't take long before she and Simone were widely accepted by the dock workers, and the crewmen of various vessels they helped to unload on a regular, or semi–regular basis. Older men came to admire them like they were their own children. Younger men laughed, joked and gambled with them; and on more than one occasion, became defensive of them when an insult or derogatory phrase slipped past a drunkards lips. Both the workers and Syandro taught them how to fight albeit in different ways. The workers and Syandro taught them to brawl and drink, unlike Syandro however; the dockworkers taught them unconventional methods; and strikes to be added to their formal training. The two girls ate and drank with the men on a regular basis; and they appeared to have finally, fully, earned the respect and admiration of most that worked or frequented the docks. Franchesca didn't feel threatened or afraid in their presence, and it was nice to be thought of as an equal, or close to it. Every so often, one of the men or boys would say something stupid, which got a laugh by Simone and her. Once the laughter had finished, the two girls proved they could do whatever it was that the men thought they could not. There were occasions where strength was involved, and the girls had to bow out. That was alright in their estimation; because, on more than one occasion, the girls bested them in matters of speed, and wit. When Syandro came around, the men would laugh and joke with him as well. On a few occasions, Syandro and a dockworker sparred, crossing blades and all the while; Franchesca and Simone observed. The two were well taken care of and made many friends during their short time in Marcilona. Franchesca felt richer than she'd ever felt in her father's home in Forn. When Franchesca was asked about her past, she was honest. She told the workers of her noble heritage, her relation to the queen of her country; albeit a distant relationship. Franchesca told them about Claude, about her distaste for her parents and the reasons why. Every dockworker appeared to understand. Strange how, folk her father and mother looked down on for not having the benefits of a so–called proper education or background, were more understanding of such simple things. Though they understood, many did say they thought her mad for abandoning her family's fortunes, for a life of hoisting cargo and breaking open crates. Franchesca simply smiled and told them she felt richer here than in the parlor of her old home, and she meant it. Just as she'd done with Simone, Franchesca offered tutoring to any who asked for it. If they wanted to know anything, and if it was within her power to teach; she taught them when she could. It was amazing what could happen and how you related to people, bonded with them; when you removed the barriers. Some time ago they stopped seeing her and Simone as, fragile little women and started seeing them as members of a crew, members of a team. The thing's the two of them had done had earned them respect, but the more time they spent with the men, the more they came to be seen as just two other members of the crew. Of course, Franchesca and Simone themselves changed as well. Simone no longer resembled the slender youth she had been, when she first encountered Franchesca in the streets; or had first met the dock workers after stowing away. Regular meals and the labor of hoisting and hauling changed her from a thin slip of a waif to a lean; lithely muscled woman. In Franchesca's estimation, it was a body built to inspire lustful thoughts and begged for those thoughts to be acted upon; and many nights, they had been. She herself had changed, no longer carrying the small bit of paunch she had been so self-conscious of when she'd first let Simone see her naked. Franchesca felt she'd grown into herself, working the docks; and not just her body, but her entire self. As her stomach began to flatten, and the muscles in her arms and legs became more defined she felt peaceful; more confident. She didn't feel as awkward here, even though she didn't speak Castel as well the natives. Franchesca's cheeks didn't color as much, and she could laugh at herself when the occasion called. Her awkwardness around Simone had ebbed as well. The two worked side by side, laughing and wisecracking with their fellows. Together they hoisted cannons, and cargo on ropes. They carried boxes and crates down into the holds and helped to pull ships into the dock. If there was work to be done, they did it; and their physical appearance showed it. Every time a ship sailed into the harbor baring the flag of Forn, Franchesca's heart froze. What it if was them? What if her father sailed after she'd left to find her? Her father wouldn't just let her escape; he would be hunting for her. He was hunting for her. What if they docked and found her? Perhaps it was Quentin, that treacherous leach. If it was, this would be the best place to kill him; especially with so much help around, Franchesca told herself more than once.

One night while she, Simone and Syandro drank at the Green Eyed Cat; the strange well-dressed man they met upon their arrival, stormed in. It was clear to see he was angry, though, at that moment, they did not know what about. The man laid eyes on Syandro and stormed over. As before, he was accompanied by a large, broad-shouldered behemoth in plate armor. However, the black eye and fat lip upon the well-dressed man's face were new. As he got closer, Franchesca could see that he also had large black bruises peeking out from beneath his collar along with a swollen nose. The well-dressed man grabbed Syandro by the back of the collar and hoisted him to his feet, before shoving him.

"You filthy worm!" The man hissed as he pressed Syandro's back against the wall of the tavern.

"Is there a problem Anton?" Syandro grinned confidently as he squared his shoulders and stepped forward away from the wall.

"Your father ripped me off." Anton growled; as he pointed a slender finger at Syandro. Something about the man's fingers reminded Franchesca of spider's leg. Just as the merchant's fingers had back in Forn. Maybe all merchants had their fingers shaped by some sinister power as a prerequisite in order to fill their position she mused as she continued to watch the scene. Maybe it was to make them more menacing?

"Don't look at me. I don't even know what your business with my father was. How should I know if he ripped you off? Why should I take your word anyway?" Syandro asked with a sly smirk. Anton pointed to his face and scowled.

"You can take my word because the man the merchandise was promised to, a very dangerous man, by the way, did this!" Anton barked. Franchesca watched as a smile crossed the man's face, as he leaned closer to Syandro.

"I'll get the last laugh though; I told the man all about you. I told him who delivered the merchandise, and I told him where you might be found. When he comes to find you, remember, if your father hadn't double–crossed me, you wouldn't be in this mess." Anton whispered ominously.

"You inspected the shipment yourself if you will recall." Syandro reminded. "So if anything happens—I'll make sure he knows you tried to play him false—either that or I'll let him know that you're too stupid to have comprehended what he wanted. I'm sure he will get back to you." Syandro replied with a smile as he shoved Anton backward. Anton sneered as he stepped back and walked towards the door.

"If it takes me the rest of my life, I'll find a way to get your father for what he's done." He hissed as he left the tavern. Syandro returned to his seat giving no indication he was bothered or alarmed in the slightest and finished his drink.

"What do you think happened?" Franchesca asked. "What could your father have possibly..." Franchesca began.

"I don't know. But I have a feeling that little snake is crafting something and I would like to find out what." Syandro replied calmly. His level of calmness surprised her; if it were her, she wouldn't be so calm.

"We might be able ta help dere." Simone said with a smile. "The workers at the docks know where his storehouses are. Fancy sneakin in an' finden out fer yerself?" Simone asked. Syandro grinned and raised an eyebrow.

"I'll meet you both back here tomorrow night; let me know what you find out." Syandro whispered as he placed a few coins on the table to tip for his drink. He walked out to the street; scanning left and right, before stepping out of the tavern. Whatever very dangerous man Anton had said was looking for him, evidently had Syandro stepping on the cautious side.

"That was a clever idea." Franchesca smirked; moving her chair closer to Simone's. She leaned in so they might be able to continue their conversation in privet. But as she looked around no one else was paying attention, they were too caught up in their own business.

"I'm doin it in part bacause I tink he's not bein quite honest 'bout sometin." Simone replied. She knew it hurt Franchesca for her to say so, but caring for someone meant telling them hard truths. It meant being honest, even if sometimes they might wish you'd lie." I don' know what's goin on—but I jus' 'ave a feelin." She whispered. For a moment Franchesca wondered if Simone could be right. Was Syandro involved? If so, to what end? Moreover, what was he involved in? Perhaps his father had done whatever it was he had because he felt there was no choice. Still—something was strange. Whatever the fake was Syandro's father certainly must have known it would be found out eventually. Why would he put his son in danger? Perhaps Anton was just an ass with a grudge, and the first target in sight was Syandro. The more Franchesca thought about it, the more she found herself agreeing with Simone. Something smelled funny where this business was concerned—though it hurt to think that her friend might be involved in it. Simone drained the contents of her cup and placed it back on the table.

"Come on; let's go get some rest." Simone said quietly.

* * *

After asking around between their new found friends at the docks, Simone and Franchesca learned that Anton had two warehouses; which he used to supply two different shops. One shop catered to the poorer of the city's citizens; while the other was an emporium of artifacts and goods, meant for wealthy clients. Their attention was peaked when one of their friends told them, once when he assisted in a delivery he noticed a book through a hole in the crate. He went on to tell them that the symbol on the book sent chills down his spine—and that it somehow made his nails itch. From what their source had told them, it sounded as if Anton dealt in sorcerous books; or forbidden texts of some kind. Things now began to make some sense to Franchesca. If by chance Anton was dealing in forbidden artifacts or heretically blasphemous texts, it made sense that Syandro's father would try to pass off a forgery. Perhaps hoping that Anton would be caught with the books, forgery or not—it would lead him to a noose; or the stake. He never counted on the books being delivered. Now it seemed Syandro was caught in the middle; but what—or who, was he caught in the middle of? Franchesca tapped her chin as she thought. He was indeed hiding something—but perhaps he was doing so to ensure his safety and that of his father's; not to mention to keep their family reputation and status intact. Whatever the case, Anton needed to be dealt with—as did the man now hunting Syandro. That night when Simone and Franchesca awaited Syandro's arrival at the Green Eyed Cat, Franchesca began formulating a plan. Simone tapped her on the shoulder and pointed, as Anton strode into the tavern.

"Strange dat he isn't bein followed by dat big fellow he usually 'as hangin round like a shadow." Simone whispered. Franchesca couldn't help but agree. Not only was it strange the man wasn't accompanied by his bodyguard when a supposed angry customer was out looking to vent his frustrations. Not only was the lack of bodyguard for a paranoid man strange; but Syandro hadn't shown up, and the hours were passing quickly. The two watched as he sat at the bar and ordered a drink. Anton was remarkably calm for someone in his position. Something was very wrong. At that moment, a man and woman stepped through the door and made their way over to him. Franchesca couldn't make out what they were saying, but the conversation didn't appear to be overly heated. The woman wore a long shawl over her head that tied around her neck. The man was cleanly shaven except for a neatly trimmed and maintained goatee. His hair was short and neatly combed, but something about him seemed out of place. There was most something about the man that was just odd.

"Let's follow em." Simone whispered, and Franchesca nodded. It took a long while, but finally, the three left and strode into the city streets. Simone nodded, and the two of them rose from their seats and followed the nobles out of the tavern. Luckily, all of them entered the same coach waiting outside the taproom. The driver cracked a whip, and the carriage rattled off down the streets.

"What do you think is going on?" Franchesca asked as they followed after the coach. She hoped this would be a short trot. Thank the gods they were staying back in the distance which would actually let them trot rather than run full out. Working the docks made her more fit, but she doubted she was that fit. More to the point someone would notice two women running after a coach.

"I'd say nothin good. Looks like dat Anton fellow made nice wit' somebody. An' dat somebody rubbed my nerves tha wrong way." Simone replied as they watched the coach turn a corner. It had been difficult keeping pace with the carriage—especially given the length of time it took for the coach to reach its destination. Franchesca and Simone had been following for what must have been an hour, perhaps longer. How many leagues had they traveled? Franchesca panted as she and Simone ducked into an alleyway. The muscles of her legs ached and burned. I hope I never have to do anything like that again she thought as she fought to catch her breath—rubbing her thighs to relieve some of the ache. Simone poked her head out and looked as the coach finally came to a stop. Thanks be to the Heavenly Lady; Franchesca thought silently. They were outside a warehouse.

"You're sure you have the bastard?" Anton asked as he emerged from the coach. Glancing back at the two who were only now emerging.

"Aye; got em last night. Stop worrying that prissy head of yers." A deep voice responded. "Should have just cut his throat and been done with it. Not like anything can be fixed now." The voice added.

"Let's just get this done wit." The girl replied as she stepped out. "Dare's more than one way ta get a letter. Show em we got a pretty little noble lad and they'll give us what we want. Konrad 'ill get es due."

"Ever the optimist, El." The deep voice barked back. The night air was split by the sound of creaking hinges as they entered. Franchesca and Simone watched as the large man they'd seen from the tavern pull the hair from his head and wipe at his bald pate. A wig and a decent one at that Franchesca mused, watching him toss it to the ground. Whoever these people were they were professionals. Did that mean his facial hair was fake too? Perhaps a careful bit of glue and hair trimmings, and lamp black to make it more convincing?

"Sounds like they got him." Simone whispered glancing back to Franchesca with a sigh. Things would turn out this way after they'd run gods only knew how many leagues. They were tired, and their muscles ached. Now it appeared as if they would need to engage in some sort of fight. At the very least they would need to run again.

"I heard. Let's figure out a way in." She whispered back. The two made their way around to the back where they thought they might find another loft. Franchesca hoped that Sayndro would be alright. Such urgency only strengthened her resolve to find a way in, and to be quick about it. Hopefully, before it was too late.

Chapter 10

Syandro lifted his head as he heard voices drawing closer. Wonderful—my hosts have arrived, he thought to himself. It was a clever thing to attack him while he slept. He had awoken in darkness with a splitting headache; sometime after the sun had broken over the horizon. A sack was tugged from his head and the glare from that morning's brilliant light sent a fresh lance of pain through his eyes and into his head. When the burlap sack was pulled off of his head, he saw two people he had never seen before. They did nothing but conk him on the back of the head once again; sending his world spinning. Now he heard a voice he did recognize—Anton; that snake, this was his doing, Syandro was sure of it.

"Why in the depths of the sea hells, did Rolf attack the damned ship that was carrying goods belonging to Konrad?" A deep voice asked.

"No one accused Rolf the Black of bein a bright un. Besides—you know that Konrad declared it open season for any aspiring to gain entry to his fleet. Can't fault the poor bastard for tryin ta snag a prize, Konrad would be proud of. Course, Konrad would be proud—after he cut the bastard's sack off; and ad it tanned to use as a coin purse." A woman answered. Syandro's mind recalled one of the faces he'd seen earlier.

"The man was just trying ta pay his way in." The woman continued. "It's just a good thing he failed."

"Hello, Anton." Syandro grunted as he watched him step forward. "I would offer to pour you a drink—but I don't know where you keep them around here. I wasn't given the tour." Syandro said, despite the pain that blazed through his head.

"This the one you were talkin about?" Syandro watched as a huge, broad-shouldered man stepped into the light. His shoulders appeared as if one could use them as an anvil. Surely it was impossible, but Syandro would have sworn

154

that the man's ancestry must have included some sort of rock formation; due to the broadness and denseness of his frame. The fact that his head was bald and shiny probably didn't help the comparison.

"You're sure that they'll pay a price fer him?" The large bruiser asked with his tree–like arms crossed over his chest. Syandro looked at Anton in a puzzled fashion.

"What have you been telling them, Anton?" Syandro asked with a smirk. "Surely you told them that my father was sailing—out on an expedition to the Tomblands?" Syandro smiled as an eyebrow climbed towards his hairline. The effort of doing so felt as though he'd been walloped in the temple by a tree, but it was worth it. Besides the pain was starting to fade. If he could keep them busy, he might have a chance. Deflect and keep them talking he thought to himself. The anvil shouldered man and woman glanced at him, then over to Anton.

"Still trying to do anything to save your own skin?" Syandro asked with a chuckle—realizing after he'd done it that emitting any sort of sound was taking things a bit too far for the separate pulse thumping in his head.

"I am sure your father is not the only one who would pay for your safe return. Your family is renowned through these lands. Great hero's of Castella."

"True—but do you really think the royal family will pay for my return? Important—yes; but far from, the no doubt, lofty price you've promised for me. Of course, while they have me; you slink away with your tail between your legs and hide." Syandro replied. Syandro peered around the room and noticed two shapes moving in the rafters. The brute's female companion looked at Syandro before allowing a sneer to slither across her lips. She wasn't all that bad looking. If the situation were different, and he were perhaps searching out a bit of fun—or some companionship for a night she might be ideal.

"What might I ask is your name?" Syandro inquired as he took in the woman with an appreciative gleam in his eyes. Her head had been shaved except for a long strip of red hair at top and back; which grew into a long mohawk and horsetail style which was bound close to her scalp. The bald sides of her head had been tattooed with various sailing scenes and motifs. She was buxom, average height and solidly built; the type of build and tone achieved through a life lived climbing, fighting; and living lean and hard. She studied him curiously with a wolfish upturn to one side of her mouth before pointedly ignoring his question.

"Why don't you just take him, if they don't give you what you want, then you have a new crew member." Anton said with a shrug as he stared his intimidating, and no doubt dangerous escorts. Syandro looked behind the three of them as Franchesca and Simone crept their way down from the rafters. He watched as Simone picked up a plank of wood and ducked behind a large stack of wooden crates. It was brave and foolish; Syandro thought. A smile crept across his lips and tugging at the corners of his mouth ever so slightly—I like that in a woman he mused silently.

"Not a bad plan." The woman whispered to her broad-shouldered companion. "After all, we can say thanks ta Rolf the goods were destroyed. We give em this un here and call it square." The woman continued. "One way or another—he gets somethin. He can trade the lad for coin, or can crew em." She said with a shrug. Syandro rolled his eyes. It was clear these two weren't important. They overlooked so many details he was surprised they remembered to breathe. The biggest one being, they would allow the person who ripped them off to get away. Anton—Syandro would be damned if he let that worm get the best of him.

"You know as well as I that he's gonna want blood—and we know whose." The broad-shouldered behemoth replied. His gruff voice sounding like paper being eaten by flames. Franchesca helped Simone wedge the board beneath the stack of crates and added her weight to the downward push. The boxes creaked for a moment before tumbling down in a loud, calamitous clatter. The broad-shouldered man turned on his heels and drew a pistol from a holster that hung from his belt. He watched as Simone and Franchesca scattered from behind the boxes and ducked behind a pillar with an unlit lantern hanging by a hook. The behemoth glanced over his shoulder at Anton.

"We told ya make sure ya we were alone!" He bellowed with a fury which made stormy seas feel calm. Before Anton could speak, the broad–shouldered man set off to capture the rodents who dared to spy.

"Deal with em Ella." The thickly muscled brute grunted dismissively as he tugged a broad–bladed knife free with his other hand. Syandro watched as Ella turned her attention to Anton quickly, and smiled. She pulled a pistol from a sash about her waist and shot him in the meat of the thigh. The sound was practically deafening as the thunderclap of the pistol's discharge bounced off the walls of the warehouse. Anton screamed as he clutched at his leg— crumpling into a ball on the floor. Without missing a moment, and fully realizing when to capitalize on a distraction in a fight—Syandro threw his weight in the chair and managed to bowl over Ella. Her pistol dropped as Syandro's chair took her out at the legs. She screamed in pain as the wooden frame crushed her legs in the most uncomfortable arrangement. Syandro shook himself as best he could, creating more agony for the woman trapped beneath.

"My apologies—I do always try to be a gentleman. But you really left me no choice." Syandro said as she hissed in discomfort. It did not take long before Ella pushed the chair off of her legs. In a fortunate turn of events for Syandro; the chair proved rickety enough from his previous exertion upon it; when Ella cast it off of her, she did so with enough force that the chair collapsed. Syandro rolled out of the splintered wreckage of the chair and picked up one of the broken legs. Ella reached for a second pistol and as she drew it and leveled it at Syandro—he swung the leg of the chair. Ella shrieked out in pain as the wood cracked across her hand. The pistol went flying from her grip and sailed through the air before crashing to the floor. As the pistol landed, it went off. Syandro threw himself to the floor out of instinct. There was a sound of glass shattering, before a dull trickling sound. Ella pulled out what would have been a cavalry saber if she were a horseman. Since she wasn't a astride a horse, however—calling it a cavalry saber didn't seem truly accurate. A saber then Syandro sighed inwardly. She swung wildly at Syandro who danced back, sucking in his stomach as she swung. As she overreached, Syandro brought the leg of the chair down upon the crown of her head. As she threw her hand up in pain; Syandro rushed forward and grabbed her sword arm. As swiftly as he could manage, he kicked Ella in the stomach and punched her in the ribs; seeking to loosen her grip on the blades handle. He was close, but she clung to it stubbornly. Syandro cracked her across her sword arm with the chair leg and immediately felt her grip go limp. He stepped back and leveled the blade at her.

"It seems the odds are in my favor." Syandro smiled. Ella sank to her knees and smiled, while Anton cried in pain trying to pull himself up using one of the thick pillars. Ella produced yet another pistol from a holster on her back and pointed it at Syandro.

"They almost favor you." She hissed as she cocked the hammer.

* * *

"Come out ya little rats! If ya make me hunt ya, I'll gut ya and play with yer bloody insides." A broad piece of wood cracked across his face with an audible ear ringing thump. As his vision cleared, he watched a girl drew her leg back and kicked him square in the groin with as much force as she could manage. Nausea overwhelmed him as he sank to his knees, dropping both his pistol and knife. Franchesca dove for the knife he'd dropped and scooped it up quickly; while Simone grabbed the pistol. The man squinted, trying to see through the pain that clouded his vision.

"Ya little bitch—I'm gonna hollow ya out and use yer skin for a cloak." He hissed.

"Then I'm gonna see ta yer little bitch friend, maybe let the crew—" The pistol shot cracked, and the man's raving's ceased; as his brains leaped from his head to decorate the wall.

* * *

Syandro dove at Ella. His weight bowled her off her feet. She fired as she was knocked down. Suddenly one of the pillars was alight. It did not take long before the whole building was engulfed in flames. Syandro lifted the sword to bring it down for a life–ending stroke, but Ella's knee found a mark in his softer tissues below the waist. With a gasp, he fell limply and rolled off of her; clutching himself as he coughed and sputtered. Ella peered around quickly before cursing and running towards freedom. She ran past Franchesca and Simone towards the door of the warehouse, and back towards the coach. Franchesca flipped the knife around and grabbed it by its tip before flinging it as hard as she could at the running woman. It came on instinct, and she thanked the gods that the dockworkers had shown her how to throw knives. She wasn't very good; as her current shot attested—but at least she had some sense of what she was doing. She heard a shout of pain as the blade sank into Ella's shoulder—but the injury didn't stop her from escaping. It would have if she'd hit where she'd meant to. Simone ran over to Syandro and helped him to his feet, while Franchesca ran over to Anton.

"Please! You must help me!" He shrieked. Franchesca picked up one of the pistols from the struggle and placed it at his feet.

"You got yourself into this mess... you get yourself out." She growled as he picked up the other pistols and holstered them in the waistband of her britches. Plumes of smoke now rolled angrily within the warehouse, making it difficult to see. Her eyes burned and breathing was becoming an entirely different challenge.

"Franchesca! This way!" Syandro's voice called out before erupting into a coughing fit. "Stay low!" He called back. Luckily the doors of the warehouse had been thrown open by Ella in her haste to escape. Franchesca shuddered to think of what the situation would be like if some of the smoke wasn't escaping. It was already terrible enough—however, she'd learned long ago things could always get worse. As they fled into the streets, they heard one loud thunderclap of a pistol shot.

"Couldn't have happened to a nicer fellow." Syandro coughed. Alarm bells rang and shouts echoed far and wide. It did not take long for water brigades to start tossing water upon the flaming timbers. With the distraction of the fire; Simone, Franchesca, and Syandro faded away into the city streets. In a city fire was a concern for everyone. Buildings nestled close together waiting to grab the flame or provide a nesting place for embers. Fire spread like a plague, fire was a plague—and it was treated as one.

"Think that they'll be looking for us?" Franchesca asked as they walked. Syadnro shook his head quickly.

"No. It will look like some crooked merchant taking his own life. They will make their own conclusions." Syandro whispered quietly.

"This works in our favor—but will work less so if we continue to hang around here." He added, making a motion with his head; indicating that they should be on their way.

"Now, I do not know about either of you—but I need a drink. My head is killing me." Syandro told them as he rubbed the back of his head. So far his goal of trying to impress Franchesca hadn't been going well in the least. She had saved his life only moments ago, and before that proven her martial skill. Or at the very least killed a man he himself meant to kill in order to show his own martial skill—along with his heroic nature. His head ached, and his stomach heaved angrily at the thought of his failed plans. She must think him a fool. No doubt she thought that he needed her protection more than she needed his. Things had not been going his way. Syandro hadn't even convinced Franchesca to take up residence in Castella. The opportunity was presented when the captain of the Gilded Merchant offered her a position at the docks. He tightened his hands into fists over and over; as the thoughts of his recent shortcomings chewed at his pride like a dog gnawing on bones. How was he to impress her now? How was he to make her see him; and his feelings? What would cause her to gaze at him with the same desire he had for her? Syandro hissed to himself as he drummed a finger upon his leg.

What would his father say to him? Most likely his father would tell him to find another to turn his attention and desires on; in doing so, it would make her jealous. However, what Syandro admired most about Franchesca was that she was so very different from other women—she wouldn't become jealous. He knew that already. Syandro rubbed the back of his head as a fresh wave of pain coursed through his skull. Perhaps the time to think about such matters was tomorrow—when his head was better equipped to deal with such painful thoughts. His muscles ached, and his ears still rang from the pistol shots that were fired. As for everything below his waist; it was better not to think about the blow he'd sustained—for when he did, he could feel the agony surge through him once again. Perhaps tomorrow he would take time to visit a healer. After being trapped in his head, a prisoner to his thoughts of failure; and the pain flowing fresh in his veins with every step for what seemed like hours—they finally arrived at the Green Eyed Cat. Franchesca escorted Syandro to the table; he usually sat at while Simone brought over three mugs of ale. The three spent the next hour drinking, Syandro's pain dulling with every drink he took. Though he sat and joked along with Simone and Franchesca— he wished all the while that someone else had found him. He wished that anyone else had freed him; and fought with his captors. Something crossed his mind then. His captors had mentioned something about Rolf the Black, and Konrad. Syandro smirked to himself. It was time he went hunting. He had no ordinary game in mind; however, but a man. Not just any man either—but the man that had tried on multiple occasions to kill him; or ensure some harm befell him and anyone around him, even if he was not directly responsible. He intended to go pirate hunting, and he'd start with the most dangerous one of them all—Konrad the Mad Dog Kursz himself. It was perfect. He could become a leader; an adventurer. He could make the world safer. Syandro could leave his mark on the world and Franchesca would see him do it. He looked over at Franchesca and Simone.

"Do you two fancy an adventure?" Syandro asked as he took a long swig from his mug. They eyed him as if puzzled. If he could find backers, and raise some coin, he could rent or buy a ship. He could take to the seas and become the terror of pirates everywhere. In doing so, he could cast a light upon himself and shadow would fall over Franchesca's feelings for Simone. She would be his, and Simone would fade back to being nothing more than a friend. Syandro could show his bravery; his intelligence, and his cunning, not to mention his martial skill. Yes—this was indeed a wonderful plan.

Chapter
11

"You failed?" His scratchy raw voice asked with barely contained anger as he drummed his fingers on the handle and pommel of his sheathed blade. He looked on as Ella sank to her knees. She was silent for many moments; gazing up at the impressive figure before her. The room filled with the sound of her breathing, as well as his own. Her shoulder ached, the damned chirurgeon she'd been able to see was a drunkard and a bastard. The wound wasn't on her shoulder she would have inspected, cleaned and stitched her own wound. Would have—if she could have reached it. She'd gone to see a back alley doktor who most likely made her injury worse. She could still feel his greasy hands prodding her naked back. Could still hear his labored breathing as he looked her over. It wasn't that she minded—as long as she got something from showing off. The bastard had ogled and still had the stones to charge her full price—hardly fair since she would be appearing in his dreams tonight, or shortly before. The least the fucker could have done was given her a break on the cost of business.

"It... appears that Anton was, less than honest." Ella replied more fear in her voice than she would have liked. "The noble's father is currently out and about in the world; there was no one to pay the ransom." Ella nodded. Her captain strode forward laughing wildly. Drool and foam forming within his mouth and dribbling out. A wave of disgust churned through her stomach— much as it had every other time she witnessed Konrad erupt into one of his various fits. There was good reason Konrad Kursz was called the Mad Dog. When he lost himself in a fit of laughter or anger he would hiss; bark, and drool. He would froth at the mouth and howl in battle. He'd growl, and shake his head wildly, and he was utterly vicious. His uncontrolled ill–kempt mane of dingy steel gray and iron back hair hung down below his neck—looking somehow between a stringy mess, and an oily rat's nest. His hair mangy as it was streamed behind him in battle or in the sea winds. In the stillness of the meeting place—his hair lay still allowing the drool to run into his beard adding to his disturbed and wild appearance. His eyes were chips of gray slate; and his face bore all of the unforgiving, unyielding compassion of a granite wall. He crossed his thick battle scared arms over his chest and glowered at her. Disgusted though she might have been, there was no denying that Konrad made for an intimidating sight.

"So two brats broke in to save..." he began as he drummed his fingers on the pommel of his blade.

"Their friend—I can only assume sir." Ella interrupted bowing her head slightly. It was the wrong thing to say—hells it was the wrong thing to do, and she was aware of that fact the moment she'd done it. Ella watched Konrad's lip curl up into a feral snarl.

"As I was saying" Konrad barked angrily. "Two brats broke into the meeting space—which can only mean they followed you. They killed Vickem, and the boy bested you in a fight?" Konrad asked.

"That's about the way of it." Ella replied. "I would have enjoyed shoving my blade into his skull, or to put a shot through..." she stopped and sneered as she thought.

"Or to put a shot through his tender parts. After all, he is a Castellian; I've heard they especially enjoy their rutting." Ella hissed. Konrad waved his hand dismissively.

"We will think of how to repay him and break a profit before we leave." Ella nodded trying to appease her captain.

"Shut up. Your voice try's my nerves. What we—do you think you'll be leaving? There is no we. I'm heading back aboard The Mange, and we will find another one of those paltry letters. If I can't then we simply head back to Tornusia. I grow tired of these lands and these waters. I set off tomorrow. I can always find another letter if I can't—I can always find another way to start my plans."

164

"But... sir if ya just give me a little time, let me prove to ya that I can grab you a letter of colorless flag. If I can nab you one from Forn, you'll have one from all the realms of men—ya can start the war just like ya wanted. Ya can swoop in and plunder and pillage ta yer heart's content. I want my own ship; Vickem was a blasted idiot. Rolf was impatient—they wanted ta be pirates in the fleet, but they never ad the big picture in mind. Our kind could rule the sea—we can pluck ships right out the waters, and when the ships ave all but gone, then we can rule the lands as we see fit. We can build a nation; we can be rich." Ella pleaded. She watched eagerly awaiting for Konrad's answer.

She wanted her chance to shine. She wanted her chance to show him what she had to offer; most importantly she wanted to captain her own ship. Ella was tired of sailing under the command of idiots, and reckless bloodthirsty halfwits. To live a life on the seas you needed a certain amount of bloodthirst, that was true; but you also needed cunning and patients. Ella recognized that trait in Konrad. He was battle crazed true, but Konrad had a much bigger, much more glorious plan for all pirates. She wanted to be a part of it.

"Fine," Konrad sighed as he threw up his arms with a wheezing laugh. "Ya get yer time; all the time ya want. I'll put it another way; El. I'll set off tomorrow aboard The Mange, and you can stay. Ya can stay until ya steal a ship." Ella's eyes were wide with shock.

"Ya can find me back at Tornusia—when ya can finally set sail that is." Konrad sneered showing off malice that prowled within.

"But sir..." Ella began as she took a step forward.

"Use yer wits; show me you are indeed better than those you sailed under. If ya can manage ta snatch up a letter and cobble a crew together, then meet me back at the safety of our precious paradise. Consider it yer provement; if ya must." Konrad rasped; his salt and iron black beard, matted and wet with saliva and drool from his crazed laughter. Ella looked at Konrad's powerful, well-muscled form. His thick arms remained folded across his broad chest. He could tell Ella wished to protest more but noticed she kept her arguments contained and stifled. She inclined her head politely and sighed. It may have been her imagination—but the wolf teeth within his mouth seemed to shine as he smirked.

"As ya say." She nodded. Konrad smirked as he turned and walked away, the thick soles of his boots thumped against the ground.

"I'll see ya around the seas. Just hope ya don't land on the wrong side of me. I'm a territorial dog after all—and I'll bite you same as anyone else." Konrad threw his head back and laughed. Ella clenched her fists tightly. After a moment her anger subsided. One did not aspire to sit upon the Throne of Tides without ambition—a firm will and a willingness to shed blood. For the time being, Konrad sat atop the highest perch a pirate could aspire to. Ella wanted that perch. At the very least wanted a place so close to that perch, she could eventually seat herself upon it. After all—she did not lack patience. Ella nodded and adjusted her belt with its empty pistol holsters.

"Seein as how yer gonna be leaven me stranded here; would ya care ta be sporting and give me a pistol, with at least one shot?" Ella asked. "Mine got lifted during the commotion." She smiled as she held open her arms. Konrad paused and sighed. It was a pirate custom. When a crew or captain decided to maroon someone upon a deserted island or stretch of beach, they were left a pistol with a single shot. It was to be their way out if no rescue came, or if food and water were hard to come by. The city might not have been a deserted island; or a desolate stretch of wilderness—but she had nothing. No money thanks to that damned chirurgeon; no stashes, no resources—and no companions; she was alone. The least Konrad could do, would be to abide by the custom. Ella didn't know what she would do with the pistol and shot. True, she could use it as an easy way out; she could also use it in a daring robbery and gain herself some coin. If she had a pistol, then she at least had options, means of some kind.

"I'll give ya the pistol. The shot and the rest are up to you." Konrad told her as he fired off a pistol into the ceiling. Under the circumstances, Ella really had no choice but to accept the offer. A pistol shot would be easier to procure than a pistol itself—especially seeing how she had less money than a leprous whore in a high–end brothel. Yes; much easier to sneak a lead shot and powder than a pistol, she told herself as she tucked the pistol into a holster at her waist.

"I'll see ya around—or not." Konrad nodded as he continued to walk away. Oh, you'll see me, Ella told herself. I'm the one who's going to knock you off that lofty perch of yours. I'll be the lord of pirates; while you drink seawater with Stromboze. Ella turned with a smile and ducked out of the back of the warehouse, to blend into the crowded streets and disappear into the Castellian night.

* * *

Syandro went over his plan once more. He took a drink from his cup and smiled. As he painted a picture of them all becoming wealthy heroes and famous intrepid adventurers molded in the image of his father. He admitted to the extreme danger of his idea, but also told them it would be a chance of a lifetime. Franchesca and Simone took a long gulp from their tankards before looking to each other.

"Just let me see if I understand you." Franchesca asked as she set her cup down. "You think it will be a good business venture to hunt the most bloodthirsty pirate sailing the seas of the world in an age?"

"I am sure there are plenty of other pirates who are even more bloodthirsty than Konrad." Syandro replied quickly. He paused realizing that particular argument might not be the best way to garner support. In the spirit of an adventurer, he continued. "Never the less think of it, Franchesca... we would be hailed as heroes..."

"Or fools, an' dead men." Simone chimed in as she leaned forward. Syandro acknowledged the point with a shrug and a nod. His honesty was refreshing, so was his optimism. He believed they could do this.

"Remember Franchesca—riches can be spent; glory fades in the eyes that are not your own... but adventure, nothing can take that away from you—it will always be yours. You will always hold that memory within your being— within your soul. The knowledge you take from experiences is life changing.

What is life without chance? Would you be here without chance?" Syandro pointed out with a tone of calmness that only helped to reinforce his point. He was right of course. If Franchesca hadn't heard his impassioned thoughts upon the subject of life; adventures, and taking chances aboard his father's ship, then perhaps she would never have mustered the courage to have snuck out and met with Simone that night. Maybe that was overly dramatic. She'd intended to meet Simone regardless. His words had somehow stoked the fire and turned it into a blazing inferno they helped to smother the worry she felt over doing so. Perhaps though, she would have never told Simone her feelings when she came to realize them for what they were. Or maybe she never would have confronted and disobeyed her parents; leaving her former life of overly pampered, stifling luxury behind. Franchesca turned to Simone with a smile and a shrug.

"He does have a bit of a point. If it weren't for taking chances or embarking upon adventures, I wouldn't be here with you—with either of you." Franchesca pointed out as she took a drink.

"Yes; I am suggesting we go after Konrad Kursz. I am suggesting that we command a ship and a crew, and send his pitiful pile of timbers and twine to the bottom of the sea. Leave his crew for food to the sharks and the sea drakes—and we bring Konrad's head back on a silver platter." Syandro grinned as he held up a tight fist and gazed at it dramatically as if he were taking part in some staged drama that was just for them. "If I can secure an audience with his and her majesty; and plead my case I am sure they will give me the necessary documents, and the necessary supplies to set off." Syandro told them. He grinned.

"I would actually be getting the very thing those imbeciles tried to gain when they abducted me." He explained with a sigh. "Thank you both for your timely intervention by the way." Syandro added with a smile that made his stomach crawl when it caressed his features. It burned his innards to have to thank them. He wanted them to have to thank him. Wanted Franchesca to need to thank him. He took a drink and set his tankard down.

"What say you? We can do this. All of us— let's make a name for ourselves... let us claim our glory—or die trying. Let the history books record that three heroes set out to the sea and brought down the great terror known as Konrad the Mad Dog Kursz. His words did inflame a passion within her. A love for adventure; and glory Franchesca felt reasonably sure she'd never possessed in excess until that moment. She'd taken a big step when she fled home, but it still felt safe. She had Simone; she even had Syandro, to a lesser degree. She supposed she still would, at least she would still have Syandro; this was his idea. She wasn't sure how Simone felt about this. When she stopped to think about it, there had been plenty of danger. That merchant in Forn who nearly killed the two of them, the pickpocketing; stowing away aboard the ship. By the Heavenly Lady, the battle with the pirates. But all those times they hadn't been looking for trouble. Now they would be searching it out. Still, there was something about it which appealed to her. She sighed—gods there must be something wrong with me; she thought. Franchesca sighed and looked at Simone who shrugged.

"Don' see why not." Simone replied as she drained the contents of her glass and set it down." Might be kinda nice ta get noticed fer somethin. I guess a little adventure wont hurt no one—cept doese dat don' come back." She chuckled. "I'll go... if Franchesca goes." Franchesca nodded. Syandro might not have truly wanted Simone along, but up until that moment when she spoke the words, he realized there was something else positive about his idea. Some people might not be coming back; perhaps he and Franchesca would end up together anyway. It would be fate if something terrible befell Simone. He felt bad for thinking in such a way, but not bad enough that he was willing to push the thought from his mind.

"I guess its unanimous then." Franchesca nodded as she drained her cup. Syandro raised his up, toasting their new endeavor.

"To our very own adventure." Syandro toasted as he swallowed the last of the contents from his cup.

The days that passed since their decision in the taproom were rather uneventful. Franchesca and Simone continued their work at the docks, saving as much coin as they could manage while Syandro awaited an audience with the royal court, in order to discuss the merit of his plans; in the hopes, they would finance him. Truth be told, Franchesca was unsure of how she truly felt. Would she indeed set off with him? She had told, him and Simone, she would. That brought with it another point of concern; did Simone truly wish to go? What were her feelings on the matter, her real thoughts? After all, she admittedly didn't feel fond of Syandro; and had difficulty trusting him. Did she actually trust him? That certainly bore greater concern. People could have trouble trusting but still trust, but when Simone said she had difficulty trusting Syandro, was that just her polite way of saying she didn't trust him at all? Franchesca had never actually asked Simone what she meant. Perhaps Simone's whole reason for going was to keep a watchful eye on Syandro and Franchesca? She knew Simone trusted her at least thought she did. Maybe she only agreed when Franchesca did so because she wished to keep her safe. Syandro dangled the promise of wealth and fame within arm's length of them, and they seemed all too eager to reach out and grab it. Maybe Simone did want to improve her prospects. Perhaps working at the docks wouldn't provide her the life she desired for herself—or for Franchesca. Gods above she hoped she didn't make Simone feel like the life they had now wasn't good enough. Maybe they should talk before they left; before they committed themselves fully to this endeavor. Simone tugged on a rope helping to bring up a net full of wooden cargo crates. She and two others held the rope firm as two behind them tied the line to a post on the dock. Once secured, Simone let out a sigh and wiped her forehead with the back of her palm. It was hard work, but she enjoyed it. She liked being noticed as valuable based on her deeds, and her performance; rather than because she had a pair of tits. They saw her as an equal here, just as they saw Franchesca. It was nice to have worked to accomplish such a thing. What would happen if they set off with Syandro? Would they be equals then? Simone spat a gob of saliva into the water as she cracked her neck. Who would run the ship? Who would they sail with? Whatever the answer—Simone knew it would be in hers and Franchesca's best interests to make sure a few of their friends from the docks and taverns were given positions on the crew.

If there was funny business afoot, then it never hurt to have people on your side, at least enough to give you a fighting chance. Simone nodded as she sat on the dock and looked out over the main port of entry into Marcilona. The two massive pillars with there gigantic bronze statues reaching towards the bright sunny sky. The waters were shimmering like a sea of diamonds and sapphires— and suddenly Simone felt a want for those very things. They were the things she knew she would never be able to acquire as a simple dockworker; but sacking a pirate's ship, one could easily acquire a gem or two. Simone wanted to give Franchesca something better than what they had now. Not that what they had now was terrible, not by her estimation; but Franchesca was different. She was special; she came from wealth and luxury. Franchesca deserved those things. She wanted to give Franchesca the things she deserved; she'd run away with her and Simone wished she could pay her back in some way. The life Franchesca left behind had been a life she, herself dreamed of on multiple occasions before they'd met. Simone knew wealth, and status didn't amount to happiness—nor was she so naive to believe that they didn't play their parts. She just wanted to give the woman she loved something, better than what they had now.

Franchesca deserved something, for that matter—so did she. Her father had always said if there was no risk then there would be no reward; if all was easy, then all became worthless. It was one of his finer moments of parenting, perhaps his only shining example worthy of remembering. The fact that he was stone cold sober when he said it seemed to drive home how important the statement was. Perhaps that was the one thing her father truly wanted her to learn. When you hear of something hard, or nigh impossible—jump at the opportunity to challenge yourself, and you will be rewarded. I will be rewarded Simone told herself. She turned and looked over her shoulder and studied

Franchesca as she supervised the unloading of crates. She will be rewarded tenfold for her faith in me, Simone thought as she rose to her feet.

* * *

As the hot day faded into crisp night, Simone and Franchesca sat at a table in the Green Eyed Cat. They drank their strong ale and ate their fill on the Dockmans Pie. A pie made with pork sausage and chunks of whatever seafood could be easily obtained. This particular occasion found prawns and octopus in the spicy; salty, and garlicky broth. It was workers food, and something about it seemed comforting to Franchesca. As she ripped off a chunk of crusty bread and dunked it into the thin gravy, Syandro entered the tavern with a broad grin stretching from ear to ear. He held up an envelope, sealed with silver wax and nodded as he sat down.

"It would appear we are in business, my friends." He told them proudly. "I am to be given command of a ship named, The Quest. There will be two small companies' of the royal military forces aboard and the rest to be filled to my desire." Syandro explained as he ordered a drink. "It seems that the royal family wishes to see Konrad's ship at the bottom of the sea rather urgently. As such they have allowed a company of Conquistadoro's and a small group of royal Pistolero's. In all, it only amounts to fifty men; but it is truly nice to have friends in high places." Syandro laughed.

"I'm sure it will be easy to fill the rest of the crew positions." Franchesca told him as she took a bite of her food and a drink from her mug. With such backing from the royal family and a contingent of actual military soldiers, it would seem far too excellent an opportunity to pass upon.

"Aye; I tink a few of tha lads at tha docks might enjoy tha opportunity ta slip a little extra coin in deir pockets." Simone nodded. "I'll arrange ta talk ta a few of em den whatever don' get filled from tha docks; we can 'ave people sign on at deir fancy." Syandro nodded, the idea appeared to be solid. His audience with the royal's granted him more than he thought he would be gifted. With two highly trained and well–versed units of war; Syandro was sure that this time he would be the one to impress Franchesca. At the very least, perhaps she wouldn't have to save him again. Syandro didn't know if his pride could take another blow. The three of them made plans to meet at the docks in two days. Syandro headed to a print shop and ordered a few recruitment announcements to be printed; which would be posted, in various locations around the city. Print presses were new, and the shops a bit, but the cost was deemed worth it for their new venture. Syandro wanted his new undertaking to be a success, and any edge he could give himself he would take.

Franchesca and Simone spoke of the upcoming recruitment, so that word would continue to travel around the city. Simone pulled a few of her and Franchesca's closest friends aside, and before long she had them agreeing to take part in the voyage. Word spread like wildfire, through the docks, and through the more destitute districts of the city. Taverns and inns were humming with news about the daring voyage being arranged by Syandro and the royal family. When the time came for Syandro, Franchesca, and Simone to meet at the docks, mobs were shouting their willingness to take to the seas. Many followed behind Syandro as he walked the docks striding along purposefully. Today was the day he would lay eyes upon the ship for the first time. A grand three masted war galleon; its sails a rich dark purple, furled and kept up, just waiting to be set loose to catch the wind—like a hound waits to be fed. Franchesca gazed up in awe at the ship. Though it was not the biggest ship she'd ever seen, it was indeed a sight to behold. Its timbers painted a rich wine red, while the railing stood in dark contrast with its coal–black color. On one side of the ship alone she counted ten cannons; she knew that thanks to symmetry, the vessel sailed with at least twenty others. That wasn't counting the weaponry at the ships bow and its stern armaments. She wondered if Konrad really had a chance. What was it his ship boasted with regards to weaponry? She hadn't ever seen his vessel before. She'd heard roomers; she doubted they were accurate though—for in the heat of battle all was chaos. Adrenaline was peaked, and folks saw things that weren't there or told fish tales to make their escapes seem more harrowing. How could someone count all of another ship's cannons? There was no time for extended observation. Besides if she remembered the stories right, his ship boasted somewhere around sixty cannons. A fireside tale if ever there was one—this vessel though was real, and it was in front of her.

"It's magnificent." Franchesca gasped in wonder taking a step towards it to get a better look. She could hear the creaking of the ropes—lines she reminded herself. On a ship, they were called lines, that's what the workers told her.

"The ship will be loaded fully by tomorrow." A proud raspy voice said. Franchesca turned and watched as a man in military dress spoke with Syandro. "My men and I look forward to sailing with you. If you are anything like your father, this should be quite a rewarding voyage." The man chuckled, and Syandro laughed.

"Let us hope. Thank you Lieutenant Captain Cornando. I shall allow you to ready yourselves and your men; we leave tomorrow as soon as we are able. Cornando's men brought over a small desk and stool and set it in front of Syandro; along with a ledger, quill and ink pot. Cornando turned and billowed out to the crowd.

"Alright—anyone wishing to sign on for this little pirate hunt, this is the place. The crown has promised a signing bonus of two gold lyros and three silver pilaas. Anyone wishing to sign up, come forward and make your mark. If you can not write, speak your name and it will be written for you!" Cornando began directing people into as much of an orderly line as could be managed. It was like a circus; all jostling bodies, shouting and cursing. The ledger passed first to Simone and Franchesca who wrote their names upon its parchment pages. The two of them were given a small canvas pouch that contained their signing bonus from a large chest; which had them pre-portioned out. Syandro signed next, and then the soldiers. After that the records were rounded out with the dock workers Simone persuaded to join. Soon the line of bodies stretching along the docks and into the city streets began to move. One by one, men came forward and signed their names.

Those that did not know how to write had their names written down and were ordered to place a small mark of some kind next to their name, indicating the crewmen hadn't written it himself. It appeared accurate records needed to be kept. Perhaps for the notification of families, should something unfortunate befall any of the men aboard? No doubt due to the fair and equal division of spoils from captured ships. Not only would the crew need to be paid appropriately, but Syandro explained the royal family of Castella expected a return on their investment as well. Franchesca watched as names, heights, and a full inspection of limbs and digits were noted in one leather-bound book after another. The quayside was hot—sweat rolled down foreheads, the line kept moving. One by one position was filled. Then Simone saw an unexpected sight. She nudged Franchesca with her elbow and pointed down the line. Franchesca nodded; her heart quickening in her chest. Franchesca and Simone walked over and whispered their findings to Syandro. They had company—unexpected, and undesired company. Syandro motioned for Cornando to come towards him. Syandro knew surprise was key, but having numbers on your side did not hurt matters either.

"Bring her over. Do it quickly, and be on guard." Syandro whispered. Cornando nodded and gave a silent signal to his men, and they set off down the long line of sweating jostling bodies, waiting to sign the ship's manifest.

* * *

Her plan came together quickly. Ella cracked her neck as she waited in the long line to sign on. Word reached her a few days ago that there was going to be a hunt for Konrad. Moreover, she overheard that the one leading the hunt was the youth she and Vikem had kidnapped. That plan failed due to Anton's stupidity. Her plan now was to get noticed, that wouldn't be difficult. People tended to remember the faces of people who tried to kill them. She knew the young man would remember her; in point of fact, she counted on it. She planned to talk her way aboard the expedition. Who better to lead a hunt, than someone who was acquainted with the prey personally? Ella's needed to get aboard, and feed Syandro false information about various safe harbors; Konrad had docked and made port in. If she managed to do so, long enough, perhaps they would cross paths with a ship from Forn. Then she could feign knowledge of the ship, saying it was one of Konrad's. Ella would get them to attack the vessel and when they boarded in the heat and chaos of the battle, securing the documents she needed would prove to be easy. Folk pretending to be pirates were an easy enough lot to spot on the seas; least if you were a real pirate. After that—it was a simple matter of stirring up a mutiny, men at sea were easily enough persuaded to change sides. The promise of a few extra coins—or something shiny, usually made men think differently. For those that were a little more stubborn on coming around, there was always the manipulating of egos and promises of respect; or the promise of warm flesh and a night of pleasure. If her plan worked out, she would soon have her own ship and her own crew; after all, once the documents were in hand and the mutiny begun, it would be easy to kill Syandro and take the ship for her own. Ella glanced around and noted the numerous men dressed in military garb striding towards her. She smiled a self–satisfied smile; so far things had worked. She'd been spotted at least. She was one step closer to grabbing the document that would prove herself to Konrad. She would be a captain in his fleet—or would it be her fleet? One thing at a time, she told herself calmly. Once all was said and done, and the war started, she planned to knock Konrad from his throne. She watched out of the corner of her eye as soldiers surrounded her; hands resting upon the grip of their sheathed blades.

"You there; come with us." One of them ordered. His tone made it abundantly clear it wasn't a request—at least not a request she could refuse and keep all of her limbs attached. Since she didn't feel like spooling in her guts; or picking up her own arm Ella did the only thing she could. The only thing that would allow her plan to move forward.

"As you say, sir." Ella replied politely. She hated playing the humble one who was given orders and obeyed. She was powerless, however; and very outnumbered, so she swallowed her pride and fell into step after them. The men marched her towards Syandro and the table.

"It seems quite odd that you should show up here, only days after trying to kill me." Syandro told her raising an eyebrow. His eyes searched her up and down appraisingly, wolfish grin turning up his lips in satisfaction. She'd tried to kill him, came damn close—he could appreciate that in a woman. He quite enjoyed a scrapper for a tumble in the sheets on occasion, but this woman was no Franchesca.

"It wasn't my fault; it was just business. I don't ave anything against ya." Ella replied with a shrug. "Least not personally." She told him. It was a lie. Any woman with two bits of gray, dark meat in her skull to bang together could've seen the way he stared at them. She didn't mind using what the gods gave her to get what she wanted—of having men underestimate her because she had tits. It was part of the secret of being a woman. Any woman worth her salt should love being underestimated and should know when to use what the gods bestowed on her to get her way. But they should never be happy about being carved up like a trussed goose. Time and place and all that Ella mused as she observed him. Her gaze calm, and dispassionate. Besides, if a man were smart, he wouldn't tip his hand in such a fashion. Ah, the foolish lusts of men she thought briefly. The youth finally broke away from his appraisal of her, his voice bringing her out of her thoughts.

"Tell me—do you really think that you'll be getting aboard this ship, and joining this crew?" Syandro asked angrily shoving his thoughts of her aside. She nodded and smirked.

"Wouldn't ya like someone who's familiar with the places Konrad likes ta frequent? Someone who knows the waters, he likes ta haunt an hunt?" Ella asked. She paused for a moment—knowing that she needed to add to the lie and do so in a grand fashion.

"Look—I know I tried ta kill ya, but I'm stuck with the bastard too. Stuck, doin every thin he wants. That bastard yer friends killed was the captain of a ship I served on—a captain who served under Konrad's command. I want ta pay the bastard back with a blade in the gut." Ella growled. "It ain't easy ta get out from under Konrad's boot, but if ya have me, I can ave my freedom back." Ella explained; which was not entirely a lie. Syandro tapped his chin and took a deep breath and became lost in thought. He turned his head and caught the sight of Simone and noted the look playing within her eyes. Perhaps Ella would indeed have a few uses; he was sure he'd find something for her. Syandro nodded slowly. She was getting through to him, which was a good sign. Perhaps a little extra sweetening might tip the scales in her favor. "Besides, have ya ever captained a crew? Or sailed fer an extended length? I ave and I can help aboard; an help give ya captainly advice." She'd tossed the bait, and judging by the slight rise in his eyebrow and twitch at the corners of his mouth; he'd bit down on it.

"Very well—however, there will be some conditions." Syandro began with a sly smirk. Ella locked her eyes with his, for a moment the air became tense. Suddenly her face split into a grin, and she bowed politely.

"As ya say, sir." Syandro passed her the ledger and the quill. Ella dipped the tip into the ink and signed. When Syandro looked at the ledger, he read out her name.

"Ella the Red." One of the soldiers gave her the same small pouch that contained her signing bonus. Ella bowed once more.

"Strip her of her weapons." Syandro ordered. Ella chuckled as she held up her arms as the soldiers began unbuckling pistol belts and her sword belt. One of them patted her down; it was not long before he reached her feet and ran a finger around the inside of her boot. There he found two more knives.

"That's everything, sir." The guard saluted; before stepping back to a position to keep her in check, should she become unruly.

"Lock her equipment up in the armory." Syandro nodded to the guard. "Welcome to the crew of the Quest." Syandro said. Two guards laid their hands upon her shoulders and held her firmly. Suddenly Ella's stomach lurched within her body. "Take her to the brig." Syandro ordered. His voice cold as steel and measured with a deliberate amount of authority, that he seemed to savor as the words rolled around within the walls of his mouth. Ella growled as she met his gaze. She did not resist. Though she loathed the idea of being a prisoner, her plan was still working. She was aboard the ship; she was part of the crew, and it would not take long before she would begin to play her game in earnest. As she was led away, she smiled. It would not be long before she cut that brat down. The Quest would be hers; and after that, Konrad would fall.

Chapter 12

Simone and Franchesca looked around in awe; they had been given one of the officer's cabins. The ship's master cabin was awarded to Syandro, as his right due to his captaining of the vessel and partially financing the expedition. The second of the three officer's cabins had been awarded to Lieutenant Captain Cornando, though Syandro gave Simone and Franchesca higher positions aboard the ship. Syandro gave the watch and overall security of the ship to Lieutenant Captain Cornando, using the royal military to keep the order and calm about the ship. Syandro appointed Franchesca to the position of Quartermaster; and delegated Simone take the role of First Mate, though doing so made his stomach clench. His first thought had been to make Franchesca the First Mate and make Simone the Quartermaster. However, knowing they would need to take stock of supplies and knowing that would require some degree of knowledge of numbers—and a degree of learning, he decided Franchesca better suited to the post. He supposed there might be others better suited to the position, but Syandro realized how it would look if he offered no consideration for Simone and simply cast her aside, favoring Franchesca above her. That ruby haired woman watched him like she was waiting for him to plunge a knife into her back.

Despite his frustration of placing her in such a position, Simone fit the qualifications rather well. She had a way with people, with the more common men of the ship. She could joke, and swear as well as any of them, and wasn't afraid to speak her mind. It didn't take long for everyone to embrace their designated positions. Each filled them aptly, and the first few days of the voyage drifted by without calamity or commotion, as the waves of the sea drifted below. Syandro looked over the map which sat unrolled upon the desk in his lightly furnished cabin. Soon it would be time to have Ella brought up from the brig. Syandro didn't want to take any chances; he could afford to wait a few days before bringing her up to consult her. Before they set off from Castella, Syandro plotted a course which would lead them back closer to Forn. After all, that was where they first ran into one of the Mad Dog's peons— perhaps there would be a few straggling mutts' stalking the waters still. Syandro planned to make this fact known to Ella. He supposed he needed to tell her, how would she guide them to their ultimate goal if he wasn't upfront? He was no fool—it was certain the woman would lie to him more often than she told the truth. It was plain to Syandro; she hid another motive; though he couldn't guess what it might be at this time. Nevertheless, he watched her closely. He positioned one of Cornando's men down below to watch her at all times. Just because she might have motives of her own, did not make her any less of a useful tool. Her motives and her actions might perhaps have a bearing on how she would come out of her current situation. Treachery would be met with death, and mild dishonesty would simply mean Syandro turning her over to be jailed as soon as he was able. Or perhaps he would set her adrift in a rowboat after he claimed his glory. Such things were to be decided later and were to be judged based on her usefulness. Despite the knowledge that she would be less than forthright, Syandro was very aware there was a great deal he could learn about his prey, Ella. He smiled as he looked down at the map with the Navigator.

"We should perhaps bring her up sir. Forn has a few good coves and islands nearby where it would be easy for a dog like Konrad to hide. Best we know where to look so as to be prepared and save ourselves from an ambush." Syandro nodded thoughtfully.

"Have her brought up." Finally, he would have a chance to put his wits and will up against another. Let the game begin, he thought.

* * *

Ella sat in the brig spinning the silver pilaa that was part of her payment. It'd only been a handful of days since they set out from Castella—and the only way she realized this was the few meals she received since being locked up in

181

the perpetually chilly, darkened brig. A thin paste made from foodstuffs and sources she didn't care to think about, served as breakfast and lunch. They took mercy on her and had decided that supper should thin, plain tasting soups, made from fish and rice. She had eaten worse aboard other ships, and had climbed through the ranks while suffering in silence; why should this be any different? She listened as the timbers of the ship groaned while the wind and sea rocked it like a baby in a mother's arms. Ella listened as the squeak of hinges cut through the silence of the brig. "Let me guess—that preening little lord requires my assistance now?" Ella called out as she heard heavy footsteps approach the soldier standing guard by her cell.

"You guess correctly." A voice called out as the guard stepped forward turning the key in the lock. There was a cold hollow click as the mechanism opened. The guard drew his blade and pointed it at her. Ella picked up her silver coin and stuffed it back into her leather coin purse, the only thing of hers they'd allowed her to keep. The guard led her over towards the stairs, and they ascended through the holds of the ship. Accompanying him was a man she'd only glimpsed at the docks before that moment, he'd been standing with that young asshole she tried to kill. He was clearly very official, very military. It didn't take long before she was led to the ship's main cabin and stood before Syandro. The man that accompanied her and the guard from the holds walked over and stood by the desk, upon which rested a sprawled map. Syandro beckoned her closer, and after a shove from the guard, Ella strode forward. She'd have to kill him when the chance presented itself. Hopefully, it would.

"You called for me?" Ella asked sarcastically, taking in Syandro as he stood over the desk and the map. She studied every move carefully; after all, that is how one insured their survival. She studied her opponents and allies alike. As she studied Syandro, she allowed her eyes to take in the strange balance of spartan military necessity with a sort of minimalized opulence which seemed to define the captain's cabin, and his wealth back in Castella. The essentials made as exquisitely, and as ornately as possible. Hand carved and polished wood; a sturdy table– richly stained, and comfortable fabrics decorated the cabin. It would be a nice prize indeed; it made her want control of the ship even more.

"We've set a course..." Syandro began glancing from her to the map spread on the table—subtlety beckoning her to study it.

"Sounds stupid of ya seein as how ya wanted me ta tell ya where Konrad might be." Ella scoffed as she looked at the map.

"As I was saying—we have set a course for the coast of Forn..." Syandro began once more eyes narrowing in frustration.

"Why would ya do a fool thing like that?" Ella asked, raising an eyebrow. "Ya think ta catch Konrad round the waters of Forn because that's where Rolf attacked ya, so ya think that if ya head over ta where you were attacked, ya would catch him?" Ella burst out laughing. "Konrad promised a spot in his grand fleet ta anyone who brings him a letter of open flag from Forn; he wouldn't risk his own neck ta get em." Ella replied. She looked down at the map and chuckled. "Ya think he would be hangin round them islands and waters; just a stone's throw from the mainland don't ya?" She asked crossing her arms, accentuating her ample chest. If he was going to look, she was going to remind him of her charms—and she had many.

"Konrad might not be there, but perhaps another one of these hopefuls will be. If so I can get information about Konrad and his movements as well." Syandro replied, his eyes doing a quick scan of her figure.

"Aye—true that might be. If Konrad ever shared his movements with anyone except those he absolutely needed to, and those he absolutely trusted—that's precious few people, and certainly no one who ain't in his fleet." Ella replied, taking a step closer to the map and looking it over. "The man is a bloodthirsty bastard, but he's not as dumb and foolhardy as ya would wish." Ella told them. "It's approaching winter in these parts right?" Ella asked with a smile. Syandro nodded slowly as he looked at her.

"Konrad is gonna sail for warmer waters—better pickings. Konrad knows the turnings of the seas and the best places ta in the world at the various seasons. Just like a farmer knows best when ta plant and harvest—only difference is, we harvest others works, and we do it on the seas." Ella explained with a chuckle.

"So then, where is Konrad likely to be at this time of year?" The navigator asked as he looked down at the map. The navigator, a grizzled military man by the name of, Pero spoke his thoughts aloud; as he tried to piece together the puzzle being laid before them. "Warmer waters, which would mean he..."

"'Has sailed half way round the world. Yer best places ta look, are The Spiced Sea, and the waters of the Jade Straight. Ojin and Dea make fer good ports and plentiful waters round these times. Course there is also Kaffra, and the seas belonging to the Crescent Kingdom."

"You have just given us half the world to search." Syandro retorted angrily. He watched as a mocking smile crawled over Ella's face.

"Aye—ta hunt a pirate ya need a bit of luck. Ta hunt Konrad Kursz—yer gonna need an act of Stromboze his self. Ya might have fared better if ya had a fleet yerselves." Ella nodded. Despite the outward appearance of anger, Syandro showed to the room; his mind was quite calm. He told himself Ella was unlikely to be forthright; he knew that much—therefore he knew not to put much faith in the first things she told him. He discounted that Konrad would be anywhere around The Spiced Sea, or the Jade Straight for that matter, they were the first waters and first continents named, which meant they were the first things that came to mind. With Syandro trying to decode lie from the truth, it still did not leave him much new information. He looked at the maps and tried to discount the obvious. He wouldn't be near Dea or Ojin—perhaps the waters around Kaffra and the Crescent Kingdom. Of course, that also left more questions. Maybe Konrad steeped himself in bloody rumors and mystery because he anchored near the Tomblands. If that was the case, perhaps his father had already dealt with him. Syandro hissed within his head. It was too early to decipher Ella's tells and signals of betrayal. There was more than one way to light a fire, Syandro reminded himself. For the time Syandro would play along—and play the fool. In a game of strategy and deception, when one's foe thought their opponent a fool, they became lazy. Their guard slipped and became lax as their cockiness and bravado grew.

"We adjust our course." Syandro nodded to the navigator. "Make for The Spiced Sea with all haste. We will sail through them, then the Jade Straight." Syandro nodded as he traced the route on the map with one of his thin fingers. Ella noted the ring that adorned it, gold and bejeweled with a shimmering emerald. A fine price she thought to herself, looking at it in passing, as a smile curled the corners of her mouth. The finger it was resting upon would make an excellent charm of its own. Soon she assured herself, soon.

"Am I dismissed, sir?" Ella asked with a cocky sneer. Syandro glanced at her then at the guard and the navigator.

"Both of you leave us." Ella peered over her shoulder and watched as the two considered each other briefly before simply bowing and exiting the cabin. So the lad's in charge, but they don't know if they should be listening to him, interesting Ella thought. At the very least they feel uncomfortable leaving him alone with me, and I'm unarmed she mused. She would have to remember that for a later time. Syandro sat behind the desk and offered Ella a chance to sit.

"I would imagine you haven't much enjoyed your time in the brig." Syandro began as he folded his hands and placed them on the desk.

"Was it supposed to be enjoyable? I thought the point of the brig was ta make ya miserable and punish ya." Ella snapped as she slouched in the chair. "Still—I've been in worse places than yer brig." Ella replied. It was true; she'd seen taprooms worse than the brig. Her main concern in her cell aboard Syandro's ship was the shitty food and the mind–numbing boredom. At least when she got bored, she could sleep, and if the food was too terrible, she could skip meals to make things interesting for herself.

"I am prepared to give you a position aboard, other than an internal cell inspector..."

"Fancy way of sayin prisoner." Ella shot back.

"As I said—I am prepared to give you a position; however, I can quickly change my mind." Syandro told her with a tone of threat in the timber of his voice. Ella held up her hands and nodded. He wasn't particularly threatening, but it would be best for her to give the appearance he was. "However, the trick is finding a position I can be assured leaves little opportunity for sowing seeds of violence and discontent against me. A position which will see you go without a weapon—as you can imagine that leaves me in a position of thought. Where shall I put you?" Syandro smiled as he tented his fingers.

"Offhand and seeing yer expression I'm thinkin yer gonna march me up ta the crows nest and leave me there." Ella replied. He was such a preening little shit. If she had her way she'd pull his tongue through his ass hole and be done with it—of course, she could try and pull it through the hole at the other end.

"I had thought of that yes." Syandro began. "However, I have little faith in your alerting me should danger be on the horizon—especially a ship of ill intent. Besides which, seeing you up there for such a period would cause my crew to think me cruel, and without mercy. Their hearts would bleed for you, and before long a mutiny would erupt—without your voice urging them on." Syandro told her as he poured a goblet of wine. He handed the cup to Ella before pouring himself a glass. The youth was an idiot. What would she gain by failing to alert them to an enemy ship, she was as good as trapped on the damned vessel with them?

"No, what I have in mind I would imagine is as unpleasant as anything I could put you through, without being cruel. You will be the ledger man's assistant; you will keep track of the wages of the crew, and the coin box on board. Should we cross paths with a ship that means us harm in the victory that will undoubtedly ensue—you will log the spoils and prizes. You will tally the dead, and the wounded, take note of what we take away and begin dividing it equally amongst the men." Syandro took a drink as he noticed her smile.

"What's to keep me from rippin ya off?" She asked as an eyebrow began to climb towards the panicle of her mohawk maned head.

"Any discrepancies will be met with punishment, of course. For example, if you should feel your palms begin to itch, and have a desire to take on some extra coins for yourself—you will receive five lashes; a second offense incurs ten. Should incidents continue to occur I will see to it you are hung from the prow of the ship. You will be chained and kept in the office, with enough slack upon the chain to walk about the office." Syandro smiled. "I am after all not unkind." He remarked with a wave of his hand as though he were being generous and handing out a princely sum.

"I will arrange for a blanket to be brought along with something to rest your head upon. Does this arrangement sound fair?" Syandro asked. Ella smiled; it wasn't as if she had much say in the matter. She could agree and sleep in a place that offered more comfort than the brig—or she could stay down below in the cold, cramped cell.

"Sound's perfect." She grinned as she downed the wine and placed the glass on the desk. Now she would go cross-eyed looking at rows and stacks of numbers. Syandro called the guard in and proceeded to give him instructions about taking her to the ledger room aboard the ship. As Ella was escorted to her new prison, she smiled to herself. It might have been a small thing to everyone else's eyes; and perhaps they would see it as a failure—those people were remarkably short-sighted, Ella thought to herself. All she needed to do was keep her goal in mind, and she would not fail. The shackle made a metallic clicking sound as it was locked around her ankle. She looked at the links and followed the trail to the large pillar in the center of the room that kept the ceiling above her head. Once it had been locked, she gave an experimental tug with her leg and listened as the chains rattled and clanked. The guard tossed a blanket to the ground along with the straw-stuffed pillow. Ever so humble, Ella thought to herself as she took in the surrounding room with a glance. Still a prisoner—but a prisoner in a warm, slightly more comfortable cell, she told herself with a shrug. She waved her hand to shoo away the guard with a scoff. Ella placed her feet on the desk with a contented sigh as the soldier who had once been her guard, exited the office, she smiled. Soon—Ella reminded herself, soon. One of her slender fingers pulled at a thin bit of metal from its hiding place in her hair. Ella placed the metal into the keyhole and began to prod, and twist the metal rod in the mechanism. Her experience paid off, and in a few moments, her ankle was free of the shackle. Despite the new found freedom, she remained in the office. The time to make her play for the ship hadn't come yet—for now she found it best to rest and enjoy her newly found crumb of freedom; best to let Syandro think she was in his clutches. Just as she let all the others think they had dominion over her. Ella smiled, everyone who thought they were her superior—or held her captive in some way, was now dead. Never underestimate the power of ambition and patients, she told herself with a chuckle. Ella looked at the pile of ledgers on the desk and began flipping through one distastefully. This is going to be more tedious than I thought, she told herself, as she glanced at the columns of numbers. She closed the book with a light snap and dropped it on top of the pile. At least for the moment, all she really needed to do was wait.

* * *

Franchesca leaned against the ship's railing, peering out into the endless sapphire seas. They'd been sailing for months, and still, they hadn't seen a trace of their prey. The seas were a large place; she told herself with a sigh; as the ship bobbed along, as gently as a flower caught within a rippling pond. Despite not having an encounter with Konrad, or any ship seeking to sail within his fleet, there were moments of tension. A few times the ship's crew had gotten into heated brawls, which saw Franchesca dealing out a punishment of five lashes to the instigators. She looked down at the whip hanging from her belt and sighed. It was her least favorite duty; nevertheless, she knew such things must be done. A task, she never thought she would've needed to learn, let alone actually carry out in all her life. With a bit of luck, they had just managed to reach the Spiced Sea by the winter. Franchesca smiled as a warm breeze rustled her hair and washed over her skin.

If she were in the waters or near any of the contents within the close proximity to Forn, the wind would not be nearly as pleasant. Still, despite the warmth of the breeze during the daylight hours, the nights were not without their chill. The Spiced Sea was aptly named. The warm air itself was perfumed with the very spices and that were harvested back upon the Deain shores. Of course, it was not the spices alone which helped to give the sea its name. Leagues and leagues of its shoreline were thick with abundantly fragrant trees—their scent a heady musk mingling with the crisp salty sea water. As with all things the further one sailed from the shores, the less they could smell the warmth of the cultivated spices and the trees, but given their current position—sailing perhaps a league from the very shores of Dea the scent was like a stroll through an apothecary's garden. The smells and aroma's of the mainland tickled their noses, beckoning them to dock. Syandro confessed to Franchesca and Simone, as well as his most trusted officers that he knew Ella's guidance, in this case, was false. She understood his explanation of playing the fool and allowing Ella to become cocky. But she didn't truly understand why they remained in these waters as long as they had. It had been a month of patrolling the coast of Dea, and still, they waited. Franchesca thought it best to make port, at least for a few days. Then, they could gather some information. Just because Ella was playing them false did not mean another source would. For all, they knew there were merchants from Dea who wished to hear of Konrad Kursz's demise. Syandro said he would think on the matter, but that was days ago. When Franchesca inquired about her idea again, and Syandro had said he didn't want Ella to figure out they knew she was playing them. Now Syandro sat in council with Cornando—no doubt asking his opinion on the matter. Franchesca knew what Cornando would tell him. The men needed at least a few days of leave. They needed to drink away their frustrations and feel the land beneath their feet at least for a day. Most of these men weren't professional sailors. A majority of them were simple dock workers. Cornando had told her as much only a few hours ago before he'd gone in to meet with Syandro. Franchesca felt Simone pass her hand over her back before she too began to lean against the railing.

"Tink we'll be droppin anchor?" Simone asked with a grin. Franchesca simply shrugged. Syandro became so busy; they hardly held any sort of counsel together. Franchesca couldn't remember the last time she simply sat down with her friend, rather than her captain. It was hard to tell what he was thinking about.

"I can't even tell what he presumes to think anymore." Franchesca replied with a sigh. "He used to listen to me; perhaps things are harder than he first thought." She added quietly. Simone spat over the side of the ship as the war galleon swayed. Franchesca smiled. No matter how often she saw Simone spit—which was quite often, her mind was taken back to their first night together; when Simone had taught her how to spit. The memories that came when she reflected on that first night brought her a sense of peace and made her smile. During times such as these, it was a welcome change. It was hard to believe how much had happened since that night. It was harder to believe how long ago that night truly was. Franchesca chuckled as she looked down at the rolling blue sea. She heard a parade of heavy boots behind her and watched in silence as a group of Conquestlara's escorted Ella up from the ledger office. So it would appear Syandro intended to play her game a bit longer, Franchesca thought. Cornando opened the door to the captain's cabin and stepped aside, allowing the group of Conquestlara's to pass. He looked over at Franchesca and motioned for her to make her way over to him, which she promptly obeyed.

"Syandro wishes you to sit in on this meeting." He told her, his rough and scratchy voice, sounding like stones being rubbed against each other. Franchesca nodded as she walked into the master's quarters. The door closed behind her.

"We've been here for days, and still no sign of Konrad." Syandro said, putting up an excellent front of anger.

"I told ya he might be here, not he would be here. I also told ya ta sail through the Jade Straight. Said he'll sail round the coast of Kaffra..." Ella protested crossing her arms once more. For a change, he was much more subtle in his ogling.

"This list of yours seems to grow." Syandro growled as he changed his look from ogle to menacing. "I want something I can go on; I want a definite source of guidance. I grow tired of gambling—and tired of feeding someone who is of no use to me." Syandro hissed. Ella simply shrugged.

"Don't know what ta tell ya. Ya can sail through the Jade Straight; maybe by the time ya make yer way back ta Forn, it will be round the spring. Konrad likes raiding ships from Forn round springtime. Says the wine they carry has aged just enough." Syandro looked over at Franchesca. So long had they been at sea that even Syandro's ordinarily neat and primed appearance was starting to slacken; his once clean-shaven face now shadowed and dark with unshaved stubble. Even the sides of Ella's shaved head began to grow out. Ella watched as Syandro looked over at Franchesca. She grinned observing something there. Perhaps it was time to start making subtle moves.

"Quartermaster—what do you think of our current situation, and have you any advice on the matter?" Syandro asked with a smile. He looked back and watched Ella turn away.

"May I speak freely, sir?" Franchesca asked. Syandro nodded. "For the sake of morale and for other practical reasons, I believe we should make port in Dea, at least for a few days. Allow the men to rest, and allow us to resupply. After that..." Franchesca looked at Ella then at Syandro who also stared at her. She could tell Syandro wished her to keep up his game of allowing Ella to think them fools. "After that, I believe we should sail through the Jade Straight and make a brief pass along the costs of Kaffra and the coasts of the Crescent Kingdom. If we have not found him by then, I think we should sail for Forn and adjust our plan accordingly." Franchesca answered. Syandro scratched his stubbly cheeks and sighed.

"I agree with her sir." Cornando nodded. Syandro took in a deep breath. He'd wanted to dock as well, but he wanted to leave it to a vote in front of Ella. He wanted her to believe none knew they were being played as fools. It appeared to work.

"It seems that there is a unanimous agreement, and I will agree to it. Make ready—we sail for the ports of Dea." Syandro said with a sort of quiet pride. Now Franchesca understood. He needed to have others of rank make the suggestion in front of her. Then Ella would believe Syandro was conceding to the needs of his crew, rather than her scheme. Franchesca bowed as did Cornando.

"I will tell the crew." Franchesca told him as she turned on her heel and left the cabin. She hated that she'd played along with Syandro's plot. For that matter, she hated playing a game she wasn't told the rules of. He was playing this game without her. Syandro was planning moves without her, without Simone. Weren't they all in this together? Still, she supposed she owed it to him to watch his back. She did know Ella had something up her sleeve. Franchesca bit her lip as the door closed behind her.

"Shall I take her back to the ledger man's office, sir?" Cornando asked. Syandro sighed and turned and nodded. "Make it so." He whispered. Ella sneered as she was led away back to the ledger man's office.

Chapter 13

The ship had been docked in Dea for a week, and it seemed there were no urgent plans—or need to set out immediately. The crew drank themselves into stupors and caroused from inn to inn; brothel, to brothel in shifts. Those not carousing were busy loading new supplies and cargo, and those not loading supplies; exhausted themselves in every other way one could think of. Fist fights were arranged for gambling purposes, as were fights with weapons, however, the rules for those fights was to first blood. Men boxed, played darts and threw dice, trying to gain a few extra coins to further indulge themselves in whatever vice caught their particular fancy or whim. Ella, however, remained confined to the ship and merely looked out from the deck at the bustling docks. The smell of sweat, heady spices, musky colognes; and floral perfumes hung thick in the air—even from a distance, she was made to observe. The weather was hot and humid, and bugs remained a constant annoyance. Ella noted the men as they cavorted about the docks flirting with the various women and watched their shows of strength, listening to a thousand tales of bravery and bravado. It was all incredibly dull—but there were a handful of people she watched closely. Most of these tales were designed to leave their fellow's in awe, or impress passing women—intended to charm them out of their fine underclothes and into a bed. Ella heard things like this before, some of which were even spoken in her direction. Those efforts always ended the same way, she laughed and crushed the ego of the men trying to seduce her with tales of their own bravery; or she put them to the test. Usually, that ended with them getting their asses kicked and leaving with some broken bone and some spilled blood for nothing. Since their docking, Ella observed the interactions of all the ship's officers from a safe distance—always when they thought she wasn't paying attention.

There were no great secrets discussed; at least not that anyone would pick up on. Syandro however, had a great deal he wished to keep hidden. To most, his secrets were just that, secrets. But under her watchful observant eyes, Ella saw through his carefully constructed veneer. She studied how he spoke to Franchesca; she noticed the movements of his body when he thought no one around except for him and Franchesca. Evidently, Syandro forgot she always lurked somewhere. He appeared as an overly boastful and proud stag, or a bird splaying out his brightest shining features to attract her attention. His demeanor changed when Simone approached; or when he observed the two of them speaking to one another. The stag lowered his proud head and brooded—hell, he pouted like a petulant, spoiled bitch; which always made her smirk. The bird's brightly colored feathers of personality and charm darkened into black storm clouds that threatened to burst open with a flood of hot rage and frustration.

Perhaps such things went unnoticed because Syandro was surrounded by men, and men noticed matters of the heart only when such things affected them personally. Otherwise, they were as dense as iron; or perhaps the others were too involved within their own minds and tasks to pay as much attention as she did. After all, she was a prisoner. She'd seen men turn their heads up proudly like that, only a handful of times, heard them posture and appear overly competent for one reason. It appeared young Captain Syandro was showing off to get Franchesca's attention. The only time men acted like that was to get women to notice them. Ella snickered to herself when she was alone at night or behind his back during the day for that matter. Though Syandro told her she would have to pull her own weight, since arriving at port, he refused to let her leave the ship; though he allowed her out of that damned ledger room during the daylight hours. That was perhaps the smartest thing he'd done thus far—in her estimation. While they were docked, he appeared to trust her even less. Which made sense in a way, after all—for all Syandro knew she had contacts and friends in Dea, who she could use to get a message to Konrad. Syandro was right in that respect after all. Ella did have more than a few contacts in the lands of Dea. Certainly none she would call friends, however. She had few of those, none truly; if she were honest with herself. I've always been too ambitious for friends, they hold you back. It made sense to her to keep herself closed off because one day she might have to kill a person she called a friend. Why get emotionally invested if you were going to have to kill the bastard? It made perfect sense. Though she wished to believe him so, Syandro was no fool; yet another cold fact she had come to grudgingly appreciate. Ella suspected that he knew the routes she spoke of were false, and designed to mislead him. If she was correct that posed a problem. But problems did have solutions, and after so long watching and waiting. After days and weeks of observation and the listening to personal interactions, Ella crafted a solution to her problem. She watched intently as Syandro strode over to the ship's rail and looked out over the docks. She followed his gaze, and sure enough, his eyes beheld the sight of Franchesca. He held her in his gaze, as she gave directions and looked over the newly obtained supplies.

"Ya watch her a lot, don't ya?" Ella asked. It was less a question and more of a statement. Syandro glanced over at her and then turned and looked back to the docks, with a scoff. The words seemed to catch him off guard; they made him flinch. Most importantly, he jumped slightly.

"Am I ta take that as a yes?" She asked with a sneer. Ella noted Syandro drummed his fingers against the painted and lacquered hardwood. Now was the opportune time—the time to plunge the dagger in, and twist it mercilessly.

"She doesn't love ya. Ya know that, don't ya?" Ella saw a wave of rigidity passed through Syandro's well defined, richly garbed frame. He was as tense as an overstretched sail. Now was the time for her to drag the blade along.

"And she's never gonna." The way she said it—the certainty of the statement, and the timbre of her tone; sent a brief tremor through him, as if he'd been given the heaviest and most crushing of weights to carry. Worse—it was a weight he'd come to suspect was true. People loved lying to themselves, for reasons Ella couldn't quite figure. She studied him for a moment, his back ramrod straight; his muscles taught with impotent anger. To his credit she noted—he'd known his efforts would never bear fruit. She saw the fire in him as he fought against himself. He fought against what he knew to be a lie and fought to at least attempt to make his desires manifest. No—she would not stick the knife in and twist yet—but she would drag the blade across the wound.

"What do you know of it?" Syandro hissed as he stepped forward angrily. His hand flying to the grip of the blade that hung at his side. Ella chuckled. Not a cruel chuckle, nor was it nervous; merely a chuckle of feigned astonishment. It surprised her how men could be so damned stupid. What did she know of it indeed? She was a woman; she knew a woman's feelings and how they thought. Though men liked to think themselves complex, they really weren't—at least none of the ones she had met. She wasn't saying they were stupid; they did a remarkable amount with the limited thought process they possessed. But eating, fucking, sleeping—and telling lies, only took one so far— had taken some men farther than most. Still such a limited thought process, in her experience that was men in a nutshell. She'd heard a saying somewhere, behind every great man was a woman. If the quote was to be accurate, it should say, beneath every powerful rutting man, was a woman. Men rarely listened to anyone behind them, hells they barely listened to anyone beneath them. At least after they'd finished, they were easily manipulated, or beforehand. It was easy to get a man to do what you wanted if you breathed in his ear heavy enough, and said something raunchy enough. Ella shook her head and stared at him with a grin.

"Contrary ta what ya think—I am a woman. I know the signs, and I see the signals." Ella told him gently with a small shrug. Now she would begin her own game in earnest. She would pull out the dagger bind, and salve the wounds with words and promises drenched in honey, and affection. She would heal his broken heart, and nurse his bruised pride, only to knock him down once again, when the time came. While she bound his hurts, Syandro would coil around her little finger like the pathetic worm he was.

"I see in her much of myself—least what I was." Ella went on; her voice was soothing, just shy of seduction. "Ya think its easy bein under the bastards? I've ad ta answer to?" She even managed to force out a tear. Good acting on her part, she thought.

"The polite smiles and nods—understood bonds of friendship, even though I see much of myself in her—I've more in common with you." Ella choked. She looked Syandro up and down. Ella could tell that he was buying it. If he didn't buy the lie yet, he would soon; it was all but inevitable. Give a man's ego a trip to the whorehouse and inflate it and he'd swallow anything you put before him.

"All ya want is someone ta heal ya. Ya want someone ta notice yer love fer em. Ya want em ta know that yer the one who's worthwhile—who'll show em the world and all its glory. Someone who will stand beside ya—be yer partner."

Syandro's hand fell away from the pommel of his blade and hung limply at his side. Her words caressed and slithered around in his brain like a snake. Though the smile didn't manifest on the outside, she grinned like a cat that discovered a mouse trying to drink from its bowl of cream.

"How. . ?" Syandro stuttered. His eyes holding desperation deep within them. His pulse pounded frantically.

"I know ya want her, maybe ya can ave her yet" Ella replied sweetly in a tone Syandro didn't think her capable of possessing. At that moment all he wanted to know was how. How could he make Franchesca his?

"Well?" Syandro asked. His Castellian pride and bravado melting away like ice over a forge. Pathetic—she thought, the word echoing in her skull. Show a man he can fuck his problems away elsewhere, and you've turned him into a drooling moron. Ella extended her hand and clasped his gently. He flinched momentarily, but suspicion faded when she smiled at him when she held his hand tenderly.

"Show her what ya ave ta offer." She told him gently moving closer into his personal space.

"I've tried..." Syandro began to protest. Ella shook her head and placed a finger to his lips.

"No..." she picked up his hand and placed it on her chest "show her through someone else." Syandro looked at her hesitantly. "Sometimes all a woman needs ta come round to an idea, is ta watch someone else. She might not think she wants ya now, but maybe if she see's ya taken she'll change her opinion." Ella told him. She could see his breath growing heavy. She could see Syandro's heart hammer within his chest, as pride, desire, and suspicion warred within him. He fought to keep himself from trembling. There was one way to remove his suspicion, and that was to acknowledge other falsehoods.

"I know I've led ya on a goose chase—I'm not a fool enough ta think that ya believed me or ya think me honest. Yer probably thinkin I'm just tryin ta play ya a fool again, but I'm not." Ella told him as her voice dropped to barely more than a whisper. Now was the time where those comforting tones took on the honey of seduction.

"All ya have ta ask yerself is—what do I stand ta gain from lyin bout somethin like this. I'm not askin ya ta remove my chains; I'm not askin ya ta let me run free the ship... I'm simply tryin ta help ya get what ya want." She told him gently. Ella leaned in and planted a faint soft kiss upon Syandro's lips. So soft it was like the caress of a ghost's touch. Add the bait to the hook, and toss it overboard, and something would bite because it couldn't resist. He'd taken the bait. Syandro pulled her closer and returned the kiss with feverish want. Though half of his mind recoiled, rebelled at the action. In that moment he was lost, he was desperate. There was a saying in Castella, desperation leads to surprising roads, and often times broken bones. It was commonly used to explain a man or woman cuckolding their lover, and the usual reaction of one party upon finding out. Syandro was nothing if not desperate—and this road was nothing if not unusual. He wanted Franchesca so badly he could practically feel it. His desperation even surprised him. Ella felt a wave of joy rolling from the tip of her head to the soles of her feet. Now she had him.

* * *

Franchesca pounded on one of the thick wooden crates and listened to the thump. Two crewmen, who she and Simone had known when they worked the docks in Castella, approached her with two large burlap sacks.

"That's eighty pounds of rice. If we can keep it dry, we'll have no shortage of food." She sighed. Another crewmember brought over a crate filled with potatoes and smiled, as he set it down beside a box containing jars of pickled vegetables. Since their arrival, it seemed that they were buying the entirety of the markets of Dea. Rice, beans, grains; pickled vegetables, and pickled eggs. There were chickens in flimsy bamboo cages and even three live goats which unfortunately would not live long, once they set off to sea again. They bought dried, salted lamb, duck, and goat, which the people also smoked; so the meat would keep longer, and to make the preserved food taste better. Franchesca would have lost count of how much food she'd overseen loaded onto the ship, if she didn't keep a meticulous record, it turned out a bit of her father rubbed off on her. It turned out that buying goods in Dea was an investment with an extremely high yield. Goods were inexpensive, and it appeared the people of the markets were willing to part with their goods for the most trivial of things. Franchesca watched on one occasion as a crewman traded a bit of scrimshawed bone for a small keg of strong liquor; which he and a few friends made short work of. Despite this, it seemed that the men maintained a deep respect for the people they interacted with, and that respect seemed to be returned by the natives. She'd heard one sailor explain that the people of Dea believed wholeheartedly their gods roamed their lands, and called them not to be greedy. Common beasts could make a living, they as higher creatures were called truly live. To that end, they placed less value on money, and more value on making trades for unusual items, or things they could leave as offerings to their many gods, of course not everyone followed such a path. As with everywhere in the world, there were exceptions. Franchesca found it interesting but felt like she should be doing more for those she was buying goods from. Simone clapped Franchesca on her shoulder and smiled.

"What ave we taken on taday?" Simone asked wiping the sweat from her forehead and cracking her neck. The heat hung close and made one's clothes stick to the skin. It was no wonder the locals dressed in such lose, thin flowing garments. What she wouldn't give to be able to purchase some of those garments right now. Sweat beaded on her forehead once more and began dripping off her skin as the sun gnawed on her pale skin.

"Almost a ton of food; we've picked up a few weapons for the ship, arranged for a few minor repairs—all for a pittance." Franchesca sighed. She felt like she was ripping these people off. Perhaps their soil was more fertile, or maybe their crops yielded large amounts of produce. Perhaps the locals believed and trusted in their numerous gods to ensure the vitality of their crops. Whatever the case might be, she felt guilty at the inexpensive cost of the goods. If her father ever found out how cheap goods were here, he could expand his business and further strengthen his finances.

"Some people don' place much value on money—I believe, dat ya were one of em." Simone chuckled.

"I am, but this seems mad. This would cost us triple at another port, perhaps even more than that at Forn or Castella." Franchesca replied a lump becoming lodged in her throat. It seemed at any moment things would turn and they would find themselves being charged more than they could pay.

"Don' scowl at good fortune when it looks at ya." Simone told her with a squeeze on the shoulder. Franchesca shrugged, she looked back towards the ship, her heart skipped a beat. She nudged Simone in the ribs with her elbow. Simone scolded and protested, but Franchesca merely pointed to the scene unfolding on the ship's deck. Locked in an embrace with Ella stood Syandro. Standing wasn't what he was doing—not by half. It seemed far more active, far more seductive than just standing.

"I knew dere was somethin wrong bout him." Simone hissed gazing on in wide–eyed wonder as Syandro pulled Ella deeper into their kiss.

"Perhaps he thinks if he seduces her he'll get her to spill her secrets." Franchesca told her quietly. "There has to be more to this than what we're seeing." Franchesca continued. "He wouldn't be stupid enough to let her have the walk of the ship... would he?"

"Doen't look like he's usin much in tha way of his brain—least, not tha one dat sits in dat particular space up north." Simone nodded her expression grim.

"Good ting we made sure ta keep some friends on board." Simone whispered.

"Looks like we're gonna need help watchin our backs." A chill ran through Franchesca, she didn't want to think Simone was right, but something's were hard to ignore. She just witnessed Syandro embracing and kissing a woman who not only abducted him but tried to kill him. Perhaps it was that Castellian passion he spoke about so often. Whatever the case, it was odd and unsettling. Perhaps Simone was right in bringing along men whose loyalties were more closely aligned to herself and Franchesca. A handful certainly seemed better than none now. How I hope he has a plan, Franchesca thought to herself as she turned her attention back to her duties.

* * *

Simone upended her tankard and finished off the strong drink within. Her eyes shut, out of reflex and she shook her head. One thing to say about this place was that the alcohol was strong, perhaps stronger than any drink she had tried before. The locals told her that the liquor was made from fermented goats milk, honey, coconut milk, and fruits. Whatever they truly made it from, it felt like liquid fire going down; and tasted rich and sweet when it touched the tongue. It was clearly easy to overindulge. Illustrating this point were several crewmembers either passed out upon the straw–covered floors of the tavern, or the handful that continued to walk into the same wall as they attempted to find the door to leave. What startled her was that she'd entered with these men, and watched them drink. The ones thumping into the walls repeatedly, only had four tankards; the ones sprawled on the floor only drank two extra. Simone took note of that and set her second glass down, quite content to be a lightweight. She suspected there might be an ingredient the locals didn't reveal—for her body felt numb, and her head felt as if a blissful fog swirled about within the confines of her skull. A feeling the likes of which she'd never experienced when she was drunk before, and she had been drunk many times. In all honesty, she didn't feel drunk, she didn't sway or stumble on her feet, nor did she lisp or slur her speech. Whatever was happening was quite enjoyable. She touched Franchesca on the shoulder and smiled.

"What do ya tink of disstuf?" Simone asked. Franchesca only had one drink and decided to wave off any other attempts at filling her glass, politely.

"It's quite nice... quite strong." She giggled, only now was she beginning to feel the faint fog swirl within her brain, and the wonderful feeling of her fingertips feeling as though they were far removed from her hands. At that moment Syandro walked in and smiled as he walked over to a seat next to Franchesca.

"Partaking in some of the local drink I see." He ordered one for himself and smiled as he took a drink and winced. "That will cleanse the body and soul, make no mistake." He said fighting the urge to clear his throat and cough to rid himself of the burning sensation, as he set his drink down. Franchesca stared at him curiously, as did Simone.

"Is there a problem?" He asked feeling a strong urge to pick up his drink once more. He thought about taking a long swig but knew that would end poorly. If he did so it would keep him busy; if he got drunk he wouldn't care; he'd be relaxed—more relaxed at any rate.

"What were you doing this afternoon?" Franchesca asked, allowing the hint of a wry smile to play across her soft lips.

"What do you mean?" Syandro asked, even though he could fully piece together what she was talking about as he took another drink—a longer deeper drink.

"We saw you with Ella—in quite a friendly showing." Franchesca replied quietly. "Please tell me it's because you're trying to draw information out of her." She whispered. Syandro merely shrugged as he set his drink down.

"The seas are a lonely place, and I am assuming that you ladies have no desire to…" his eyes flitted back and forth allowing a mischievous grin to play across his handsome features. The grin was far too sincere for Simone's taste. As if he were asking and pleased he'd gotten to do so because he'd found a way, sneakier than snakes ass to do so. His grin almost asked if silently if he might watch them.

"She tried to kill you." Franchesca interrupted. She wasn't about to indulge in a discussion about her and Simone's activities. By the Heavenly Lady, it had been quite a while though. Not the time she reminded herself. Of course, its hard to do anything when you're on a packed ship—filled with rowdy sailors. Damn it not the time Chesca she scolded silently. Using the name Simone had given her was a mistake, and she felt the fire burn within her heart and felt it spread lower. She chided herself one last time and forced herself to focus—and to set her drink aside.

"I am aware, you are right, however…." Syandro lied. He was not intending on pulling information, or the truth out of her. If such a thing happened, then that was a pleasant bonus—but it was not his main focus.

"I do hope it will loosen her tongue, pun not intended. Perhaps I should say I hope it loosens her honesty—though I suppose that is not much better." Syandro scratched his now clean–shaven face. Time upon land had done him some good. He looked to be much more refreshed, clearly he took the time to visit a bathhouse and indulged in a soak and shave. He looked more rested and more relaxed than they had seen him in months.

"Still, if I can have a bit of… companionship." He said with a very impolite sneer. "Why not take full advantage of the opportunity." He felt Franchesca's hand on his, and his heart pounded. The simplest touch of her skin was exhilarating.

"Just promise me that you'll be careful." Franchesca told him gently. Syandro nodded as he upended his tankard and shivered. You're the one who should be careful, the thought flashed through Syandro's head only for a moment, and he felt shamed by it. He quickly let out a sigh of disappointment that built within. It wasn't the response he hoped for, but she was worried about him; it was a start he supposed. Ella told him to be patient. It had always been something he struggled with.

"We should be making ready to leave within the next two days." He said as he pushed his empty tankard away and gave no indication that he wished it refilled.

"The cargo is loaded, and the reports from the workers on the ship say they will be done by sundown tomorrow." Franchesca answered. Syandro nodded.

"Then we shall make ready to leave at first light the day after the repairs." He said and rose from his table, taking note of the men sprawled all around. "I will see you back at the ship quartermaster, and first mate." He smiled and bowed. "Franchesca—Simone." He said as he turned and walked out. Something sat oddly in Franchesca's stomach, and judging by the look on Simone's face something felt off to her as well.

"All we can do is wait..." Franchesca said quietly, as Syandro departed the tavern. A chill settled within the marrow of her bones.

"An' watch our backs." Simone nodded. "Come on; I've got sometin ta show ya." Simone smiled as she made her way towards the door.

"What is it?" Franchesca asked she rose slowly, unsure if the alcohol would suddenly take some drastic effect. She hadn't had much, but this drink was nothing to be trifled with.

"Don' worry—it'll be fun, I promise." Simone assured. Somehow that didn't ease Franchesca's nerves, nor did it answer any questions. Still, Simone never hurt her or brought harm to her in any way—at least not on purpose. The business with the shop owner could hardly be anyone's fault. Maybe more her own than Simone's if she looked at things from all angles. Franchesca sighed; but followed, feeling more eager with every step.

* * *

Franchesca winced as she poked her shoulder. The newly tattooed flesh was still as tender as a baked piece of fish. It hurt like hell and felt as if she'd been beaten with a switch about her right arm.

"I told ya it would be fun." Simone smiled as she sat next to Franchesca beside the ship's rail.

"Yes, the most painful night of fun I've ever had." Franchesca replied with a lopsided smile which faded into a wince. It had been Simone's idea the night before they go and receive their first tattoos. Both of them asked for a collection of script and runes of the Deain sea god, to honor their time spent in Dea, as well as to hope for the continued guidance and protection of whatever god watched over the seas. Tattoos were a tradition amongst sailors, and Simone thought it fit to embrace the tradition now that they served aboard a ship. Franchesca had to admit she felt more like a proper, and professional sailor now. Not only did she feel that she'd found her calling—if she were honest, she did enjoy the freshly inked scars upon her body. She didn't enjoy the throbbing ache of bruised and punctured skin, however. Fortunately, taking a few large sips of the ship's rum supply numbed the pain to a dull, yet constant pinprick. Since setting off Syandro chose to remain in his cabin—a change that undoubtedly had more to do with the company of Ella than anything else. There was a crash of thunder above, as a streak of lightning split through the clouds. The patter of rain came gently at first, then grew in volume until it became a full–fledged down pouring. The seas grew choppy, and the ship was pummeled, as waves of increasing size and strength beat against it.

"Ship ho!" The voice from the crows nest bellowed down as the crew member gave a yank on the rope to ring the small bell to alert the whole of the ship. Franchesca and Simone shot to their feet and dashed towards the ship's bow. The door of Syandro's cabin clattered open as the spotter in the crows nest called out again. Through the pouring rain of the storm, Franchesca could make out a hazy ship silhouetted against the horizon. Black striped sails straining in the wind were the only things Franchesca could make out with any sort of detail.

"Spyglass!" Franchesca billowed, with as much authority as she could muster. She held out her hand and felt the cold brass of the looking glass against her palm almost immediately. "I can't see a flag on her. Just the sails." She growled. Perhaps they stumbled upon Konrad's ship after all. "Battle stations!" Franchesca shouted.

"You lot heard tha quartermaster! Get ta yer stations double time!" Simone shouted as she waved her fist above her head and pointed with her other hand. High pitched tin whistles blew, and there was a mad rush to man every gun and retrieve weapons from the armory. Syandro stepped up beside them, and Franchesca passed him the spyglass. He put the device to his eye and studied the ship on the horizon. Franchesca noted that Ella stood behind him. He passed her the spyglass.

"What do you make of it? Is she one of Konrad's?" Syandro asked. He studied her carefully, a test of sorts. He aimed to tell by her reaction if she told him the truth or not.

"Aye—a ship called the Blind Bard. Rumor has it the current captain... piloted it out of an elf merchant captain's hands." Ella replied with a shrug.

"I would say you are trying to place politeness on the word of murder. No matter how you dress the words, it is still the same thing beneath." Franchesca said with a scowl. Ella simply shrugged.

"Pirate, remember." She reminded with a smirk. "With this storm bearin down ya don't have a chance of catchin er. Not if ya want ta keep yer ship in one piece." Ella said only loud enough to be heard over the pattering rain.

"Full sail!" Syandro billowed. It seemed as though he were ignoring Ella's commentary. Maybe he didn't believe her, after all.

"Give chase, and get us within range!" He roared. Ella looked at him as if she had been struck with a very large fish across the face. Trying to catch a ship of Elven make was indeed going to be a challenge. Elvish ships were sleek and quick; they moved through the waters like oiled sharks—but Syandro would take the challenge if it meant getting closer to Konrad. He hurried back to his cabin as his order was repeated all along the ship. Men let loose the sails, and the stiff storm gales tugged the ship forward.

Men lurched and grabbed on to taut lines or railings to keep themselves upright. Those that couldn't grab onto surfaces propped themselves up against area's wide enough. None aboard were keen on the idea of falling overboard in this weather; none were keen on falling overboard period. Once inside his cabin, Syandro strode over to the wall where his sword belt hung upon a peg.

"What are ya doin? Why aren't ya listenin ta me?" Ella asked angrily. "Yer making me look like a fool; what's more is yer makin yerself look like a fool!" She hissed. Syandro turned to her and smiled.

"My apologies darling—but I have to assume that you don't want us to catch any of your former brothers in arms—and would still attempt to dissuade us. It will look far better for you if we gave chase, catching the ship is irrelevant; at least at the moment." He grinned. Ella shook her head and sighed. There was truth to that statement to be sure. She didn't want him to catch any of Konrad's men. She knew what would happen if Syandro made Konrad mad enough. She could kiss the time needed to board a ship from Forn goodbye because the Mad Dog would come stalking the seas—though this could bode well for her. Maybe she should reveal the names of a few more ships to Syandro? Let him get a taste of bloodlust—the more he believed he was accomplishing, the more she could twist. If he sank one or two on her word and locations she told him of; she gained his trust. With his trust, Ella could make mention of a ship in Forn. She could spot a vessel with the papers she needed for Konrad, and goad the prideful youth to attack. It wouldn't take much—especially if she proved to be honest. Perhaps it was time for another change to the plan. As Syandro went to leave, she wrapped her fingers around his arm and pulled him back. Ella looked him dead in the eyes, fixing him with a look of longing and seduction.

"I'll make ya a deal." She whispered with a smile as she took a step forward. The movement caused him to take a half step back and nearly pinned him against the wall. He couldn't say he minded, parts lower certainly didn't mind her nearness as they stirred.

"Go on." Syandro nodded. His heart raced—he didn't know if it was eagerness to hear what Ella had to offer, or if it was the excitement of the upcoming battle, but his heart pounded. How long had it been since he'd had a good fight? Syandro pulled himself back to the moment at hand and took a breath, fixing her with an unblinking stare.

"If ya catch this ship—if ya skink it, that'll be all the proof ta know I'm on the winnin side. Ya show me I'm on the winnin side—I'll give ya complete honesty. I'll give ya the waters yer most likely ta find Konrad's ships in. I'll give ya them first because I know ya won't believe me if I tell ya its Konrad. Let me earn yer trust." Syandro smirked and couldn't help but laugh.

"You're already on the winning side, but the offer sounds fair." Syandro nodded quickly licking his lips. He turned to bound to his station, to ready himself when Ella reached out to him once more. Her hand closing around his arm with an iron grip.

"And one more condition." Ella interrupted. "I want ta fight." Syandro sighed and after a moment relented. He was eager. It had been too long since he tested his skills. It would be a nice chance to show off. Not only could he finally show off for Franchesca. This would also be a perfect opportunity to demonstrate his superior skill to Ella—and shame Simone. Talk about killing a flock of birds with a single stone he mused. He'd show Franchesca and Simone they'd gotten lucky when they'd saved him.

"You stay close to me, understood?" He said as he stared at her, warning her without needing to say more than he already had. His look was enough to convey his point, or so he thought. Ella thought it the expression of a youth well and truly out of his depth, struggling to swim. She grinned and bowed her head politely in deference.

"Oh, I'll stick close alright." She grinned as she grabbed hold of Syandro's hair tugged his head forward and kissed him deeply. I'll stay close enough to slip a knife between your ribs, she thought with a smile.

Chapter 14

The Quest had given chase to the ship, Ella named as the Blind Bard, for days through the waters of the Jade Straight. The men broke away from their battle stations within the first hour—as there were no signs of the chase coming to an end. And indeed it hadn't; just as Ella admitted, the slender hulled elvin ship was fast; far faster than the bulky Quest. The storm with its swirling winds only helped to hinder Syandro's ship. It seemed the longer the chase lasted, the tenser the crew became. All of them waited anxiously to see one of Konrad's ships flounder. Each was eager to engage in some activity other than minding their stations and the tense drudgery that the chase seemed to instill. Finally, after six days and nights of dogged pursuit, the Quest finally managed to get within range of their prey. The cannons thundered, and at once there seemed to be a calmness that settled over the ship. It appeared for days that they might lose the vessel they chased. Now that they knew they would do battle—it removed some of the collected tension that held the ship's crew. No hunter wanted to watch its prey escape, not when it was so close. Syandro ordered the ship's sails to be brought up to half mast, to make the sails a smaller target and the wheel turned hard and swift to port. He'd remembered the jargon for left and right aboard a ship easy enough. Port had four letter's just like left, starboard had more than four, just as right possessed more letters than left. The Quest cut left and its heavier, thicker hull battered into the sleek Elven ship. There was a raucous cheer as the ships collided. It might have been foolish to ram another ship out here on the open seas, so far from a safe place to drop anchor. The extent of the damage would not be known until after the ensuing battle.

Franchesca found herself muttering a silent and hasty prayer to the Heavenly Matron, that the ramming maneuver wouldn't cause significant damage to the ship's integrity. She followed with a prayer to the Shield Maiden for courage in the events which were to come. Cannons thundered once more, peppering the Blind Bard. Screams could be heard from the crew of the enemy vessel as flying splinters tore through eye sockets or other tender areas of flesh. The company of Pistoleros opened fire from their positions aboard the Quest. The elite sharpshooters of Castella reaped a terrible toll. It was easy to spot where their shots struck, for the scene resembled nothing less than fireworks of gore, and death exploding. Franchesca watched as the backs and sides of heads burst apart in a spray of crimson and brain.

Men fell dead to the deck in a pool of blood, as another volley ripped through their numbers. Suddenly the skies above became darker than they had a right to be. The hairs on Franchesca's arms raised as the winds began to swirl into an icy gale. A bolt of lightning struck the water, scant feet from the ship's body. What by all the Gods was that? She glanced down at the water where the lightning bolt struck and saw that it steamed and boiled, with even a few dead fish now floating upon the seas choppy surface.

"Reel em in! Real em in you dogs!" Franchesca recognized Ella's voice as she shouted the customary abusive praise of pirates, only to continue to give orders over the din of battle. Syandro stood next to her and waved his Castellian–rapier above his head. The blade was similar to a typical rapier, possessing a good amount of flexibility, and made mostly for thrusting; but it was slightly thicker than a standard rapier. It also possessed a spear–like point which was wider and bore a slight curve on one side. The thickness allowed it slice through bone as well as thrust through tender flesh.

"Pull them to us! Let's test their metal!" He roared the cannons barked once more, and the Quest rocked as the iron shot struck it. Franchesca knew that all the prayers in the world wouldn't keep the ship from being damaged from being damaged by cannon shot. Panic began to mount. Gods—what if they sank out here? As the ship rocked violently, a few crewmen close to the sides fell over. There was a loud splash followed by the booming of thunder. A bolt of lightning arced down and there was a momentary shriek followed by the smell of burnt overly sweet smelling meat. Franchesca peered over the side of the ship and saw two black and charred bodies floating lifelessly. She felt Simone nudge her. Simone smiled at her and took a deep breath.

"Ready?" Simone asked raising her eyebrows and grinning mischievously. In truth, she was terrified. Less so for herself—always less so for herself. No, she was scared for Franchesca. Maybe if she were honest, she was a little afraid for herself. Not all of the butterflies fluttering around in her guts could be for Franchesca. Could they? Ok gods damn it, she was more than a little afraid. It felt like a betrayal to admit it to herself. But if one couldn't be honest with themselves what hope did they have to be honest elsewhere?

"As I'll ever be." Franchesca replied. With a loud wordless shout, the two of them rushed forward and leaped over the side of the rails. They rolled onto the deck of the ship and sprung to their feet. Franchesca plunged her blade into a stranger's gut. She'd just killed, again. The feelings of nausea that washed over her before didn't do so now. She wondered what that meant; for only the briefest of moments before she parried a strike aimed at her neck and severed an arm at the elbow. One by one the crew from the Quest leaped overboard to land upon the deck of the Blind Bard, and the sounds of death and pain were conducted into a terrible symphony. Syandro fought a few paces away—his steel a blur of polished silver steel light as he parried, dodged, sliced and impaled. Soon the silver was covered and dulled by thick crimson blood. Pistols barked like rabid hounds and men fell clutching legs, arms; shoulders and stomachs. Franchesca felt her hair stand on end once more. She looked over her shoulder and noticed a woman scantily clad in strips of well–worn leather and ragged scraps of tunics and leggings. Her head sported thick dreadlocks; some of which had rings and other trinkets embedded in them. She leveled a long pole topped with the blade of a pirate cutlass. Energy swirled around the steel as she cackled wildly.

"A sea witch..." Franchesca gasped. She felt a hand tug her down violently as a beam of lightning cracked and arced past her. Franchesca looked over and smirked at Simone. She had pulled her out of the way.

"I'll kill ya both, and I'll give yer corpses ta Stromboze ta chew on!"
Franchesca and Simone tugged pistols free from the bandoleers strapped across
their chests. In unison, they both fired off their shots and watched in horror as
a wave of seawater arced up from the waters below and swallowed up the lead
shots.

"Yer gonna have ta do better than that." The sea witch shouted as she
stepped forward slowly. With a casual wave of her hand, a powerful stream of
water caught one of the Pistoleros square in the chest, knocking him
overboard.

"What do we do?" Franchesca asked as she rose to her feet. Glancing about
the deck observing the scene unfolding around them.

"Guess we charge an' hope fer tha best. Maybe if we get in close, we'll 'ave
better luck?" Simone nodded. The two of them charged forward and began
aiming cuts and slashes where ever they saw an opening. The sea witches
martial prowess was astonishing. She parried and deflected every blow aimed at
her. It was reflex and speed. She knocked aside Franchesca's blade and tripped
her with the haft of her staff, before parrying Simone's strike and kicking her in
the stomach. The sea witch brought her blade to Simone's throat and held it
there a moment. She savored the fear in her eyes. As she drew the blade back to
plunge it through Simone's soft neck, she gasped in pain. Their foe became
distracted—which Franchesca used to her full advantage. She scrambled to her
feet once more, her legs throbbing from where the sea witch used her staff to
knock them from under her. Franchesca lunged forward desperately, and she
took a measure of relief that her blade found little more resistance than weak
flesh, as it plunged through the woman's chest. The sea witch gasped as
Franchesca twisted the blade before ripping it free. As she went to turn around,
Simone rose and hacked the sea witch's head from her shoulders. A precaution
Franchesca thought for the best. One couldn't be too careful with magic users,
she supposed. They smiled at one another and nodded. The two of them
watched as Syandro continued his fight. His blade, dealing death with every
movement he forced it through. Its point slipped past hasty parries and sloppy

guards. These men were used to brawling and hacking; slashing engagements, where the one who hit hardest and quickest walked away still breathing; and mostly unwounded. Syandro however, was a skilled swordsman, and showing his skill with brutal efficiency. As he went for the killing stroke on his opponent, a blade crashed against his. A slender man with dreadlocks and a long beard smiled at him. All around him men backed away out of intimidation, or out of respect, Franchesca could not tell. Syandro only grinned.

"You must be the fool who attacked my ship." His voice that of a log being devoured by flames; crackly, rough, and acrid.

"Captain of this stolen vessel I presume, and the whipped hound of Konrad Kursz." Syandro sneered leveling his blade and shifting his weight into a ready fighting stance. The very picture of a serpent ready to strike.

"I'm no one's whipped dog boy, and you'll be findin that out the hard way." The captain drew a second saber and began a barrage of furious swings in Syandro's direction. As the blows rained the other battles being fought seemed to halt. It appeared as if everyone was holding their breath in anticipation, waiting to see the outcome. Ella watched carefully. She paced behind a crowd of the Blind Bard's crew; stalking, like a wolf. The captain locked his blades with Syandro and sneered.

"Pity ya have to die this way boy." His sneer melted away when he saw Ella pacing. His moment of hesitation ended his life. Syandro planted a kick in the captain's stomach and batted his blades away. Syandro rammed his blade into the captain's stomach and gave a hard tug upwards. He twisted the blade as he ripped it out and looked around. Ella pushed her way through the crowd and stood by Syandro.

"You...treacherous little snake. Konrad will gut you like a fish when he finds you." His voice was wet and raspy as blood filled his mouth. Ella knelt next to the dying man and grinned.

"Konrad's sands have all but run. I'm makin sure I live." Ella grinned as she leaned in closer and pulled out a knife. "It will save me the trouble of killing

Konrad myself." She whispered as she slipped the blade into his throat and tugged it free. There was an arc of crimson that spurted against her face as he began to choke, something that didn't seem to bother Ella in the least. She wiped the blade on his ragged clothes and turned to Syandro with a smile. "Orders, captain?" Ella asked calmly as she stared at Syandro, appearing to all those around her like a gore–splattered ghoul.

"You all have a choice! You can lay down your weapons, and crew upon my ship. Or you can die with the likes of your captain there." Syanrdo looked around and sneered.

"Which do you choose?" There was a unanimous decision as the sound of weapons clattered to the deck and men knelt.

"Your days of serving Konrad are done! From here out—you serve me and my interest, is that understood?" Syandro asked with a grin. Grim, slow and silent nods were the only thing that served as the sign of communication any of the former crew of the Blind Bard gave in response. The dead were left where they lay, and the new crew members were brought over to the Quest. Only a handful remained—perhaps fifty at first glance, Franchesca knew she would have to get a more detailed and accurate number later. The Quest's sails were unfurled once more, and they were on their own, leaving the damaged ship adrift on the stormy sea. After a few days of tension, the crew seemed to ebb. The old crew came to adjust well to their newest additions. Whatever valuable goods were held aboard the Blind Bard, had been plundered and brought aboard the Quest—including any food which was needed to feed the newly collected mouths; black powder to replenish and indeed add to their stores, and more than a few strong boxes laden with wealth, as a way of financing their newest recruits. The ship limped through the waters of the Jade Straight while carpenters did their best to make necessary repairs. Damaged was patched with tar, pitch and spare wood, sails were stitched and mended with extra canvas taken from the cargo hold of the Blind Bard. The battle with the pirate vessel saw a cloud of shrapnel slice through the sails, and within the swirling windstorm, the rips only became larger. The Quest was blown around like a leaf on the wind before falling into a river only to be carried by the current. Fortunately, due to the surprise of Syandro's attack, they remained relatively unscathed.

Franchesca gathered with Syandro and Ella after the encounter. The turn of events saw Ella naming captains that worked for Konrad—as well as their locations. Franchesca's instincts told her she should not trust a single shred of information put forth by Ella. She made Syandro aware of her thoughts as well. Syandro however, shrugged off her concerns. He pointed out, even if Ella were to give false information they would still be sailing around aimlessly searching for Konrad—or any other members of his fleet. It was a fact Franchesca had to admit was far too accurate for her liking. Ella's word really didn't mean anything—nor did it not; she only knew possibilities, likely hiding places. Pirates weren't likely to hang around one area for long, waiting to get blown out of the water. Her word was little more than a possible edge a hint in a goose chase; Syandro had told her on the seas nothing was a certainty. Franchesca supposed that was doubly true when one was hunting pirates. Bands of men who made their living, lying, cheating; and murdering where ever fate saw fit, to curse those unfortunate enough to cross their paths, and retreating long before anyone knew who or what they were. There, however, was something to be admired amongst them; they did not simply resign themselves to fate willingly. They tried to change the course of their lives, and their fortunes. Franchesca had seen it first hand. In Forn, Simone was poor, and in turn, was viewed with mistrust and disdain by those who might have just had one or two drops more of luck than she did. Out here on the seas, she was an equal—she had a position of power. She was respected; her previous circumstances didn't matter and all of this because she and Franchesca dared to change the course of their lives. Franchesca looked up at the scarred sail as it rustled in the wind. Off in the distance, she watched as a fin broke the surface of the shimmering water as the sun began it's decent. The sky was yellows, rich reds; and fiery oranges which stood out in a stark and beautiful contrast against the sapphire seas. Syandro told her that they should sail towards The Silk

Lands, a land more commonly referred to by its trade goods than by its actual name of Chuhuay. Of course, Franchesca knew that Ella had something to do with that decision. She told them one of Konrad's men favored hunting ships in those waters. Franchesca glanced back and noticed Ella standing upon the quarterdeck next to Syandro. One eye gazing through a spyglass; as she turned slowly scanning the distance. Franchesca watched as Ella said something; which was met with a small nod from Syandro. She wished she was close enough to hear. Franchesca had a sinking feeling about all of this, but Syandro didn't seem to believe her. Syandro waved to her and motioned to his cabin. Franchesca nodded slowly and made towards the door. She wondered why she should bother sitting and speaking with him. There was no chance he would listen to her. He never did any more, and it galled her—though Franchesca couldn't say why it did so much. Perhaps it was because she knew this would all end in tragedy.

"We should be sighting our prey by tomorrow." Syandro told Franchesca as she sat across from him in his quarters.

"Is that what Ella told you?" She asked as she took a drink from the glass of wine he had poured for her. Syandro nodded as he reclined in his seat.

"I can't help but notice you have given her quite a few freedoms. Is she no longer your prisoner with whom you consult?" Franchesca asked placing the cup down and pushing it away from her.

"Oh no—she is still very much a prisoner with whom I consult..." Syandro began, quickly seeing by the expression upon her face she wasn't convinced.

"A prisoner with a weapon, and free reign of their prison?" Franchesca asked steepling her fingers. Syandro simply smiled. He didn't let his joy become unmasked. She was getting upset—she was noticing him. She was beginning to hate Ella for having his attention, and affections. Ella was right after all. Sometimes, one just needed to lose something they thought they didn't want, to show them how much they truly did want it. A little while longer and she would be his, she would be begging for him.

"I can fend for myself—as can you, and Simone… and anyone else aboard this ship." He assured with a nod as he picked up his glass and took a sip. "Whatever measures I can take to loosen her tongue and make sure it stays loose, seem a small price to pay. At least for the reward, such actions promise to yield." Syandro added with a confident smirk.

"Do you really think I don't know she is trying to toy with me?"

"You both seem as if you are quite comfortable with one another." Franchesca observed quietly. "I wonder if perhaps you are enjoying being the plaything." She added as she took a sip and placed the glass on the desk and looked up at him with an arched eyebrow, and a disapproving glare.

"Keep your friends close and your enemies closer. How much closer could one be than a lover?" Syandro replied with a calm smile raising his glass. It must be a Castellian saying, Franchesca thought to herself—or perhaps a bit of personal philosophy. She was beginning to think Syandro insane.

"I believe she wants Konrad dead—though for what ends I can not say for certain. Though, I lean towards the thought that she aims to kill me after. I'll help her kill Konrad, for the enemy of my enemy is my friend; and I can see fit to use her expertise. However—once my blade pierces his heart, I won't believe a word from her lips. Until then she has some uses." Syandro smiled. Gods—he sounded so cold, so calculating. If what he told her was true, then he could use people and not care. True Ella had tried to kill him, and she deserved to be punished for that—but Syandro almost made Franchesca believe Ella might walk free after this was over. What did that woman think? Had he always been so cold? This was a side of him Franchesca hadn't seen before—and never once before this moment did she ever think twice about calling him a friend. Now she wasn't sure if she wished him to be close to her. Was he always so manipulative and conniving? Who else was he using to further his own ends? What else would he do to further his own ends? Or perhaps the sea in its current course and all of its trials and events had deranged his mind. Franchesca couldn't say, all she could say was she was happy Simone had the foresight to assemble crewmen who were loyal to them and would watch their backs. At this moment she didn't trust Syandro to watch her back—not anymore.

"I understand you must think me terrible." Syandro told her quietly; as if he were somehow reading her thoughts.

"I am not a terrible person—and this is outside of my nature. However, I will do whatever I have to do to survive and see Konrad brought down—that is my nature. That is at the very heart of my purpose." Syandro told her gently.

"I don't know what lurks in Ella's heart. Perhaps once Konrad and his ship sink below the surface, she will change. The only way to truly find out is to kill him." Syandro nodded. Franchesca shrugged. She never had more distrust for him than she did in this moment. Her skin crawled and rebelled at his nearness. Her spine wanted to ooze from her body, as his honeyed words seemed to snake their way through her brain and down her back, like a physical thing.

"Do as you see fit—you are the captain after all." Franchesca told him. Her throat felt dry, and her tongue felt like lead, but she forced the words out into the open.

"Lead, and we will follow." She nodded as she stood from her seat. She wanted to be out of the room, away from Syanro. She needed to feel the air upon her skin; perhaps it would clean away the feeling of utter wrongness that clung to her like an old cloak.

"I just ask you to be careful—watch your back... more importantly" she said quietly "watch your crew members back." Franchesca left the room, closing the door gently behind her. Syandro did indeed watch at least one back as it exited his cabin and smirked. Once Franchesca was free of the cabin she shuddered, the thought of topside and fresh air forgotten, she made her way to the cabin she shared and the warm embrace of her blankets and of Simone. Such a thing would do more to clean the feeling brought on by Syandro's words than fresh air ever could.

* * *

Ella watched Franchesca exit Syandro's cabin. She watched as Franchesca retreated below deck. No doubt to enter her own room. Ella waited before making her way to Syandro's quarters.

"Another meeting without me?" She asked in the same manipulative sweet tone she had done days ago. Like she gave a damn—well, perhaps that wasn't true. She did like to keep an eye on Syandro—liked to make sure his mind remained firmly within her grasp.

"Ya wouldn't be trying ta get rid of me would you?" She smiled as she sat across from Syandro. She allowed herself to say you instead of ya and batted her eyelashes as she sat in the chair in a way which accentuated her—if she were to say so herself—ample breasts.

"Of course not, I only informed her that we would be sighting our prey within a day. I want my crew ready for the battle ahead." Syandro told her. Ella stood up and sauntered over seductively, sitting down on the desk smiling at him. She reached out and tugged his shirt from his chest and grinned.

"Guess its best then if we take what we can for today." Ella whispered as she leaned in and kissed him. "After all—we don't know what tomorrow brings."

"Hard to argue with logic such as that," Syandro whispered. He grabbed her cheeks with his thumb and forefinger and stared into her eyes.

"I want you to know this of me, Ella." He whispered with an arrogant sly smile.

"If you think to kill me, either through your friends or by your own hand... you will find yourself wanting for limbs." He smiled as he leaned in and kissed her. He truly was a fool, Ella thought to herself as she slipped her tongue past his lips and into his mouth.

Chapter 15

Reikert cleared his throat. It echoed in the empty throne chamber. He wasn't nervous, as most people in his position should be. Or wasn't as nervous as he should be. Few people could deliver bad news to the man he was about to deliver it to and not piss themselves. Reikert served with him for years and could read him well enough to know when to deliver news—and when to wait, besides someone had to deliver the news no one wanted to hear. It might as well be him.

"We're receiving word that more ships of your fleet have been sunk sir."

Cold fury washed over his features, as the corner of his mouth lifted into a snarl.

"Name them." Konrad growled as he sat atop the Throne of Tides, gripping the armrests furiously.

"Our contacts say that the Black Star has been sunk. Word is that The Fang—the Albatross, Crimson Knife; and the Griffon have all been sunk as well." Konrad hissed at the news. They weren't his best ships, but they were his ships; damn it—his property, under his command. Someone dared to strike out against him?

"Reikert—ready the Mange. Someone seeks to hunt me, and I would not want to disappoint them by hiding." Konrad growled. Reikert merely nodded as he turned and strode out of the throne chamber. It was never wise to attempt to talk Konrad out of a course of action, especially when his temper had risen. Konrad reclined on his throne, the Throne of Tides and growled. His heart pounded angrily within his chest, and long strands of drool seeped from the sides of his mouth. When he found those who were sinking ships in his fleet, he would flay them and wear their skins as cloaks. He would turn their guts to garters and distribute them to the whorehouses across Tornusia. The women would flaunt them as freely as their tits—and all would hear the stories of what happened to all those who entertained a thought about destroying what belonged to him. He was Konrad, the Mad Dog Kursz—he owned Tornusia everything and everyone on it. His name and reputation spread fear on every sea, and every coast dreaded the day he would dock at their ports and come ashore to take his pleasure. He was the reason wives of merchants made passionate love to their husbands the night before they set sail, for fear of not seeing their loved ones again—at least alive. He was the reason whores prayed for the safety of the sailors aboard those ships, the men they loved—though they dare not speak it—and the men who loved them back fearing to let them know. He pillaged, and he raided, he took what he wanted, and he didn't care whose blood he spilled to get whatever he desired. His will was iron and his determination unbreakable, the salted sea water that coursed through his veins had seen him climb his way to the Throne of Tides. He had a grand plan, and he would not see his war undone before it had a chance to start. It was to see the downfall of empires; he wanted anarchy, the likes of which hadn't been seen before. He vowed an age of piracy—an age where the strong lived because they fought to survive. A golden age where anyone could have anything they wanted—so long as they could spill blood, fight and kill while staying alive long enough to hold onto their prize. Konrad vowed that dream to be so the day he watched his father hang at the order of some paltry king. He would see the rule of the wealthy destroyed. The only way someone deserved true power is if they took it for themselves. How many mutinies did he root out like a pig hunting truffles? He deserved this. I will not be denied; he thought to himself as he slammed a fist on the well-worn arm of the throne. He stood up quickly and strode from the chamber and began his walk to the docks.

"I'll see every last one of them dead." Konrad hissed.

* * *

"We should begin to head towards Forn." Ella told Syandro as she drummed at the pommel of the blade that hung at her shapely waist. She'd proven her trust, and her loyalty. Or so Syandro thought—so she wanted him to believe. If she said so herself, a damn fine bit of acting, even if she did only say so herself. If only a career in stage performance paid more, she mused silently. Ella led them to one ship after another. She fought like a madman and killed many of her former comrades. Or so she had Syandro believe. The truth lay somewhere in–between. She'd been part of Konrad's force just as they had, that was the only truth she baited upon the hook when she told Syandro that she killed many of her former companions. The fact was she knew perhaps one or two men, and they were the captains she'd sailed with before they found a spot in the Mad Dog's fleet. Her plan worked better than she hoped. She'd been patient, and now Ella planed to reap the rewards. Slowly and carefully she steered them back towards the waters of Forn. After sailing much of the free world, and sinking five more ships—Syandro and his two women commanders hardly noticed where her plan seemed to be leading them. They still paid no attention. Ella was subtle when she needed to be—a woman could get her way by being direct, but where was the fun in that? Where was the accomplishment? Ella stood upon the threshold of getting command of her own ship. All she needed was to find an appropriate ship from Forn. Once that was done, a quick knife across Syandro's throat and she would be in command. She planned to deliver the letter to Konrad personally. He would have to grant her a position within his fleet then. After she became a commander in the fleet, she would arrange an unfortunate accident to befall Konrad. They would all pay for underestimating her. Konrad's plan was simple, steal the letters of open flag from ships belonging to every nation and use them to begin a war amongst the powerful countries. He would give those letters to his captains and tell them to go out and plunder their weasely black brains out. When he had the nations believing other nations were attacking friend and foe alike and that anyone could be next, he would lead the charge with his own hand–selected pirates. When the nations of the world heard pirates were on the prowl, they would pay them off, because they couldn't afford to split their attention. Konrad also believed with his men diminishing shipping and naval power of the world; they would have no choice but to contract ships from Tornusia. The nations would be stopping piracy by funding piracy, in more ways than one. Divide the world, attack it while and where it was weak and assume control. Ella believed there was more to the plan, but as she told Syandro; Konrad was not particularly forthright with information.

"Why would we do that?" Franchesca asked as she peered up at Ella. Suspicion still shown in her eyes, Ella thought perhaps there always would be. There would be no convincing some people. Ella grinned—that one and the red–haired tart were the smart ones. Of course, it didn't help their captain tended to do more thinking with his cock than his head. So the girls would be suspicious; until Ella proved to them that their suspicions were deeply rooted in truth. Then they would just be vindicated. Of course, after the two were vindicated, she'd have their pretty head chopped from their shoulders—pity that. Ella did have to admit she admired Franchesca and Simone. If only they'd chosen the correct side, the things they would have accomplished would have been a sight to behold. Even Konrad would try to get rid of them as soon as he found the most savage way. True, she realized that if Franchesca and Simone joined her, the danger to herself would have been increased tenfold, but everything had a consequence.

"Konrad has been searching for the last thing he needs to begin his war." Ella began. "That thing is found in Forn."

"What is it?" Franchesca asked quizzically as her eyebrows climbed, like rangers scaling a cliff.

"Let's worry about reaching it before we get in ta specifics." Ella nodded as she glanced up from the map and the charts she was studying. "I haven't led ya false yet; I think I've earned a bit of trust. I just need ya ta get us there as quickly as possible. I heard the last captain I put my blade through mention something about waiting for Konrad in Forn." Ella smiled, as she planned to sweeten the trap and make it irresistible. "He said Konrad was sailing for those waters shortly. If we hurry—we can be there waiting for him." Ella glanced between Syandro and Franchesca.

"Make our course. Let's head to Forn." Syandro said quietly. Franchesca bit back a curse. She was cautious about sailing to Forn. What if her parents were still searching for her? What if she was recognized? A sound of alarm broke her away from her thoughts.

"There's Darkwater right ahead!"

Ella was the first to burst from the room and headed up to the ship's quarterdeck. Syandro and Franchesca following right hind her, though neither of them were entirely sure what was happening. Neither of them had ever heard of Darkwater before. A great writhing coiling black mass sat atop the water. A long inky tentacle shot out and plucked a low flying seabird from the sky. There was a muffled squawk, and a splash as the mass pulled its prey down and drowned the creature.

"By the Heavenly Lady!" Franchesca gasped, she was still not entirely sure what she was looking at. Whatever the thing happened to be, there seemed to be some sort of awareness, or intelligence, because it began to ungulate to draw itself closer towards the ship.

"If that gets hold of the ship we're all dead." Ella hissed as she darted back and forth between port and starboard trying to take in the situation. This was no time to make a mistake. A mistake here kill them all—and kill them all in the most terrible of ways.

"What are you talking about?" Syandro asked with a chuckle. "It's only as big as the ship's wheel, something like that can't cause enough damage to sink the ship."

"Ya don't understand—Darkwater is like an iceberg. It might appear small on the surface but below..." The ship rocked suddenly and the sound of cracking, splintering timbers interrupted the conversation; seeming to prove Ella's point. "Fuck me!"

Ella dashed towards the wheel of the Quest and turned hard to starboard, trying to pull away from the thick mass that sat atop the water. To Franchesca's eyes, it resembled tar or some sort of sewage sludge. There were startled shouts as sailors stumbled, or fell and thumped against the deck.

"What is this?" Syandro shouted as he braced himself. Ella hissed in frustration, though she turned the wheel as hard and as fast as her arms were able to work, the ship seemed stuck. Damn this sea cow—it couldn't turn worth a shit, couldn't even move worth a damn, thought Syandro bitterly.

"No one really knows." Ella growled as she released the wheel for a moment. The ship lurched suddenly, the substance forcing it to an unnatural, violent stop, an eerie calm descended over everyone who still stood upon the deck. Men lay utterly still, and most did not bother to pick themselves up from where they had fallen. Suddenly, with the roar of sea water, the ships back half was sucked down violently. The angle of the vessel steepened and only seemed to grow steeper still. As if the mass grabbed the hull and now sought to suck the ship's entire bow below the water. For a moment the front most part of the ship hung in the air useless, but Ella did not release the wheel. Instead, she tightened her grip on the pegs of the wheel, her knuckles white with fear and effort. She had come too close. If the ship stayed in this position for too long, the forward weight would cause it to splinter, and break in half. It couldn't end now—not like this, she said as she looked at the skyward pointing aft. She turned her head and looked at Syandro.

"Tell the men ta grab any oil we have aboard, a keg of rum… anything flammable and throw it overboard, before tossin somethin that's on fire. It's the only way we're gonna get free." Ella hissed as she pounded the wheel. The ship seemed to be sucked lower for a moment, seemingly before the Darkwater lost its grip. The ship crashed down, and a great wave lapped against it. Men screamed as they were knocked overboard by the sudden motion and the violent spray of water that resulted. Franchesca was thrown to the deck violently, as was Syandro.

"Franchesca are you alright?" Franchesca cast her gaze upward and saw Simone clinging to the rigging for dear life; still, she managed a roguish and mischievous smile, before her foot found purchase and she was able to adequately secure herself.

"A little bruised, nothing a drink or two won't fix!" Franchesca shouted back making sure to keep her wits about her.

"Grab all the oil you can! Rum, gunpowder anything that can be set fire to; grab it and make sure you get it into the Darkwater, or as close as you can!" Syandro shouted as he picked himself up. He grabbed a lantern and hurled it towards the black tar–like mass. A slender, slick tendril that had been rising withered away as the lit lantern sailed into the tarry mass.

"You heard him, lads!" Franchesca shouted. "If you want to live, get the supplies double time!"

"Move the lot of ya!" Simone shouted down as she began her descent. The deck became unfettered bedlam, as men rushed to and fro, seeking out anything that could stoke a fire. One of the crewmen struggled up the steps with a full keg of the special alcohol from Dea; a site to which Franchesca couldn't help but chuckle at. It was heaved over the side of the ship. The coiling mass grabbed it and held on to the barrel while the waves of the ocean rippled, bobbing the mass and its newly collected prize up and down. The strange substance crushed the barrel as easily as a dried leaf. The contents of the barrel floated atop the viscous morass, still more of the liquid sprayed into the sea surrounding the Blackwater. Franchesca rushed down the stairs as best she found herself able, trying to cope with the bobbing and swaying of the ship. She grabbed two lanterns and their small casks of lamp oil and flung them at the dark mass. They stuck in the black tarry substance, and one by one more men threw flammable materials overboard.

"Get a lantern or a candle that's already been lit!" Ella called out from the quarterdeck as she turned the wheel with as much speed and urgency as she could muster. Franchesca peered around and grimaced. She could only see one lantern that was lit, hanging over the doorway to the lower holds. As she ran towards it, the ship lurched once more, and she found herself falling backwards as the planks of the ship were brought up at a sudden angle. Franchesca hardly had time for a quick prayer to her goddess, to spare her life and keep her safe, as the ship continued to get sucked down. She watched in terror as a crewman slid down the deck twisting and turning until his head hit the main mast and split open like an overripe tomato. With some scattered sense of self–preservation, Franchesca flung out an arm. Her fingers only just recognized the course sensation of rope before she closed her hand around it and gripped for all her life. Franchesca dangled over the side of the ship, her heart pounding so feverishly she could feel it in her ears.

"Franchesca!" Simone shouted as she gaped at the perilous situation. Syandro looked on as well, his pulse racing. Was he about to lose Franchesca? Not if he could help it, he swore to himself. The ship righted itself ever so slightly, and Syandro only had the briefest of moments to assemble a plan. With a half–formed idea, he released his grip and fell towards Franchesca. He caught one of the ropes and wrapped it around his forearm before striding towards her. He reached out his hand—sweat pouring down his brow, his arm feeling like it was going to be pulled from its socket.

"Grab my hand!" He shouted. Simone had tied a rope around her waist and slid towards the two of them. She noticed out of the corner of her eye that a coil of the Darkwater was drawing closer to Franchesca's foot.

"Franchesca grab on! It's gettin ready ta drag ya down!" She screamed, panic edging her voice. Franchesca glanced down and wished she hadn't. A long and narrow, inky black tentacle lifted itself from the mass. The ship rocked again, the sudden violent motion beating Franchesca against the ship's hull trying to dislodge her. It knocked Syandro and Simone's legs out from beneath them, as well as the air from their lungs as they slammed into the deck.

"Grab on!" Simone roared as she took in a small breath and shot her hand out eagerly. It felt like fire, but she did it because she needed to. Tears born from pain trickled down her face as she fought for breath. Franchesca reached out—but to no avail. She was a fingers length away from being able to secure a hold on Simone's hand. Franchesca peered up at Simone helplessly. She was going to die. It was hopeless. She could just let go. How bad could death be? It might hurt for a moment—but after that, it was over. It was peaceful. She could just drop. Franchesca glanced to Simone once more.

"Don't even think it!" Simone scolded as she tried to lurch forward just enough to grab hold of Franchesca. Syandro loosened one coil on his forearm and slid down. He reached out and grabbed hold of Franchesca's wrist. She looked up at him with panic–stricken eyes. Where had those thoughts come from? They'd come over her so suddenly? It had to be the terror, for as soon as his hand grabbed her wrist the feelings were gone. He smiled at her.

"I've got you." He assured. Syandro pulled Franchesca up just enough that Simone could assist him. The mass released the ship once again in its efforts to get a better grip. Franchesca felt her legs dangling over the side and the force on her stomach as she hung there. Syandro and Simone pulled her back aboard, as she pulled her foot back over the side of the ship, they noticed the inky tentacle retreat back down into the mass of goo. The three panted and laughed, the thrill of their near–death clouding their minds. Syandro glanced back towards the wheel and saw that Cornando gripped it and had it as far left as it could go. Where was Ella? As if answering his question, her voice boomed through the nervous chaos.

"Take cover!" No sooner had the words been shouted, than there was an almost deafening *whomph*—followed by a massive explosion. Franchesca, Syandro; and Simone felt the heat from the blast and the hungry flames as they curled themselves up where they lay. The whole front and left side of the ship were illuminated and caught in a raging firestorm. There was a heavy thud next to them, and Franchesca risked peeking. She watched as Ella threw herself to the deck and curled up into a fetal ball.

The ship rocked as another explosion split the air. At that moment, Franchesca noticed something. They were moving. Were they free? Cornando—who kept the wheel pegged hard to starboard, now eased back as the wind caught them and carried them from the clutches of the Darkwater. There might have been a cheer from the crewmen if the victory truly had a chance to sink in. Franchesca panted heavily, feeling her heart in her throat and her stomach. Her eyes opened experimentally, testing for light and signs of disaster.

"We're alive?" She whispered, more of a question than a statement of fact—showed how surprised she was. It all happened so quickly, and she wasn't truly sure what happened. Syandro picked himself up and offered a hand to Franchesca and Simone.

"You... saved us." Franchesca said quietly as she helped Ella to her feet.

"Ya sound shocked." Ella smiled. Her trust was all but earned, by her estimation. A pity it wasn't about saving their lives and more about saving her own. There were things that needed to be done, and dying wasn't on Ella's list—not yet anyway. Still, the act of self-preservation helped her cause; because it had saved everyone else, Franchesca and Simone included. She doubted that she had much to fear from Franchesca and Simone now.

"Let's make our way ta Forn." Ella said fighting to catch her breath and slow her pulse. It appeared to be a battle she was having difficulty gaining the upper hand on.

"Tell the scouts ta mind the waters. Darkwater can spring up from nowhere—and if it's spotted, make course away and give it a wide breadth; as wide as you can." Ella panted the excitement of her recent activities still thundering through her veins.

"Though... I think we're going ta need to resupply." Ella told them as she turned and gazed out over the field of debris floating and burning where the mass of Darkwater had been. Syandro nodded. A ship without beer or rum, especially without black powder for their weapons, was a mouse fleeing from a cat into a den of snakes. If the danger didn't come from outside, it would come from within.

"We'll make course for the closest port and resupply there." Syandro answered addressing Franchesca. "Are you alright?" He asked with a smile as he touched her shoulder. For the first time in weeks, Syandro appeared to be the man she recognized. He appeared to be her old friend. The very same man she'd left Forn, and set out from Castella with. She nodded quickly. He might look the same—but looks had nothing to do with the way one thought or the things one said. True, he might appear the same, but Syandro had changed.

229

He'd shown her that already. She remembered his cold way of speaking, about how he could get rid of Ella after their hunt was over.

"I'm alright, thanks to you two." She smiled. Simone nodded and patted her shoulder. With all that had happened recently, she didn't want to think more than she had to—didn't want to remember. She'd been inches from death, moments away and she knew it. Franchesca's heart pounded like wind buffeting a sail, and she felt shaky, but at least she felt something. At least she was alive; a few others didn't have such luck.

"Let's be sure. We'll go an' 'ave tha ship's churgeon ave a look at ya." Simone led Franchesca off patting her shoulder gently. Simone peered back over at Syandro and Ella and for a moment, wondering if perhaps she had them both figured wrong. Franchesca smiled and shook her head.

"Watch them close darling." She whispered to Simone and gently touched her hand.

* * *

Konrad gazed at the wire thin, old man standing before him. His long salt and pepper beard was scraggly and patchy; while his skin appeared pale and unhealthy. His hands were calloused, and his skin bore patches of discolored flesh and raised scars where he'd been burnt, or come into contact with something hot. Sections of his body even bore the marks of well scratched and well–picked scabs.

"Is my weapon ready?" Konrad asked gruffly as he crossed his ample arms over his broad chest. The thin old man cackled and rubbed his crooked, bony fingers together. He hated coming here. Hated this man's mad genius, for mad he truly was. His presence made Konrad's teeth itch, and his spine ache.

"Down to business, yes, yes as always. Konrad is straight to business." The man squawked. In a voice that made one wish they were incapable of hearing sounds above a whisper. Konrad had always thought that the man resembled a twisted bird. More oft than not, the man walked hunched over with his arms held behind his back giving him the appearance of stubby, featherless wings.

His nose was long and beaklike too—and his lips seemed narrow and pulled forward, and age had pulled them down slightly. Konrad even noted that the wretched old man's tongue was strange, too fat and wide to fit in such a narrow mouth. Konrad felt in himself the strong desire to gut the madman where he stood. Many claimed that Phizemann was insane, that he'd not birthed a sane thought in years. Despite this, Phizemann proved to be a brilliant alchemist, and a more than capable of understanding the ways of the magical arts, even if he couldn't manipulate the winds of magic as he claimed. His mind, though wracked with insanity; was capable of coming up with new and strangely genius weapons. It was for these reasons that Konrad stayed his blade. Phizemann earned his place; Konrad supposed he could tolerate a few eccentricities. Even if being overly generous with the definition of eccentricities—for Phizemann, indeed was mad.

"Do you have it or not? I wish to set sail as soon as possible—and I want the bastards that think they can sink ships belonging to me, to suffer and rot." Konrad growled. Phizemann cackled once again, his strange voice sending a chill down Konrad's spine. Stromboze's blunted mercy; his mad chortle even sounded like the call of some strangled bird.

"Aye, Phizemann has it, yes he does. He has the weapons Konrad wished him to make." The old man used a strange mixture of hopping and walking over to a corner of the workshop. He ripped a tarp off a collection of barrels and laughed madly.

"Found a way of making Darkwater a weapon I have, just as Konrad requested." The crazed old man reached over to a cage and plucked a fat white rat from it. Giggling like a child being tickled by his mother, Phizemann dropped the rat into one of the buckets. A small splash followed by two frantic squeaks, before the splintering of bone; filled the suddenly silent chamber. It was Konrad's turn to smile. Phizemann scratched his graying beard with his leathery hands chuckling wildly.

"Do as I'm bid, yes, yes, Phizemann always does as he's told." Konrad waved the man off as he stepped closer to the barrel. Phizemann's bony hand reached out and grabbed Konrad's wrist.

"No, the dog must be careful yes, yes careful. The Darkwater senses when prey is near; yes, senses when it is close. The water would grab the dog, yes grab him and..." Phizemann stopped, and a look of pure madness and joy sparkled to life over his aged bird–like features. He made a strange squawking noise as he released his grip on Konrad's wrist and brought both of his hands together before bursting them apart with a laugh. Konrad knew it was the madman's way of saying that the Darkwater would kill him in terribly unpleasant and gruesome way.

"What is left that needs to be done, old man?" Konrad asked as he rubbed a hand over his scarred features. Phizemann scratched the top of his balding head with a crooked finger. His look was one of deep thought—and horrible mind melting insanity.

"Yes, yes, Phizemann knows the next step. To ready, yes; to prepare the charges for Konrad's voyage. Lids must be made, yes, crafted of lead. It holds the Darkwater at bay, makes it sleepy; yes—dormant like a fat, well–fed cat." Konrad rubbed his face and nodded. He doubted that lead was all that was involved. There must have been some alchemical secret, or mystical step involved. Lead was too easy for anything that rolled around within the confines of Phizemann's skull.

"How long?" He asked. Phizemann turned and appeared to be counting the barrels, laughing every so often. There were very few people Konrad felt uncomfortable around, Phizemann occupied the very top of that list, though Konrad never let it show. Showing someone a sign of discomfort or fear planted the seed of weakness. It gave them the opportunity to play upon your fears. In the presence of a madman such as Phizemann showing fear or discomfort could do far more harm than even Konrad could comprehend. It was why he always stood confident and commanding. His shoulders square, to show off their full broadness—even if his guts churned within at the sight of the tittering old man before him.

"Two days, yes, two days and they can be loaded on the dog's ship." Phizemann flashed a rotten–toothed smile and laughed. "Eager, yes. Yes, the dog is oh so eager." The mad alchemist chortled rubbing his hands together.

"Yes, he is." Konrad growled. "I shall leave you to your work old man. Make sure they are ready in two days..." Konrad glowered over his shoulder. "Or you'll find yourself in one of those barrels." Phizemann laughed wildly as if he'd heard the funniest joke in the whole of the world. Tears of insanity streamed down his cheeks as he threw himself to the floor and rolled in a fit of laughter. And people think I'm mad, Konrad thought to himself as he exited the room. He found himself eager to sail once more—too long was it since he'd felt the waves churn beneath his ship, or heard the snap of canvas in the breeze. It appeared that the world had forgotten about him. Ships sailed without fear, and that needed to be remedied. When was the last time he heard the cannons aboard his ship fire, smelled the acrid stench of the spent powder? When was The last time he felt a blow crash against his blade and felt the effort needed to hold it before creating an opening and gutting his attacker like a pig? Someone out there was attacking ships under his command; the thought caused his hands to ball into fists. Apparently, he'd not left a lasting impression. There was time enough to change that—and change it he would. None before him found a way to turn Darkwater into a weapon, not one they could wield anyway. History would remember him, even if he had to write the pages in blood himself. He would be remembered as the man who brought down the economies of entire continents. He would be the terror of nations, a nightmare for coastal towns and seaports. He would create a world where everyone was equal—a man made himself and decided his own fate. A world where anyone could have anything they wanted, as long as they could defend it and take care of it; by the sweat of their brows, and the strength of their bones.

Now someone fought against his dream, how unfortunate—for them, Konrad thought to himself. He sailed the grandest ship through the waters of the sea, and soon he wouldn't only be the king of pirates sitting atop the Throne of Tides—he would also be, Konrad the Mad Dog Kursz, who shaped the world into an image pleasing to him and crowned himself king of all he laid eyes on. King, until someone had the power and strength to strike him down. Konrad tightened his grip on the leather wrapped handle of the blade that hung at his side and sighed. How he ached for the spray of the sea and the surging movement of a ship being taken with the winds. He achieved his current position through patience and planning. Waiting two days before he set out seemed unbearable now that those words had a chance to sink in. Perhaps he should do as he always had done when forced to wait. Stow his anger and his frustration away and unleash it in its full furious frenzy when the slaughter began. Konrad paused for a moment and tapped his strong jaw in thought. Perhaps a different approach was needed. He could send his most trusted captains out to comb the seas, or to terrorize them. Maybe the time to start his war had finally come. Konrad smiled as a long strand of drool dripped from the corner of his mouth. He had enough flags from the nations of the world. He possessed enough letters of colorless flag that any of his pirates would appear to be given legitimate work. None would know until it was too late. Relations between once friendly nations would strain and break. Between using his men pretending to have papers given to them by nations and flying the nations flags and acting as false agents, as well as using his men as his own. Using them as old–fashioned pirates, nations would pay a levy to pirates to leave them alone. They would pay the pirates to leave them alone, so they could defend themselves against a threat he created—a threat which would see nations employ his men for warfare. It was complex, but it was genius if he said so himself. He would make the great powers of the world finance piracy; and Tornusia would grow, as they fell before his blade and his cannons. The world would be his. Yes, his time had come at last. Stromboze rarely ever presented opportunity so clearly. Though being patient had its virtues, Stromboze was the god of pirates. His way was not to wait forever; his way was that of a hunter or a wolf. You wait until you spy the weakness, then you attack and bring down your prey. Konrad cracked his knuckles and his neck. It's time to send his heralds into the world indeed. He howled as he walked down the hallway. Reikert rounded a corner upon hearing his captain.

"Orders sir?" Reikert asked with a slight tilt of the head. His hands were clasped behind his back. It was always best to show Konrad you weren't a threat, best to show a sign of submission. Working with the bastard really was like learning your place with a dog. A dog that would rip your guts out, if you didn't learn your place fast enough.

"I want my most trusted captains to sail into the seas—and I want them to take any ship that crosses their paths. Sack it and do not stop until my war starts." Konrad growled.

"They shall be the ones who make all aware of my war. In two days I shall sail once more, and I will smell terror upon the waters as I do."

"I will do as you say, sir." Reikert nodded, now keeping his shoulders square and straight. When the Mad Dog gave you an order, you showed you could handle the responsibility, and he was a careful observer.

"And one more thing..." Konrad said with a smile. "Fetch the sea hag; I've a task for her as well." Konrad relished the look upon Reikert's face. Reikert, much like all upon Tornusia, feared the sea hag. She could be as cruel and as unpredictable as the seas themselves. Many believed she lived upon the lands of Tornusia, long before any nation's ship, or pirate dropped anchor. She claimed no allegiance to Stromboze nor any god that could be reckoned by those claiming the island as their home. If ever asked, she would merely cackle and repeat the same thing; my gods are the tides. Many avoided her hut, fearing to set foot near it. It was rumored that many a sailor met a grizzly death at her hands. For as many that feared her, there were others that merely thought her mad like Phizemann—though even they knew better than to think of either of them as harmless. Madmen and women rarely proved to be harmless.

"As... you order sir." Reikert nodded, trying to untangle the knot that twisted in his guts at the request. Someone out there had forgotten their place, but he would remind them. Konrad nodded and waved his hand; dismissing

Reikert, to do as he was bid, which he promptly obeyed. Until his audience with the sea hag, Konrad had other business which needed tending to. It was high time he studied his charts and made note of the attacks upon his ships. Perhaps it would give him a heading. If not, it mattered little to him—for he would see them burn just as he would see the world burn. I'll have the grandest treasure a pirate could have, Konrad thought to himself as he made towards his chambers. I'll have everything.

Chapter 16

The candles flickered as he traced his finger over the path on the chart. There seemed a pattern, of that he was sure. As for which direction the pattern was moving, that was harder to tell. Konrad scratched his bearded chin as he looked at his maps and charts. A knock at his door distracted him, Reikert entered quickly as he looked up from the maps strewn across the table.

"She's here, sir." He announced fearfully. Konrad gazed back in a puzzled manner. How was that possible? Hardly any time had passed since he'd given his order, and she was a hag. She couldn't move fast as that, surely. A humpbacked frail, looking old crone slid out from behind Reikert. A gap–toothed smile tugged at the corners of her normally sagging, perpetually scowling mouth.

"Not often does a dog give summons to its master." The crone said haughtily. Her voice sent a shiver down the spine—a voice like sea water slapping against rocks, or the sound of hulls splintering against a cliff. She moved past Reikert with a forceful nudge leaning against a gnarled driftwood staff. It produced a hollow thump as it hit the floor. The top of the staff was threaded and laced with various fetishes that clacked and jangled and clattered hollowly as she moved. Her hands appeared to be little more than bone with leather, stretched so tight and thin over them that it left one wondering if merely touching a quill nib would tear through the beaten hide she called skin. Her arms were thin, the skin of them appeared to be melting from her body; all adding to the wrinkles that showed her considerable age. She smelled of seawater and fish; her hair sparse, as it appeared, appeared as little more than spiders webs that clung feebly, or perhaps stubbornly to her skull. Maybe she simply refused to allow the last of the pitiful strands to fall from her head, and instead was using them as a show of her power. Konrad bowed his head and smiled a gesture that was met with a sharp thump as she hammered the butt of her staff against the wooden planks in protest.

"Save your preening false gestures of humility. I don't need you to remind me of your place." She hissed angrily. Her voice sounded of a howling tempest from behind closed shutters and locked doors. Once again her scowl took up its customary place across her face. "What do you want dog?" the crone asked bitterly. It might have been his imagination, but he felt as if she wished to spit on him.

"I wish you to offer me counsel—and I wish your assistance." Konrad smiled as if he were not being scolded like a misbehaving child. He allowed the stones she cast his way to find their mark, without speaking in anger; such was the wise thing to do. He knew that—but by Stromboze's insatiable greed, did that gnaw at him. If he weren't so attached to his life, he would be tempted to show her how it displeased him. The sea hag spat on the floor before cackling.

"And why should I help the likes of you who pretends to be my master; he who is frightened when shown otherwise?" She asked glowering at him. Konrad felt his anger being fanned by the woman's words and actions. She gazed past him, taking in the charts on the table and chuckled. "Ah—you need a course. What direction to turn your wheel and aim your sail for cold revenge." She smiled deducing the reason for his audience with her.

"Aye—but I've also have need of your talents in other areas." Konrad bowed. It galled him to be humble. He could feel his gorge rise as she berated him. How he wanted to pin her to the floor and flay her skin from her bones. He could gut her like a fish or strangle her with her own entrails. Of course, she could simply strike him down with the power she held. Perhaps it wasn't the act of being humble that galled him—it was the fact he could do nothing. Somewhere there is always someone stronger; upon Tornusia that was Ayzza.

"The tides grow tired of indulging you Konrad sea pup." The woman growled. Eyes narrowed in disgust as her gnarled hands clutched her driftwood staff.

"Perhaps, but Stromboze has seen fit to guide me upon..." The hag spat once again and waved her bony hand at the mention of Stromboze's name.

"Bah! Stromboze, is a paltry god of half–truths, just like you and your ilk. He has his place within the tides true, but he's not nearly important as you wish him to be. I guess you both have that in common—you're not nearly as important as you think yourself to be either." She scowled. At that moment Konrad wanted to rip his gray greatcoat from his shoulders and throw the garment over top the frail looking old hag and strangle her with his own two hands. Still, he held his ground—though she appeared old and frail, the woman remained a force to be reckoned with; and more than once, Konrad wondered if perhaps she was the embodiment of the seas given flesh.

"Have you the payments for my services?" The crone might have despised him, but she served him at least after trying to emasculate him and showing her discontent first.

"I always do Ayzza." Konrad acknowledged as he pulled a pouch of gold coins from his trouser pockets. He held the jangling purse out in front of him and smiled. Ayzza grabbed the pouch. As her thin bony fingers closed around the leather purse—a vision flashed through her mind's eye, quick as a blink. She witnessed fire and the sight of sinking ships all around. Splintered timbers bobbed upon the waves. Maimed bodies drifted carried by the whims of the sea. Ayzza sneered as she studied Konrad. Death was coming to claim him, or so she hoped. There had been a few times when Konrad somehow managed to change the course of his fate. Strokes of luck perhaps or perhaps the fates of man remained as constant, and as changing as the tides. They are always flowing, they can be predicted—but the smallest of things cause the greatest changes to occur.

Ayzza reached into her threadbare cloak and pulled an old pouch. Its contents rattled dully. As her thin fingers tugged the leather cord, she dumped out a small collection of bones into her frail looking hand. Not just bones, Konrad noticed. Crab claws, fragments of shells; even a few teeth from various sharks, and other predatory sea beasts. If he wasn't mistaken, he swore a

239

preserved tentacle from an octopus. Ayzza strode over to Konrad's sea chart. She clasped her hands together, holding the contents of her pouch tightly. She shook her hands while muttering in a strange language that Konrad was unable to place. Everything about the language seemed to flow and swirl and crash like water and wind. Though no extra moisture glistened upon her lips, he swore to Stromboze's sodden halls, her words bubbled and frothed.

"Ask your question." Ayzza said as she shook her hands over the map. Her voice shook him out of his thoughts of the strange language. Was this the language of the sea's—or of the sea gods themselves? Konrad blinked, time enough for that another sunrise.

"Where will I find those responsible for attacking my fleet?" Konrad growled as the thoughts of his destroyed property came back to the forefront of his mind.

"Touch my hand." Ayzza gestured with a subtle nod of her head. Konrad reached out a hesitant hand and touched Ayzza's leathery skin. A hollow clatter broke the silence, as she opened her hands over the map and let the contents fall from her hands. The bones and teeth seemed to make a rough path, before creating an almost half circle about Shark Mouth Cove—a small collection of islands in between Forn and Tornusia.

"You have your answer—and your course." Ayzza nodded.

"What else did you want?" Konrad pulled his blade from his sheath and held the razor–edged steel before him.

"I want you to craft a poison, and I want my blade to sit within its venom until I set sail. I want one scratch from this blade to bring my foes the slowest and most painful of deaths." He sneered viciously. Ayzza took the blade and chuckled. She merely bowed her head and leaned against her gnarled staff; petty, so very petty. She'd, of course, left out what else she had seen in her visions. There was no sense in telling him everything.

"As you wish," She whispered as she limped from the room. The thump of her staff echoed down the hallway.

"Is it wise to trust her sir?" Reikert asked as he stepped in and glanced at the map. One of the candles flickered out—releasing a small gray–blue trail of smoke from its expired wick. Konrad smiled as he cracked his neck.

"It's wise to trust no one. However, there are occasions where you must overreach yourself. I know very well that the sea hag hates me. It's because I know this fact that I can better watch for the knives coming at my back." Konrad explained as he drained a tankard of ale that sat next to his charts.

"If you say so, sir—something about her puts a chill deep beneath my skin." Reikert grimaced at the thought as if Ayzza was standing, arm's length from him.

"Am I to prepare the Mange for a journey towards Shark Mouth Cove then?" He asked, looking at the map where the small bones, teeth and shell chips lay. Konrad reached out and lifted the bottle of Castillian rum on his map table, and pulled the cork free with his teeth.

"Indeed, with enough supplies to keep us anchored there for a time." Konrad pointed. "I don't trust that my prey will be waiting for me like a sheep in a pen. I should expect I will need to wait for their arrival."

"Aye, sir—is there anything else you will require of me?" Reikert asked. Konrad smiled and shook his head.

"No, for now, you may take your leave." Konrad waived him away. "Be ready to sail in two days, and be ready to kill any who stand in my way once we find them." Konrad hissed as he upended the bottle and took a long pull.

* * *

Ayzza eyed Konrad's blade. She had laid the item upon a warped and twisted driftwood table. Candlelight flickered upon its smooth, steel surface. As she loomed over the polished blade, she saw her face. A face worn and weathered, deep creases lined either side of her mouth; and bags cascaded like waterfalls from beneath her eyes. How long had she lived? It was a question she had asked herself over and over. Though her mind was as sharp as it was in her more beauty bearing years—the question of her age seemed to have no answer she could correctly recollect. Old enough to remember a time before the pirate lords of the world decided to lay claim to the island that had always been her home. Ayzza reached out and touched the cold steel of the blade and sneered. Here she was—an ancient, doing the bidding of young boy by her reckoning. He wasn't more than thirty summers, and she answered his calls as a child answers the summons of her parents. Is this what has become of me? Ayzza asked herself. She frowned at the reflection that stared up at her from the polished blades surface. Ayzza dropped the blade into a wooden barrel and began her work. What Konrad demanded was going to take a considerable amount of expensive and difficultly obtained materials to accomplish, and she imagined a great deal of time. The hag reached her withered, leathery hand into a glass box she had at the other end of the room. She pulled out a slimy, transparent jellyfish; with a black heart–shaped mark upon its bulbous bell–like head. The creature wrapped its stinging tentacles around her arm, but Ayzza felt nothing. She was of the sea; creatures such as this posed no threat to her. She grabbed hold of her staff as she dropped the creature into the barrel with Konrad's blade. There was a thump as she mashed the creature, known as the blackheart jellyfish, to a pulpy paste. She stirred the tip of Konrad's blade through the paste scowling all the while. The woman reached above her and pulled down two vines of dried seaweed; known as seahemlock, and dropped the sea plant into the vessel before reaching and grabbing a crab–like creature, known as the seawidow, from a jar. Ayzza upended the jar and smashed her staff down once again until the materials began forming a clump of goo. She dragged the blade through the slime—sighing angrily as she did.

How could she answer to this pup? She spat into the vessel. As she watched the poisonous slurry coat the blade, she remembered the sights she had seen within her mind's eye. The ruin of ships and carnage of floating butchered bodies, floating in the sea. She remembered seeing a mass of blackness upon the surface of the waters and the thunderous cracking of ship timbers, as the black mass coiled around them and pulled them beneath the surface. Men screamed before a loud gurgling sound filled the air as they were pulled down below the surface of the water. Naturally, she told Konrad none of what her vision showed her. She recognized a flag that flew in her vision; the flag was Konrad's. She saw it in the center of the fray explosions which lit the banner in a backdrop of bright orange flame. It stood in the center of the black mass, and there was a fierce fight raging upon its decks. Ayzza watched as two shadows battled against Konrad. A moment later there came a third and Konrad held his own. Ayzza clutched the handle of the blade, gripping so tightly, her knuckles turned white. Her mind retreated inward, taking her back to the raging battle. The sound of steel clashing against steel, rang within her mind like the harbor bells.

Suddenly she watched as Konrad had a blade punched through his heart. In a last dying show of spite, he raked his blade across one of the shadows. It was then that Ayzza was able to discern some detail. It was a woman—young by her reckoning, and young when compared to Konrad as well. She could hear the girl scream in agony and watched as she clutched her arm. Blood flowed freely from the wound as her body was consumed by the burning fires of pain; the poison coated blade would create within her veins. She was going to die. Ayzza glared down at the instrument of death. She wished she could have made out more details—the woman was young in her vision, but she couldn't tell how young. The beating of her heart slowed to an aching crawl seizing in her chest.

Konrad must be killed. It was time for the tides to change. She dropped the blade back in the barrel and stepped back. Ayzza watched as a crab started to creep across the sandy beach floor of her hut. With the speed of a woman less than half her age, she plucked the crab from the ground before banging the creature's shell upon a stone that served as her chair. She sank down and peeled back the shell of the now lifeless crab and began plucking its pale white meat from within. Her eyes remained fixed upon the barrel, as if in a trance. The poison coating the blade was a nasty piece of work. The poison held every particularly vicious poison and toxin that she was easily able to get her hands on. A single flesh wound would see the body emptied of blood, for nothing could make the bleeding stop; and the pain would be indescribable. The victim's body would feel as if it were being consumed from the inside out by the roaring flames of a forge. Eventually, the lungs would refuse to inflate, and veins begin to dissolve. Its corrosive nature would eat away at the wounded rotting flesh, until there was naught but exposed the bone. All things change as the seas—even visions, Ayzza thought to herself as she pulled one of the crab claws free. Let us just hope that Konrad does not return and that his fate is finally sealed, she thought. Nothing would please her more.

* * *

"We'll be approaching familiar waters soon." Syandro said with a smile as he leaned against the rails. Franchesca sighed and shook her head.

"Before leaving my parents and striking out for myself, the only familiar waters I ever saw were the harbor waters." She replied. She knew he meant well, but it appeared as if he had forgotten just how closed off her life previous to this grand adventure, had been.

'Well—Ella assures me that the best place to scout is Shark Mouth Cove. Apparently, it's a frequent stop for smugglers and a good many ships pass by it." Syandro nodded as he glanced back at Ella, who piloted the ship. Syandro studied Franchesca's expression.

"Do you miss land?" He asked. Franchesca shrugged.

"A little, not so much that it ruins my life." She replied softly. "I think I'm just about used to things out here now. Use to doing things on my own... I just can't seem to place the same amount of trust in Ella that you have." Syandro smirked raised his shoulders with a calm, detached indifference upon hearing her protest.

"As I've said before, it's not that I trust her completely, but a suspicious lead is better than grasping in the dark. You might not miss land, but I find myself missing firm packed, unmoving soil more and more each day. I want this to be over as soon as possible so that I can set foot upon it again." Franchesca smiled at his honesty.

"I'm not cut out for a life living at sea." He admitted. For the first time in a long while, Syandro looked upon Franchesca and felt relieved. He didn't know when exactly, but his feelings of longing and jealousy seemed to have faded. His heart didn't ache for her, nor did his thoughts run rampant within him; wondering what it might be like to feel the smoothness of her flesh beneath his palm. He couldn't recall the last time the sound of her voice sent a chill of excitement down his spine; it seemed that finally, he had some peace. In two days they would arrive at Shark Mouth Cove. Or so they hoped. Their encounter with the Darkwater had done more damage to the ship that Franchesca could recall. Holes were hastily patched, but the damage was well beyond the skill of the ship's carpenter, at least with his current supplies. The men complained of being wet and cold, as sea spray and water found openings in the splintering timbers; gaps, and holes. The ship's rudder had taken a thrashing, having large chunks ripped from it and a good portion of it was cracked off when the Darkwater had grappled the vessel. After their encounter, Franchesca searched through a few sea manuals in the ship's library, hoping to find mention of the force that almost destroyed the ship and nearly claimed her life. Unfortunately, she had found precious little information. Many scholars, mages, and sailors wished to know more about the deadly patches of Darkwater. It didn't help that the ship's library was something of a gross overstatement—for a library it was not. The so–called library consisted of little more than two bookshelves, most of the shelves holding more books on sea life and destinations than anything else. Still, there was some information to be had. Some books claimed it was a living thing; others said it was simply a form of water. All of the sources warned of it and instructed to give it wide breath when spotted. The texts she had read also spoke that fire was the only way to truly rid yourself of the plight, given the fact that it existed in water only showed how dangerous and hard to kill it was. Whatever the substance proved to be, living creature—or some other strange thing produced by the water Franchesca hoped never to see it again. She reached over and rubbed the ache out of her shoulder before patting Syandro on the back. He had undergone some other changes since she had seen that cold, detached change in him. He somehow seemed more at ease.

"Watch yourself, and remember you're watching over everyone else as well." Franchesca reminded. Syandro chuckled. Trust her to place extra weight on his shoulders.

"I'm going to have a look at the supply logs, and the ledgers." Franchesca explained. Syandro nodded as he watched her walk away. He supposed it would be good for him to check his charts as well. It would be beneficial to see if there was a place they might likely be ambushed. Syandro looked back at Ella as she adjusted the position of the wheel slightly, and winked at him. He couldn't help but smile. Not for the first time, he found himself wondering where her true loyalties lay. On the surface, it appeared that she had joined with them, that they were all in this together. It appeared that she might actually be connecting with him. She had ridden him roughly and wildly more than once, and vice versa had allowed him to control their activities on more than a few occasions.

Their talks afterward had always seemed meaningful. He had told her of his father's reputation within Castella and his recent voyage to the Tomblands. True, he did leave out his father's true destination; and the real purpose of that voyage. No one needed to know of that. Syandro hadn't been aware until now just how much Franchesca had drifted to the back of his mind and how much Ella seemed to be stepping forward. Perhaps that was just the chaos of all that had happened. The rush of battles and near catastrophes brought forth reserves of passions and the nights they had spent, were as passionate and consuming as any he had ever had, or dreamed of before. Sometimes it wasn't even the nights. The two might disappear into the captain's cabin for a few hours at random only to stumble out reeking of sweat and sex. Still, that did not make Ella loyal. Syandro tried to think about how he felt about the possibility of her still being a spy for Konrad. He was surprised to find that the thought of her betrayal hurt him deeply. For a lingering moment, he paused to consider the implications of what that in itself meant, and he was not at all sure he liked that thought.

Chapter 17

Konrad departed Tornusia without fanfare; it seemed to be the custom of the independent island. The last of his cargo had been loaded only a few hours ago, twelve barrels filled with Darkwater, sealed with lead tops; inscribed with all manner of sigils and wards to keep the substance from destroying the ship. As soon as the barrels were stowed aboard, he was ready to take to the seas to punish those that dare struck out against him. Konrad had the forge master create a special weapon in which to fling the barrels. It looked much like a large ballista crossbow; only instead of firing long massive spears of wood, it would hurl the barrels into the sea and towards his prey. The tests saw the improvised machine working quite well, given the short amount of time that had been afforded the engineer. Ordinarily, Konrad would have liked to give the forge master, and the weapons crafters more time to fine–tune their machines, but that was a luxury he did not have. True, he could have waited for his revenge until the engine had been tested and refined; but he chose not to, Stromboze favored the bold. Someone was out there attacking ships of his fleet, his property. That someone needed to be taught a deadly sort of lesson, Stromboze also rewarded those who punished the wrongs against them quickly.

The machine worked well enough in the few tests they'd been able to run. It proved simple and quick to operate; two of his men would turn the wheels of the ballista bending the arms of the machine while another brought over the barrel of Darkwater. The group would hoist the barrel up onto the track of the machine. It was essentially a combination of a bow and a slingshot; with the arms having a leather sling between them that would fling the barrel overboard through the large gap at the front of the machine. The wind tugged at the gray sails of The Mange, pulling it from the harbor and out into the sea. Waves churned and crashed; they roared dully as Konrad listened to the waters lapping up against the shore of the beaches of the island. The sound was growing fainter and quieter with every passing minute, soon the island that dominated the horizon became little more than a fleeting dot; dwindling into a speck. He would not set eyes upon Tornusia again until he'd dealt with this upstart. He smiled at the thought. Fair well, for now, a smirk crossed his face as he thought of all he accomplished since he'd taken the Throne of Tides for himself. He killed his former captain, in a magnificent bit of bloodshed, if he said so himself. He became the undisputed lord of Tornusia, and any who took upon a life of pirating paid a tax to him; lest they find themselves hunted by the Mad Dog.

He'd discovered a Khaos cult upon the island and had rooted them out viciously; a cult whose ranks included his very own brother, Fridricht. Konrad had enjoyed locking him away in the brig beneath the palace. The punishments he visited upon his brother were so magnificent that, at night he could still hear his screams. In that time he'd also been feared and reviled; as a stalker of the seas of the world. A sinker of ships and a killer of men, with bloodthirst so insatiable that no quarter was offered, and a legion of sharks followed his ship; attracted by the crimson pools he would leave, content to feast upon the corpses of the crewmen he killed and threw overboard. Some of the stories were exaggerated, but Konrad saw no reason he should put a stop to them. Let the seas believe he traveled with Stromboze's very own hounds at his heels; it served his purpose. He was a killer, a hardened man with a short temper and salt water in his blood. He gave no quarter and expected none in return. Tornusia was his seat of power, but the seas were as much part of his kingdom as the island itself. Evidently, the world had forgotten that.

"Let me see every sail full, you gods–damned spineless maggots!" Konrad roared from the quarterdeck as his meaty hand wrapped around one of the wheel's pegs before he gave it a slight turn.

"Full sail you heard him! Full sail you whelps!" Reikert repeated as he stood by his captain. He'd stood by Konrad's side for years. They both set foot on their path to piracy at the same time, and there was much respect shared between the two. Reikert got away with saying things to Konrad that would have seen another man flensed and his hide used to patch the sails. Konrad liked Reikert after a fashion; not enough to trust him, because Konrad could ill afford to trust anyone. It's why when Konrad sailed, Reikert stood at his side. The last thing he wished to do was sail back into the port of Tornusia and find that his friend replaced him as its ruler in his absence. Konrad had killed to seat himself upon the Throne of Tides, and he would do so again in a heartbeat, it was just much easier to kill someone you didn't know as well. It was easier not to have to do it in the first place. There had been times Konrad thought of killing Reikert; he still entertained the thought from time to time, it made him smile more often than not. After all, what better way to keep men on their toes than to kill someone they all assumed was safe because of his friendship? He wondered what that would do for his reputation. He wondered what Reikert's last words might be. Would he be a screamer? Would he see it coming and resign himself to his fate, how much would he bleed if he just decided to open the bastard up right now? Konrad never referred to anyone as a friend, unless he'd been about to kill them; afterward he'd speak his feelings after all then they would never be able to repeat his feelings to anyone else. It saved them both; if any found out that Konrad had friends, it would paint a target on his back; and he would be killed one way or another. He would be killed because a crowd of sharks would smell a weakness to exploit, and he would not allow himself to be exploited in any way. His so-called friend would not fair much better and would follow shortly thereafter. It was also entirely possible that if he ever called another a friend, they would do the bloody deed of killing him themselves. Though he liked Reikert, something within Konrad kept him from calling the man his friend even within the silence and howling fury of his mind. As it stood, Reikert was more use to Konrad alive than dead, perhaps that what was it he thought to himself. The man has proven his merit time and again. Perhaps that made him, more of a tool to be utilized; yet another weapon in an extensive arsenal. Maybe that's what friendship meant to Konrad.

"Besides, it would take too long to break in a new boson." Konrad whispered. Reikert glanced over his shoulder. He was doing it again; Konrad was talking to himself. When a man spoke to himself, it never boded well.

"Did you say something, sir?" Reikert asked; though he heard what Konrad said in his mumblings.

"I said, it would take too long to break in a new boson." Konrad repeated. At least he could be commended for his total honesty. Giving voice to his thoughts of killing various members of his crew kept them on their toes. They might not always know where they stood in Konrad's favor, but sometimes he gave them a clue.

Reikert chuckled mostly to himself; it wasn't the first time Konrad entertained the thought of killing him, and he doubted it would be the last. Perhaps one day he actually would, when it seemed, he became too dangerous to the Mad Dog.

"Full mast and prepare yourselves for Shark Mouth Cove!" Konrad shouted, before throwing his head back and letting loose a wild howl. His crew joined in, and for just a moment it seemed as if there were a pack of wolves, as well as other baying beasts loose upon the seas. The sails snapped and rustled in the wind and Konrad Kursz, the Mad Dog of the sea, was loose upon them once more; hunting his prey.

Chapter 18

Franchesca sat at the small table that served as the desk in the relatively cramped cabin she shared with Simone. She scratched her head as she studied the book propped open on a stand; along with the collection of parts from the pistol she'd deconstructed. Simone entered the room and chuckled.

"Are ya still tryin ta figure dat ting out?" She asked as she walked over and sat on the narrow bench that served as a bed.

"I think I've almost got it now." Franchesca smiled as she slid the pistol's metal barrel along a carved wooden grove.

"How are things topside?" She asked without looking back as she examined her work momentarily before turning to Simone with a pleasant smile. Simone shrugged as she sank into a chair.

"I tink it's goin alright. I ave a feelin more dan a few of tha crew are enjoyin 'aving land baneath deir feet again. Syandro seems ta be included in dat lot. He's been sittin on tha beach wit' his lookin glass all day." Simone replied as she slouched in the chair and pulled a dagger from a sheath held against her thigh. Simone examined the dagger closely before reaching over to a small table that stood next to the chair. Franchesca however, found her eyes roaming Simone's thighs. Simone picked up a whetstone and began sharpening the dagger.

"Batween ya readin bout tha Darkwater an' readin dat... gun book ya 'ad yer nose in a book more dan any other place." Simone smiled with a wink. Franchesca laid the pistol down on the desk and turned with a smile.

"I'm sorry..." Franchesca began slowly as she made to rise. She truly had been neglecting Simone. She hadn't been doing it on purpose. Franchesca always had been the type to get swept away in whatever occupied her mind. If she encountered a problem her mind began working on how to solve it, sometimes it worked harder, and longer than she realized. Her tutors thought it would serve her well if she could learn to control it. Her parents worried that it would be a flaw any potential suitor would see. Well here she was now, she hadn't learned to control it, and it appeared that Simone indeed found it bothersome. By the Heavenly Lady's silver radiance she despised anything that meant her parents were right. Franchesca opened her mouth to speak again, eyes pleading.

"I ain't sayin I'm upset. I like beddin a smartie girl; like avin her bed me to." Simone smiled as the whetstone sang across the steel. Simone peered down the blade again and batted her eyes playfully at Franchesca. A wave of relief surged through her. She was only kidding. Still, Franchesca's heart raced. She did wonder if she was upsetting Simone. After all, with all the time, she'd spent searching for answers as to what Darkwater was and the time she spent working on her guns she must have become lost in herself for quite some time.

"Ave ya found any more out?" Simone asked not giving her a chance to chase down the thought further. It was something she was grateful for. Franchesca smirked as she turned and gazed at Simone fully. By the Heavenly Lady's silver light she was alarmingly beautiful, stunningly vibrant and filled with life. There was a quality about Simone that was intoxicating; some indefinable thing that pulsed and thrummed within her, and drove Franchesca to smile even when she felt she didn't want to. Somehow Simone made things better, made them right. It was the only way she thought to describe it.

"No, I haven't, at least not anymore about the Darkwater. It seems that people don't live long enough to study it in detail. Though there are hints at a few people who might know; unfortunately those people are long since buried; or not on the best terms with the race of men. Though there's been mention of at least one scholar in Austinea, who is regarded as much of an expert on the stuff as one can become; at least without fully understanding something. He's at least made a few better-educated guesses. Though even he says, take his guesses with healthy doses of skepticism and salt." Franchesca explained.

"As far as working on weapons... I would say I've learned a bit. If I knew a blacksmith and a forge master I'd be able to make the parts I need and repair a few of these pistols I've come across." Franchesca told her with a sigh.

"Do you think that Ella is telling the truth?" Franchesca asked quietly. She didn't like having to talk about these things with Simone. She wanted their time to be joyous, wanted them to have fun; not worry about who was plotting to kill them in one way or another. It might have been unrealistic; and Franchesca admitted she was still young, that she was inexperienced in the way of intimate relationships. Though she wished that their time together could be nothing but bliss and wonder, she knew that was unrealistic. Franchesca supposed that it was nice that she and Simone spoke openly about the fears and the darkness that surrounded them, but everyone wished for a happy, carefree life. Simone paused in her sharpening and sighed.

"I honestly don' know. Seems ta me she's in tha best position fer playin people fer fools." The sentence was ended with Simone running the whetstone back across the blade.

"She saved our skins an' held tha helm during dat whole episode; even tried ta get us clear. If ever dere was a time when she was gonna earn trust, would 'ave been in dat moment." Simone continued.

"Do you trust her?" Franchesca asked. Simone laughed as she paused again, her emerald eyes meeting Franchesca's.

"I don' trust dat one as far as I can spit. Don' sapose it matters much, not if she's proved wrong 'bout dis. Though... I tink we're gonna be seein 'er true shades soon, an' I get the feelin dat dey ain't gonna be pertty." Simone slid the dagger back into its sheath and placed the whetstone back on the table. She stood up and walked over to Franchesca and pulled her from her seat, both of them giggling. Simone leaned in and began to kiss the girl she loved, but no more than a moment into the display of affection there was the sound of the ship's bell tolling, followed by a loud banging at the cabin door. Simone sighed as she looked into Franchesca's eyes.

"Are we ever gonna get tha time?" Simone asked in an exasperated whisper. Franchesca smiled and planted a gentle kiss upon her soft lips.

"What is it?" Franchesca asked as she opened the door.

"Ship spotted miss. Looks like a big one." The crew member said in a voice shaky with excitement, and a glint of anticipation.

"We'll be up on deck in a moment Almin." Franchesca nodded. The broad–shouldered man saluted and turned as Franchesca closed the cabin's door. She walked over to the chair she had been sitting in when Simone had entered the room and took up her sword belt. Now attached to the belt were three pistol holsters, each of which was the home of a readied pistol. Franchesca plucked up her heavy coat and slipped it on hastily as Simone finished securing her sword belt. Simone gave the knot an experimental tug and nodded once she was satisfied it would not slide from her person in the heated excitement of whatever were to come.

"After you darling." Franchesca said with a smile as she kissed the top of Simone's hand. As she glanced up into Simone's eyes, she gave a delightful upturn to one side of her mouth; which indicated that there would be a wonderful sort of mischief once this was all over. Simone returned Franchesca's grin with a smirk, and the two of them rushed topside.

* * *

It was the moment Ella had waited for. After days of waiting and scouting ships that had crossed their path at Shark Mouth Cove, she had finally seen one she could turn Syandro's attention on; without suspicion being placed upon her, at least not until it was too late. She stared over the rails as swarms of men rushed to their rowboats that'd only moments ago been beached upon one of the small islands surrounding the cove; as the men scrambled to get back to the ship. The ship she laid eyes upon, was a galley favored not only by merchants; but pirates who were just getting their start. She spied six cannons in the lower decks. Two smaller cannons were mounted upon the back of the ship at its quarterdeck. Easy pickings; Ella thought to herself as she rubbed the bare skin on the sides of her head. It would be easy to convince Syandro that the ship was a pirate ship, what better way to throw suspicion than by appearing weak and under armed? She would tell him. Knowing full well that Syandro expected one of Konrad's most dangerous ships; after all, that is what she had spoken of, Syandro hung upon her every word. Even the name carved into the wooden hull of the ship spoke vaguely of pirate nature. The Thunderborn, she whispered under her breath. Ella glanced over as Franchesca and Simone made their way towards the quarterdeck. Syandro climbed over the side railing as swiftly as he could manage.

"What did you see?" Syandro asked as he took the looking glass from Ella's proffered hand.

"It's a ship called the Thunderborn. One of Konrad's most trusted ships; it's kept lightly armored as a means of keeping it hidden from suspicious eyes. Make no mistake though; the captain is cunning as a fox and bloodthirsty as a marauder." Ella told him. When one dealt in lies, they came easy; and they came fast to the mind, just as hers had done. Franchesca's spine began to prickle with unease, as she turned her gaze to Simone. She knew the same sensation of unease clamped down upon Simone's nerves as Ella spoke words. Franchesca asked for the spyglass and held it up. As she studied the ship in the distance keenly aware of her hearts pounding, she listened to Syandro and Ella talk.

"I think you must be mistaken; its flying Fornish colors..." Syandro began shrugging his shoulders and waving his hand dismissively.

"What better way ta get eyes ta look the other way? You got any ideas about what to do, miss?" Ella asked. There was a thread of truth to that, Franchesca would not deny. Still, something felt very odd about this all of a sudden. Birds took to the air from the trees that dotted the cove, as if knowing what would ensue. Syandro looked at Franchesca for many heartbeats. Her look told him of her thoughts on the events unfolding. With a heavy sigh, Syandro nodded.

"Make way, get us within range." He told Ella. Franchesca watched as Ella smiled with no end of satisfaction. With no small amount of frustration, Franchesca and Simone relayed Syandro's orders to the crew. Shouts of acknowledgment rose up from the deck; each in a different voice, and in moments the Quest sailed out of Shark Mouth Cove. Franchesca stood at the prow of the ship watching as its bulk cut through the sea. Hopefully, this would prove once and for all that Ella was the predator in sheep's clothing. Little did Franchesca or anyone else for that matter know, Ella held yet another trick up her sleeve. When backs were turned, and she was sure everyone had set about their tasks and was too busy to notice, she pulled a small phial from within her sleeve. Ella unscrewed the cap and hastily placed a few drops on her finger, which she quickly rubbed over her neck. The rest she drank in a hurried gulp. It was something she had kept hidden for a long while. A potion she went to great lengths to procure while the ship was docked in the lands of Dea. She might have been confined to the ship, but a few whispered words to one of the crewmen and a bit of coin passing into his fingers; as well as the single act she would subject herself to, were enough to sway him to get her what she wanted. It was said that Dea was one of the few lands that the ingredients could be found, thus one of the only places it was able to be made. It was as much perfume as a potion; a single smell could rob a man of his will. Its combination of rich musk and flower–laden scent fogged the minds of those in close contact, making them easily manipulated. She had heard it lowered inhibitions. It didn't control the mind, but it made it very hard for the victim to string a clear and coherent thought together. Ella smiled as she dropped the phial overboard and walked towards Syandro. She patted him on the back and pointed towards the ship with a smile.

"Soon you'll be in range, and soon the attack will begin. It's a good thing ya have the upper hand with surprise." She smiled.

"I only mean to get in close so I can scout, to see if what you say is..." Syandro halted in the middle of his sentence; as if he had been pole–axed. Ella smiled as he stared at her. She leaned in close and kissed him gently at first, and after a tender moment encouraged the kiss to become more aggressive. He had an objection just a moment ago; but now, he simply felt content to try things Ella's way.

"Fire on the ship." She whispered. "Kill the captain; claim the glory that waits for you." Her accent suddenly shifted and seemed altogether more gentle and noble.

"Show Konrad, who the real terror of the sea is; show me." She continued in the same seductive whisper. Syandro stared at her wide–eyed and was lost for words. His heart pounded, blood thundered and surged within his ears, making him all but deaf to the world around him; everything sounded so faint and far away, everything except the honey coated voice that belonged to Ella. Her words coiled around his mind, and his heart felt like it might burst if he did not obey her. If he could not make her happy if she was displeased with him what would she do? She would leave him. He would never see her again. His fingers might never touch her flesh, and he would never taste her kiss again. He could not stand that thought. He had already lost Franchesca; he couldn't lose Ella.

Syandro would not let that happen. Syandro blinked a few times and considered the ship off in the distance. She would leave him if the ship got away. Or was it if, if what, if he didn't tell them? After a moment the only response he managed was a nod.

"You have to tell them, darling." Ella coaxed him gently touching his face softly with the hand that she had placed a drop of the potion on. The scent filled Syandro's nostrils, and the need for it grew; he craved it. Syandro turned swiftly and began gauging the distance.

"Cannons make ready!" Syandro shouted from atop the quarter deck. His back straightened and his legs spread shoulder–width apart. The very picture of a commander who should be obeyed. The very image of a confident man who'd left youth behind and who appeared to have been captaining ships all his life. Syandro tilted his head back and flared his nostrils.

"Sir, is that wise?" A raspy voice asked. Syandro turned and beheld the sight of Lieutenant Captain Cornando, the man in charge of his contingent of Conquistadoro's and Pistoleros.

"Prepare your men, Lieutenant Captain; I expect no quarter to be given." Syandro told him with an excited firmness. Cornando thought the order odd; Syandro had always allowed those who surrendered a place aboard his ship. Because he'd always seen sense in refilling the ranks of the men who had died with new crew members.

"But captain, I don't think..." Cornando began, Syandro rounded on the veteran with a scowl and eyes that could have been wreathed in flame, had he been some Khaos creature; rather than the mortal he was.

"I gave you an order! Are you refusing to obey it, sir?" Syandro hissed. Ella stood behind Syandro and smiled at Cornando.

"No sir," Cornando replied quietly as he rubbed his hand across his now bearded face. The grizzled veteran shouted out orders to his men as he descended the steps of the quarterdeck to the main deck. He walked along its length instructing his men and ordering them into positions where they would be most effectively used in the battle ahead. Cornando himself strode up and stood behind Franchesca as a large cloud of sea spray showered the deck. "I fear our captain may need our assistance before the end." Cornando growled as he rested a hand upon the blade sheathed at his side.

"I've thought that since that bitch came aboard." Franchesca replied. She gripped the handle of the blade that hung sheathed at her side. Franchesca wondered if she had it within her to give an order she did not believe in. Could she, and what would happen if she refused? Franchesca peered back and watched men returning topside from the armory; axes, pikes, sabers, knives, and billhooks in hand. Others came up baring flintlock pistols and a few long; especially expensive, flintlock rifles. The men aboard the ship were ready to kill and maim. Franchesca wondered about the crew of the other ship, wondering how or if they knew of the death approaching them. Were they truly members of Konrad's fleet? If not, did they deserve to die? Franchesca's heart sank. What was happening? Everything was falling apart around her. She was going to be an accomplice to murder. Men were going to die in cold blood; she would confirm the order that would see Syandro and his men down the road to piracy.

"Make ready to fire!" Franchesca heard Ella bark as she patrolled the deck of the ship. For a moment, and only a moment, brief and fleeting, Franchesca felt Ella's eyes cut through her and watched as a smile of malice spread across her face. Franchesca took a deep breath as her heart thundered within. She would not have to give the order. She would not be the one condemning the crew; she would not be a cold–blooded murder.

"Almin!" She shouted as she stepped back from the prow. Before she shouted a second time a tall man broad of shoulder; with sweaty sun–kissed skin, lacking hair upon his head stepped forward.

"Yes, miss Franchesca?" He asked in his thick Castillian accent as he bowed politely.

"Find Simone; and all the men whom you trust, and who accompanied Simone and me upon this voyage out of loyalty to us. Tell them that we will remain aboard in reserve. We hold the Quest, but I will not board that ship, and any loyal to myself and Simone will follow mine and Simone's example. Understood?" Almin bowed deeply and nodded.

"I will do just that miss. We shall be the reserve." He nodded as he ran off with haste to inform those Franchesca had instructed.

"Do you think it wise?" Cornando asked. As he stood next to her watching as the distance between the Quest and the Thunderborn shrank.

"I don't know if it's wise or if it's foolish... it is simply my decision. I'll not attack innocents in such a ruthless manner." Franchesca replied softly. Cornando sighed.

"You are a noblewoman; it would be far better if you were in command of this vessel." Cornando nodded as he drew his blade from its sheath.

"Fire!" Syandro's voice rang out from the quarterdeck, loud enough for all topside to hear. A hundred more mouths relaid the order as the thunderous barking of the ships cannons began. Franchesca glanced back over her shoulder and caught sight of Simone who merely nodded. Franchesca knew that Simone and the men the two of them trusted had received the message she had ordered Almin to give them. Smoke billowed from the mouths of cannons, creating a layer of acrid fog that fell over the ship. Men shouted and screamed, waving their weapons around joyously awaiting the chance to strike at flesh and bone. Cannon crews reloaded. Powder monkeys the nimble, quick youths who'd signed up and who were responsible for bringing powder to the guns; worked in teams to haul barrels to the deck, placing them where the cannon crews could access them with greater ease and quickness before they darted down into the holds once again. Franchesca felt sorry for those youths their job was one of the most dangerous, and they were the youngest. Despite the chaos, she found herself praying for their safety hoping none would be maimed, that none would lose the innocence of their minds this day. Men with fingers caked in blackness from handling gunpowder and cleaning out the soot of the cannons continued their work. It was like watching a machine. A machine that served to bring death and destruction; each man, each team, made up a cog in that killing machine; and it sent a chill down Franchesca's spine.

Syandro's order to fire rang out over the deck once more, and the screams of the dying echoed the sound of splintering timbers of their prey. Franchesca watched as the men Ella claimed sailed a pirate ship, hurried to ready their cannons to fire at their attackers. These were no pirates, and their weapons crew was poorly trained. Ella had played Syandro for a fool.

"Get down!" Franchesca ordered as the first shots from the Thunderborn were fired. Men threw themselves to the deck, and the ship rocked. Men died screaming as shrapnel in the forms of finger length splinters and twisted metal debris, tore into their bodies. A few of the cannon shots tore gaping bloody holes through men's torsos who had failed to drop a moment in time. Blood showered the deck, and the sounds of men in their death throes clawed at the ears. What had Syandro done; Franchesca felt her heart sink as the cloud of smoke cleared only to be reborn again with the firing of the guns?

"Ship!" The lookout in the crows nest shouted. "Ship; Ship commin up behind!" Franchesca picked herself up from the deck and rushed to the side rail hoping to catch a glimpse, but the thick cannon smoke made it all but impossible to see more than a few feet out. Once it cleared, she saw what approached. She gawped in wide—eyed shock and muttered a silent prayer to the Heavenly Lady; praying that those she cared for would come through this unscathed, and alive. Though, as it looked at the present moment, it seemed unlikely her prayers would be answered. *Syandro, what have you let her get us into?* She wondered silently as she made her peace with the idea that they could all very well die this day.

* * *

Ella heard the shout from the lookout and promptly snatched up the spyglass from Syandro's hand. Her heart was pounding. *No, this was wrong, all wrong.* She searched out over the sea scanning it carefully. Then she saw the sight that made her heart sink and her stomach knot. It was the Mange! Konrad was here but why, what brought him here? She swore under her breath as she watched the massive bone ornamented frame of the Mange surge through the water. Then a realization settled over her that turned her blood to ice within her veins. He was patrolling the seas looking for whoever it was that had sunk the ships in his fleet; ships that he felt belonged to him, whom he let other men captain. What would happen if Konrad found her aboard? What fate awaited her if it was found out that she was the one who led Syandro on his hunt? Konrad enjoyed when his men showed ambition, but he had never tolerated the destruction of his property. He had made the captains swear oaths of loyalty to him; he even had them swear that they were the captains, but if they wished to sail in his fleet than the ships they captained belonged to him. He was the pirate lord, and he made sure everyone beneath him knew it; their ships were his, and their lives were their own. He welcomed them to kill each other in the name of ambition, but to destroy his ships was most certainly a death sentence. He could not catch her; she refused to allow that. Ella had come too far to allow herself to die at the hands of the man whom she was trying to prove herself to. It seemed it was time for another adjustment to her plan.

"Pull them in you swine! Pull them in!" Ella roared frantically gesturing towards their prey. Despite her effort, her voice was cracking with fear and panic.

"What about the other ship, miss?" A crewman shouted as he struggled to be heard over the cacophony of battle.

"Follow the orders and thrice damn the other ship!" Ella shouted back as she waved her saber above her head. The crew did as they were ordered and hurled a number of grappling hooks to bring their prey closer. She glanced over her shoulder as Konrad's ship drew ever closer. For the first time in a long time, Ella found herself praying that her schemes would play out without a hitch. Somehow she doubted that would happen.

* * *

"Ships insight sir, it appears as if we've interrupted a plundering." Reikert said as he handed Konrad the spyglass. Konrad held the device before his eye and smiled.

"What are your orders, sir?" Reikert asked with a slight bow of the head. He had been with Konrad long enough that such a question was foolish, but one never assumed to know Konrad's desires. Even in this very predictable instance.

"Ready the crew for all—out war." Konrad replied with a growl. He let out a wild howl as he shook his head to and fro. Froth flecked his lips and ropes of drool slid from the corners of his mouth to moisten his wild beard.

"No quarter you whelps! Ready yourselves for a bloodletting! There's two ships worth of spoils ta be had! Spare no one and take everything!" Reikert shouted as he ripped his sword from his sheath and pointed ahead.

"Ready cannons!" Reikert growled as he descended the quarterdeck and did his best to stir Konrad's men into frenzy. It took little to accomplish such a task. Konrad stood at the wheel, one of its many pegs grasped in an unyielding grip. Standing next to Konrad was a woman scantily clad, and draped in what appeared to be a fishing net; caked in seaweed, and other assorted maritime and oceanic debris. Dried starfish, and seahorses and even a few bits of deep ocean coral all tangled within the net. The woman was young, and attractive; though that attractiveness hid many dangers. A witch of the seas, well versed in the magics of the ocean and a priestess of Stromboze himself. Konrad always had at least one sea witch accompany him on his voyages. Pirates were a superstitious lot, but in Konrad's case, it had little to do with superstition and more to do with adding another weapon to his arsenal. It made good sense to bring along someone who held the ability to fry someone with a bolt of storm lighting at the far end of the ship, an effective weapon and a potent tool of terror and intimidation. If Reikert remembered, it was Konrad, who once said having magic on your side always gave an edge. Though that quote could have come from the histories and none aboard would know, save Konrad himself. It was hard to argue with the results, however. There was a deafening roar as the numerous cannons on the Mange were fired. Some shots went wide, but a majority of them peppered their targets as the ship began a slow turn. Konrad was looking for the best spot for his vessel to join the battle and to deploy his new weapon.

"Brace for impact!" Konrad shouted as he turned the wheel. He would make a place for himself in the raging battle. His calloused hand wrapped around the pegs in the wheel and he held them firmly as he howled like a mad wolf.

"Get ready you pack of scabless dogs; loose the harpies, the time to reap blood and plunder is upon you." Konrad shouted as the ship drew closer to the raging battle.

One of his crewmen pulled a canvas tarp from a large block of cages; as soon as the light fell upon the beasts, they shrieked and screamed. They flung their emaciated forms against the iron bars of their cages swiping with talon and chomping with mad fury. The beastmaster took out a coiled whip and cracked it over the cages; before prodding the beasts with the goad, he carried with him. It was a terrible nasty tool; barbed with sharks teeth and coated in jellyfish venom. A prick would leave an open wound which would sting and drive a beast to a mad frenzy from the pain, just as Konrad liked. Konrad glanced over watching as the beast–master prepared his charges for the fray. Once they were close, they would be released so that the creatures wouldn't turn on his crew. Konrad was in luck; it seemed his presence would go unnoticed, he drew closer and closer. He imagined that the ships were so engaged with one another that they could not fire upon him, lest one get the advantage. However, one ship did have the advantage—his ship. Approaching rapidly and unopposed, Konrad the Mad Dog Kursz prepared to ram the battling ships.

Chapter 19

Franchesca heard the bark of cannons and gawked in the direction from where they called. She looked on in horror as one bright muzzle flash after another sparked in the distance. There was a third ship, a massive ship. Decorated with bone, and grizzly macabre trophies; its prow made to look like a gaping mouth filled with rows upon rows of razor sharp teeth, huge coal black and dingy gray sails straining in the wind bringing the massive collection of lumber and manpower closer; second by passing second, heartbeat by heartbeat.

"Almin!" Franchesca shouted as men rushed to and fro. Suddenly the Quest shook violently. Clouds of splinters tore into the air and through any flesh that happened to be in the way, or in the immediate vicinity. Franchesca threw herself to the deck and covered her head with her arms; hoping that would keep her safe. Screams filled the air, and the ship rocked once more. She heard splashes as men, or chunks of timber were blown into the water by the barrage of cannonballs. Franchesca didn't deny that there were probably a few of the crew who threw themselves overboard in their search for safety rather than risk being blown apart by cannon shot.

"I'm here miss!" Almin shouted. Franchesca dared to peak, though her heart pounded as her mind struggled to take in the scene of carnage and chaos that surrounded her. She swore she heard her own heart in her ears. She was alive; praise be to the Heavenly Lady, she was alive.

"Get as many cannons as you can to fire on that ship!" Franchesca shouted. That order made sense, and she found herself surprised at how quickly she'd just adjusted to being trapped aboard a ship that had just been peppered with cannon shot. No sooner had she been proud of herself for her quick concessive clear thinking, than she saw her approaching end; only after her moment of triumph would she meet her end—it figured as much. Her blood froze in her veins and time slowed to a crawl around her. She saw an iron cannonball flying through the air heading right toward her. She was sure; her life would end in only a moment. A heartbeat perhaps less was all the time left to her upon this world. At least she put up a brave face before she died, it was more than most had the chance to show. With her heart frozen she watched as the approaching iron shot passed only a scant hands width over her prone form and splintered the deck just a few feet away from where she sprawled. Almin launched himself up and roared out Franchesca's orders. Franchesca blinked for a stunned moment; her mouth was dry, and her bladder loose. Her trousers blessedly still being dry was the smallest of miracles that had just occurred. She picked herself up and began shouting frantically before rushing over to one of the few cannon crews she could see in the raging chaos. She wasn't even sure if what she was saying made sense—as if some deep inner part, a part of her she'd not known existed, took over and the rest of her struggled to keep up. Few of the men remained on deck; most boarded the Thunderborn with Syandro and Ella as they engaged in battle. The Thunderborn faired no better in the volley though; and as Franchesca gave a quick glance, it appeared to be listing to the left. Those men that remained upon the deck; who still remained upon the ship, were loyal to Franchesca and Simone. They were their friends and companions. Men they ate and drank with while working the docks at Castella and all of whom considered the two women family. That's why they were here; they were a family sticking out this adventure together, looking out for their loved ones.

Human debris and shattered human forms littered the deck as it was stained bright red with the blood of those dismembered by blade and cannonball alike. Franchesca helped turn a cannon on the main deck about to face the approaching ship—no sooner had it been dragged into place than she ordered it fired. The shot was flying straight for its hull, not a fatal shot; but scoring a hit was something. If she could get more cannons to fire, perhaps they stood a chance at buying time. She wasn't sure how the men below in the cannon deck faired; if they could get their cannon's firing, they might have a chance. Her heart sank when she witnessed a great geyser of sea water rise and swallow the iron cannonball they had just managed to fire. One by one, other cannons fired in the direction of the approaching ship; each time a wall of salty sea water rose up to shield the vessel from the projectiles, and each time she felt her heart sink beneath the waves as the sea water swallowed the cannon shot. Franchesca once again cast a glance down at the deck of the Thunderborn and spotted Syandro. He was a maelstrom of death, and well-aimed sword strokes cutting down all who his gaze fell upon. Fighting a short distance away from him was Ella—a blur of fury, more of a brawler making crude slashes and swipes than a true sword fighter. One could tell Syandro was a well-practiced swordsman; one could tell Ella made a living killing. She maimed and butchered any opposition, with brutal hacks and disemboweling slashes. She watched as Ella sidestepped an attack and sliced through the face of her attacker; leaving a grisly line of exposed bone, leaking brain, and a ruined eye. Franchesca glanced back and looked on in horror as the massive ship closed in. It was too late.

"Brace for impact!" Franchesca shrieked, as she ducked low and grabbed on to the cannon she stood by. A crack like thunder echoed as the massive ship rammed the Quest. Timbers splintered, and the seas churned and sprayed. Ropes and cables snapped and buckled. Beams fell from above, some falling wide and landing in the sea, others fell and killed crew members unlucky enough to be in the path. Franchesca gawked at the behemoth-sized vessel as it came between the Quest and the Thunderborn. She peered around frantically to see where Simone crouched. Franchesca found herself praying more fervently than ever that Simone still lived. A hand clasped her shoulder firmly. She jumped, having been startled and glanced back.

"I tink we're in some trouble." Simone shouted over the din. She was caked in dust and black powder residue, but what a sight to see. Franchesca's heart beat quickly, she was overjoyed to see her; but had no time to say anything, and the only reply she could muster was a quick smile. "Any ideas?" Simone asked as she gazed up at the mountain of bone decorated timber. Almin pulled himself over and squatted beside them, gazed at them saucer-eyed.

"Orders, miss?" He asked in a daze, no doubt wondering how they could hope to be victorious against such a ship. Franchesca gazed in stunned silence. The ship towered over the Quest, and it would take time to scale—to arrive at the top of its main deck. What would happen when they reached the top? What horrors would they face? Franchesca turned to Simone and then to Almin.

"Get the cannons ready to fire. I want to fill that ship with as many holes as possible." Franchesca told them firmly.

"Aye, aye miss." Almin agreed. He stood up and began shouting her orders to the remaining crew, all cannons to fire upon the ship of their newly arrived foe. The Quest rocked once more throwing men off their feet. There was an ominous clatter followed by an unnatural and uncomfortable silence. The air thick with expectation, Franchesca stood next to Simone; each was waiting with bated breath for what was about to happen.

There came a shrill bestial and primal cry, the likes of which Franchesca had never heard before in her life. Male and female shaped creatures leaped to the sky, held aloft by broad leathery wings. Metal collars glinted upon their pale necks, complete with chains attached to them. The rustling clank of the metal links accompanied the dull thuds of their bodies as they landed.

"Harpies!" Almin shouted. Franchesca had read of harpies in myths and legends; as well as in the great tails of heroes who journeyed to distant lands; she'd even read about them in books detailing and describing dangerous creatures of the world. Never in her life did she expect to see one in such close proximity. One of the creatures landed six paces away aboard the deck of the Quest, staring at Franchesca almost dumbly.

Its eyes, though appearing to be no different than her own; say perhaps for the fact that they were slightly larger—gazed upon her confusedly. Its slightly elongated face resembled human if a human had mated with a dog. Its pale skin seemed to be drawn tightly over its gaunt frame, the creatures' ribs clearly visible. It hunched over, keeping its weight divided between its strange, goat-like legs. Its feet ended in three toes tipped with razor–sharp talons; which

269

allowed it to settle on its haunches with great ease as well as being able to grip tightly upon the ship's rail.

With a sudden sharp realization, the harpy pulled itself from its daze and let its predatory instincts take over once more. It released a shrill cry and leaped towards Simone, gliding on its massive outstretched membranous wings. It pulled its legs up in front of it and readied itself for impact. With a shout, Franchesca tackled Simone to the deck, feeling the wind of the passing harpy as the beast glided over them. Franchesca rolled on her back and tugged one of her pistols free and fired as the creature pulled its wings back to fly upward. With the clap of gunfire, there came a screech of what Franchesca could only imagine was pain, as the lead shot tore through one of the wing membranes on the harpy. Franchesca dropped the pistol and tugged a second free, pulling the hammer back as the thing pulled into the air with a howl, with a second clap of thunder and a loud bang from behind her. Franchesca turned and saw the barrel of Simone's pistol belching out a billowing acrid smoke cloud; a dead harpy lying a scant handful of feet away. Most of its head was missing; blood and what tiny bit of brain the creature had, spilled out onto the timbers of the deck. Franchesca noticed the beast plummet through the air, approaching one of her crewmen who swung at others as they approached. The harpy dove rapidly towards him, bore left at the last possible moment. The gust of its movement and a quick change in its direction caused the crewman to lose his balance momentarily. Before he could right himself a second harpy came from behind and latched its claws upon the man's shoulders, as it flew away there was a scream of anguish as the beast tightened its grip on its prey, its razor sharp claws sinking into the sailor's shoulders.

"They're everywhere!" Franchesca shouted as she saw another make a line towards her. When it was within range, she pulled the trigger on her pistol and noticed as its head exploded and its body tumbled ungracefully through the air before falling into the sea.

"Ave ta kill em one at a time." Simone replied with a laugh; as she pulled a throwing knife free from a sheath on her belt and lobbed it towards one of the monsters as it streaked past. Franchesca turned and spied Almin slicing through one creature's wing. As it fell to the deck, he brought his blade down and severed its screaming head. No sooner had he dispatched one harpy; than another swooped in from behind and pulled him up into the air.

"Almin!" Franchesca shouted. She gaped as Almin thrust his blade upward searching to inflict a wound upon the creature. The attempt was desperate—and unsuccessful. Almin noted the large meat hook like talons gripping and gouging his flesh. Every flap of the harpy's wings brought fresh waves of agony, the likes of which he struggled against. Almin gritted his teeth and made a decision—a desperate, foolish decision, but the only one that would get him free and keep him alive, he hoped. He gripped the handle of his sword in his other hand and howled furiously; more in an effort to distract and let the adrenaline surge through himself than another purpose. He swung his blade twisting in the harpy's grip and severed his arm a short distance below the wrist. Gods help him, but he tried to get the harpies leg as well, the beast seemed to sense what Almin was doing and adjusted its grip so that it would remain unharmed. With a shout of pain, he plummeted from the air and landed with a thud against the deck of the ship. The small grace was that they had not gotten very high with Almin's considerable extra weight pulling the creature down.

"Simone, we have to get to Almin!" Franchesca shouted. Simone had drawn the second blade she'd procured some time ago, and swiped at the harpies as they came towards her. Great furrows were opened along their chests and legs. If there was an opening, she made a point to attack. A few of the beasts had even lost a leg or a foot in their attempt to carry Simone off.

"Alright, lead on!" Simone answered back as she swiped and removed a head from the diving body of a harpy. As they moved along, dodging and slashing at any of the harpies that crossed their paths, thinking the two of them might make easy meals, Franchesca gazed at the horror. Blood dripped from their maws, and fresh meat was stuck between their razor–edged and needle–like teeth.

271

Franchesca split one from crown to throat; while Simone plunged one of her blades through another creature's chest, piercing its heart. Finally, they were within sight of Almin. He lay at the foot of the steps leading to the quarterdeck. Hovering over him was the largest of the harpies; settled on its haunches—leaning over using the small claw–like hands that topped the corners of its wings, acting as a second set of feet as it walked forward on all fours. Its face was scarred, and it appeared to be missing half of its nose, what remained of it sniffed the air repeatedly. The creature's chest also had been heavily scarred, looking as if perhaps he had been whipped or beaten with a switch. The beast growled in warning, flashing a mouth full of jagged needle–like teeth. The small claws atop its wings scratched and gouged the wood of the steps, as it hissed trying to intimidate any who approached away from its meal.

"You think you scare me?" Franchesca scoffed as she leveled her blade at the monsters head. Its thick muscled chest heaved in irritation, as it flattened its pointed ears to the side of its head. Its exposed breasts, which disturbingly bore too much resemblance to Simone's or her own, hung proudly free; baring the scars which had been inflicted on it. Franchesca risked a glance down at Almin and saw that he was breathing—albeit very shallow and faintly.

"Get out of here miss…" wheezed Almin before erupting into a coughing fit. His eyes were closed tight against the pain that threatened to engulf his entire body.

"No, not till I get you safe." Franchesca replied calmly, turning her gaze back to the harpy's dim and predatory eyes. Little understanding flashed in those beady orbs, just hunger and a primal ferocity that would see it fed—or killed. It didn't look as if it cared which was its reward—but thought that a full belly might be in its future. It let out a shrill cry as it snapped at the air; making a full display of its fangs.

"Mi…" Almin tried to protest. He wasn't sure he could. Cutting off one's hand tended to take a lot out of a fellow. Or was it better to say take a lot off of a fellow? They shouldn't waste their time on him. Almin cleared his throat to speak again, feeling white burning waves of anguish shoot through the raw nerves of his stump.

"It's not open for discussion." Franchesca added firmly interrupting Almin's protests. The harpy narrowed its gold–flecked eyes as a long strand of drool dripped from its mouth. No doubt any bite from a mouth like that would fester quickly; and painfully. Franchesca sneered in an effort to keep her courage up, and immediately wished she hadn't.

Quicker than Franchesca thought possible for a beast of its size, the harpy leaped and planted a foot in her chest—its razor–like talons making gouges and cuts upon her skin. She fell to the deck winded as the beast landed past her before charging towards Simone. As Simone charged the creature to swipe at it, the harpy leaped into the air and made a sharp turn and tackled Simone. There was a dull thud as the two of them rolled along the deck of the Quest. Simone rose slowly and trudged over to Franchesca swiping at the beast as it came near. Franchesca sat up with a groan. How Franchesca loved her, but it was the wrong choice. Simone should have pressed the beast; the creature was determined to make one of them a meal. Franchesca didn't give it any more thought, sure that she made more than a few foolishly wrong decisions today. Her vision swam, and her whole torso felt bruised and painful. This must be what getting kicked by a mule feels like, Franchesca thought to herself as she winced; placing a hand on her chest.

"Get down!" Franchesca heard Simone's shout a scant second before she threw herself overtop of Franchesca and knocked her back to the ground. Franchesca grunted as her battered torso hit the deck once more, in a less than gentle way. The massive harpy drifted overhead hissing and howling as it flew over and missed its prey. It released a screech to express its anger. Simone pulled the third pistol from Franchesca's holster and smiled.

"Sorry love; but tink I'm gonna need dis." Simone stood up and trained the pistol on the beast as it banked through the air to make another pass. Franchesca propped herself up on her elbow and grasped at another pistol laying only a few inches from her hand. There came a loud, shrill howl; as the harpy came in for its second pass. Simone fired the pistol, and the beast dropped from the air, tumbling and rolling as the lead ball impacted its shoulder joint. It rose once more and loped towards them howling and charging.

"It jus' won' give up!" Simone growled in frustration as she quickly bent down and picked up her second sword.

"I think it's the patriarch—I think that's what they're called... the patriarch or the matriarch—if it's female." Franchesca could see the breasts wobbling as the beast loped towards them, but wasn't sure if that was a defining characteristic of these beasts. She had seen breasts on all of them.

"I don' tink dis is tha time fer a lesson." Simone chuckled as the creature closed the distance, it leaped into the air shrieking and howling. The same familiar clap of thunder alerted all to a pistol shot as Franchesca squeezed the trigger of the pistol she'd found. Thank all the gods it had been loaded and praised them double that it worked. The harpy's cries became dull and muffled as the shot tore through its thick neck. Its metal collar did nothing to shield it from the impact of the pistol ball. Shrapnel ripped the beast's flesh, and though it slowed, it still managed to charge. Simone sidestepped and brought her blades down and hamstrung the creature. It fell to the deck and looked up at them, eyes blazing with fury. It let loose one final hate–filled, defiant shriek; before Simone severed its head from its shoulders. The two of them limped over to Almin.

"Is he alive?" Simone asked as she knelt down. Franchesca placed her fingers over Almin's mouth and felt the warmth of his breath wash over her skin and nodded.

"He's alive but weak... I don't know how long he'll hold on." Franchesca replied. "You brave idiot; why did you have to do that, at this time?" Franchesca asked with a nervous laugh.

"I wasn't gonna get eaten by a glorified, plucked bird." Almin replied with a weak fluttering smile.

"I'll get em somere safe." Simone began with a nod. "You kill tha bastard dat tried ta flounder us." Simone added as she and Franchesca helped Almin to his feet. Blood oozed from his stump and pattered against the deck of the ship. He appeared ashen, Franchesca worried that Almin would not survive this; worried that she and Simone would not either.

"But..." Almin began to protest weakly. His eyes fluttered—gods he felt cold, and his head felt foggy. Was it his imagination or did his eyelids feel heavier?

"Go will ya, we'll be fine." Simone assured as she patted Franchesca's shoulder.

"Go on or yer gonna miss yer chance." Simone nodded. Franchesca stopped to pick up her pistols and slid them back into their holsters. Maybe she would have time to reload them; if she was lucky, but that wasn't a thing she was counting on. As she rose from retrieving one of the pistols, she felt the signet ring she had stolen from her father; bump against her chest. She glanced down and held it; along with the coin she had placed on a strip of leather and took a deep breath. Up until that point she hadn't given it a second thought. If only her father could see her now, Franchesca sighed. He would be more displeased than ever. Somehow that brought a happy grin to her face. As she slid the last pistol into her holster, she turned and shouted.

"Make sure my books are safe!" Franchesca gawped, did she just say that? They were in the middle of a fight for their lives; Almin was quite possibly dying—and she worried about her books? A breath burst from her lips; she couldn't even tell if it was amusement or surprise at her own petty worries. There were more important things going on, but she couldn't help herself. Well, I'm an idiot; she thought to herself, no doubt Simone thought so too at this moment in time.

"Aye; right now, go on!" Simone replied; with a grin. She shook her head, no time to dwell on minor oversights, she had to focus. Franchesca marveled at the size of the ship. She knew somehow just by gazing at it that the ship was Konrad's.

It was built to impress, built to impose and intimidate. How by the gods did one get so many bones? Franchesca winced, climbing to the deck would be suicide; there were still harpy's flying about searching for easy meat, not to mention there would be crew members swarming looking for foes to cut down. One could not be more vulnerable than when climbing the side of a pitching and bobbing ship. Franchesca smiled, some the gun ports, unfortunately, were open, and the climb would be a relatively short, quick one; and of course it would be easy to open up the window and slip into one that wasn't being manned. Alright then, Franchesca told herself as she approached the railing of the Quest. Her pace quickened, and she leaped atop the rail with her left foot and pushed off with her right. Quickly her hands found purchase on a narrow ledge that ran around the ship. She might not have known how Konrad had gotten all of the bones that decorated his ship, but in a way she was thankful; because they gave her no shortage of hand and foot holds to climb into the cannon ports. Franchesca held on for her life as the ship rocked in the choppy waters. She managed to pull herself up and quickly noticed a cannon port. She gazed into the belly of the beast, into the breach with a deep breath to muster herself. Right; she whispered as she pried open the door flap and hastily crawled inside.

* * *

Ella stabbed an onrushing swordsman in fancy nobles dress garb. She plunged her blade into his gut with a sneer before twisting and tugging the steel free. Ella lopped off the man's head before he toppled to the deck of the ship that he was charged with protecting. With a flick of her wrist, she sent blood spattering from her blade. Then she noticed it—the captain's quarters; only a handful of paces away. If she could make it, she had no doubt that the papers she'd planned to secure would be found. She was so close she could taste her victory. The scent of blood and gunpowder filled her nostrils while the sound of agony, death—and clashing steel carried on the air to her ears. How sweet it is; Ella told herself as she rushed towards the door and kicked it open. She heard a muffled gasping shout of surprise. The sound of someone who knew their life was in danger and was told not to make a sound. That kind of thing never did work right. When you told someone not to make a sound; then left them alone in a room to have a door kicked down, what did they always do? One couldn't help but be surprised when the door was booted in; one couldn't help themselves, sound's were made. Ella closed the door gently and sashayed towards the gaudy and massive desk, deliberately letting her boots thump loudly, and her hips sway. Her nostrils were assaulted by the smells of uncontrolled fear which mostly included musty urine and foul excrement. Ella pulled a small hatchet from a loop on her belt and slammed it into the wood of the desk. There was a gasp from below, and a man crawled from beneath the desk. It did not take a mind reader to know what he was hoping and praying for. All he desired was to get away.

"Do ya always shit yerself when ya have company?" Ella asked as she calmly perched on the desk and crossed her legs with the sort of mocking seduction she'd practiced for years. "Or do ya shit yerself when yer in the company of ladies?" She continued taking a moment to pause to lean over and push her arms closer together to accentuate her already full breasts.

"People... please..." he stuttered and stammered sweat beading and rolling off his forehead like raindrops.

"Please don't hurt me, take what ya want; I'll give ya anything ya want. Blah blah blah; I've heard it all before." Ella replied as she inspected the man who lay curled up on the ground, no doubt he was more miserable than she was. He was closer to the scent of his own foul shit—he was curled up in it; as well as steaming piss stained clothes and fearing for his life, she only had to listen to his pleading, and smell him.

"I'll tell ya what I want, shit–britches." Ella said as she tugged her hatchet free from the table. "If yer quick enough bout it I'll let ya live—yer trousers might be packed with shit and might be gettin a little cold from yer own piss; but you'll be alive, sound fair?" The man nodded so quickly it was surprising his neck did not break. "I want yer letter of empty flag." Ella told him calmly.

"Wha... what?" The man asked fearfully, even though he'd shot up to his feet and was rummaging through stacks of papers and scrolls which littered his cabin.

"Ya might know it as a letter of colorless flag. Ring any bells?" Ella hissed. "Lets ya be a pirate fer yer paltry little shit hole of a nation." The frightened man grabbed up a handful of papers and held them in front of him.

"How... how... did you know I had one?" The frightened man asked. Ella simply smiled. He lost the battle even before he thought to begin to try and play. After all, as soon as she'd asked he'd already risen to his feet acknowledging that he had one in his possession while denying he did in the same breath. Fear really did make idiots of people. Ella guessed that when this man asked for the letter, it'd been the bravest thing he'd ever done. What a sad little fool he was.

"Ya have yer empire's flag at the half position, only time someone does a fool thing like that is when they got a flag of their own they want ta fly higher. Yer a merchant ship, armed like yer expecting trouble, and yer ridin low in the water, meanin yer carryin more than ya set out with. I also saw a few cutthroats walken yer deck through the spyglass. Ya fancy educated lot think us pirates is a dumb barbaric lot." Ella smiled as she snatched the letter away and stuffed it beneath her shirt and against her breast. She couldn't help but notice the man staring; suddenly less concerned about the documents he had given away—or the hatchet and blade in Ella's hand.

"True; some of us are a dumb barbaric lot... I ain't one of em." Ella growled, she pushed the man's head up by the chin and smiled. He smiled back at her almost easily. All his fear forgotten. What a fool he was Ella reminded herself as she stared at him.

"So... so you won't kill me?" He asked her almost joyously; seeming to forget that he had voided his bowels and bladder only a handful of moments before. Ella allowed him to meet her eyes and smile at him as she returned it.

"Ya did very well..." her grip tightened about his chin and cheeks. He squeaked in pain. "But I'm still gonna kill ya." His eyes went wide, and he tried

278

and pushed himself away from Ella and her grip, but not quick enough. Her hatchet cleaved through the crown of his head, and her sword came up immediately after and removed his head from his shoulders. Ella smirked and threw her head back with a lunatic laugh. Now she just had to reach Konrad and present her gift. The very thing she'd promised him that she would deliver. She would hand it to him, and they would kill together once they sailed back to Tornusia, Ella would have her ship. A ship earned with patience; wit, planning, clever lies; blood and half–truths, and when all else failed, some well flashed tit and ass.

A woman had to do what she had to do, and though a woman's charms only took her so far they were still tools at her disposal, and she made it a point to use them. Ella would sail under Konrad's command and be part of his grand fleet. History would remember him for a bloodthirsty madman; but the histories would remember her—Ella the Red, for her quick thinking, her prowess in battle and as the greatest pirate to ever sail the seas of the world. Or they would, once she slipped a blade into Konrad's back. Thanks to the dead man at her feet, her plan was that much closer to being completed. Ella turned on her heal and strode through the door; the battle still raging in every direction around her, yet now it all seemed muffled and so far away. She brought her blade up at an overhead slash to block, while she removed a man's hand at the wrist with her hatchet. As he cried out, she plunged the blade into his throat and twisted. Within a moment he drowned choking on his own blood. One by one any who crossed Ella's path were dispatched, cut down quickly; and brutally. Skulls caved in by the head of the hatchet or simply run through by her sword. Limbs were hacked, slashed and maimed; heads fell from shoulders, and free–flowing blood painted a picture illustrating the losses of life. Ella quickly clamored over to the mast of the Thunderborn. She twisted her arm in a length of rope and held tightly before she kicked the lock of the gears that held the counterweights in place. Quick as cannon shot, she rose up and swung for a place to land on Konrad's ship. Ella managed to reach out with her leg and step out on a small platform close to the bow of the ship. She climbed the last few feet and stood upon the deck of the Mange. Even aboard Konrad's vessel, there was a maelstrom of battle raging. Outclassed men fought against savagely hardened killers, each one screaming and dying as the pirates of Konrad's crew dismembered them. It was like livestock marching to the slaughterhouse, and Ella remained unfazed. A dark shape seemed to tower above all others. Perhaps because her eye was drawn to him or maybe because Ella knew that he was the last obstacle standing in her way. Konrad stood in a bloody field of severed limbs and broken dying souls. He was in his element delivering death and terror upon the seas, and all who dared to sail them without his blessing.

"Come on ya scalded rats! What are ya? Are you men or are ya mice?" Konrad roared as he grabbed a man's wrist and repeatedly hacked at his shoulder until he cut through the man's torso, leaving two lifeless halves of meat. His free hand, when not grasping limbs to be severed or blocking blows; rested upon the pommel of a second blade still sheathed at his waist. Ella made her way over towards him a broad smile on her face as she reached to retrieve the papers she had worked so hard to get her hands on.

"As I live—breathe, and kill; if it isn't Ella." Konrad chuckled.

"I thought you had long since died." He laughed as he split a man's skull open and let his brains slip from the fresh hole in his head out onto the deck.

"What are you doing here anyway?" Ella extended her hand and passed Konrad the sheet of paper with a smile.

"Getting what I worked for." Ella pressed the papers into Konrad's hand and grinned. The world slowed. When everything appeared to go her way, just when she thought she'd won. It all fell apart.

"You treacherous little whore!" Ella's heart sank, only because she recognized the voice because the owner of that voice could ruin everything for her. Ella drew her blade once more and stepped away from Konrad and grinned at Syandro.

"Ya didn't think there was anything real here, did ya?" She asked." Yer, just a young kid playin at bein a captain..." Syandro's heart had been ripped apart.

He had thought that perhaps there was something, a small something beginning to bud and blossom between them. In her company it made the loss of Franchesca not feel as such a blow; now those wounds sank in with fresh fervor and salt. Gods, he was a fool thrice over.

"I sank every damned ship you led us to! I followed your word and your counsel on everything!" If he were going to be proved a fool, he'd see her be made a fool as well; and worse. His pride would allow no less. Ella's heart sank as she listened to Syandro. Not because she felt anything for him, she never had. He had let the cat out of the bag. He had just fucked up everything. Her dreams now were naught but smoke and ash to be blown away upon the wind.

"I was the captain, not you!" Syandro shouted furiously. Konrad's bushy eyebrows climbed toward his wild hair upon hearing news of the revelation. Someone had played with a Fornish gambling wheel, and bet all their money on black; but the marble landed on red, which came over Konrad's vision now.

"Hold on to your tongue lad." Konrad growled as he pulled his second blade free of its sheath. Ella glanced back as she heard the steel hiss as he freed it from the simple leather sheath. The paper she'd worked, and schemed so hard to get her hands on was now sliding across the deck of the Mange moved by the sea breeze.

"Are you saying, you lot sank my ships—and are you saying that this one here; this tavern whoring bitch right here, led you right to them?" Konrad growled. His face was growing red with barely contained anger, and the strings of drool that so often appeared at the sides of his mouth when caught in the grips of his red fury began to fall. Syandro pulled a short dagger from his belt and held it in his off hand.

"I am saying exactly that." Syandro hissed as he put his weapons up into a guard position. There was a heavy boot thump, and Ella gazed at the corroded blade held in Konrad's hand. Though it was rusted and stained in appearance, the razor's edge appeared sharp as new. She knew it would cut flesh just as well as a fresh blade from the smithy.

"You scabby little turn cloak." Konrad snarled at her as he leveled his stained blade towards her.

"You should know above anybody that I don't tolerate those who destroy my property." He stepped closer and took delight in the darting of her eyes, as they glanced from him to his blade; back to the young man who was clearly ready to jump into a fight he had no hope of winning.

"I hate when people lie to me and expect to be rewarded for it. Tell me wench, am I to reward you for your troubles? The trouble of lying, or the trouble of keeping your dishonesty's in order, tell me which shall I repay you for!? Shall I pay you a ransom for the ships of mine you sank!? Or for my men, which you saw fit to butcher to craft the pedestal for you to climb toward your lofty ambitions, which would you like payment for Ella the treacherous!? Ella the Red—for the blood you spilled of my men in the hopes of furthering your aspirations, while you lay on your back and let this man between your legs, I'll see to it that your corpse is picked clean by the scavengers of sky and sea. You thrice timing whore bitch, now you die!" Konrad shouted.

With a simple flick of his wrist, he struck a wound—no more than a scratch by pirate's standards, upon Ella's forearm. She hissed and grabbed her forearm, feeling the blood flowing through her fingers and staining the sleeve of her shirt. It was deep, but her pride would only allow her to call it a scratch.

"Don't get too comfortable with the mortal realm." Konrad hissed as he held his blade before him and smiled. "There will be poison; and a painful death, a death that best fits a traitor such as you." Konrad smiled wickedly. He turned on his heal without saying a word and blocked a blow from Syandro. With his second blade, he swept away the dagger that was stabbing towards his heart. Ella felt her vision blur—and pain; she felt pain, the likes of which was indescribable. Fiery needles of agony swept atop the surface of her skin while liquid fire surged through her veins. Her fingers felt icy cold, and her veins were blacker than a starless, moonless midnight. She felt her mouth go dry and a terrible thirst overtake her. Her hearing seemed to fade in and out; in one moment everything sounded far away and muffled as if every mouth was gagged and had a pillow stuffed over their face while being locked away in a trunk. The next moment sound amplified, threatening to burst her eardrums—becoming so loud that she thought about ripping her ears off with her own two hands. That bastard, she thought to herself as she trudged forward, that miserable, cruel bastard. Every muscle felt as if it were made of lead and stone. Every fiber of skin, bone, and nerve fought against her commands to move. Still, by force of will alone, Ella pulled her sword from its sheath and shuffled forward. Slowly, step by agonizing step, Ella made her way towards Konrad. If she was to die, then Konrad was to die as well.

* * *

By whatever grace clung to her, Franchesca did manage enough time to load a shot in one of her pistols. Though she wished she could have loaded all three; she dared not try to load the other two, not in the current state of things. Skulking through an enemy ship with men bent on doing harm and worse, was not the time to press your luck. The holds of Konrad's ship were indeed massive. It appeared as if the ship and her crew could be at sea for a whole year if not, multiple years without having to make landfall to replenish supplies. After a few moments of sneaking about, Franchesca finally found the steps that led towards the topside—or so she prayed. Up was at least the direction she needed to travel. As she placed a booted foot on the first step, she heard the sound of rapidly thumping feet above. She cast her gaze around quickly and made a hasty decision. Franchesca retreated down the steps she'd begun to climb; and wedged herself beneath them, squatting down trying to make herself as small as possible. Perhaps they wouldn't notice her. Men of Konrad's crew quickly descended the stairs holding a wounded comrade. Maybe there is honor among thieves, Franchesca thought. She watched as they placed him down on the timbers and stood over him. They shrugged at one another before one of them; a large man with a shaved head and a long walrus type mustache pulled out a knife and slit their wounded comrade's throat. Franchesca realized she was wrong in her earlier judgment when she thought there might be something resembling honor among them.

"One less set of hands diggin in our share of spoils." He continued as he stared down at the corpse of his crewmate.

"Aye, he was wounded badly enough anyway. It was only a matter of time—a nice act of mercy, Ritzmund. Now back to our posts. Gotta be ready ta go collect our prizes. I'll wager there's a pretty trinket or two aboard those vessels yet."

The second man wheezed out a chuckle. Franchesca scowled as she pulled a knife free from her belt and drew herself closer to the steps. She waited until the two men were where she needed them to be, and then she struck. She stabbed through one of the gaps that were just large enough to get her hand through and stabbed the one called Ritzmund through his barefoot. The thick man let out a scream and tumbled backward down the steps, his foot spurting blood in an arc. Before his companion knew what had happened, Franchesca stabbed into his ankle. He howled in agony and fell forward. He watched Franchesca pull herself from beneath the steps.

"You little bitch." Franchesca just grinned at the wounded man lying a short distance from his companion. She had cut through the back of his ankle, and his eyes watered fiercely as he gawked up and cursed at her. Franchesca shrugged as she put her blade through his heart. She walked over to Ritzmund and knelt beside him and reached out to draw the blade across his throat. He shot his hand out and held her wrist firmly. With a grunt, he dragged her off her feet. Franchesca felt a surge of panic that the bulky man was about to tug her arm from its socket. As her back hit the floor, Ritzmund pushed himself to his feet. With an angry growl, he stomped down at her head; with his unwounded foot. She noticed him wince, however, as his weight shifted to his wounded foot. Franchesca rolled quickly, but as she did, his large foot kicked her in the ribs. Her lungs emptied in a rush and panic filled her brain. With the air driven from her lungs, she was easy prey. As she struggled to breathe,

Ritzmund grasped a handful of her long, raven locks and tugged her head backward.

"Should lock you in a hold and let the lads have a turn with you. Nothin keeps em happier than bein with a woman. Long times at sea; ya know don't ya." He sneered. Ritzmund backhanded her across the face as he tugged her to her feet by her hair. Franchesca spat in his face with as much fury as she could manage, she was still struggling to pull air into her emptied lungs. A wad of saliva and blood spattered upon his scared face. Ritzmund's response was a simple and brutally effective headbutt. Franchesca's world went bright white for a handful of moments before spots of blackness danced before her eyes. White hot pain danced through her brain like a drunken longshoreman. Her knees threatened to buckle, and everything below her eyes felt as if it did not even exist.

"Is that the best you got?" Franchesca mocked, though her speech was slurred. Though it was brave, and foolish as she certainly knew, she thought that perhaps she would infuriate him into making a stupid and careless mistake. It was a possibility of course, but so was her untimely death at his hands. She spat on him once more, and his reply might as well have been the same. Ritzmund backhanded her so hard the world went spinning—as did she. She stumbled towards one of the stacks of wooden crates.

"You still think this is a game little one?" He paused for a moment and eyed her; noticing the golden ring and coin that hung around her neck by a length of a simple leather cord.

"Ah, there are indeed pretty little trinkets ta be had." A cruel and lewd smile crossed his features as he looked her up and down as if for the first time he truly took in her features.

"Some even more precious than that bit of gold strung round yer neck." Franchesca turned her head to the side and spat once more. Though her ears were ringing, and her head was splitting, she refused to give up. If she gave up now, she was as good as dead. If she gave up; she'd be wishing for death long before it came to embrace her.

"You have to get me in a hold alive first." She sneered defiantly. Franchesca wished she'd managed to keep her grip on her knife, but her fingers had loosened when Ritzmund had tossed her. By the gods, that was probably wrong. Her grip probably faltered when he had backhanded her. It had only been a handful of moments, but her memory was spotty—of course, being stuck in such a violent manner tended to have that effect. She knew she needed to think of something. There was no way she could outmuscle him. Though she couldn't match him physically blow for blow; if she could get her hands on something to use as a weapon it would increase her chances of survival. Adding to the desperations was the fact that Ritzmund, though aptly broad and muscled to play the role of a brute, was quicker than his appearance made him out to be. He closed the distance faster than she could blink and held her up over him by the throat. Her legs kicked and flailed—while her fingers desperately attempted to pry his from her windpipe. Her eyes bulged, and the corners of her vision began to blur and darken, she could feel her grip on reality start to strain. It took enormous effort to keep from blacking out in Ritzmund's iron grip. Perhaps she could reach her pistol. Franchesca had hoped she wouldn't need to use it so quickly upon entering Konrad's ship. Especially since she didn't know what else this vessel had in store. She could just feel the butt of the gun with the tips of her failing fingers. She was so close, so very close; but Ritzmund's grip restricted her movement, but she refused to resign herself to death. As her eyes began to roll back in her head, she made one last desperate grab for it. Ritzmund saw her tug the pistol from its holster and tossed her. She bounced with a dull thud off of a wall of the ship and fell to the ground. Something in her brain kept the pistol in her hand, locked in a death grip. To lose her grip on it meant death; meant worse—much worse. It meant being kept in a hold to be used as a bed slave for the crew of this damned ship. She'd die in the end, but not before being tortured, and wishing for it ten thousand times over. Even though her hand was wrapped around the handle, the impact caused her finger to tug on the trigger, and with a loud thunderclap, her only shot was expended. Her salvation; her only shot for survival, had just disappeared in a plume of expended black powder, and smoke. With a gasp and a cough, Franchesca pushed herself to one knee; sucking in air greedily. She groaned and pushed herself to her feet as Ritzmund strode towards her.

"No shot left in that little pistol of yers? What a shame." He laughed. A thought raced through her mind as quickly as a flash of lightning. If Ritzmund appeared the part of the oversized, under–brained brute, perhaps he would play the role fully—if she pressed it. It was a gamble; it was worth a try. It was the only thing she had left.

"Aye, poor little me out of shot... or am I?" She asked with a wheeze as she pulled a second pistol from her holster, and leveled it at him. He paused as Franchesca's thumb pulled back the hammer. He watched as a smug smile lined her face. She hoped her luck would hold and he would not call her bluff. For the moment she had bought herself time to plan her next move. Precious little time, but it was time all the same, and it was indeed precious to be alive. Ritzmund spat a gob of saliva to his side and scowled at her.

"Behave yourself, or I'll give ya a nice lead shot in yer tender parts there." She smiled as she lowered the gun towards his groin. Ritzmund reflexively tensed and took a step back." Now you're going to get over there and sit yourself down, and I am going to go up those steps. After that I'm going to kill your captain..." at the mention of the last, Ritzmund laughed heartily.

"I hope ya have more than just the one shot." Franchesca smiled as she waved the pistol guiding his sizeable frame past her. As she watched him; she noticed he was growing more and more pale.

"I would wish ya luck if ya hadn't just threatened ta shoot me in the stones. Either way, my coin is on my captain." Ritzmund shouted as she walked up the steps to the next hold.

"If he's as dumb as you then I've already won." Franchesca called out with a laugh as she shut one door." My pistol was empty." She heard Ritzmund's heavy stride pounding across the floorboards as she shut the second of the doors leading down to the lower hold. She slipped a thick beam of wood through the handles to barricade it and listened as Ritzmund pounded angrily against the timbers. Now to find Konrad; Franchesca told herself, as she pressed herself into the shadows cast by the various crates and cargo containers. She knelt and reloaded her pistol and sighed. Her heart galloped within her chest, and she wished more than anything, at that very moment, that Simone was with her. She gripped her father's ring hanging on the leather cord around her neck and sneered. She held it for a moment and breathed deep. I'll do it on my own, she told herself; I'm no spoiled princess—no helpless rich girl. I'm going to show you; she whispered as she clutched the ring, speaking to no one except the memory of her father and mother before she continued on her way.

Chapter 20

Syandro's blade clashed and rang against Konrad's. Syandro could not remember the last time he'd engaged in a fight that demanded his total and utter concentration. Usually, he allowed his training to take over. He shut his thoughts off and didn't have to think. People were predictable, Konrad was anything but. He didn't truly remember the last time his skills were tested so— nor could Konrad for that matter. Syandro's ornately guarded parrying dagger held Konrad's discolored blade; as Syandro aimed a slash with his thick Castellian rapier, hoping to score a disemboweling cut across Konrad's midriff. Syandro's blade held enough material to it that such a thing was possible; though it required quite a bit of strength of arm. Konrad took a step back and batted aside Syandro's slash, but didn't anticipate the dagger coming towards his suddenly unguarded side. Konrad spun to avoid a grievous wound, instead the dagger bit through his long coat and tore a large furrow.

"You fight well for one of such youth." Konrad sneered. There was a twisted sort of happiness that played through his eyes and across his features. "Trained with the Castellian Blade Dancers didn't ya? Shame you will have to die, and piss away all their hard work." Konrad said as he lunged forward and began a savage barrage of strikes. He tried to keep his mind blank; along with his expression, hoping that Syandro would search for some reading of him— some prediction of his next move, only to be betrayed. The fighter who kept his feelings and thoughts locked behind closed doors and who avoided thinking, was more often than not, the victor in Konrad's experience. Fights were savage things, born of well-trained instinct, and memory of muscle—and Konrad had trained. It didn't appear to be working, however. Syandro himself seemed to betray no thought of his next strike or thrust. It was as if the two were simply locked; living from moment to moment, where death lurked perhaps only a heartbeat or stray eye twitch away. Their minds simply observed one another with casual detachment, rather than thinking of their next strike.

"I suppose I should say you fight well, for one of such... age." Syandro replied as he leaped back, allowing Konrad's next swipe to miss by a wide margin. Syandro turned his head and watched as Ella aimed a clumsy downward stroke towards Konrad's head. Konrad simply stepped back and glanced at her. The cold, detached glare of a snake; that had poisoned its prey and now waited for its venom to take hold. Konrad sidestepped her and sneered. He merely shook his head as he looked at her pain–wracked form, up and down. A feverish outpouring of sweat had begun to ooze from her skin; making her look as if she'd been dunked into the sea. Konrad saw her breathing coming in ragged, and uneven hitches—wheezing and crackling like dried leaves on a gravel path; under the fall of a boot with every rise and fall of her chest. She looked like she wanted to say something, wanted to curse him. He knew she wouldn't because it would be too much effort.

"You're not worth my time El... Yer already a dead woman walking." Konrad mocked wryly as he swung once more for Syandro. Konrad lunged one blade aiming for Syandro's stomach; while the other licked out wide, searching for a blow to his shoulder. Syadnro blocked both and spun away from the steel.

"You must still fear her." Syandro panted with a smirk. "You avoid her like the plague." Sweat trickled down the side of his head, but his smile remained as confident and as roguish as ever.

"I've more pressing matters to tend to." Konrad replied; allowing his eyes to lock onto Syandro, as the sea wind ripped at his cloak. Ella glanced down at the growing spot of blackened flesh where Konrad had scored a wound against upon her. Blood wept from it as puss wept from an infected wound or an overfilled boil. The pain was nothing short of anguish. In her travels, whenever she strode through a city, she'd overheard mothers speaking of the great pains and difficulties of childbirth. She remembered them saying, it was the most painful experience they'd ever faced. Ella hissed as fresh waves of fire boiled up her arm; before flowing through her body, and seizing her guts in a vice–like fist of lead. That pain was surely nothing compared to what flowed within her now, and she would stake her life upon it as fact; what little life she had left anyway. She believed Konrad's boast; she knew she was dying. This anguish couldn't be overcome and leave a body intact, let alone a mind. Her joints felt like boiling pits of magma; while feeling like winter's chill had latched upon them at the same time. She burned like a raging forge—only before feeling as if she was standing stark naked in a howling winter blizzard with the next thump of her heart. It was utterly maddening. With every passing moment, the strength was eaten away from her limbs. This wasn't the way it was supposed to be. Konrad was supposed to die; not her, damn it, Ella thought to herself angrily. She was supposed to be made captain; she was supposed to be given a chance to earn fame, glory, and renown. Books were to remember her and her great deeds, among the first would be of disposing of Konrad and outliving him. The gods were fickle beings, Stromboze in particular. Perhaps she'd built such an unachievable dream within her mind that she was destined to fail.

A hacking cough wracked her chest and blood flew from her mouth; with each explosion of air that was squeezed from her lungs. For a moment she thought she'd been shot, such was the pain in her chest; such was the amount of blood raining to the deck around her, but there was no bullet hole; just that sanity devouring pain. Her eyes felt dry, and her lips felt cracked, and Ella was sure they were bloody as well, but her life's blood did little to nothing to wet them. Damn the gods—especially, Stromboze; and damn Konrad. She might not outlive him, perhaps she wouldn't be captain, but Ella had decided upon one course of action that no sea gale would be able to change course. If she were going to hell, she would be the one to take Konrad there. Not that preening weak hearted Castellian brat—her Ella the Red, the woman who'd schemed and plotted and made it this far. She pushed herself to her feet, the sensation of molten lead burned through her entire being and charged forward. Though every nerve of her very soul was afire and weighed down with steel; burning like a pyre, she would force herself to do this. Konrad glanced back at her and growled. His blades struck the blade in her hand, and his eyes widened slightly in surprise. Ella forced her muscles to obey and pushed them to move faster; even as agony threatened to claim her mind. A primal roar of fury was expelled from her lungs; even as blood dribbled free from her mouth, it coated her lip and chin. She swiped, slashed, pivoted, and parried. With a shout, Syandro rushed forward and joined in the assault. Konrad growled furiously he did his best to protect himself.

"I'll make you regret killing me up until your dying moment!" Ella shouted as she swung wildly. Blades clashed all over the deck of the Mange as well as down below aboard the Thunderborn and the Quest, in a song of steel and death.

"Reikert!" Konrad shouted above the din of battle as he booted Syandro in the gut and held Ella's blade against his own. "Make ready to fire the black bow, and set sail! I'll kill these fools on the open sea if I have to!" Konrad shouted as he strained his muscles to shrug off Ella and buy himself space. Konrad observed his boson disembowel a foe before striking out with a meat hook like weapon which tore out another man's throat with savage efficiency.

"Aye, sir!" Reikert shouted as he ducked a blow and buried his hook weapon in another sailors gut, before giving it a brutal diagonal tug and a vicious twist. "You lot come with me." Reikert ordered as he strode past two of Konrad's crewmen as they finished their opponents. The doors leading below deck were thrown open, and the small group descended to the lower decks.

* * *

Simone lowered Almin down by the door of the cabin she and Franchesca had shared through their voyage.

"Wait 'ere; I'll only be a second." Simone smiled before patting Almin on the cheek. He scoffed as he rolled his eyes.

"Course, where the hell would I go?" Almin asked in a weak voice, with an even weaker smile. Simone darted inside and strode over to the table where Franchesca placed her books. Simone unceremoniously scooped them into a canvas sack and threw it around her shoulder. She hoped that was everything;

part of her wondered what by the gods, she was doing grabbing books when a man was bleeding out his life just outside the door. Still, she knew those few things Franchesca brought with her meant the world to her. They were the only material things she owned in the world now. She knew this and wanted nothing more than to keep them safe; now all she was able to do now was hope she grabbed everything of Franchesca's; as well as hope that she moved fast enough that no harm would come to Almin. Well no more harm than had already happened to him. She supposed that meant making sure he lived. To make sure of that she better move.

She walked outside and knelt next to Almin. She placed his unwounded arm around her neck and stood up supporting him as best she felt able. Thank the gods working on the docks had strengthened and toned her muscles. If Simone had been asked to do this before she and Franchesca left Forn, it might have very well been impossible.

"I do not mean to pry Miss Simone, but perhaps we might be of assistance?" She overheard a familiar rough, raspy, and accented voice ask. She glanced over her shoulder and was greeted with a sight that made her heart leap with joy.

"Cornando if ya an't a sight fer sore eyes!" Simone exclaimed as he walked over and helped in supporting Almin's weight.

"Where is Miss Franchesca? I seemed to have lost track of her in the battle." Cornando asked as a few of his disheveled men strode forward to aid him.

"She snuck aboard Konrad's ship at tha first moment." Simone nodded in the direction of the towering, hulking hull of black painted timber and collection of bone.

"What are you lot planning?" Simone asked. Cornando simply chuckled before letting out a long sigh.

"There is no way of saying; at least for certain. Captain Syandro ordered us to attack the Thunderborn. However, we were... interrupted." Cornando pointed towards the Mange.

"We have no orders to follow now—unless you have any miss Simone; you are the first mate, and you can give us orders." Simone glanced around taking in the situation as quickly as she could. A plan came to her. It was mad, and it was desperate; the type of plan the situation called for. They would just have to hope it worked.

"Ya know how ta sail, an' captain a ship?" She asked. A few of the sailors, who remained aboard nodded as did a few of the military men who had come with Cornando.

"Good. I wan' ya ta wait till I'm aboard Konrad's ship an' I want ya ta pull back ta a safe distance." Simone told them as she patted Cornando on his armored shoulder.

"If I don't come back—it was a pleasure." Simone smiled at Cornando. The military man smiled himself and bowed his head slightly.

"It was for me as well. Let us hope we see you again, as well as Miss Franchesca." Cornando told her quietly.

"We will see to it that he gets medical attention." He nodded before Simone found the words to give the order. She handed one of Cornando's men the burlap sack filled with Franchesca's belongings and motioned with her head.

"Jus' put em in 'dare an' keep em safe fer Franchesca." Simone told them. She glanced back and took a deep breath. I'm going to need a spot of luck she thought.

"Aye miss we'll see to it." She nodded as she walked over to a section of well-secured lines. She turned and gave Cornando one final salute. She grabbed onto a taut rope and tugged the belaying free. With its anchor gone the rope tugged Simone upwards towards the deck of Konrad's ship. Her stomach churned, and for a moment Simone felt as if it had somersaulted as she was pulled through the air. Simone tried to imagine if the way she felt now was how a bird felt as it soared through the air upon its wings. Somehow she doubted it. She had trouble believing a bird's stomach would lurch and send its nerves racing as it flew; perhaps because they were used to it. After all, they were built for it, whereas she was not. No sense in your stomach flipping onto itself every time you did what was in your nature. Whatever the case, her voyage was almost at its conclusion.

Praise all the gods for its quickness. She pulled her legs back and swung, changing her course; as the crossbeam that the rope had once secured, was loosened. As it turned over the deck of the Mange, Simone swung forward and dropped onto the deck. She tugged her two blades free and was immediately pressed upon by foes.

"Right, come on den, ya lackwits!" Simone parried the first blade before turning on her heal to slash her first attacker across the back. She listened to his scream, but he fell motionless to the deck. As she came about face once more, she lunged; one knee making contact with the wooden planks of the ship as she extended her blade through another attacker's unguarded stomach, there was no sensation quite like feeling razor sharp steel passing beyond flesh and muscle. Feeling it quiver within its target; the impact of every inch of the steel, every movement, every breath, no matter how small sent a shockwave into your hand. You felt their life, felt their breath on the most personal of levels; it was visceral. Before she rose, she blocked an overhand strike that was meant to cleave her head in half, like a melon. As her foe's blade made contact with her first blade, she lashed out at his legs with her second blade. The man fell screaming and clutching his legs; as Simone rose and stepped over him.

"Is dat tha best of ya? Are ya notin more dan spineless pups?" Simone shouted as she caught her next attacker's blade upon her own and kicked him full in the balls, before sweeping up with an underhand blow which cut through the man's face from chin to crown. As he fell back dead, she made out the sight of a raging duel. She spied Syandro and a broad–shouldered man with wild facial hair and a sweat matted salt gray and iron black hair; the exposed skin of his marred with raised scars, and tattoos. Simone also spotted Ella and noticed she was limping after the two swashbucklers.

She was clearly wounded, yet that didn't seem to stop her attempts at fighting. Simone studied Ella as she swung her blade savagely; and quickly, not unlike a dying wolf simply trying to score a wound on its prey, before it curled up and died. Steel rang like temple bells as the seas churned beneath them. Simone was unsure of what to do. There were plenty of fights to be had with Konrad's crew, and indeed the number of free crewmen seemed to be growing as they killed any who engaged them in a fight. She could go help Syandro. However much better trained he was than his foe—Syandro was unable to deal with three opponents, and five blades between them; or so Simone believed as she watched the crewmen rush toward the dueling pair. Simone took a step forward but was knocked back by a gale of wind that struck her full in the chest. As she flew backward and thumped against the deck; feeling the air driven from her lungs, she gazed up dazedly as a sea witch stepped forward.

"Konrad has enough flies to swat, little one." The woman said as she leveled a staff that was tipped with a barbed whaling harpoon. Simone propped herself up on her elbow and gazed at the woman, noticing that the other end of her staff was tipped with a cruel looking barbed hook. Simone picked herself up and shook her head as the air recirculated through her lungs.

"Right den, come on an' lets 'ave at it." Simone replied calmly as she took up a fighting stance. The woman lunged towards Simone with the tip of the harpoon, but Simone swatted the barbed tip aside. As Simone spun past, the sorceress whipped her staff and swiped at Simone with the hook. When Simone had parried, she was hit in the chest by a powerful stream of water the sorceress shot from her hand. The blow knocked the wind from Simone's lungs, as sure and as powerful—as painful as if she'd been punched by an ogre's fist. The blast knocked her off her feet, and as she hit the ground, she gasped.

The sorceress rushed over, not giving Simone a chance to recover. She stabbed the tip of her harpoon towards Simone's head, but Simone acting out of only primal survivalist instinct rolled out of the way. There was a thump as the point struck the deck; before her senses fully caught up to her, there was another strike, and she only had the mental awareness to roll once more.

"Stay still, you little bitch!" The woman roared as she planted a bare foot upon Simone's chest to hold her in place. As good an opening as any; Simone thought as she swung at the woman's leg with her sword. The sorceress stepped back quickly, giving Simone enough time to roll to her feet. As she found her footing, she found her opponent's harpoon tip leveled at her chest.

"Having fun playing at being a pirate?" The woman asked as she lunged forward. Simone batted the staff aside with her blade and opened up a furrow across the sea witches back, as she spun and danced out of the way. The woman howled in pain as she turned on her heel, but before she shifted her staff up to a guard position, Simone's blades punched through her chest. The sorceress gasped; and with her last dying effort, flung a high powered stream of water into Simone's chest. The blow hit Simone square and flung her to the ground. The world existed in dull silence as she peered up at the sky from where she lay. Her eyes grew heavy as she began to close them; a strange pain gripped her shoulder. Waves of fresh pain raged through her arm. She wanted to lift her head up; she wanted to open her eyes to see what happened, but her body would not obey. Perhaps if she closed her eyes for a moment; just a moment to allow herself to recover, perhaps then all would be fine, she thought. Simone drifted into unconsciousness with her shoulder impaled upon a broken plank of the ship's deck.

* * *

Franchesca ducked behind a collection of barrels at the sound of approaching footsteps. This was certainly taking forever. Just how big was this damned ship anyway; she thought. Franchesca could hear one of them giving a command to the others.

"Get that up topside and put it on the ballista." A commanding voice ordered. Franchesca listened to the voices of the men who'd entered the area, trying to note how many there were. She heard as much as felt the barrels shift as the men took one from the area where she was concealing herself.

"Be careful you fucking idiots!" The man giving the orders scolded. "One slip and that Darkwater will see us dragged to the bottom of the seas." He growled. Darkwater—Franchesca wondered to herself; rapidly feeling far more insecure about her choice of hiding place, as well as her proximity to something that had been a near–death experience. Franchesca realized she might have an opportunity. She stood up from her hiding place and cocked her pistol, grabbing hold of one of the barrels and leveled her gun at one of the crewmen.

"Stay where you are, the lot of you!" She ordered firmly. She eyed the man who'd been giving the commands. A blade held in one hand and a bloody hook held in the other.

"And what do you plan on doing if we don't?" He asked with a smirk as he took a step forward. Franchesca laughed.

"I'll kill us—all of us." Franchesca warned in a humorless tone, emphasizing her hold on the barrel. It was a bluff—mostly, of course. She didn't want to die, nor she imagined did the men before her, but if a barrel had to be tipped—then by the grace of the Heavenly Lady, she would tip it, consequences be damned. The men chuckled as they set the barrel down gently and turned their attention on her. She could tell they were not laughs filled with bravado, however. They were nervous; scared, she was indeed cause for concern. If they did one thing wrong, she could kill them all.

"Careful with that one... she's a real bitch." Franchesca heard a voice that made her heart sink. She glanced over her shoulder and noticed the panting form of Ritzmund as he limped forward. This was not the plan she had in mind only moments ago.

"And where have you been?" The man with the exposed steel blade asked angrily. Ritzmund scowled before he spat a wad of saliva to his left and fixed Franchesca with a glare.

"The bitch locked me in a hold below." He explained with a low growl. A few of the others laughed at his explanation. A few of them reached for cudgels, and hatchets, which were tucked into their belts; and sashes.

"What do ya say, lads, lock her in a hold? I'm sure we can find some way of entertaining her—not ta mention ourselves. Bet she's soft as a kitten once ya trim her claws." Ritzmund took a step forward, and Franchesca tilted the barrel violently but kept it upright.

"You wouldn't..." The senior of the men in the hold said as he adjusted his grip on the handle of his cutlass.

"Wouldn't I?" began Franchesca, as she drummed her fingers on the top of the barrel. She heard the creak of a floorboard behind her as Ritzmund took a tentative step forward. "I've got nothing to lose. Get back; one more step and your brains are going to leap from your head." Franchesca hissed calmly. Ritzmund began to snicker throwing his head back.

"Blow my brains out with an empty pistol? Think I'm stupid enough ta fall fer it twice?" He growled. Franchesca simply smiled.

"Perhaps the pistol is empty, and perhaps it's not. What isn't a bluff is what's in this barrel. You can thank your captain for that. So you can take a step and be shot, or perhaps you can take a step, and I'll drop the barrel and doom the ship. It is your choice—but don't think I will not follow through on my threat."

A tense silence settled over them as Franchesca's eyes darted back and forth; taking note of all who surrounded her. Likewise, the senior sailor with his drawn blade and polished hook held in his other hand glanced back and forth at the two who had accompanied him to the hold.

"It appears we are at an impasse..." Reikert began. He was cut short, as Ritzmund charged forward; his bare feet thumping and slapping against the planks. His injured foot couldn't keep him upright, and his weight caused his wounded leg to buckle. Franchesca leaped aside, scant seconds before Ritzmund's charging and collapsing bulk collided with the barrel and sent him flying into the others. There was a clatter of falling wood and a strange splash as he knocked over several of the barrels containing Darkwater.

"You bumbling shit!" Reikert shouted angrily. A peal of thunder boomed within the hold, and one of the men beside Reikert went down with a lead ball blowing out the back of his skull. As his brains showered the wall, there was a splintering crack as a barrel was crushed thanks to the force of the Darkwater. Franchesca ripped her blade free of its sheath and charged forward. The last crewman swung his hatchet. She blocked the blow and chopped through his wrist. Before Reikert could turn his full attention to her, Franchesca had darted past him heading topside.

"Help!" Ritzmund shouted as he attempted to stand in the growing puddle of Darkwater. Reikert turned and gawked at him. There was a sickening cracking sound which tore a howl of pure anguish from Ritzmund's throat. Reikert watched as tendrils of the substance formed and snaked their way up Ritzmund's muscled body. The inky tendrils twisted and crushed the bone and muscles of his legs. A quick glance down and Reikert could see the stuff spreading, and inching towards him. He backed away towards the stairs, watching as Ritzmund was choked—before the Darkwater popped the man's head from his shoulders like a cork. Reikert dashed up the steps and grabbed one of the hanging lanterns. Without a second thought, he threw it into the hold below and paced backward.

"Where do you think you're going?" Franchesca asked as she leveled her sword at him. Her voice was edged with ice so cold not even a northern winter would claim it. An authority so commanding even this man who served with Konrad the Mad Dog Kursz halted in his tracks.

"You don't understand... we have to get as far away from here as we can." Franchesca smirked. Her eyes two storm clouds which had narrowed and focused all their fury on Reikert.

"I understand, perfectly." She scowled. "You've made your bed, now its time for you to sleep in it." She told him calmly.

"If I have to kill you to get off this damned ship than that's a price I will gladly pay." Reikert nodded. He lunged forward, swinging his blade to the right. When Franchesca blocked it, she felt a piercing pain as the hook he wielded in his off hand tore into her shoulder. As blood streamed from the wound, she went on the offensive, unleashing a flurry of high slashes and lunges aimed at his midsection. As Reikert blocked the last lunge, Franchesca spun and managed to score a cut along his side. Reikert hissed in discomfort but remained on his feet.

"You're a fool!" He hissed as he took one step back feeling the sting and throbbing pain of the furrow that had just been scored in his flesh. "Do you know what evils Konrad keeps at bay?" He asked eyes as wide as a trapped animal; which she supposed he was. Though come to think of it, so was she.

"No more than he commits." Franchesca grunted in reply as she stepped forward, unleashing a barrage of fencing strikes. Her shoulder was aflame with pain but she fought on, to do anything else would mean death. As her sword locked with Reikert's, he shoved her backward.

"You truly have not the first clue!" He howled as he lunged forward; at the last moment he swatted Franchesca's guard away, and brought his hook around once more and felt it puncture her flesh. She howled in pain as he pulled it free and took a step back.

"You've doomed us all. Not just aboard this ship, but you've thrown the seas into turmoil! The one person who could control the maelstrom and keep the waters safe is aboard this ship and if he doesn't get clear... then the seas will become a battleground; the likes of which you haven't seen in a hundred years."

"Big talk from a man frightened of dying." Franchesca spat angrily. "You'd say anything to step out of the shadow of death. Worse than that, is you believe in the lies of a mad man." Franchesca nodded as she heard Konrad howl somewhere off in the distance. Reikert's pace slowed, and when Franchesca batted his blade aside, he flung his arms wide. He dropped his hook and smiled. "If you believe so, then kill me; go on. Kill me—then kill him... let's see how you fare." Reikert nodded as the sea wind ripped and rustled his clothing. He dropped his weapons to the ground with a hollow, spine–chilling clang. Franchesca held her blade inches from his chest but refused to deliver the killing thrust. She lowered her weapon and stepped back, shaking her head. "I'm not going to kill an unarmed man." Franchesca replied calmly. Reikert scowled as he stepped backward.

"It could have been me you know... once not so long ago; I could have killed him and we—I could have avoided... this." He told her as he waved his arms turning in place. They were as good as dead, and he knew it. Hungry flames crackled and leaped from the holds below; and there was an immense sound, like the breaking of an entire forest full of trees. The ship pitched violently to the right and forced Franchesca to drop to one knee. She looked up at Reikert who remained on his feet. His years of sailing rough and pitching seas became so much more evident in that moment than ever. His well worn; well earned, sea legs and a sense born from weathering a hundred rough skies, and violent storms became obvious as if he predicted the move. He leaned slightly, just enough to keep his balance and stay on his feet.

"I could have been the captain; I could have ruled the seas." He went on saying as if nothing had happened. "You are right; however... I believed his lies. I believed he was the only one who could keep the world—keep Tornusia in check. I always hoped he would keep it in check; I always helped him. Now I've helped him lay the stones on his path to ruin. I've helped him lay the stones of a new world—perhaps you can pull those stones up. Or at least build something better on top of them" Reikert told her gently. There was a thundering boom from down below and a shower of splinters and debris of the ship as it mixed in with a pillar of flame. The fire had spread and ignited barrels of powder below, and it wreaked horrible damage on the deck of the ship. Men were hurled into the air; or shredded by the clouds of debris, screaming in agony as the fire ate away at their flesh. "He is right about one thing though girl." Reikert shouted as the thunderous roar of the ignited powder faded into a dull ache in the ear. "The world... does need to change. He was no madman in that regard. "He told her as he stepped backward. Reikert glanced over the side and saw the puddle of Darkwater forming beneath the ship.

"It needs to change." Reikert repeated as he tugged a pistol from a holster in his belt and placed it at his temple.

"Don't..." before Franchesca could finish, Reikert pulled the trigger. His brains exited his skull violently, and he tumbled over the side railing and splashed into the water. Franchesca rushed over and watched as the Darkwater enveloped him and tore him into separate pieces. Franchesca watched as that same Darkwater crawled up the side of the vessel grabbing it violently, cracking and shattering wooden planks.

The ship was rocked once more as the substance pulled it to the side. Franchesca felt her feet go out from under her. With a curse, she braced her arms against the ship railing and held tightly. Was it going to end here? She wondered as the scent of sea wind and spray tickled her nostrils. She closed her eyes and took a deep breath. The weight of her father's signet ring felt like the heaviest of weights around her neck; as if it were pulling her towards the tainted water beneath. It was as if it wanted her to fail—it wanted her father to be right. He wasn't right; Franchesca told herself as she braced to keep from going overboard. No, she whispered to herself as she shook her head. The ship righted itself violently, and Franchesca planted her feet firmly as it returned to a flat plane. Waves crashed beneath the Mange as the seas churned. Franchesca peered over her shoulder and watched as the fight between Syandro, Konrad and Ella continued. For a long moment, Franchesca thought to herself. What should be her next course of action? She could lend her blade to Syandro; surely one more blade would see that fight ended quickly. If that battle ended quicker perhaps, they could escape. Where; Franchesca asked herself with a sigh as a plume of gray and black smoke momentarily obstructed her view of the fight. A stiff gust of wind blew the smoke aside, and then Franchesca felt her heart freeze. There lying on the deck was Simone. Without a second thought, Franchesca leaped into action. She ran over to Simone's side and knelt over her. Franchesca touched Simone's face lovingly, reverently.

"No; no, please... Simone—Simone wake up please." Franchesca whispered as she ran her fingers through Simone's crimson hair gently. Her heart began to pound as moments seeming to take forever passed without Simone opening her eyes. Franchesca felt her heart stop in mid–beat as Simone's emerald eyes fluttered open weakly.

"Gods! feels like I caught a beatin wit' a damned mallet." Simone whispered with a sputter. Franchesca shushed her and gently rubbed her forehead, wiping away beads of sweat and perspiration. Simone turned her head and sighed.

"I knew I felt sometin in ma shoulder." She scoffed. "Just ma luck." Simone smiled with a shaky breath. Simone felt new waves of pain rack her body the longer she remained conscious. She closed her eyes and hissed biting her lip to distract herself, as well as find some form of relief.

"I've got to get you free—Konrad had Darkwater aboard; and it... well, it's a long story. The long and short of it is that we're sitting in it now and it's going to take us down. We've got to go quick." Franchesca told her. Simone nodded.

"Tink I'll be needin yer help fer dat." Simone told her with a grunt. Franchesca nodded and after an arrangement where Franchesca told Simone that she would count to three and pull her up as smoothly and as quickly as possible. Simone nodded approvingly, and the count began. "I'm gonna need a drink, or four after dis." Simone joked as Franchesca counted. There was a sucking sound and an intense pressure which Simone felt in her shoulder. When Franchesca had pulled her to her feet; Simone felt a crippling wave of pain flow through her arm like molten rock. Her knees shuddered and almost buckled, but Franchesca supported her and kissed her cheek.

"How are we going to get out of here?" Franchesca asked. Simone panted as she stumbled and dragged her feet slowly towards an open barrel. She dipped a testing finger in and found it to be water. After a single deep breath, Simone dunked her head in and pulled back gasping deeply. Franchesca walked over and plucked a wineskin from a fallen sailor and pulled the stopper out. She took a single swig and passed it over to Simone. As Simone upended the wineskin and took a few long and deep gulps. She turned and watched the fight; heart pounding, as a feeling of doubt crept into her soul. Simone didn't know what outcome she desired as she watched the blades clash. She didn't know what conclusion would yield the best result. One thing she did indeed know for certain, they did need to get out.

Chapter 21

Ayzza gazed at the sea below the cliff, where she stood. The water foamed as waves crashed against the rocky shores below; violent and tumultuous, yet somehow calming and serene. The sea was the very picture of a contradiction. How did something so powerful, and so violent, become so calming; and gentle to the senses. Perhaps people saw it as so because they enjoyed looking out over something more violent and angry than themselves. The sea didn't kill because it enjoyed it; did not sink ships from one nation more than another—yet the people of the world called the seas a violent place, a temperamental thing. Did they do so because they sailed it? Did they taint it with their presence? Ayzza sighed as the feelings of pain grew within her. They were a dull ache now, but soon that feeling would intensify. She knew this for a fact; she'd experienced it before—a great many times before. Her arms felt tired; and her chest became tight and strained. A fog raged through her mind; confusion, anger—rage. Her heart pounded within her racing chest as if she were fighting a magic duel. It was happening; just as she'd foreseen. Part of her wished she'd warned Konrad, if for nothing else than to see the expression of fear on his face, as her due. If she was forced to go through this damned pain again, then damn it by the gods, she should've been allowed to see Konrad look like a scared child, caught red-handed filching sweets by the shopkeep. It would not have swayed his decision; Ayzza knew that much, still the look would have been worth it. When she closed her wrinkled eyelids, the vision came just as before; Konrad's departure played out before her. Soon it would be time. There would be a newly appointed occupant upon the Throne of Tides. As for who that was to be, Ayzza did not know. Of course I never do see the whole picture do I, she thought to herself.

"My time is almost at an end." She whispered feeling the rush of sea wind about her. She could smell the salt; feel the tiniest droplets of spray and hear the call of the seabirds as they glided through the air. It was a gentle moment, one she had experienced many times before; those moments before her rebirth—before her cycle began anew. Each form different, as different and unpredictable as the very seas she was so much a part of. I am the embodiment of the seas made flesh, Ayzza told herself. Her weathered and wrinkled hands curled around the staff that she walked with. She knew every one of the raised gnarls, and knots she'd run her aged hands over, by heart. Every crevasse and dip within the wood contained a memory; not all were pleasant, but they were there none the less. She played the guide to all who sat atop the Throne of Tides, a warning to all who thought themselves the sea's master; but none were the masters of the sea—no matter how fiercely they pretended. How she longed for the cycle to be at an end.

She did not want to be trapped within the confines of flesh any longer. Why must she look after and guide those who cared nothing for the seas she shepherd? Someone must, Ayzza told herself as the muscles within her arms burned. No, no that wasn't right, and she knew it. Deep in her marrow, she knew that to be false. Once she'd known her purpose, but by the gods, by the salt of the sea, she could hardly remember how long she'd been trapped upon within the confines of flesh. She'd been trapped with all of its frailties; including the frailty of memories for longer than she remembered—well longer than she cared to remember. Something within her told her it was an important purpose, a great purpose; but all mortal men said that of themselves did they not? Am I truly any different, Ayzza mused silently turning the thought over in her head as the pain within her body mounted? Why didn't the gods tell her before they saw fit to rebirth her? Why would they allow her to forget? Surely that would cause more harm to their grand purpose. A searing bolt of pain lanced through her chest causing her to wince.

"Soon," She whispered to the sea wind that rushed over her wrinkled skin. Her heart became heavy as she stared out over the churning azure field below. Ayzza felt her body growing heavier by the moment; with every passing heartbeat; her eyes grew heavy. She leaned upon her staff limping closer to the edge of the cliff. She always hated this part. After the calm, the storm; so they said. The same proved true of her many rebirths. After those fleeting moments of calm, came an intense pain; the pain of one in their death throes—as if one suffered a prolonged illness. Muscles grew tight, and breath came ragged and short. Shorter and shorter they came every time while trying to take in a deep lungful. Ayzza's breath crackled as she began to wheeze. She could feel her breath rattle as it passed through her mouth; she even felt it within her chest. As if someone were shaking a dried seed pod that'd not burst open to release its new life upon the world. Ayzza held her driftwood staff in a white–knuckled death grip. Not long now; she thought as a burning feeling gripped her chest— no not long at all. Her shoulders tensed and her back became painfully tight. If I'm going to be put through this once again, I'm doing it remaining on my feet; she told herself in a determined voice. Her breath wheezed and rattled, and she began to breathe faster and shallower; her heart burned, and her chest ached.

Ayzza closed her eyes, and hot tears flowed down her wrinkled cheeks, drawn out by the pain. Despite this, she smiled as her aged ears heard the waves crash and roll beneath her. Seabirds lent their noises to the squall. Now she picked up the faint whisper of the gusts rustling and drifting through the branches of the trees. Her bones felt brittle—yet heavy as weights of iron and lead. Her fingers and other joints felt stiff and useless, Ayzza wondered if she could move herself even if she wished it. Finally, it happened. Her heart froze completely. As it stopped, fiery agony was set loose and rampaged within her chest. Her eyes flared open as if in shock, and she gasped. As her heart seized, Ayzza tumbled from the towering cliff; her driftwood staff frozen within her dying grasp. She crashed into the churning seas below. Her ancient body sank beneath the crystal blue churning waves; and Ayzza was no more—at least for now.

Her last thought as the waves claimed her was an all too familiar knowledge that she would be reborn, once more. Reborn to see through a task she couldn't begin to recall after more than a hundred years—after more than two hundred; and after more than ten of these pain wracked rebirths. The next occupant of the Throne of Tides was coming, and she must be ready for when they needed her. I must be ready; the thought washed over her like the waves of the sea. Perhaps they will guide me as much as I guide them. She didn't know why that thought occurred to her, didn't know if it was truly her own. The thought seemed to belong outside of her head—as if it had been suggested by some invisible force—some outside voice, it faded to darkness; and, silence lapping water like the rest of the world as she slipped beneath the waves.

* * *

Ella let out a howl of pain as her breath strained. Her lungs refused to obey her will and desire for them to inflate. Gods, it felt as if they were melting within her damned chest. A strange panic filled you when you discovered no matter how hard you attempted to breathe you would not be able to. The sensation of choking on nothing was indeed a strange one. The feeling of holding one's breath when they weren't trying to do anything other than inhale, tortured the soul and mind. Ella had known long before Konrad struck the blow upon her, she would die; though she thought that day was far off. Even when he told her she was going to die, she'd made her peace with it. Though if she were being completely honest, she believed it at least a partial bluff. Hoped it was a bluff, in part at least. She should've known better—Konrad didn't bluff. She thought that there might have been time to get to some port and see a churgeon; or if it came to it, cut off her damned arm. Stromboze piss, why didn't she do that before now? Because she was a fool because she thought it less serious than it turned out to be. This death was crueler than she thought possible. She glanced down at the hand that held her cutlass; the poison had eaten away her flesh and muscle down to the bone over most of her arm. Her hand had long since gone numb; as did a growing portion of the small remainder of her arm spreading to her shoulder. She poked what little of her flesh remained; tenderly, with her other hand. Ella groaned as she staggered forward. Konrad swept away a series of attacks by Syandro, before booting him in the stomach. As Syandro doubled over, Konrad howled as he readied himself to deliver the killing blow. Konrad's blades descended, but Syandro blocked them. After a short and frenzied attack, their blades were locked once again, neither one willing to slacken their resistance. The duel was unlike anything Ella had ever seen before. She only wished she wasn't half delirious with such pain so she could see it through un–maddened eyes.

"Come now boy; you're good as dead." Konrad hissed as he pushed Syandro back step by step, blades still locked tightly. The muscles in his arms burned more than they had in a great many years. It'd been some time since he engaged in a fight that tested him so severely. He couldn't imagine that he was the only one feeling weary. Surely his opponent's muscles must be just as sore and just as tired; perhaps more so. After all, the boy was giving ground when pressed; if ever there was a sign of fatigue, that had to be it. Then Konrad saw it—could feel it, a small tremor as his opponent's arms began to shake with the strain as he pushed back with his blades. He listened to the faint tap of the steel of his opponent's blades as they rattled against his own. He glanced at Syandro's arms and noticed the shaking with renewed predatory eyes. The fight was as good as over.

"You're tired I see." Konrad said. Syandro sneered as he swung his blades aside and broke the hold. As Konrad's arms were thrown apart, Syandro swiped at his chest. A deep furrow opened, and Konrad howled. That preening little shit—was it an act? No, it couldn't be an act. Damn his doubts to the bottom of Stromboze's hells; with the traitors who fail, and fall in their efforts of betrayal.

"Castellian steel... the finest steel in the world." Syandro smirked as he took a single step back. Konrad glared angrily as he lifted one foot up; he suddenly staggered and gasped. Why was he in such pain? It was a scratch. No—no this was more than a fucking scratch. Konrad looked down and noticed the blade protruding from his chest. Syandro glanced down as well before looking over Konrad's shoulder at Ella; who grinned in a most satisfied manner. She might have been as good as dead, but Konrad had made the mistake of thinking a dying woman was nothing to fear. Syandro heard the wet squelching noise and watched as she turned the blade in its new fleshy sheath. Konrad howled in pain and grabbed at the exposed steel jutting from his chest, before falling to his knees with a dull thump. He slumped to the deck, eyes glazed and wide open. Ella herself was unable to stand any longer and collapsed in a heap.

"I... I... told ya that ya would regret—killing me." Ella hissed through gritted teeth as she clutched her arm. She tried to make it sound as tough as she could, but she slurred the words as much as hissed them; with any real venom still left within her. Syandro watched as blood flowed in great stringy rivers from the corners of her mouth and her breath becoming nothing more than irregular spasms. He rushed over and cradled her head and wiped her forehead.

"Would ya let a lesson sink in; you whining big–eyed pup?" Ella scolded as she gazed up at him blood falling from her mouth with each movement of her lips. "Don't ya know I don't love ya... and I never did?" Her voice sounded strong and clear, but it wasn't hostile. It might've been his imagination, but to his ears, it sounded as if there were notes of regret laced in her words. Syandro allowed himself a nervous and uncomfortable chuckle.

"Yes. I understand that I think part of me always understood that but didn't want to admit it." Syandro whispered as he knelt slowly by her side. Ella peered up at him in a puzzled fashion. She made to speak again, but Syandro held up a hand.

"Everyone deserves to see a friendly face before their passing." Ella laughed as more blood fell from her mouth, intermingling with drool.

"You're no pirate boy; yer not cut out for it." Ella told him. He watched as she tried to fight it, but a faint smile tugged at the corners of her lips, and her eyes began to mist. Syandro heard the sounds of footfalls coming up from behind him. Ella nodded and raised a weary finger at the two who approached.

"But those two are." Ella rasped as she raised a trembling hand and pointed at Simone and Franchesca. "They had me figured out... ya should ave listened..." Syandro sighed and shook his head. "I used you as much as you used me." He replied. Ella snickered at his confession, which she could tell he didn't truly believe. Even in her last moments he blustered and lied. Say what you will about Castellians, their pride never allowed them to be outdone.

"If ya can lie ta yerself like that... maybe there's hope fer ya yet." Ella gasped; showing him, she knew the truth and hinting that if Syandro looked deep, he knew as well. Simone pulled a dagger from a sheath at her side. Syandro shook his head.

"Traitor's deserve no mercy." Syandro whispered as he laid Ella's head down gently. Ella smiled and gave a short nod.

"There's hope ta make ya a pirate left yet." Ella rasped before taking in a sharp and ragged hiss of a breath. Syandro took the dagger from Simone and stared at Ella. He knelt down once more and placed the dagger's handle into Ella's palm.

"And there's hope of a different sort for you." Syandro whispered as he rose. He made a polite bow of his head and smiled. Another explosion rocked the ship violently and sent Syandro and the others diving to the deck for cover. As timbers thumped and splashed into the water or collided off the timbers; a rain of fine splinters fell around them. Men leaped from the deck to the waiting sea waters below, only to find themselves in a much darker predicament. As the noise of the explosion quieted, Syandro picked himself up and helped Franchesca and Simone upright.

The ship was sinking fast. Every few minutes there seemed to be a new explosion as the flames ignited powder reserves, stored below. It was most assuredly a strange situation. Would they sink before they were blown apart or would the ship be ripped apart and crushed by the Darkwater; which was even now spreading as they debated their next course of action?

"Difficult to believe it will end like this." Syandro sighed as he eyed Simone and Franchesca.

"If we can get to a rowboat, we might have a chance of getting out of this. It's a huge gamble, but I've never felt more comfortable gambling in my entire life." Franchesca nodded towards one rowboat holding precariously close to a growing patch of bright orange flames.

"We'll be needin ta row pretty hard, and pretty quick ta catch up wit' tha Quest." Simone nodded as she joined Franchesca in walking towards the small vessel.

"I warned em dat dis could take a turn." Simone smiled as she held her still throbbing shoulder. Franchesca glanced back at Syandro who stood beside her. "Bet evrybody's glad I told em ta pull da Quest back now." Simone said as she and Franchesca worked to loosen the ties that secured the boat: so they might lower it. Her shoulder ached fiercely, but the will to live proved to be the best anesthetic she could ask for.

"Are you up for some rowing?" Franchesca asked with a grin. Given how she truly felt, she thought the grin, a rather good bit of acting; she felt the terror was hidden rather well.

"I'm up for anything that keeps me alive at the present moment." Syandro said as they hastened into the small rowing boat. Syandro surveyed the deck before settling into the small craft, and there he saw her. It'd been a sloppy job, but given her state, it was probably the best she could manage. He took a deep breath as he fixed the image of Ella, her face a picture of serenity and his dagger jutting from her chest; at least she'd chosen to end her pain. He gave a slight nod. That took care of that then, he thought.

"What are you looking for?" Franchesca asked as she followed his gaze. She simply turned her head to avoid the sight. "R... ready?" She asked as she placed her hand upon the rope. He nodded as he took up position to help her. Syandro and Franchesca began lowering the vessel down via the ropes and pulleys; while Simone sat in the middle to distribute the weight as evenly as possible. Another explosion rocked the ship, this one so violent that it shook the ropes free of their hands. The small vessel raced towards the sea recklessly, without their synchronized efforts to bring it down. A loud thump echoed, as the little craft battered off of the side of the Mange, as it heaved.

"Hold tight!" Syandro shouted as the rowboat descended quickly—too quickly. There came a great splash as the nose of the boat plunged straight down into the choppy sea waters, like the tip of a knife. The boat launched back out hastily, seeming to be spat out by some undersea creature; as it rocked from side to side threatening to shake the three of them out. Franchesca unlatched the oars and dipped them into the water hastily. No sooner had she begun exerting her muscles, forcing them to work harder and quicker with every passing moment—there was a splash right beside them. The gasping gawping form, a sailor, threw his arm's up over the side and tugged himself upward, trying to get into the life–saving vessel. His movements and frantic flailing resembled a fish trying to pitch itself out of the ocean and land itself on their boat. His weight and panicked movements almost capsized them.

"Please! Save me, don't let me die like this plea..." his frantic cries for salvation were cut short when something dragged him beneath the water. A spreading stain of crimson showed up beside the boat and as Simone peered over, she watched in awe as the shadowy form of a shark thrashed its tail and swam away. All around, men were snatched below the water's surface; in some cases, it was the Darkwater, in others the predators of the sea, who saw fit to partake of a rare feast. Franchesca watched in terror as she pulled on the oars, putting some distance between them and the death throes of the ship. There came another explosion, this one more powerful than all the others, its size sending vast rippling shockwaves that jerked the small rowboat in all directions. Franchesca's eyes widened as heavy iron cannons were flung through the air as if they were no more than a toy, thrown by an angered child. They splashed down, sending enormous fountains of water spraying into the sky; landing back in the churning sea, with a sound of clapping hands, as the water drops pattered against the water's surface once again. The Thunderborn began to sink beneath the waves being pulled down by the wandering tendrils of Darkwater; as timbers cracked violently. Finally, after what seemed an eternity—all became quiet, and all was calm. Syandro glanced down at the small bit of wood that served as a seat aboard the rowboat and sighed.

"I'm sorry I've gotten you both into this mess." He told them quietly as he looked around. It had been some time since Franchesca passed the oars over to him. A mess it most certainly was. He didn't know how many members of their crew remained alive. Syandro scowled as he took a firmer hold of the oar and began rowing. He was a terrible captain, truly terrible. Even in this, Franchesca bested him. Worse still, Simone bested him. A girl from the streets, even this guttershite who had nothing; proved better than him at captaining a ship and giving orders. He was Syandro De Madonia, a member of a high noble house of Castella; indeed a pride of a nation, by his father's bravery and blood. Had none of this been passed into his veins? Was his mother's line so weak? No, he knew the answer to that already. What by the gods was it then? Was it him? Gods it was him wasn't it?

"I think we all played some part in getting us here." Franchesca replied as she peered into the blue depths. She was being charitable—very charitable. As the captain it had been his responsibility to see to the safety and welfare; indeed, to the very success of his men and this endeavor. He'd failed at that, because of his pride. Was it his pride? Perhaps it was his lack of direction. A lack of focus. Syandro's stomach tightened. He didn't know what it was that had led him astray; but whatever it was, he'd mucked up his grand plans marvelously. The sun shown overhead and beat down on them; there was a soft breeze that rushed over them as they drifted. How long had that entire affair taken? It had been sometime around the early afternoon when it all begun. If they were to judge by the sun, it was perhaps the middle of the afternoon now. Gods did it really begin and end so quickly?

"Wonder where 'dose lads got ta." Simone sighed. She kicked herself and called herself a fool for thinking that they would wait around for them. What kind of fool waited around when there was Blackwater spreading around you, and you had no way of knowing once you were clear? She muttered a silent curse as she brought the toe of her boot down with an angry thump. The gesture wasn't much, but given the small space, it was the best she could do without capsizing the boat; stomping a hole through it, or even kicking one of her other companions.

"I don't know if arriving back on board would solve anything." Syandro sighed. "I opened fire on a merchant ship; of a friendly nation... I don't think I

315

would find much welcome back home." Syandro shrugged his weary shoulders, in between the steady pattern of pulling the oars.

"Why not jus' tell em it was Ella? It was her fault anyway." Simone nodded as she rubbed the back of her neck, reaching around with her unwounded arm. Franchesca rose to her feet slowly; so as not to alarm them, as well as not to tip over the tiny vessel, and pointed off in the distance.

"Look, look over there." She exclaimed happily. Simone began to squint her eyes, and Syandro paused rowing and searched over his shoulder. There on the horizon was the familiar, if not battered form of the Quest. "We've found them!" Franchesca exclaimed. With renewed determination and vigor, she and Syandro rowed. Their muscles powering the boat smoothly; and moment by moment, stroke by stroke, they closed the gap towards the ship they knew as home and the crew they knew as family. Once they arrived, there would be a host of questions Syandro would need to answer. If not answer, at least consider answers to. First and foremost amongst them would be, was he fit to lead? True, it'd been Ella's idea to fire upon the merchant vessel of a friendly nation; her and whatever damned beguilement she used, but that still posed a problem. He was the captain. He was supposed to be above such things. His underlings were there to confer and consult, not make the decisions without him. Syandro scowled; fortunately for him, his efforts in rowing hid his face of anger, disguising it as a face of effort and exertion. Ella had damned him; in more subtle ways than he could imagine, and he followed along, and for what? Gods thrice damn him for his stupidity. Had it made Franchesca jealous? How Syandro wanted to leap over the side of the craft and sink in the sea until one of the beasts found him. Perhaps they would devour him, and his torment and mockery would finally be at an end. No, it was never that simple. No, he wasn't a captain, not now. He was like a cheap whore in a brothel. He knew he was going to get fucked; he just didn't know how.

* * *

"Look, there, sir!" One of the sailors pointed towards the distance. Cornando placed the telescoping spyglass to his eye and scanned the area where the sailor pointed.

"It's them!" He exclaimed joyously. "By the heavens and by my Castellian eyes and soul; they did it." He said happily.

"Drop anchor; we await their return." Cornando shouted as he strode about the quarterdeck. In a half hour, the crew was reunited with Simone, Franchesca, and Syandro. They embraced the two women happily upon the heavily wounded ship and extended their hands to their captain.

"We feared the worst." Cornando said as he embraced each of the women happily, before snapping off a crisp salute to Syandro. "What of Konrad? What of..."

"Konrad and his ship lay at the bottom of the seas and Ella with him." Syandro said. Cornando gazed past him to Franchesca and Simone, who nodded in confirmation of the account Syandro had just given. There was a thick silence that fell over the ship. Though they had achieved what they had set out to do, this was far from a happy occasion. Many of their friends and companions were lost. Their ship was damaged, and barely afloat; each silently thanked the gods for that miracle. Making things worse, the crew witnessed their captain being manipulated. Syandro sighed as he looked out over all of them. He could tell they had seen it—could tell they had heard every word, by the way, they eyed him. There was suspicion lurking in those eyes.

"I am truly sorry for the misfortunes I have put you all through. I leave our next course of action to your decision." Syandro told them quietly. Cornando stepped forward and scanned the crew. Franchesca stepped forward and cleared her throat as she held up her hands for quiet; intending to be heard over the lively discussion that had broken out over what their next course of action should be. In that momentary lull in the chaotic debate, Franchesca heard cries for help. She held her tongue for the suggestion she'd been ready to voice, as she listened. Franchesca turned her head, and a short distance a ways floundering within the waters was a young woman. Men peered over the side as she floundered and flailed.

"Get a rowboat down there!" Franchesca ordered. With as much haste as could be made, men scrambled over to the ropes and began lowering the small rowboat from the wounded Quest. Franchesca leaped in along with two other men, as the ship finally touched the waters of the sea. With all haste, the men rowed over to the drowning woman. Franchesca shouted for the woman to hang on—that they were almost there. Just before the boat reached the woman, her head sank below the surface. Franchesca shrugged off her coat and leaped into the water, diving below to retrieve her. The crew of the rowboat looked over the sides, trying to peer into the blue deep, hoping to catch a glimpse of Franchesca or the drowning woman for that matter. They held their breath, their hearts pounding more and more quickly with every agonizing second that passed.

"Where is she?" One of the men asked as he lowered himself down cautiously and placed his head down, hoping to gain a better vantage of the depths below.

"Do you see her?" The few men in the boat asked as they scanned the water, a deep sense of dread growing within their chests. Franchesca kept her eyes open as she swam. The water stung, but her eyes remained open despite her strong desire to close them. She swam down and shot her arm out to grasp the drowning stranger's unconscious, drifting arm. Her lungs burned, and her mind raced, but still, Franchesca wrapped her fingers around the woman's wrist. She pulled the woman closer and kicked her feet furiously, using her one free hand to rake the water away from in front of her in a desperate attempt to reach the surface. The woman suddenly grasped Franchesca's arm. Sparing a glance down, she noticed that the stranger's eyes were opened—more than that, everything slowed to a crawl. Her lungs didn't seem as fiery hot and tight; indeed everything seemed lighter as if she were on dry land in a gentle breeze. Franchesca was aware of the woman's gaze upon her, baring more weight than she could stand. She closed her eyes, and suddenly the calm faded and all fell to heaviness once again. Franchesca kicked once more, putting all she could muster in an attempt to reach the surface and breathe the free air; to fill her lungs. A strong sensation of calm, and a voice seeming to say her name; told her to be at ease and be at peace. Seconds later she saw the azure blue surface of the water and the sunlight which illuminated the sea. She broke the surface with a gasp and pulled the stranger towards her. The men in the boat reached out and took the woman aboard gently and laid her down. Franchesca gasped and panted as she sucked in more and more air.

"We thought we lost you down there, Miss Franchesca." One of them said as he helped her back aboard. Franchesca smiled. That would have been a strange turn indeed. Surviving an encounter with Konrad Kursz, and his titan of a ship; only to drown saving a woman. Thankfully fate hadn't seen fit to play so sick a joke.

"Almost, and none of that Miss stuff, you know better." Franchesca joked as they helped her into the boat. Once she was back inside, she gave the speaker a playful punch in the shoulder. The stranger gasped before coughing and spluttering up mouthfuls of briny water. She coughed out salty sea water as Franchesca rubbed her back and helped her sit up.

"I don't know who you are—but you have my thanks." The woman said in between gasps. Her sodden clothes clung tightly to her slight and willowy frame and felt as if they were made of dragon skin, for all the water that had saturated them made them cling. The woman's voice sounded familiar, Franchesca thought.

"You may want to hold your thanks." Franchesca smiled. "I'm afraid our ship isn't in the best of conditions, and we are well out of range of many welcoming ports." Franchesca confessed as the men began to row. The woman simply smiled as they drew closer.

"Still I can find you a dry set of clothes, and you'll have a dry place to sleep; as well as warm food to eat, meager though it might be." Franchesca nodded, with a smile she hopped offered more reassurance to the stranger than fear.

"That is indeed most kind of you. It seems I have much to be grateful for. I am in your debt stranger." The woman gazed at her. Franchesca extended her hand.

"My Name is Franchesca." The young woman grasped her forearm gently and shook politely.

"I am Ayzza." She replied almost in a whisper. A grin broke out over her pleasant features. "I thought I had heard your name over the sounds of my coughing and spluttering, but couldn't be sure." Franchesca grinned back at the woman and nodded. "That's me." Another small bit of coughing wracked Ayzza's frame and the men rowed back towards the wounded Quest. Franchesca looked back towards the ship. Gods, what was she going to find upon her return? When she'd left, the air had been tense and on the verge of going up like a powder keg. The men were furious with Syandro, she couldn't rightly say she blamed them; but by the gods, she didn't want to see him dead for his mistakes. He didn't deserve that. At least she didn't think so. Franchesca looked over at Ayzza and gave her what she hoped was a pleasant enough smile. Then a thought crossed her mind, where had this woman come from? Perhaps she was aboard the Thunderborn. Franchesca hadn't ventured aboard, so she did not rightly know what sort of people were aboard. Had she swam? That certainly was a long way to swim. Perhaps she'd gotten tired, and that was when she had begun to flounder? Poor woman, out here all alone; pulled from the sea, where she would have been easy prey for sharks. Franchesca wondered what Ayzza must have been thinking, were any of her family still alive? She appeared to be about as young as Franchesca herself. Once she got a nice meal and a change of clothes, perhaps things would right themselves. Ayzza eyed Franchesca—studied her, discretely. At least she hoped the look was discrete. The girl was not what she was expecting. Though the gods rarely gave her what she expected. She was pleasant enough, but what did pleasant have to do with the Throne of Tides? What did that have to do with keeping the pirate lords of the seas in line, of guarding the treasures of the seas? Yes, she might have had the heart, but did she have the wit, the strength? Gods, she was only a child.

Ayzza peered down at her hands truly taking in their form for the first time since she'd been reborn. She hated the pain, hated the drowning—no matter that she'd gone through the experience an uncountable number of times, no one got used to dying. By the gods, her skin was smooth, taut and supple.

She glanced down; her cleavage had a pleasant swell as well; firm, but not ridiculous. Fifty years ago, she'd been reborn to a shell with breasts that bordered on the ridiculous. These were wondrously manageable, downright utilitarian. They would not impede, and would not distract. Somehow she got the feeling she was going to appear very attractive. I'm going to have to do a lot of fighting, aren't I? She mused silently. Casually, Ayzza allowed herself to glance over the side of the ship into the cerulean waters of the sea. Her eyes widened for a moment. She looked as young as the woman who had pulled her from the sea itself! How was she to be taken seriously when she seemed to be no older than seventeen summers? I look like a child, she thought bitterly. Ayzza bit her lip for a moment as she thought, that might not have been a bad thing. When she had lived during Konrad's tenure, she was a crone. Her mind recalled the bone aches, the foggy memory—though she would never admit to such in the company of another. Perhaps this youthful form would have its advantages; though surely there would most assuredly have its disadvantages. I hope I don't get moonbloods again. It was an experience she'd only been cursed with on a handful of occasions, and cursed was an apt description. Even the thought of the horrid cramps and feelings that came with them made her feel nauseated. The one positive was that her magic's had always been stronger at that time. She felt that weaker magic reserves and weaker magical strength were a fair trade-off to never experience such things again though. Gods! Please don't let this be a cycle burdened, and cursed with moonbloods; it's pointless since I can't breed anyway, she thought as she watched the ship's form grow larger as they drew closer. The riddle still stood before her, however—or more accurately sat before her. Why a child?

Chapter 22

Once aboard the battered Quest, Ayzza received a change of clothes. They were a well–worn patchwork of rags and scraps, but they were clothes; if only in the loosest sense. They bore a striking resemblance to a jester's motley, rather than anything a self–respecting sailor might wear. Edges were frayed and rough, the bottoms of the leggings were tattered and ragged, but at least they were dry. Ayzza smiled as a bowl of warm, seafood stew was brought over to her; where she huddled upon the deck of the ship. She'd listened to men argue and bicker over where they should sail. Ayzza knew, of course, there were only two ports realistically within range to their damaged and fractured pile of timbers. Though there was only one port that she intended them to sail to. There she only intended for them to sail to the port that which needed them most. She didn't know the reasons exactly; she just knew that fate had chosen one aboard this ship, to be the new occupant of the Throne of Tides. They needed to sail to Tornusia, and that was exactly where she would get them to sail. She was the embodiment of the seas, its guardian; created by the sea gods themselves, and Ayzza felt it time for a change. Konrad had fallen, just as she'd foreseen; before her rebirth. It spoke volumes where the sea had chosen to resurrect her. It would not take much for her to steer the vessel towards Tornusia. Or so it appeared at the moment. Men were anxious to get underway. The crew wanted to be somewhere—anywhere else, but stranded here, waiting for the next storm that might send a rogue wave that would drag their damaged craft to the bottom of the sea. But she needed to wait, needed to be patient. She needed to speak with the one she knew held enough sway over the crew to get them to sail where they were needed; to get the men aboard to do what they needed to do. Ayzza knew she would see Franchesca again. She had not foreseen it, but she knew it deep in her bones. It was a sort of intuition. Was this that damned woman's intuition people spoke of, did it honestly matter? She wondered if every time she was reborn if she became more and more human, and therefore less and less like what the gods intended her to be. Ayzza pushed the thought aside. It might perhaps be foolish to read into it; they were on a ship after all; while the vessel was fairly large, it wasn't vast. It was no great stretch of the imagination that their paths would cross aboard. Ayzza sighed; until then, she would wait and observe. She watched Franchesca and noticed she spent much of her time in the company of another woman, with fiery crimson hair, whose shoulder was bound in bandages. Ayzza nodded and smiled to herself; yes, this is what Tornusia needed.

"Ya don' 'ave ta worry, I'll be fine. I got it looked at, wit' as much peckin; pickin, an' pokin dey did, I'm sure dey got evrything. Basides wit' as much asit stung, an' burned when dey poured dat stuff over it; had ta have been cleaned." Simone chuckled reassuring Franchesca, adding a gentle squeeze on her lover's shoulder to emphasize her point. Syandro became more of a recluse than ever in the time after the sinking of Konrad's ship. He sat within his cabin; though as for what he was doing none were able to say with certainty. Almin convalesced on a small bunk down below. His arm wrapped in bandages that were changed every day, when the stump that remained of his hand was treated with a salve designed to stave off gangrene and infection. His wound had been treated with a mixture of tar and pitch that most sailors used to seal their larger wounds. This was of course after the churgeon sealed the wound by searing it with black powder. When Franchesca and Simone first went into visit Almin, he told them he would never eat pork again; as he held up the stump of his arm. The churgeon thankfully had enough poppyspirits to keep the worst of the pain at bay. He lived, though by his own words felt weak and helpless. He told Franchesca when she'd come to visit, that the pain was the most torturous part of the affair. It was constant and intense; even with the poppyspirits. The poppyspirits might have handled the brunt of the pain, but Franchesca still believed there was pain searing its way through what remained of his arm. More frightening was when he told her that sometimes he still felt his hand was attached; and that sometimes he felt the limb and appendages still itch.

Even when he glanced down to reassure himself that it was no longer there he still felt the desire to scratch. Almin told her that it was slowly driving him mad. He had an overwhelming desire to scratch and remove the itch he spoke of, but there was no way of doing it. During their talk it almost brought Almin to the point of tears. Franchesca ordered the ship's churgeon to apply a poultice made with poppyhoney and black ivy to the stump along with the salve's already being applied to help with the pain. She also told the churgeon to give Almin another, stronger, tincture for his pain later in the day. As she went to leave, the ship's churgeon pulled Franchesca aside just beyond the door and began a hushed conversation with her.

"I don't know how long he will last if we don't find port—and a more skilled healer." He whispered. "Aye—he's a strong lad, true enough; but he's not through the worst of the woods yet. The medicine and pain tincture's I have at my disposal can only do so much." Franchesca took the news in with a heart that began to grow heavy and feel twice its weight within her chest. She let out a sigh and rubbed her head.

"How long do you figure he will last?" Franchesca asked in a whisper. "Your best and most optimistic guess." Franchesca nodded. The churgeon sighed and scratched the top of his sweaty head before ruffling his thick mutton chops.

"Days... perhaps, a week at the most. I will do all I can, but I cannot guarantee his survival with what I have at hand." He nodded before turning and heading back into the room to tend to Almin and the various other men who bore some sort of wound. Franchesca turned and saw the shadow–cloaked form of the woman Ayzza standing at the top of the stairs. Franchesca walked up them slowly.

"There is a way... a port, naught but a handful of days away." Ayzza told her quietly. "Might I speak with you?" Ayzza asked with a smile, knowing she now had Franchesca's attention. The hairs on her head stood on end whenever she stood close to Ayzza, though she struggled to place a reason as to why.

There was something eerie about the woman; a strangeness that was difficult to define. Franchesca nodded but held up her hand with a single finger raised.

"On the condition, that Simone is an audience as well." Franchesca nodded upon seeing Ayzza agree. Franchesca nodded towards Simone and beckoned her forward, and the three made their way to the ships chart room. Once inside Ayzza requested that the door be locked behind, only then would she speak.

"Now you said there was a port close by?" Franchesca asked with a sly smile. "Somehow I get the feeling there is a catch... there usually is I have found recently." She'd learned much being out on her own. She learned even more during the disastrous voyage Syandro had put together. If only he listened to her about Ella. Why didn't you, you stupid man she asked herself. Franchesca blinked; realizing her thoughts were quickly running down the forest path leaving her behind. No doubt they'd find their rabbit hole if she didn't take charge. She cleared her throat.

"A sly and sharp mind, you have; and quick wits." Ayzza grinned as she watched Franchesca walk over to the chart table. Franchesca and Simone watched as she took a deep breath and looked down at the maps as if studying them.

"Aye, an' I get tha feelin yer, not all ya appear ta be yerself. Sometin iffy 'bout ya, near as I can figure. Got a feelin about ya dat I can't quite figure." Simone said as she crossed her arms giving a short, curt nod of her head.

"I mean you no harm, which is to say that I bear you no ill will; as for those in this port I can not speak for all. Some will mean you harm; some will not. But yes, your keen mind has deduced that the situation is not as easy as simply sailing forth into this new port." Ayzza said gazing back and forth between them. Something about her glare made Franchesca feel uneasy, judging by the single step back Simone took it was safe to say she felt the same way. Never the less, she was in charge now. She had to be firm; she had to be in control. No matter how much that thought scared her—and it did. Franchesca decided she couldn't let herself show fear. She could let her stomach get tied in knots, but she had to stay in control. At least as best I can for my first time in a situation like this she told herself nervously.

"Let's wave aside the cobwebs of banter and get to the point if you would be so kind." Franchesca cut in with a sigh. Step into the boots fill the role she kept telling herself. Act brave long enough, and it will come. I hope, Heavenly Lady; let it be so.

"I speak of Tornusia." Ayzza told them as she straightened herself and squared her shoulders. Ayzza looked at each of them proudly, back ridged as a steel bar. Despite Franchesca's brave face, she felt more than a little shocked at the announcement.

"You want us to sail to a pirate's hovel, a lawless wasteland to have our throats cut or worse?" Franchesca asked raising a querying eyebrow. Had she truly just heard the woman right. Sail to Tornusia? They had just killed the most bloodthirsty pirate lord in an age—their iron–fisted overseer, and now she suggested they sail to his home port? It would be easier to set a burning brand to what powder they had left and cut their own throats.

"Are ya daft woman?" Asked Simone, her eyes wide with surprise her arms were no longer crossed. Now they were pressed to the side of her head. Trying to keep her brain from swelling at the idea of sailing off into such a bad idea; or launching into a tirade. Ayzza sat in a chair and released the breath she'd been holding, smoothing out her borrowed clothes as best she was able.

"Right now it is the only port that will welcome you with open arms. How many ships in passing had their captain's eyes looking through their spyglasses? What of the sight of your captain giving the order to fire upon a ship of a friendly land? What awaits you, should you dock in Forn? What awaits you if you dock in Castella? Never mind the thought of making it back to Castella; with as damaged as your ship is, I doubt you'd make the journey. Besides, which neither would your companion down below?" Ayzza replied calmly. Franchesca cleared her throat and sighed before looking at Simone.

"Right now you have a grand opportunity; you would be wise not to squander it." Ayzza told them with a pleading note in her tone. Franchesca studied her curiously as did Simone.

"What do you mean?" Franchesca asked as she sank into a chair of her own. Simone did the same. Her heart began to race. Almin did need help, and he needed it as quickly as they could get it. If for no other reason than to keep a friend alive she should listen to this woman. Though her mention of a grand opportunity was also more than a little intriguing.

"Tornusia is in a time of transition. Konrad Kursz is dead; the lord of the pirates is gone. Even as we speak, the Counsel of the Black Flag will be gathering to talk over Konrad's plans; with him gone they will need to elect a new captain upon hearing the news, a new master to sit upon the Throne of Tides."

"What does any of this have to do with us?" Franchesca asked leaning forward. How she wanted to bite her lower lip. She could do that right now couldn't she? This was her first meeting in charge of anything. It could be a quirk, something she did when she thought. Except she didn't want to chew her lower lip to think; she wanted to chew it because she was nervous. Was this woman serious? Go to Tornusia—them? This crew against an entire island of pirates? The thought brought a fullness to her bladder she was sure was not there a second ago.

"The world needs the likes of you—Tornusia needs you. Like it or not, the Throne of Tides needs an occupant. Being from Tornusia myself; I can say that you can change things. You or Franchesca could be the ones who sits upon the Throne of Tides. You could write the laws of the sea, and the codes of honor; you could be the noble change that the seas need. What will be set loose upon the seas, what terror or madness will come to pass if another takes charge? Aye, Konrad did keep an order of sorts; now that he's gone, the world will need someone to take his place. To bring true order again, for the greater good." Ayzza explained. Her words held a certain bit of logic that was what freighted her so.

"What of the others? What about the navies of the world? Surely nations can look out for themselves." Franchesca said, looking over to Simone for support. She could see her love was just as confused; but just as intrigued as she was about what Ayzza spoke of. It was the first time, perhaps the only time either of them had been told the world needed the likes of them.

"Aye, after a fashion but what of the poorly equipped vessels? The depleted navies? Those nations that do not offer aid to others; due to spite or wounded pride? Like it or not pirates serve a purpose. They are sheppard's of the sea; the waters, and all the nations of the world their flock, and their hunting grounds. Take control Franchesca, be the hand of order; the voice of diplomacy and reason. Earn not only the respect of your crew but of the world. Take up residence in Tornusia and take your place upon the Throne of Tides. Write your name in history, nowhere does it say that your name must be written in blood if you are a pirate or captain of a free navy. Show the world—show them." Ayzza exclaimed, and Franchesca's mind raced. There were thousands of possibilities swirling through her head. Could she? Should she take Ayzza's advice to heart? Did she even truly want to? What would happen if she did this if she listened to Ayzza how would her life change? Franchesca's heart raced, her mouth felt dry, and her head heavy under the pressure of these revelations, and the passionate pleading Ayzza had voiced so enthusiastically. It was a chance to show the world; a chance to make something of herself, all on her own. It was a chance to show everyone what she could do.

Everyone—or my father, she asked herself? Did it matter, Franchesca thought? Proving herself to her father, or proving herself to the world; she liked the sound of both. Her own family history would record her as an ungrateful madwoman, who threw away her father's coin and legacy for the woman she loved and the life she desired. Though how important was her family's name truly? If she grasped this opportunity, Franchesca had the chance to carve not only her name in history but that of her family's. It would live forever; she would rise to heights greater than her father. Her legacy and her deeds would eclipse his own. At least she hoped. The last thing she wanted was to become infamous or prove her father right. Could she do it? Or was her father, right? Was she a foolish woman who'd thrown it all away and would end up a guttershite, or worse, because she didn't have his patronage; because she didn't have the husband he'd chosen? Would she succeed? By the Heavenly Lady's holy light could she actually do this? Could she actually succeed? What if she did? Such a thought filled her with want and desire. She could change things. She would prove herself; she could prove herself. It made her heart flutter to think that she had the chance to rise so far above the likes of her father, that she'd be able to look down upon him. Not only could she rise above his legacy and self–made fortune, but rise above it all doing as she wished; loving who she loved, doing as she pleased. She would be able to step out from his shadow and make a name for herself on her terms, and there was something satisfying about that. The words Syandro once spoke aboard his father, Cyrillio De Madonia's, grand ship when she and her family had been invited to tour it, began to tickle their way back into her mind. She found herself, remembering what he told her. Life was an adventure; she told herself slowly repeating what she heard almost a year past. Life is an adventure; money dwindles; influence waxes and wanes like the moons, but an adventure is something no one can take from you. They only end when your life does, and then you have a new one. What was this but another adventure? An adventure she thought after a long moment of silence. All Franchesca ever wanted was to live her life, on her terms. She'd been true to her desire. She made difficult choices, cast aside wealth and opulence for hard work and toil to earn honest coin. A pittance in comparison to what she left, but it was enough; it was always enough. Life was an adventure, or so Syandro had told her once. It was because of that, because of him and his words; she embarked upon her own adventure. Now her journey, her life led her here. Franchesca considered Simone out of the corner of her eye and sighed. Without those words, Franchesca wouldn't have had the courage to have gone out into the city to meet Simone. They might not be together if it hadn't been for her deciding to take a chance to; as Syandro said, experience an adventure.

"Let us speak to each other; you will have our answer later." Franchesca nodded. Ayzza rose from her seat and closed her eyes gently before bowing at the waist.

"I look forward to hearing your decision." She announced politely. She unlocked the door and smiled back at them as she exited the room. The door closed behind her as she made her exit and Simone rose and strode over to the chair Ayzza occupied only moments ago and sank into the seat. That chair sat across from Franchesca, and Simone gazed at her. Simone saw the thoughts dance through Franchesca's eyes and her expression, though it was distant and far away lost within a fog twisting and turning down winding paths. She might not have known the exact nature, but it was easy enough to make a guess as to what they were. She wasn't an idiot. No doubt Franchesca was going over the possible scenarios within her own head. Examining them from every angle possible.

"What are ya tinkin?" Simone asked with a grin. Franchesca shook her head to break free of her thoughts and become more present. She sighed as she looked at Simone, before rubbing her forehead.

"I'm not entirely sure." Franchesca confessed as she ruffled her wavy black hair, before letting out a moan of frustration. "We're trapped here, between a rock and a hard place. All thanks to that bitch Ella, and her twisting of Syandro. "It perhaps wasn't fair to blame her; Syandro had a part to play as well. He should have ignored Ella's advice; should have seen she was using him. He could have listened to her, could have listened to Simone—but he'd refused. But try as she might—Franchesca just wasn't able to blame him, though she didn't rightly know why.

"It seems the only course that we can set that will see us alive is to head towards Tornusia. But what awaits us there? What of the men?" Franchesca asked as she rubbed her head.

"Ya know well as I do dat tha men would follow ya nywhere ya asked em to. Dey know ya 'ave deir best interests at heart." Simone assured. Franchesca peered into Simone's emerald eyes and bit her lip nervously. She might have been nervous, but it never failed to send a chill up Simone's spine, when Franchesca bit her full lips.

"What... what do you think we should do?" Franchesca asked as she leaned back and met Simone's eyes. If there was one person who she trusted without reservation is was Simone. The two of them were in this together. The crew might well abandon her. Syandro might very well hate her; it was getting increasingly difficult to tell. But she and Simone would see each other through the roughest times.

"I'd say sail ta Tornusia. Dat one is right, jus' bacause Konrad was a bloodthirsty mad bastard, doen't mean evry one of em is. Ya could be queen of tha bleedin seas, sell yer ships fer escorts. One sellsword is as good as another; men do it on land, why not on tha sea?" Simone chuckled with a shrug.

"Ya could set down some order, 'an some laws; don' imagine it would be easy, but ya know I'll be right 'dare wit' ya. So will tha men. Yer a good lass, ya got a strong an hard head, a good brain an a good heart. Gods know if it wans't fer ya doin what ya 'ave, we wouldn't ave made it dis far." Simone told her gently. Franchesca loved her. Simone was so modest. Truth be told she believed if Simone hadn't been with her the crew would be long dead, and Syandro besides. Simone was quick to see in Franchesca what sometimes took her a moment to see. She guessed it worked the other way too. Simone was leagues smarter than she believed. Here she was getting carried away with the situation before her and Simone stripped all the trappings away and laid it bare and simple. Damn, she was over thinking—again; Franchesca scolded herself briefly.

"Do you think she's right?" Asked Franchesca as she reached out and placed her hand on Simone's.

"Aye ta a point—like it or not tha world needs just a bit of rule bendin, an' law breakin. A little bad behavior is necessary. Ya know dat, after all when ya first hit tha streets wit' me ya 'ad ta help me pick a few purses ta eat. Tha world is full of sitations like dat. In times of war, nations are gonna need tha smugglers fer slippin past tha blockades; else lots of innocent people die. She's right dat pirates serve a purpose, evryone 'as a purpose... don' we choose what we become in tha end?" Simone asked. Franchesca stared at her and smiled—suddenly feeling the pressure and weight fall away from her shoulders and heart, her mind suddenly clear and easy.

"I don't know what I would do without you, my love. You truly are wiser than you realize." Franchesca told her as she rose from her seat and walked over to Simone and kissed her gently.

"I 'ad a good teacher." Simone replied with a reassuring smile as she placed a hand on Franchesca's face staring into her eyes.

"So, are ya gonna do it? Are ya gonna sail fer Tornusia?" Franchesca took in a deep breath and finally allowed herself to bite her lower lip.

"I'll propose the idea—but I will leave the decision to the men. A vote, for that, seems most fair. We've all been through these trials together. We face any new ones together; they have a right to speak their thoughts." Franchesca confessed. "But I'm going to tell them exactly what you and Ayzza told me. What we become in the end is up to us, but the world needs a change."

Simone nodded and smiled. "Aye, it does." She replied running her thumb over the top of Franchesca's hand. They were sweaty and caked with filth, yet their eyes sparkled with the possibilities of what lay ahead.

"And you will be right by my side. If I'm to sit anywhere or become anything—I want you and only you, to be beside me; cheritte." Franchesca told her peering back at her.

"Always will be, cher." Simone replied as she leaned in and kissed Franchesca's pale lips.

* * *

The next day Franchesca called the crew together. While she stood upon the quarterdeck, the men stood on the main deck and conversed amongst themselves waiting for her to begin. Even Syandro exited his cabin, though only slightly so. He leaned against the doorframe; one hand resting upon the pommel of his blade while the other wrapped around a bottle of wine. Any who caught a glimpse of the cabin beyond where he stood were able to see that Syandro vented his frustrations within the confines of the cabin.

Slash marks were scored into the wooden panels. Maps, books, and sheets were littered about with no regard. The stubble of a growing beard, which Syandro had ignored, and continued to neglect to shave; grew from his youthful features. He tilted his head back and took a long swig from the bottle before turning his head to spit onto the deck. Let Franchesca worry about what to do next.

He'd gotten them this far; he reminded himself bitterly—his mistakes, his recklessness, and stupid pride. What would his father say if he laid eyes upon his son now, what would he be feeling? Shame, Syandro whispered to himself as he took another drink. I feel shame over what I've gotten us into, why wouldn't he? I ignored every bit of advice and wisdom he ever spoke to me, Syandro thought. Once the bottle was drained, he threw it over his shoulder back into the room and sighed. An impossible situation—yet he felt more confident that Franchesca would find a solution to the mess he'd gotten his men into. No. Not his men—he told himself; her men—they'd always liked her, always favored Simone and her over him. They served under Syandro, but they were loyal to Franchesca and Simone. They always had been, he was just too much of a fool to see it.

Pride might have gotten the better of him in many situations, but this wasn't one of them. In this case, he knew better; he was able to admit he was not fit for this sort of thing. At least he now—that particular lesson sank in deeply. Sailing for countless months, keeping men's spirits and morale up, working like a dog in the hopes of a reward. Syandro took in a breath and hung his head. How his father must look upon what became of his son, it made him shiver with disgust. At least he knew it was better for him to step aside—perhaps that was his only saving grace. He was sure his father would think so. His father told him that everyone had a place and served a purpose. Some are better at a particular task than us, let them do it; trust them and use it to your advantage. Perhaps there is hope for me yet; Syandro smirked slyly as he watched Franchesca approach the damaged railing. Standing behind her, off to one side was Simone. Where Franchesca was, Simone was usually not far behind. Also following behind her was the woman whom they'd found lost at sea; Ayzza; if he recalled her name correctly. Syandro crossed his arms over his muscled chest and leaned against the door frame, letting it support his weight. He had far too much to drink, and he knew it, but his recent failures and debacles hit him hard. At least if he leaned upon the door frame and kept his movements to a minimum, he would not make a fool of himself. The last thing he needed was to fall down drunk in front of these men. He might still piss himself while leaning against the door, but if he did, perhaps no one would notice because he was moving so slowly. As it was, he was all but invisible. At least that was something to hope for should such an event happen. Gods, had he fallen so low already? He watched as Franchesca cleared her throat and held her hands up in a gesture requesting silence.

"Friends, and companions—I am here before, you to ask your opinion—to take suggestions and take a vote on our next course of action." Franchesca announced as many voices that had a remark, a thought or a joke to put forward—all spoke at once; as gathered crowds usually do—the call of seabirds adding to the lively discussion. Many shouted how they thought they were lost in a situation from which there was no escape. Others shouted their solutions, many of which were not actually solutions at all. As the debate rose in volume and intensity, Franchesca called for order once more, trying to keep control over the situation before it turned ugly.

"Let's not lose our heads over this. Unfortunately, enough heads have been lost, and enough blood has been spilled. Now, we know that our captain has made mistakes yes; he did order an attack upon an innocent vessel of a friendly nation, but that was through no fault of his own. I propose an unusual course of action, only if you will follow me, my friends." Franchesca announced. The crew waited; with baited breath as they listened to her speak.

"I propose we limp over to Tornusia, and we take Konrad's place. The seas are lawless; too lawless. I propose we assert ourselves and bring order and some small measure of law. You know as well as I do, we cannot sail home to Castella; not with as much damage as we've suffered. As it is now, we sit between two ports, Forn and Tornusia. We are not, cruel and black of heart as Konrad; nor any of his ilk before. But make no mistake lads—when we were permitted to hunt down Konrad we became pirates. How many of his ships did we sink? How many of his men did we kill, and how much of their coin did we take aboard and stow in our holds?" Franchesca told them passionately. Syandro listened to it all with a hollow pit of resentment in his gut. Even as she stood atop a pulpit and condemned him and it'd all been his fault for trying to make her jealous, for trying to impress her. She didn't condemn him, not outright—but he knew. When she spoke of mistakes, she spoke of his. He was in charge. When she spoke of failings, she spoke of his. Though she avoided speaking his name, there could be no doubt even the crew knew they beloved new leader spoke of him. Syandro let out a sigh; he supposed he couldn't blame her. Though he was surprised, he never thought that Franchesca was the type to salt a wound. Syandro quieted the rage in his mind and forced himself to listen once more. Not that he cared overly much. He wasn't here to make decisions anymore. Still, who was she to condemn him? Especially now when she proposed limping to a pirates paradise.

"There is a difference between killing pirates, and killing merchants." Cornando told her as he stepped forward. He moved through the crowd smoothly as they parted for him. He stood in front of them and glowered up at her, his gaze intense and unwavering.

"Aye, indeed there is; but what about attacking smugglers? What about keeping the waters of the world safe from those who seek to harm the shores of our homelands? What of offering our service escorting ships, or offering our services to those in need? Konrad was a bloodthirsty black–hearted beast, but he was only one such pirate." Franchesca illustrated with one finger. She pointed to all of the crew and held up her finger.

"He was one man and look at the terror he caused." There was a murmur of agreement. "I am not talking about becoming the next terror of the seas. I don't want to be the bane of Forn's trade routes, nor Castella's. I don't want to plunder Austinean ships for their cannons and weapons. I would seek to protect them from those who do wish to be the terrors of their navy's, of their merchant captains; of their coasts. I wish to protect them from plunder and bloodletting." Cornando ran his hand over his thick beard and sighed.

"You speak of a noble cause, and you speak of it with beautiful words." His thickly accented and scratchy voice acknowledged. With a heavy sigh, he nodded but placed a finger up. There was always a condition, always a warning with Cornando; with the Conquestlara's and Pistolero's¬. They would do nothing to endanger the name and honor of the royal family of Castella. How they aimed to handle the stew pot of a situation Syandro had dropped them into, was a question Franchesca wondered about.

"I will accompany you, and I will stay to see what it is you make of your noble plan, but I must return to Castella in the end. And you will allow me and my men to do so, and if you become what you swear against; rest assured I will make all known to the royal family of my land. If you wish me and my men to accompany you, then you must agree to these terms. You will have to release us, even if you know we will speak ill of you and condemn your activities." Cornando said as he walked up the steps leading up to the quarterdeck. He extended his hand. Without a moment's hesitation, Franchesca shook it.

"I promise I will not endanger your honor Cornando or that of your men. You will remain as honorable and as virtuous as when you set out from the docks with us." Franchesca smiled as she clasped his forearm with her free hand.

"We shall see. I have already lost a great deal of honor" Cornando replied softly, his gravel tone; adding more of a chilling warning than perhaps he intended. His roaming eyes alighted on Syandro leaning against the door to his cabin, and a dangerous scowl darkened Cornando's face as he glared at the youth.

"All in favor of carving out a place in the history books, any who wish to bring law to the otherwise lawless sea, speak!" Franchesca shouted. The crew erupted into a loud cheer and stomped their feet aboard the deck of the ship, creating a dull thunder that added to those who clapped their hands. She doubted there was a soul aboard who wished otherwise. Say perhaps for the unmoving Syandro. Gods—what did she do to you? Franchesca thought silently as she held him in her gaze for a fleeting moment.

"Make ready and set our course! We sail for the island of Tornusia, and we will not stop until our place in history has been carved into the songs and tales until we become legends!" Franchesca gripped the pegs of the ship's wheel and gave them a hard turn as the men aboard rushed to their stations and readied their ship to sail once more upon the pitching; rolling waters of the uncontrollable seas. The turn was perhaps a bit much. She worried the moment she'd done it that the rudder might've broken, in her effort and flare of being dramatic. Syandro sneered as he leaned against the door frame, keeping himself upright as the ship turned. So Tornusia was to be their course, their next port as well as their lively hood. She had towering aspirations; Syandro had to admit that much about Franchesca. Even before she left her comfortable life of lace and her father's shadow, she spoke to him of grand aspirations. It was one of the things he loved about her. It was nice to see that she still dreamed big. Let us just hope they bear fruit darling one, he thought to himself with a chuckle. He watched her at the helm of the ship; perhaps there was a way for him to redeem himself and his pride after all. I guess we shall have to wait and see what new adventure awaits me upon the island of pirates; Syandro thought as he stumbled and shuffled back into his cabin. He slammed the door behind him and moved awkwardly towards his bed. He collapsed onto it and reached down searching for another bottle of drink. No sooner had he brought the bottle up, he lapsed into unconsciousness. Claimed by the alcohol and the rocking of the ship, he drifted into a dreamless sleep awaiting the next of his own life's adventure.

Chapter 23

By dusk of the fourth day, the bustling ports of Tornusia were in sight. All was quiet, though something nagged within Franchesca; something trying to warn her that the quiet wouldn't last long. She felt Simone squeeze her shoulder reassuringly. There'd been a few close calls on their admittedly short voyage to the island. On the first night a terrible storm hit, it battered the ship terribly. It took all hands, all their wit and focus on making hasty and shoddy repairs; to assure they could still sail through the worst of the storm. For a long while, it appeared as if the storm might actually claim them. They made it through, having to stretch their patchwork and move repairs from one damaged section to a new, even more, damaged section. The lower holds held ankle deep water, and it felt more like walking through a marsh than the holds of a ship. The food stores in the lower hold did not make it through the storm and were destroyed, and much to the dismay of the crew; much of the ships ale and other drink stores had been lost. It had taken a good deal of reassurance, but Franchesca let the men know they were not far from their destination and they had enough to last them until they arrived. She hoped she'd not lied; now with land in sight, she knew she hadn't. Ayzza stepped beside Franchesca and smiled, her youthful features seeming brighter than they had in days; as she gazed upon the land.

"Home." She whispered with a contented cast to her features. Ayzza took a deep breath and nodded. New trials lay ahead, but she had a good feeling about the future—for the first time in a long while.

"For you perhaps, I haven't a clue what to do, once we arrive." Franchesca announced quietly. "You never discussed that with us." Ayzza turned and sighed as she took in Franchesca's tense posture.

"Don't worry; I will guide you. Upon our arrival, simply pay the harbormaster; and wait aboard until I return tomorrow. There are a few things

I must gather." It had been too long since Ayzza felt the reassuring and comforting presence of her staff, the driftwood worn smooth by her constant handling.

It was as much a part of her as her eyes, and though she was clothed, she felt strangely naked without it. If she was forced to remark on her clothes, they too felt, wrong. She missed her old garb, even though they were little more than rags. They were comfortable, and they were hers. These felt strange and awkward.

"After I have tended to the matters I need to attend to, I will return and guide you." Ayzza assured.

"What of the crew? They will want to drink, amongst other things." Franchesca replied. She didn't want to think about what other things the crew might want, though she knew. In truth, they were things she wanted. A warm bed, hot fresh food. Perhaps chief amongst them, time alone with Simone.

"I made no mention of the men." Ayzza announced, with a sly smirk. "I told you to wait aboard until my return." She continued. Franchesca gawked at her as if puzzled. Why should she have to wait? Why could she not go and have a drink, by the holy name of every god she knew, she certainly needed one.

"Fear not—all will be revealed upon my return." Ayzza told her with a gentle smile, as she patted Franchesca on the shoulder. Despite all of her worries, so far the docking at Tornusia had been a quiet affair. It was far less murderous, lawless; and rough and tumble, as Franchesca once assumed. It seemed like any other port in the world. Men unloaded ships; cursed gambled their pay, and drank just like anywhere else she'd seen. Some lay slumped against buildings with caps pulled down to shield their eyes from the setting sun. If she didn't see them, stirring moments ago, she would have thought them dead. When asked about their business, Ayzza stepped forward and flashed a smile and simply replied that it was their own.

Franchesca gathered that must have been an appropriate response because the Harbormaster just smiled and walked back down the ramp. Perhaps it was a pirate's line. A way of getting to dock with giving nothing away about where you'd been; what you intended, or what you carried in your holds. Well, if they wished to search their holds all they'd find would be seawater and waterlogged booze. Ayzza turned and nodded to Franchesca, reminding her of what she mentioned earlier. While the others disembarked the ship, Franchesca remained behind along with Simone. Simone didn't have to stay but chose to. Franchesca couldn't say she minded, nor could she say she pressed very hard for Simone to go off and explore. She wanted the company in truth; at least someone to stay behind. The fact that Simone decided to stay was all the better. The two of them hadn't been alone—for gods; she couldn't even recall how long, now. Perhaps that was another reason which led to Simone deciding to stay aboard with Franchesca. Whatever it was, this time would be far less solitary, and much more enjoyable now.

Few others were left on the ship—though she couldn't say for certain if Syandro took his leave of the vessel or not. Cornando sharpened his blade on the deck, whilst a few of his men spared and practiced their blade work. Francesca leaned against a rare undamaged section of railing and peered out over the harbor. Ships of all different forms and shapes bobbed in the water. For many long moments, she found herself trying to wrap her mind around where so many types of ships came from. What were their purposes, what was the story of their captains? Did they serve in a fleet? She supposed these ports were perhaps stopping grounds for many smugglers; maybe even fishing vessels docked here and did a bit of business. Not every one of these ships could be a pirate ship; surely not. Folk of the island needed to get fed, that meant that some of them must be fishing boats. Looking out over the number of ships, Franchesca felt a tug of doubt pulling her mind. Could she truly change anything? Perhaps Cornando saw through her; maybe he saw the doubt that plagued her. Were his words a warning, or an expression of lost faith?

"Something troubles you Miss Franchesca?" Cornando asked, as he stopped running his whetstone over his blade momentarily and began examining his work. If it weren't for his thick Castellian accent, she would have sworn it was Claude speaking to her. She missed him terribly. She wished he were here—he would know what to do, he could guide her.

"I just never expected... this." She replied as she held up her hands and sighed. Franchesca sank to the deck and rested her head against the wooden bars, posted every few inches; propping up the ship's side railing. The sight before her was nothing like what she expected. Where Franchesca once thought of a rundown backwater, with a collection of primitive huts and a run–down harbor, perhaps made of tarpaper shacks—she saw a large town; not unlike the ones she visited in Forn when accompanying her father on business. Though it was smaller, it was still larger than what she expected; and what she prepared herself for. It was cleaner, though it bore normal refuse; grime, and dirt like any city or place where people gathered. From her place aboard, she could see people laughing and joking. Children ran about the streets, and merchants sold their goods. She pictured this place as a lawless, filthy backwater; filled with murders, and whores. What she saw looked like what she left behind in Forn or Castella. Its architecture was a miss–mashing hodgepodge of different styles, and though it didn't always appear like it went together, somehow it found a harmony of its own. This place was a collection of many people, of many cultures; living and sharing customs. Gods—she'd been a high–necked, elitist bitch. She allowed her own preconceived ideas color her judgment about a place she'd never been to. It was the exact same thing her father had done with dockside taverns—or any taverns. Franchesca sighed as she gazed out from the ship. This was only what she could see at the docks; by the Heavenly Lady, what must the rest of this place be like? She asked herself in stark wonderment. She glanced over and watched as men lugged in a brimming fishing net; and thought herself the biggest hypocrite, and biggest idiot upon the face of the earth.

"You expected less, and you hoped that all you sought to change was laid out and founded by fools." Cornando observed with a light–hearted chuckle.

"I had certainly hoped." Franchesca replied with a gentle smile. She hated to admit it, but she could. She'd been wrong. On the surface, it rather looked as though she would enjoy it here. Fireflies lit up the growing shroud of night as they hovered over the beach and the docks. Sea Owl's let out their calls as they took to the air to do their twilight hunting.

"Tornusia was once a stop along a trade route of many nations. It was, how to put it—it was a place governed collectively. The nations of Forn, Castella, Austinia; they all had a claim upon the land and so treated it as a neutral territory. Each had a hand in building it, which is why you will notice the differences in architecture. Castellian haciendas settled next to Fornish chateaus, and those stood next to Austinean lodges. Yes? Each wrote laws for the charter, each had a governor that was part of a council, and for a time things went well." Cornando explained as he began to polish his blade.

"What happened? I must say, this is something I never learned or even heard of in my history lessons back home." Franchesca asked as she uncorked a leather wineskin that she'd been holding.

"I would imagine not. Many only teach the history of their regions and traditions to their youth, when a broader view is studied—very rarely do tutors speak of failures to the young; unless they are being groomed to take military command so that they might study the mistakes and learn from them. They teach those they groom for military command of failures so that they can learn from them and never repeat them. Why history is not treated the same way, I can only guess." Cornando replied with a smirk as Franchesca leaned over and passed him the wineskin. He took a small drink before passing it back to her.

"Is that why you know of it? Is—that why you said what you did to me?" Franchesca inquired quietly; as if ashamed feeling that Cornando had seen something within her that she hadn't. Indeed perhaps he did, perhaps he saw a girl dreaming lofty enough without the brains to pull off what she desired.

"Yes; I learned of the, shall we say corruption of Tornusia when I was younger and studying military matters. It was a great folly, so they say." He told her. "I told you what I did because Miss Franchesca, I have seen a great many noble and kind hearts set out to do great things, and create a better world around them. I have seen those same great, and kind hearts be corrupted by their own ambitions and their own successes. It is a danger that lurks beneath the skin of us all; the gods didn't craft us shining, and perfect. They instilled in us flaws, the same ones. Some are more easily seduced by them... others..." he paused and smiled as he studied her "seem to resist them until the end of their days." Franchesca felt a grin cross her features.

"I said what I did as a warning; you are flawed Franchesca, as am I. I told you what I did because; I don't care to see your name go into the history with a stain, such as Konrad's will. True enough, you have quite a load of work before you, but I do have faith in you." Cornando told her as he polished his blade.

"I only ask that you keep what I said in mind." Franchesca nodded as she took in a breath of fresh air and listened to the gentle, lapping of the water against the ships of the harbor, accompanied by the sounds of merriment and laughter.

"So, what happened—to Tornusia?" Franchesca asked as she took a drink, letting the sound of the waves calm her nerves. Cornando quietly rose from where he sat and sheathed his blade and smiled.

"That I am afraid is a tale for another time. I am going to turn in for the night Miss Franchesca; I hope you will sleep well. May the gods watch you, and may all your voyages be peaceful ones." Cornando bowed as he strode below deck to his cramped room. After that, the night seemed to pass at a crawl.

Franchesca lay next to Simone but sleep refused to come, and for countless hours she lay in her bed awake gazing at the ceiling. Her mind raced from one thought to another. One memory bled into dozens; many were of Claude. Her heart ached when she thought of him; for she missed him more than anything else in the life she left behind. She wondered how he fared, and what he was doing at the moment; Franchesca wondered such things often. Her thoughts drifted to more current matters, such as Ayzza and the strangeness of her sudden appearance once she found the Quest. Was it merely a coincidence? Franchesa sighed as she rolled over feeling the smoothness of the covers brushing her skin as she moved. Her life had suddenly become very strange and complex, and Franchesca felt herself struggling to find ways to unravel the tangled mess of confusion it had become. Suddenly her mind drifted to a darker corner; to that fateful encounter and the bastard who sought to destroy her to garner a loan from her father. Quentin, that despicable black–hearted leach! There'd been many times Franchesca hoped she would cross him upon the seas so she could cut his hands from his arms before kicking him overboard. Sharks would rush towards the scent of his blood, and they would pull him apart; he would be nothing more than an unpleasant memory. She clutched her fists as she recalled the name and her cousin's features. His face stared at her in the darkness as her mind recreated its image. His hawk–like features and blonde hair so bright it held the appearance of sun–baked wheat; his calculating unfeeling brown eyes, the eyes of a man that would kill a friend if the price was right. A ruddy dirty brown to match his soul—often it was it said, one's eyes were a gateway into their soul; Franchesca could believe that was the case with Quentin. Even her father carried more feeling within his eyes than Quentin. Cornando told her not long ago that the gods did not make humans without flaw, but hatred of Quentin was something she embraced with enthusiasm. If it took the rest of her days, if it caused her death, she would find him, and she would kill him for what he'd done. If she died in the act, at least she would die happy, knowing he preceded her. She only hoped she had more than a damaged ship to her name when she found him, so she could rub in how much more successful she had become without her parents to stomp his pride against. After all, their last encounter had been when he came to demand money from her father, Franchesca left with the intention of becoming a self–made woman. Franchesca prayed to the Heavenly Lady for a quiet mind, and a calm heart; though she knew not how long she prayed she could feel sleep tug at her. She felt Simone roll over and drape a gentle arm around her. Franchesca couldn't help but smile. At least Simone was at peace, at least she could sleep. That thought along with her silent prayers helped to relax her. Somewhere in the middle of a prayer, and the brushing of Simone's exposed flesh against hers, sleep finally claimed her.

The next day Franchesca stood aboard her ship, awaiting Ayzza's return. As she stood upon the quarterdeck of her wounded vessel, she watched as other ships sailed towards the island. Tattered sails of saffron, dingy grays; royal blues, reds, purples, and greens rustled in the wind as they moved closer. Some ships she recognized as being designed by the folk of Ojin or Dea—ships of all sizes, tall and thin maneuverable vessels; or broad fat behemoths that trudged through the water with the black flags atop their masts fluttering and snapping. Still, others looked completely alien and stranger still to her. Something told Franchesca that these were ships of greatest importance. They appeared to be better maintained and extensively armed. As she gazed through her spyglass, she could see that some sails bore strange, unfamiliar runes or lettering upon the corners. One ship even bore an incredibly intricate pattern stitched out in gold and silver thread. Where was Ayzza? Franchesca wondered as she watched the approaching vessels draw closer to the harbor.

"And you've not seen all of it." A familiar voice announced from behind her. Franchesca heart leaped in her chest and started pounding. Why did people have to sneak up on her?

"Don't sneak up on me like that." She scolded, as she glanced back to see Ayzza on the main deck looking up at her with a sly grin.

"Come with me." Ayzza told her as she clutched her staff. Franchesca studied the garb the woman was clad in. A tattered and raged bit of fabric was tied about her breasts to conceal them and secure them. A simple long brown dress was tied around her waist with a length of rope while being open to the sides. Phials of water and dried starfish, as well as other various forms of preserved sea life, were knotted and tied into the coarse rope that synched her garment about her waist. Ayzza's skin was pale and soft; it seemed to shimmer with moisture; as if she recently went swimming and came out of the water only a hand full of moments before. It'd been a long time since Ayzza inhabited a form so young and lithe. Over her many years she amassed, and crafted many different garments; each suited to the body the gods had seen fit to grant her, upon her rebirth. In her last incarnation, she looked and dressed the part of a hag. Her clothing was little more than sackcloth, baggy and loose like her drooping skin. Now, however, she was young and vibrant. Now she could wear something more comfortable. Ayzza never made it a point to dress revealing or provocative on purpose, but she did enjoy when she was granted younger forms. The clothing was lighter, more stylish; and if she so desired she could dress in more plunging necklines, and revealing cuts of fabric. Tornusia did after all have a tendency to become quite hot, and humid in the summer; on occasion, those sweltering temperatures even lasted well into the evenings, and late nights. Though she hated to admit it, there were times when playing to the weakness of men accomplished more, and with less time, and effort than it would take for her to intimidate or use her magic's to get her point across; she could reveal some skin and get whatever information she desired. Ayzza hated when such things became necessary, rare though they were. Things were on the cusp of changing upon Tornusia, but they would only change so far, she was no fool. Franchesca might be able to accomplish much, but she couldn't change everything. She was getting ahead of herself. Another drawback to being reborn in such a youthful frame, she sometimes allowed her mind to run freer than it should have. Perhaps Franchesca was not here to change Tornusia. No, perhaps Ayzza had been led to this girl so that her great purpose might finally be fulfilled; whatever that might have been. Damn these long years and the failings of fragile mortal memories. She noticed Franchesca looking at her, and simply smiled. Time and the gods will tell. The first step lies before us now. Franchesca turned to Simone and nodded. The two of them followed Ayzza in silence. A million questions raced through their minds—but neither knew what to ask first or even if they should speak. Franchesca cast her gaze about taking in as many of the new and strange sights as she could. There were sections of a thick stone wall that surrounded parts of the town. Defenses that had been built long ago no doubt, she wondered if they could still offer any real defense and if so; how formidable would that defense be? The walls were unmanned; she suspected that had much to do with the fact men were awaiting orders. Evidently, Konrad felt so secure in his rule he thought it safe to pull guards from the walls. Posts were empty; and only taverns, brothels and other businesses of that nature remained open. It would have been easier to storm in and overthrow him here than fight him at sea Franchesca thought. No doubt there was some sort of skeleton crew left about to manage some hasty defensive effort; should matters demand such, but how much of a fight would they be able to put up? Or perhaps she missed guessed, and there was more structure to the island than she first realized. Franchesca had, after all, been expecting a rundown backwater; and was greeted with a small town similar to any other she had seen. Perhaps I should stop making judgments and simply observe, Franchesca thought. Damn it you're letting your mind burrow down the rabbit hole again.

Now that she allowed her eyes to roam about, she could spy cannons and a few crews that inspected and set about cleaning them. They might have appeared sparse, but that could have been by design. Further down she spied a few mortars that looked to be undergoing maintenance; while others went about drilling with the one in charge, an officer no doubt. He shouted out angles and his men rushed to tilt the mortar properly. Franchesca listened as he would add something like wind coming in from the south, stiff gust; it sounded like a strange code to her, but it was more work of the appropriate ways of loading and firing their equipment. The men clustered, would repeat what he said and then they shifted the mortar slightly and announced a new calculation. That calculation evidently being two drams less powder and a lighter five, pound ball since the wind came at their backs. When he called out a shift in the direction of the wind from south to north they corrected again making the addition of three drams extra powder to account for the shift in the wind. Franchesca had to say it sent a chill down her spine. These were men who knew their business; who knew their equipment. They drilled over and over, and she doubted that they made many mistakes, if any at all. These men sounded as if they could outperform any team from the Austinean, Imperial Gunnery Division. Perhaps they'd been from Austinea. What surprises does this place have in store?

Ayzza led them for what felt like miles through the winding streets. In some places, there were no paving stones, and they trampled through the mud; in other parts, the paving stones were cracked and jagged. Ayzza walked through the streets barefoot and made not a single protest. It felt strange to be on land again; to not have something constantly moving beneath her feet, Franchesca thought as her boots thumped against the earth. She glanced down at the mud and dust that now covered them and smiled. It had indeed been some time. If she had an accurate recollection—it'd been nearing on a year since she had last set foot on actual solid ground. Well, close to that Franchesca thought. By the gods, had it been so long. She thought back over the past months in her head and confirmed her previous calculations. She had to confess she missed it. The reassuring firmness, that steadiness beneath one's feet was something she had taken for granted before sailing. Franchesca peered up as Syandro stepped out of a barber's shop; his once stubbly face now clean shaven, and his once disheveled appearance now appeared neat and more composed. Though his clothes were still stained in a handful of places; they somehow seemed cleaner, and he appeared to look more and more like the Syandro she set out with from Castella, all those many months ago. He held open his arms with a smile.

"Fancy meeting you here." He said happily as he walked to join them. "To what do I owe the pleasure?" He asked as he fell into step with them.

"Ayzza is guiding me—somewhere; though where and to what, I don't have much of an idea." Franchesca replied.

"You will be meeting with the others who will hope to sit upon the Throne of Tides, once they find out Konrad is dead. As I spoke before it will be a complicated manner, and you will face many challenges. The more aid you have, the better." Ayzza announced as they rounded a corner and came to a square. Its paving stones still lay neatly in the shadow of a large, slightly rundown temple; wandering ivy and patches of moss clinging to the stones. Marble statues stood atop pedestals at the bottom of a stone staircase missing limbs; their once beautiful, flawless faces now cracked or chipped. Gargoyles leering out from the architecture above also bore the scars of their exposure to the elements.

Some gazed out upon the square with half their faces, where the other half had vanished, one could only guess. The smart guess was time, the ravages of weather—and drunken piratical pistol shots. Even the steps leading to the weathered oak doors of the temple were in various states of disrepair. Some were caked with moss; others had wandering vines twisting and tangling beneath the lip of the step. Others were cracked, and in some places, entire sections and chunks of stairs had fallen away. Despite its weather–beaten surface, the temple was beautiful; and Franchesca could immediately see that there had been many minds, from many cultures, which brought the structure into existence.

Ayzza leaned on her driftwood staff with a grin. Sapphire blue onion domes topped the front two towers of the structure, while a high pointed steep roof rose in the center; most impressive was what Franchesca couldn't see. There was a stark absence of visible seams between the bricks and stones. She had only heard stories of one race capable of such a masterful work of stone and masonry, Dwarves. Franchesca wondered what deity this temple once served; since it was brought into being by many different cultures, with entirely different religious beliefs and deities. Dwarves, Castellians, Austineans; and the Fornish who chose the religions to practice beneath the roof of this grand temple. Though Franchesca knew not who was worshiped within these walls in the past; she knew to whom visitors prayed to now. She had heard his name many times in her travels, by many a bloodthirsty man who sought to spill her blood. This temple was now a house of worship for Stromboze the god of pirates—of whom Franchesca knew little if nothing about.

"I take it by others; you mean other pirates?" Franchesca gawped as she eyed Ayzza and admired the impressive architecture that towered above them.

"Indeed I do." Ayzza replied, simply casting a single fleeting glance over her shoulder as they made towards the steps.

"Are ya daft, woman! ?" Simone stammered. "What do we know 'bout bein pirates?" She supposed she shouldn't protest too much. Before she'd arrived here, hells before she met Franchesca to folk like Syandro she was one ship away from being considered a pirate. Gods, maybe she did actually know a thing or two. Besides she did encourage Franchesca to come here, she did tell her that she could turn this island around; that she could be the queen of the pirates. Gods I used those exact bleedin woods, Simone thought.

"You know more than you think. You'll have more common ground with the fellows in there than you believe possible as well." Ayzza assured without bothering to look behind her. They ascended the steps and passed beneath an arch held aloft by grand marble columns. Ayzza placed a hand upon the heavy oak doors and allowed her palm to linger upon it for a moment. She allowed her hands to drop to the heavy iron ring and tugged the thick doors open. "This is where the meetings will be held until a newly elected throne holder is chosen. Let us cross that bridge before we cross the next." Ayzza smiled as the hinges squealed. The foyer beyond was dim; the only light came from two lanterns hanging from rings in the wall to either side of the door. Ayzza paused and stared at Franchesca.

"If you are to be taken seriously, you will need a name for yourself. Konrad, for example, was known as the Mad Dog; He who occupied the Throne of Tides before him was known as Villner, The Scarred. You will meet others with various colorful names, and you will need one yourself." Ayzza told her.

"Why can I simply not be... me?" Franchesca asked. She'd read historical accounts of famous pirates known by their given names. Johan Klass was one; apparently, he was a freighting bastard who beat the teeth out of anyone he fought and found ways to decorate with them. The histories claimed he called them mouth pearls. The mere act of recalling that bit of information sent a chill through her. What if there were other men like that in there? Konrad had a thing for bones. They adorned the outside of his ship, and she recalled seeing more than a fair bit scattered as decor inside; she supposed that fit the whole dog motif. Of course, Franchesca also remembered reading that old Johan

Klass didn't last very long. He'd risen quickly, become feared quickly—and gotten himself hunted and killed quickly.

"Though you wish to set men on a new course, the name you choose is meant to keep others from knowing your true name; from keeping them from becoming too friendly with you, lest they forget you are in charge. It's meant to be a protection from the other nations of the world who would seek to bring about your downfall. An intimidating moniker shows the world you're not to be trifled with." Ayzza explained.

"It is a way of you being able to travel freely through the world; it is usually also chosen by your personality or a trait you possess. I am sure you noticed Konrad tended to howl, or froth at the mouth whenever he was lost within the fog of battle, hence Mad Dog." Ayzza added. Franchesca could see the benefit. What might her parents do if they found out she'd been made a pirate lord? No doubt someone might aim to take advantage because they knew her once. The idea of a self–stylized moniker indeed sounded appealing.

"Yer always lookin at dat gun book ya brought wit ya, and tinkerin wit' pistols; an' yer a fine shot." Simone whispered.

"True, however pistol, gun, aimwell, goodshot or fireright; isn't very mysterious—nor very intimidating." Syandro interrupted. Franchesca smiled and considered the two of them.

"Flint, however, is." She announced with a smile that showed the pride Franchesca felt in herself for her quick wit. Ayzza nodded, and Simone's smile beamed just as brightly as Franchesca's own.

"That will suffice. I must depart from you for a time." Ayzza announced quietly. Franchesca made to protest, but Ayzza held her hand up to cease any discussion.

"All will be made clear in the end. For now, you simply go in and hold your own. I am sure you will be fine once you are within. I will return, I promise." Ayzza assured with a smile as she turned and strode back the way they came.

"One more thing before I leave." Ayzza said, holding up a finger. She glanced over her slender shoulder "show them strength, courage, and confidence. Do not show them weakness; if they sniff it out in you, much will be lost." Ayzza told them ominously as she pulled the door open and stepped through into the fresh air that waited outside. The trio stood in the dimly lit entry chamber for a moment; silence seaming to radiate from the stones of the building itself in a heavy wave, chilling the atmosphere. After a few heart-pounding moments in the dim light and piercing quiet, Franchesca broke the silence.

"Let us go make a name for ourselves." She nodded as she grasped the iron ring door in front of them. As the hinges squealed, the scent of cold stone, damp and dust washed over them. One more, Franchesca prepared herself to undertake a new adventure.

Chapter 24

The sight beyond the doors was one not entirely unexpected. A lean man with sun–browned skin and a face charming enough to have gotten him into trouble, reclined upon a wooden bench, resting his head on the thigh of a voluptuous blonde woman; clad in light sheer fabrics. She fed him grapes all the while smiling and touching his raven hair, almost longingly. Every so often her hand would wander down further. Her slender fingers rubbed his exposed chest, as his fine shirt lay unbuttoned and opened hanging off him slightly; on occasion the woman's hand approached the very southernmost borders of the man's trousers, only to trace a sensuous path back up his muscular chest and flat stomach. The scene looked like a cheap painting one might see hanging in a brothel; only it was being played out before her, rather than hanging still in a frame. His tricorn hat rested upon his stomach, which jumped up and down as he chuckled at something the blonde woman whispered to him and continued tracing her hands around it moving up and down his torso lovingly. Franchesca resumed her scan of the room and saw an ebon–skinned man from the lands of Kaffra, put his feet up on what was no doubt once an altar; dedicated to a deity—or deity's, she couldn't name. His sculpted chest, which was partly visible due to the opened sleeveless hemp vest he wore, glistened with sweat, as did his smooth brow. His skin was heavily scarred, though from partaking in a great many duels and fights; or some sort of ritual scarring, she couldn't say with certainty. Some appeared to be of a ritualistic nature, and her tutors said such customs of scarring rituals existed in Kaffra. His face was clean shaven, say for a small patch on the very bottom of his chin which he'd grown into a beard; twisted tightly and bound with a leather cord, so it resembled a rat's tail. Another dusky skinned man stood behind him and to the right, his dreadlocked hair pulled back and gathered in a topknot. Bracelets of precious metals or simple braids of leather hung upon thickly muscled writs—bejeweled rings decorated fingers and collections of so many necklaces of various materials hung upon the men's thick necks they must have produced their own musical rattle when they walked. As she scanned the room Franchesca noted a few men had large, golden hoop earrings hanging from their earlobes and everywhere she looked she could see more and more people.

Were these all captains? The world could not have so many pirates sailing its seas, could it? Franchesca wondered as she gazed around taking in broad chests, thick beards, scarred and tattooed flesh of the men around her if she truly stood a chance. Well, the world was an extremely, vast place she reminded herself.

"Newcomers I see." Said the man reclined upon the bench as a woman placed another red grape into his mouth. He smiled as he chewed it. Now that Franchesca listened to him speak, she could tell the man was from Castella.

"I believe you are lost little ones. Perhaps you should return to your homes before papa and momma call in you for supper, eh?" He chuckled as if very proud of himself for his jibe; as did the blonde haired woman. Did he think he was that witty for mocking their age? The blonde woman he rested his head upon was only perhaps two years older than any of then them. Franchesca felt anger rise within her. They'd killed Konrad the Mad Dog. The man who ruled over these men, and he was telling them to run home because they were young? I'll bet we could take him she mused.

"And I would tell you to return to your whoring mother's breast, but it seems you have found an adequate substitute." Franchesca replied hotly. The words were out of her mouth quick as a blink. Ayzza told them to be strong, not to let the other's push them around. Franchesca didn't realize she had the words rolling around upon her tongue until they'd been spit out. Well, they were out now, there was no going back. Be strong Ayzza told them; so she would. The man glared at her wide–eyed as the rest within earshot who were of lighter moods, or perhaps tired of the Castellian, erupted into roaring laughter.

"Sharp tongue on that one there," The Kaffrian with his boots upon the altar, chuckled a deep, rich and booming sound; his voice bearing the heavy and thick accent of his homeland. His cadence was unusual but not unpleasant, his accent thick enough that Franchesca had to pay close attention lest she miss what he said, or miss understand. Still, she found she rather enjoyed the man's voice. It was rich as honey, smooth, and as powerful as oak. She could hear the edge in it. Not of anger or malice, but if he wished to intimidate, or if he fanned flames of rage she had no doubt his voice would show it quite admirably.

"Still, I agree with the man there. This is no place for the likes of you. You are no more than a child..." he was cut off as another decided to make his opinion known, calling from the assemblage somewhere lost within the shadows of the room.

"And you are a woman." A haughty voice added as its owner stepped from the shadows. His clothes hung loosely from his average build and unimpressive frame. A long curved blade hung sheathed at his side as he crossed his arms over his chest. Franchesca could tell by the garb he wore and his accent that he came from the continent known as Sahar, though sometimes called the Crescent Kingdom. It was called such because the crescent moon was the chief holy emblem of their god, and the folk of Sahar were a deeply and profoundly religious people. Franchesca had heard the pride of many of the men of that land ran deep and flowed strong within their veins, and that pride had a less than favorable outlook upon women. That was unless of course, they were doing things other than managing a household; raising children, keeping their husband's beds warm, and their more desirable parts available and ready for their husbands use. She knew not all in lands of Sahar, at least she surely hoped not—shared this outlook; however, the one standing before her now certainly made his feelings clear. Franchesca merely smirked at him.

"I think I've earned my place here..." the smirk's quirking their way on to numerous faces along with the quiet snickers bursting forth from many of the captain's showed their opinion on the subject.

"What is your name girl?" The Castellian asked finally rising and sitting on the bench. She watched as the man placed his arm across the blonde woman and crossed his legs. No doubt to hide the growing tightening of his trousers, due to the woman's affections.

"Not that it is any of your business, but you can call me Captain Flint." She grinned. The olive–skinned man of the Crescent Kingdom scoffed and waved his hands dismissively.

"Yet another woman playing a game she has no business playing. I correct myself a child and a woman; playing a game, she has no business gazing upon. Be gone with you; your presence is an ill omen. Mark my words there shall be nothing but trouble if you stay." Franchesca felt her rage simmer. She didn't even know this man's name, but already she wanted to punch him. It was an action that might get her killed, she didn't know how well he fought, but it might be worth it just to wipe the arrogance off of his face.

"Trouble for you perhaps." Franchesca shot back with a calm, self–assured smirk, as she met the gaze of his intense brown eyes and kept her eyes hard and cold as stone. The Kaffrian man smiled.

"Go sit somewhere and brood Saaladan. Perhaps have one of your eunuchs attend to you." The broad–shouldered Kaffrian said. His voice and demeanor making it sound as if he were scolding a child.

"You call yourself a man? What know you of pride? Allowing a Haraht in our presence when we've matters of business to discuss? What would your father, and elders say if they saw you taking orders from a woman?" Saaladan asked angrily as he waved his hands about.

"My fathers would spit upon me for listening to you, before listening to her." The Kaffrian replied as he rose slowly and menacingly from his seat and glared down at him. Gone now was the voice which gave the impression he was speaking to a child. Now every thick muscle was ready to act in a most violent and unpleasant manner should Saaladan test him.

"Secondly, the woman has not given me an order; nor has she given you one. Now I would suggest slinking back into the shadows, like the dog you are before I make you fit to join your eunuchs." The heavily muscled, scarred man growled. Saaladan spat upon the floor before turning sharply upon his heels and stormed off. Franchesca watched as the Kaffrian sank back into his seat and placed his heals back upon the altar. She'd seen her father negotiate and argue with dignitaries, and nobles before; as well as haggle with merchants and traders, but it never became as heated or as intense as this. Franchesca remembered many an occasion when he went away on business, or when he'd been called to the palace to discuss military matters; when he came home, he always complained about negotiations and the politics that came with holding such a lofty name such as his.

A smile crossed Franchesca's face as she tried to imagine her father here. She imagined him trying to argue and getting tongue–tied, and watching as the sweat of fear and frustration beaded upon his brow; all the while knowing that the muscles of his lower back and shoulders were knotting under the strain of his nerves. Yet there she stood, calm as a Fornish breeze.

"Now that the interruption has passed, I must say... Flint did you say; I have not heard mention of your name before this moment? What is it you hope to accomplish here?" The dark–haired Castellian asked.

"Do not clutter your all too precious and limited thought space upon me; it is surely at a premium. As I am sure you have all heard, Konrad is dead; I am proud to say I had a hand in his downfall." Franchesca sneered as she peered over at Saaladan. The men gathered, glanced at one another; some with admiration, and others with disdain.

"Konrad is dead?" The Kaffrian asked with surprise written upon his features. A murmur went through the halls, and it was only then that Franchesca realized they did not know Konrad was dead.

"If you didn't know he was dead what are you all here for?" Franchesca asked. Somewhere behind her, she heard the familiar scoff of the man she heard addressed as Saaladan. No doubt he was formulating a rude reply, tied into her gender and her lack of knowledge; but he was not given a chance to speak.

"Konrad issued a summons to go over matters relating to his grand plan." The ebon–skinned man with the dreadlocks bound in a topknot replied.

"He was planning on starting a grand war that would have seen Tornusia as the dominant power of all the seas. More accurately, I think, to see him as the dominant power of the seas." The Castellian added.

"He liked to tell us little parts; he didn't think we spoke to one another; because it was something he avoided. He was wrong, however. After comparing notes when coming across one another, we found we were all collecting the same things. We also overheard many drunk sailors we overheard who also happened to belong to Konrad's fleet brag about collecting flags and the very same letters of colorless flag we'd been. His secrets weren't so great, nor were they as secret as he would have wished." The Castellian shrugged." We didn't know everything; but we knew enough to know to be worried, eh. From what we believed his plan was, we thought him a fool." He said calmly allowing the woman to feed him another fat grape.

"But if one likes to keep their head attached, you pretend you don't know a thing; and you pretend that Konrad is a genius, the likes of which you have never seen." The Kaffrian who kept his feet upon the altar announced. "So instead of learning about following a crazy bastard into war, we are here now to elect a new captain." He added with a sigh of his broad chest.

"Can't say I will miss him." The Castellian added as he reached down and picked up a bottle of wine. He took a long swig before offering it to Franchesca. "If you indeed had a role to play in sending Konrad to the watery embrace of Stromboze, then, by all means, have a drink." Franchesca smiled and politely bowed her head before taking the bottle and took a long swig. Hinges squealed once again, and Franchesca glanced over her shoulder as she passed the bottle to Simone; hardly able to conceal her surprise at the sight that awaited her. Moving silently through the doorway was a tall, slender figure—an elf. Never in her dreams did she believe an elf would take a seat in a gathering of pirates. She knew little of the elder races, but what she did know; spoke to their general distaste and distrust of the human race. A loud booming voice shouted behind the door, and heavy footfalls echoed as the thick doors were shoved open. She knew little of their history other than there was a great war between the elves long ago, a war that had split their race. Her history tutors said that some elves possessed dark and black hearts and raided human shores; taking slaves, killing and burning. Her tutors learned that those who died in the raids were the lucky ones. Few who were taken as captives returned; those that managed an escape spoke of horrors beyond belief. Many of those poor souls went mad because of what they'd suffered. Aiding in their push to madness was that, few if any who heard their harrowing tale believed their ravings. Her tutors were unaware if the elves answered to one authority or if the schism created long ago had repercussions which spanned through their entire race. What they did know was that there was a mistrust that ran between the elves towards men as well.

"You lanky toothpick of a pointed eared pantywaist!" A stocky, thickly built—bushy red–bearded dwarf shouted as he leveled an axe at the elf who strode into the room. A dwarf too, Franchesca thought to herself. She knew the dwarves and elves hated each other though she'd never really heard why; she only knew that dwarves and elves got along together like oil and water. Or more accurately like gunpowder and fire.

"I'll have your blood..." the stocky dwarf roared—his stout legs carrying him quickly after the much taller longer limbed elf captain.

"You'll have nothing master dwarf, you know the code. There shall be no bloodshed during the great meetings, and other gatherings. Unless ordered and carried out by the holder of the throne themselves; and since we are without a body upon the Throne of Tides, no killing until there is a new one to replace the corpse." The Castellian replied as Franchesca handed him the bottle. The lean elf paused for a moment, but only a moment as if considering something of vague interest. It was little more than a second before he continued on his path; leaving the angered dwarf behind.

"Hang the code! I want his ears Frabranzo, and I'll have them!" The dwarf roared as he stomped forward. There was a loud crash as a door upon the altar clattered against the wall. An elderly man strode out from the chamber beyond, accompanied by two heavily armored men with halberds in hand and swords sheathed at their waists. The man was hunched over and walked with the aid of a simple staff; much like the one, Franchesca saw Ayzza use. Despite his simple staff, his dress was fancy filigreed with gold and silver and the tricorn hat he wore upon his wrinkled brow; sported tall and exotic plumage. The full feathers of some bird the old man came across in his earlier days no doubt. Blue, white and black; they waved and danced as he walked. Wisps fluttered as if waving to the assembled men casually. The man removed his hat as the Kaffrian stood from his seat and offered it to the man. Franchesca could see that the aged man's hat bore a seal that was pinned upon the right side. As he sank into the seat, the Kaffrian found another and sat.

"You will do no such thing Obman Ironbrow." The old man announced as he cleared his throat. His voice seemed stronger than his age. "The code is law; the law of our kind. There is honor amongst thieves, eh?" The old man asked as he raised his snow-white eyebrows as the man smiled a smile that was showing the absence of many teeth. "Despite what outsiders might say, thank you Kaluka for warming an old man's seat." The broad-shouldered shaven-headed Kaffrian gave gleaming smile and gave a slight bow.

"Honor amongst some of them at any rate." The dwarf known as Obman muttered as he stomped over to a seat as far away from the elf as he could manage to find. The old man placed a pistol upon the altar where he now sat. Two more men entered the room hastily and smiled. Their black hair and facial features noted them as being from Ojin and the lands of Chuhuay.

"Some of our brothers have chosen to forestall this meeting, expressing their lack of interest in Konrad's summons. Though if my old ears have heard correctly, it now seems they have forfeited their interest to sit on the Throne of Tides." The old man announced. "Those of you gathered here now may wish to cast your name for consideration—others may be allies of those seeking the throne. In the end, one of you will sit upon the throne." The old man pulled out a pair of spectacles from a pocket of his ornate coat and placed them upon his face.

"I see there are some new faces, come forward and make yourselves known; present your piece of eight." He ordered somewhat authoritatively. Ayzza never mentioned such a demand would be made. Franchesca shrugged as she removed the leather cord from her neck and untied it, placing her father's ring upon the altar before stepping back.

"My name is Flint, my companions Syandro of Castella and..." Simone stepped proudly forward shoulders square and back straight.

"Steel," Simone interrupted with a grin. It'd thrown Franchesca, but she couldn't help but admire her. The elderly lord studied them from where he sat and sighed.

"And where is it you hail from, and what is the name of your vessel?"

"I hail from Forn; our vessel goes by the name of the Quest." Franchesca announced. There was a burst of laughter from the gathered men.

"When last I checked, that vessel was the property of the royal family of Castella." The old man announced. It was remarkable how was it he knew? Franchesca felt her mouth go dry. Gods, did these men have spy's walking about in ports around the world? Was that how they were able to know about the Quest. With an internal sigh the answer became clear as polished glass—of course, they did.

"Last I saw it was a barely floating pile of matchwood, bobbing up and down in the harbor." A newcomer from Ojin announced with a smirk.

"And yet here I stand." Franchesca announced as she spread her arms wide and cocked her head ever so slightly. The elderly man simply shrugged as a large book was brought over to the altar. It slammed down with a thump. As he flipped through the pages with his bony fingers, a quill was set beside him by one of the armored men. With a satisfied sigh; he finally stopped flipping through the pages and made a note, once finished he returned his quill to the ink–pot. He waved his hands and dismissed Franchesca who walked over and stood in the company of Syandro and Simone once again.

"It's gonna be a long day." Simone whispered as she patted Franchesca on the shoulder. Franchesca wished she could disagree, but it appeared Simone was right.

"Yes, I am afraid my dear that the changing of plans can cause for a bit of time to be spent in making repairs." The old man sitting behind the alter announced as he turned to Simone with a broad smile indicating that his ears were sharper than she or Franchesca thought possible. Perhaps this man avoided firing guns, and cannons—from the looks of him, he appeared to have crewed upon ships which used catapults, and scorpions as their weapons.

"Hasty solutions do tend to make for quicker disasters and numerous corpses." The old man added as he waived his hand and dipped the quill in the ink–pot once more. Simone's cheeks darkened as she blushed and she averted her gaze catching Franchesca's eyes out of the corner of her own as she glanced down. Off to a wonderful start, she thought.

Just as Simone predicted the day was long—and loud. After the presentation of the pirate captains assembled, arguments began between them. Threats of violence; boasts of deeds and skills passed from one set of lips and another; over and over. Franchesca simply stayed quiet, choosing to observe the animosity rather than become part of it; even though she was mentioned a number of times. Simone reached for her blade only to have Franchesca place her hand on Simone and shake her head slowly. Even Syandro on a few occasions needed to be restrained. She was not sure if this was a good thing or not. Ayzza warned not to show weakness. Surely a quick temper among pirates would be considered something of a positive trait; quick to arms and all that. She'd shown she possessed a level head perhaps that was the weakness Ayzza mentioned. Failing to become part of the heated arguments, allowing insults to roll off her back like water off a hull. Should she leap over the table and deck one of them? If so she knew who she would start and focus her attention on. Others threw bait in the waters to test her when she didn't take it they were content to move on. Saaladan however, was intent on insulting her and Simone; simply because they were women. How she wanted to spit in his face and kick him in the stones. Did he really think that just because he had a cock, and they had tits, he was better? She might not have engaged in the arguing; might not have partaken in the threats of violence, but every time Saaladan opened his mouth, her fists clenched so tightly they hurt. Franchesca locked eyes with the elderly man sitting behind the altar, observing the proceedings with nigh a word said. There seemed to be an unspoken admiration of Franchesca's control of her temper. Had he noticed how Saaladan spoke about her? Had he noticed that she had not fed the man his own teeth? Perhaps it was because she was not giving the old man a headache with constant bickering; whatever the reason behind it, Franchesca welcomed the look of approval. Such admiration could only help her cause. She hoped at any rate. Gods, she didn't know what she had to do! Damn it, Ayzza had been less than specific; now that she truly thought of it. Maybe she should start to argue, perhaps; a threat or two would help her case. As she took a deep breath, the old man cleared his throat. It was too late.

"You all know the way of it." The old man seated at the altar interrupted. Though he did not strain, or rise from his seat, his tone was authoritative without showing the slightest bit of effort. Briefly, Franchesca wondered how long he'd been doing this. She also wondered what exactly this was. His eyes were hard and paused upon every assembled body in the room.

"Votes are to be cast, and I'll not sit and listen until my ears begin to bleed whilst you all argue amongst yourselves. I only have so much time left of my life. I shouldn't be forced to listen to your petty squabbles. Do any of you damn captains think of how you inconvenience me when you lot die?" The old man asked gruffly.

"Then let us cast one vote now." A steel cold, yet calm voice called from the doorway. Somehow, without alerting a single person to her arrival and without the familiar squeaking of hinges, Ayzza entered the chamber. The collective whispering between the captains sounded like the hissing of gathered snakes communing with one another.

"As good a time as any is it not? Perhaps one voice will lay the foundation." Ayzza said, her driftwood stave clattering against the ground with an eerie sort of thump. The gathered captains gawked at her wide–eyed; Franchesca caught a glimpse of the old man as well. He might have mastered his surprise more quickly than the others, but there was shock written upon his expression for the quickest of moments. What by the Heavenly Lady was truly going on here? Franchesca narrowed her eyes and pursed her lips. There was a much grander picture here than she was not seeing or being made aware of. What am I getting myself into?

"The voice of the sea is ready to declare its vote?" The elderly looking man asked as he leaned forward, grinning somewhat joyously. Something hid behind his eyes; a curiosity, and a host of questions. Franchesca assumed that he smiled because there was a momentary lull in the arguing. Ayzza nodded and smiled as she made her way towards the altar and stood before the assembled. Franchesca glanced at Simone; they both wondered what was going on. True, she knew that Ayzza was readying herself to declare her vote, but how was it so many seemed to know her; and know of her so well? What caused them to murmur within her presence? What'd the old man meant when he asked if the voice of the sea was ready to declare its vote? Was it some cult, who took leadership from Ayzza? Ayzza seemed to know about everyone in the room, and the way they spoke around her made it appear that she knew all of them very well. What was going on?

"The sea casts its vote for Captain Flint." There was a murmur of outrage from a few men; others seemed indifferent, while others gaped about in a puzzled fashion. Most notable of the outraged captains was Saaladan. The elf captain seemed to take the announcement with a strange unresisting nod of the head. The dwarf captain crossed his arms over his barrel chest and just grunted. Weather a grunt of satisfaction or consternation, Franchesca couldn't tell; and she imagined no one else could either, she assumed that was the point. After all, she heard a dwarf would never agree with an elf; perhaps it was his way of agreeing without having to actually agree.

"The elder races will not go against the voice of the sea, which the gods have made flesh. I will cast my vote for Captain Flint as well; obviously, there is a hidden glory that will rise to the surface when it will be made apparent."

"You cannot be serious Ailmyrth!" Saaladan choked as he stepped forward. He scowled as he glared at Ayzza and the elf captain. "I cast my vote for myself, and my right to rule! At the last assembly, it was between me and Konrad; I see no reason why it should not be so now." Saaladan hissed as he rubbed his face and made, what Franchesca assumed, was a crude gesture in her direction. He moved with such fury and such anger that the loose, comfortable linen of his thobe snapped like a sail.

"I think I will throw my name into the mix." Frbranzo grinned. "Perhaps if people do not wish to vote for Flint, they will at least consider someone else before the Saharian. Seems to me his hot temper will get us all in a bit of trouble. Besides, could you imagine Tornusia without a brothel to its name? I shudder at the thought." He smiled as he shuddered; followed by a polite bow.

Frbranzo tossed a glance back at the curvaceous blonde woman who sat with him and smirked, which brought out a musical chuckle from her. Franchesca took all of the unfolding events in as best she could; though her head seemed to be spinning.

"It would appear we have three names up for consideration. Are there any others, speak now or hold your tongue until the next convening, which might not be for a long while?" The old man said as held the gaze of all within the room for a moment. After his gaze shifted between the assembled; he took in a deep breath and tapped his wrinkled chin. His eyes fell upon Ayzza who met his gaze firmly.

"You feel strongly about this one?" He asked, his question seemed to have more questions lurking beneath it, as though he refused to ask them. Franchesca couldn't say she blamed him. She'd only been introduced to these men a handful of hours ago. She was young, which in their language translated to inexperienced. It probably also had the added definition of foolish. I hope I can show them Franchesca thought. Gods what was she doing here, it wasn't the first time she'd asked either—she doubted it would be the last.

"Indeed I do. If you will remember I warned against the election of Konrad, and none would heed my warning." Ayzza nodded to each of them with a sly smile.

"Aye, but you would have had us leaderless as well." A man, whose name Franchesca didn't know, called out.

"Indeed, as leaderless as the seas themselves; those very things you claim to be the masters of, yet bow to one whom you all call master. Do you not find it strange? Sometimes the best course of action is the last one you would expect." Ayzza agreed.

"I would have had you leaderless then—now I have found one worthy of the position, and worthy of the title; worthy because she knows of respect, duty, and loyalty. I watched her place her needs and wants below others who needed. She worked as one of her crew, as well as fought and bled beside them, as have any of you. I watched her place her fate in the hands of her crew and only by their leave did she arrive here today."

"Sounds as though she is indecisive, to me." Saaladan nodded as he sat down and crossed his arms over his narrow torso.

"I've heard all I need to hear. Discretion is the better part of valor, so they say. Who amongst us has weighed our odds, or cast a vote before coming to a course of action?" The old man nodded. "The new one seems to have a strong wit, and a good head on her shoulders; sharp in tongue, and strong in battle. The newcomer has my vote, which places her above the rest of you. I suggest you all talk to your crews, in a week's time we will call a meeting of our fair island residence; wherein, you will all stand before them and plead your cases, and your causes. Once the citizens have cast their votes, we'll have a new body upon the Throne of Tides. The Keeper of the Code declares this meeting concluded." The old man said firmly as he hammered a small wooden block upon the altar with the walnut stock of his pistol. As the loud bang of wood against wood faded to silence and the ancient looking man made his exit—

there were murmurs, and a great many conversations started about the proceedings.

"You did wonderfully." Syandro whispered as a few broad shouldered bodies walked past him heading towards the exit. Simone patted Franchesca on the shoulder and smiled at her, nodding in agreement with Syandro. Franchesca felt as if her stomach were a box filled with butterflies, and her head throbbed with nervous tension.

"I'm glad you feel I did well; because this is exhausting." She groaned as she rubbed her head. Franchesca felt another hand clasp her shoulder and turn her around slowly.

"You're not finished yet, child." Ayzza nodded. "Follow me; the two of you may do as you please." Ayzza told them. Simone looked on with concern.

"Whatever ya 'ave ta say ta her, ya can say ta us." Simone asserted firmly, meeting Ayzza's gaze with cold, unflinching calm. Ayzza sighed, but nodded and motioned them to follow her as she led them from the temple; Franchesca could feel the icy, cruel eyes of Saaladan following her. As they exited the temple her ears caught the tail end of a whisper; in a language, she couldn't understand. The last thing she believed she heard was a throaty muffle of an agreement. As the door closed, Franchesca felt the night air wash over her. It was the best feeling she experienced in what seemed like forever.

"Where are we going?" Franchesca asked in a fatigued voice. Ayzza smiled, there was something about the smile that made Franchesca's hairs stand on end and made her spine feel more rigid than she ever remembered it being.

"Fear not, the trek is an easy one; once you reach the end, all will be revealed." With that last seemingly foreboding statement, Ayzza led them off through the twisting alleys and streets of Tornusia; their destination still unknown.

Chapter
25

A thick palm leaf seemed to jump into Franchesca's path as Ayzza led them through a twisting jungle swamp. Collapsed buildings and piles of crumbling stone lay scattered through the landscape; as did great muck covered rocks and fallen trees. Tall reeds and sawgrass rustled as their coats and scabbards brushed against them. More than once they had heard something plop and slither into the murky water. Simone glanced at Franchesca, and both suppressed a shudder. At least in these late hours of dim lighting, it appeared murky, perhaps during the daylight hours, the water was crystal blue. It was doubtful, but she'd just been made some sort of leader for an island; she wasn't about to dismiss anything. Franchesca took in the landscape as she paused to brush the palm leaf away. Judging by the way things appeared thus far, she doubted the water was clear at all. There was a clicking and scampering sound. Franchesca pulled a pistol from her holster. She breathed a sigh of relief as she saw a lizard with its claws clutched on to a tree. Franchesca began to wonder if this little trek was going to end well; the thought of another nasty surprise made her want to lay down and not get up. Not die exactly, but certainly lie down and sleep for a good few months. She found herself hoping that there would not be any more meetings and long–winded discussions of politics while being shouted from the tops of one's lungs. From behind she heard Simone utter a curse as she hacked her way through a thick mass of tangling vines.

"It is not much further now." Ayzza assured as the sound of a squelching muddy footfall followed after her voice had faded. That's what you said half an hour ago, Franchesca thought bitterly as she stepped over a jutting tree root. Despite the ache in her feet, legs and back; along with the tired wiry tension knotted in her shoulders, and neck—the chirp of crickets and the gentle spark of fireflies made things almost worth it. Almost. What she wouldn't give to sit before a warm meal, eat her fill and curl up to sleep for three days. She didn't even need a bed; she was so exhausted the hard floor sounded equally restful. Franchesca's nerves were on alert once more, as she heard the rustle of feathers and flapping of wings. Bright luminescent eyes seemed to absorb what little light there was; peered down at her, before letting out a high pitched call. This place is more likely to scare me to death than Konrad's ship, Franchesca thought to herself. After a few more minutes and an eerie silence, they arrived at a clearing of sorts. A dilapidated shack sat in the center of the path. Its planks warped and its roof sagging in numerous places. Many planks looked as if they were secured to one another with nothing more than twine or rope. Was this place even capable of staying upright in a stiff gust? By the gods, if the three of them walked over and blew upon it would the shack crumble to the ground?

"Did a single nail go into building this place?" Syandro asked no one in particular, as he rested his hand upon the hilt of the blade at his side. It had a quaint charm to it, Franchesca forced herself to admit. She supposed ramshackled shacks in the middle of swamps could possess a sort of quaint charm. It certainly seemed like the place where a witch might live; she'd read such things in adventure stories all the time. Of course, it also looked like it could have been a place where two lovers could sneak away and lose themselves in one another for a few hours. She had been known to read more than a few penny romance stories as well, and this place appeared as if it could be a great many things; a witch's hovel, a secret romantic hideaway—even a smugglers warehouse all seemed possibilities. Each as good as good as any. Of course in the stories, not everything ended well. She was in one of those stories now— with her lover, a friend—and even a witch. Hopefully, my life isn't about to become a penny novel; Franchesca thought to herself—or worse she reminded ominously.

"This is my home," Ayzza smiled, "be it ever so humble." She finished as she walked towards its crooked driftwood door. There was a squeal of well–rusted hinges as she pushed it open and extended her hand, beckoning them in. Ayzza smiled as Syandro crossed the threshold. "To answer your question, yes nails have been used." She smirked. Syandro simply shrugged. She hadn't insisted on Franchesca's companions remaining behind after the meeting for a few reasons; it would be easier to explain it to them all at once; rather than trying to have Franchesca explain it later. There were also matters that needed to be discussed, far better to do that as soon as possible. The darkness within seemed to be a shifting mass of blackness and pale gray, offered by the moonlight that shone through the numerous gaps in the timbers that made up the shack.

A dull thump broke the silence, and suddenly the tip of Ayzza's staff began to glow. A soft white light cast away the darkness that surrounded it; allowing Franchesca a glimpse at the interior of the rundown domicile. The door was not the only thing that was crooked; the tables seemed to slope, as did the few bookcases. A few lanterns hung upon the wall hooks; which Ayzza walked over to and lit with the tip of her finger. A glowing ember of flame danced upon her fingertip and no sooner had she lit the lamp than curled her hand into a fist, and the flame disappeared as if it'd never been.

"Please, let us sit." Ayzza told them as she gestured towards a table surrounded by a few large driftwood logs; which served as benches. Unlike everything else in sight, the table seemed to be the only ornate thing that existed in this otherwise simple home filled with warped driftwood furniture. The base looked to be carved in the shape of an octopus with the tabletop resting upon its bulbous head, while its eight tentacles acted as legs. The eyes of the wooden creature were made of some smooth sea–green gem, and set with two vertical slits of onyx; polished to a mirror finish, unlike everything else which seemed to be caked in dust, dirt, and cobwebs. Sitting atop the table was a large map that'd been sprawled out; almost taking up its entire surface. Syandro paused and turned his attention to a shelf full of jars. Some containing plants in varying stages of dehydration, others contained roots or soil. Still, others held murky fluids, and different forms of life suspended in the liquids. As he walked over he studied the jars curiously; he tapped on one filled with a cloudy yellow fluid that housed a strange looking creature. He tapped on the glass jar with the nail of his index finger and jumped back with a start, as the creature within opened its eyes.

"I'll thank you not to touch anything." Ayzza scolded as she pushed her nubile frame between Syandro and the wall of curiosities. A nervous smile played across Syandro's features as he stepped back and held his hands up in surrender.

"My apologies." He bowed stepping back. He looked at his hands as if that action alone would scold them and keep them inline. After his glare at his hands, he took a military's parade rest stance, with his hands locked behind his back. It was as if that were the only way he could keep them—and therefore him out of trouble. Syandro found he had to remind himself this was no noble's tea parlor or entertaining area. This room belonged to someone just as powerful, just as important—but far more dangerous.

"With all respect—what exactly is going on?" Franchesca asked in a tone of heated temper." When we pulled you aboard, you said that Tornusia was undergoing a change. You look no younger than me, yet those captains seem to know about you as if you were constantly in their presence; as if you were some great and mighty authority here." Franchesca said in a frustrated tone taking a step forward.

"Ya also seem ta 'ave great importance; seems a bit at odds wit' tha way which ya live." Simone noted with a curt nod, taking in the ramshackled hut. Ayzza simply smiled and bade them sit around the map covered table.

"The story of my existence takes place long before any of your births, long before the births of any of your known empires." Ayzza told them. "I have watched over this island, and the seas before there ever existed a Throne of Tides; or even truly a throne of any kingdom."

"Could we please stop traipsing through the hedge maze and get to the heart of the matter." Syandro interrupted as he gazed at Ayzza, hands still clasped behind his back. The last thing he wanted was to suffer some other terrible fate. He'd suffered enough at this point.

"If you so wish; the short of the story is that the gods bound the spirit of the seas to human form. It was done so that I might watch over the seas; all that has ever been told to me is that there will come a time when it decides the fate of many. At least I think its the spirit of the seas, so much that was once clear is—not anymore. Its as if I'm looking at something through a dirty window, covered in grime and cobwebs. I've been given some great purpose; as near as I can tell it has always been tending to this island and the seas, which the pirates claim to be masters of. Somehow I doubt that is truly the case." Ayzza told them fixing each of them with a glare. Franchesca cleared her throat and regarded Ayzza in a confused manner.

"So you... are a goddess?" Franchesca asked raising a curious and arching eyebrow. Ayzza shook her head.

"No, I am only a shepherd of the seas; their wild nature made flesh and bone. I have died many times only to be reborn; each rebirth brings with it a new mortal shell and a different physical appearance; just as the sea changes, so do I. With every rebirth more of my past becomes a mystery to me." Franchesca made to speak, but Ayzza held up a hand to stop her.

"After Konrad's death, I was reborn into the form you see before you. In this cycle of rebirth, something was revealed to me. I was to come across a captain, unlike any who have come before. Voices whispered within the winds and sea waters that shaped me, when all was done, I was guided within sight of your ship. A voice within me seemed intent that I find you. I can only assume that you are the captain revealed to me." Ayzza continued her revelation detailing how the politics of Tornsia had come to involve her, she spoke of centuries of mariners seeking her blessings and favor. Though she wasn't a goddess, men knew it tended to bode well for them if they knew of one who has the ears of the gods.

"So you are a guardian?" Franchesca asked. "You watch over the seas, and the creatures within." Ayzza gave a hesitant shrug but nodded. "To what end? And moreover why are you in the service to Tornusia and its pirate lords?"

"A fair question indeed," Ayzza sighed, as she hung her head. "In truth, I don't know or perhaps more accurately; I have a vague memory of a great purpose. Something the gods knew of that caused them to craft me; to give me life. As to which gods—I cannot even truly say as there are a great many gods, and sea gods in this world. None have seen fit to speak to me since my creation, not in any clear and meaningful way. It is always riddles and guesses. To that end, I simply try to follow what I believe the will of the gods. What I feel they guide me towards. I keep hoping that each and every death becomes my last. That I might be at one with the forces of nature once again. Though every time I hope—I'm reborn. I don't know why; I have never been told—and my own questions are met with silence, remaining unanswered. I've only ever been told through stray whispered thoughts, not my own; that a time will come when I am returned to the deep... a time when the need is most dire. Not even truly the deep, the deepest deep. I've no true understanding of what that means; no true way of finding out." Ayzza told them quietly as she peered at the map unfurled upon the table.

"So den I guess tha others 'ere fall in line bacause ta cross ya would bring quite tha consequences down on dare heads?" Simone asked as she ran a hand through her red locks. Ayzza chuckled.

"They try to keep on my good side true enough, but really the vengeance of the sea is not mine to dole out. I can harness its power; and be of aid, but as far as all else, they simply fall back into their superstitions, which works in my favor. I receive respect and privacy, so I don't discourage them. I am simply someone who can call upon the winds of magic; their minds do the rest." Ayzza took a breath before she could continue a black and gray–clad assassin burst in through the rickety front door. Another assassin clad in deep, dark reds, and blues dropped through a hole in the roof of Ayzza's hut. As the two assassins surrounded and cut off the escape routes; two more dressed in stark white garments entered through the front door. They all had their heads wrapped in layers of fabric; leaving only a small opening of exposed skin around their eyes. All four of them bore a weapon in each hand, a curved knife that resembled the wickedly hooked talon of a bird of prey. With their other hand, they carried a short yataghan—a curved blade which looked ready to amputate a limb or disembowel any who stood in its wielders way.

Syandro leaped from his seat and drew his Castellian rapier and dueling knife. Simone likewise pulled her blade free from its sheath and adopted a modified fighting stance she'd learned from one of the crewmen she and Franchesca sailed with. Franchesca pulled two pistols from the leather holsters at her hips and cocked them. The assassin wearing black and gray let out a loud shriek that was echoed by his companions adding their voices to the ululating battle cry, as they rushed forward. Franchesca's pistols barked like angry back ally dogs in a thunderstorm catching two of the men in their shoulders. They paused in their tracks momentarily before leaping towards her. Steel clashed as Simone and Syandro locked blades with their attackers. The assassin in the red garb shouted a command in a language, utterly foreign to Franchesca; but if she were forced to make a well-educated guess as to its origin, she would be able to do so with ease. Of course, she'd been given the clues of their weapons and their garb; those were some rather large hints. These were men of Sahar. As one of the assassin's leaped at Franchesca, she ducked beneath a swing intended to decapitate her; she grabbed her black powder pistol by the barrel and used the polished walnut handle as a bludgeoning club. She slammed its rounded grip into the assassin's knee and was rewarded with a loud crack and a bellow of pain from the attacker's throat. As he fell, she rose to her full height again and delivered a swift kick to his head, after that he remained motionless; but the gentle rising and falling of his chest let Franchesca know that he was still alive. The attacker clad in red advanced towards Ayzza. The deceptively young looking woman merely smiled at him.

"If you are fully prepared to die, then, by all means, allow me to indulge you." Ayzza said with a smirk. For the briefest of moments, Franchesca saw a flicker of doubt play across his eyes. Before that doubt completely ate its way into his mind and wrapped its tendrils around him, he lunged forward. He swung his yataghan in an overhead strike, meaning to cleave into Ayzza's skull.

She held her staff above her head, blocking the blow; and pulled her stomach back from the swinging, claw–like dagger meant to disembowel her. She hissed a single word in a language that sounded like rocks, grinding against one another and the assassin stopped in his tracks as if he'd been poleaxed. He dropped his weapons and began patting at his clothing hurriedly; his hands flew to the shroud that was wrapped around his face to conceal his identity in desperate effort to untie it. Franchesca watched as the ground beneath his feet grew more and more saturated with moisture. Once his face was exposed, she watched as water dribbled out from the corners of his mouth. His pain increased as he tried to suck in a breath of air but to no avail. Rather than sucking in air, the inhalation caused him to gargle and choke. It was only a matter of seconds before streams of water flowed freely from his eyes; then his nose, and ears. The assassin dropped to his knees and clutched at his neck before pitching forward and succumbing to the effects of Ayzza's magic. She'd drowned the man from the inside; the thought of such a fate made her shudder. What a terrible way to go. Ayzza gazed down at the dead man with cold eyes. The icy glare of an unrepentant killer. No, not just a killer; Franchesca thought, the death she'd just witnessed was a torture, and the lack of emotion shown by Ayzza sent a chill; colder and sharper than any winter storm, down Franchesca's spine.

"Come on ya weak little shit!" Simone jeered as she blocked an overhead blow and kicked her attacker in the groin, he doubled over and gasped. Simone brought her blade around and cleaved into the side of the man's skull. There was a light ping where Simone's cutlass hit against the small metal skull cap worn beneath the wrap, but the angle of the strike still cut into the side of the man's shrouded face and neck. Simone kicked him back and slid the tip of her blade through the man's throat; as Syandro hamstrung his opponent, following with a viper like, quick thrust of his dagger that tore open the assassin's neck. The man dropped his weapons and reached for his ruined throat with a wet gurgling hiss as his life slipped away. In the lull, there was another shout from outside, and scant seconds later there were a series of dull thumps. The sound of breaking pottery split the quiet as flames began to consume the shack.

"Persistent little buggers, aren't they?" Franchesca said to no one in particular. The sound of more shattering earthenware pots clattered against the back wall of the shack, and Ayzza hissed angrily at the turn of events. Flames crackled to life; growing in their ferocity and intensity, eating at the walls and the ceiling; Franchesca shook her head.

"We've got to get out of here!" She shouted over the crackling of the hungry fire. Franchesca glanced back at Ayzza who reluctantly nodded her head in agreement. The group made their way towards the front door as an arrow flew past Franchesca's eye and lodged itself in Syandro's shoulder. He let out a hiss of pain as they rushed from the doorway and threw themselves to the ground to avoid the storm of projectiles. Syandro knelt down behind a thick root and glanced at the shaft lodged in his shoulder. He gripped it as close to his flesh as possible and broke the remaining protrusion off with his free hand. Syandro let out a sharp breath and pounded his fist into the dirt. There would be time to get this attended to by a churgeon—provided they lived through this ordeal. He fully intended to, and he would see that at least Franchesca did as well. He picked his weapons up from where he'd laid them and glanced over to see Simone pressed against a rock, while Franchesca and Ayzza lay behind a large mound of mud and reeds. Franchesca worked on reloading her spent pistols with a look of determined concentration. Syandro felt the hairs on his arms stand on end, and a tingle go down the back of his neck. The air grew cold, and there was a clash of thunder and lighting overhead. He listened as Ayzza chanted furiously; gradually flexing her fingers to make a fist. The closer her fingers drew together the fiercer the winds began to stir. Leaves rustled, and trees groaned; branches cracked as the wind howled, and gusted through the canopy and the marsh weeds. Franchesca rose from her spot of concealment as a swarm of arrows was loosed in her direction, each one flung far and wide before ever coming close to her. It would seem having this woman on our side is paying off; Syandro thought to himself as he broke from cover and ran over to Franchesca. The storm flung the arrows in all directions away from their intended targets. There were hollow thunks and thumps as the arrows were swept into tree trunks, or scratching sounds as they collided with rocks. Syandro spotted one of the bowmen and made his way over to him. The shrouded assassin dropped his recurve bow and pulled a yataghan from the sheath at his side. The engagement was brief, Syandro parried, and sidestepped his attacker's wild, panicked swing before kicking him in the knee; and plunging his dagger into the assassin's throat. He felt a jolt of pain flow through his arm as he stabbed the man. He glanced down at the broken shaft and growled. In the rush of battle; with his mind racing, he'd forgotten about his wounded shoulder. It didn't hurt, until that moment at least. A new opponent charged forward, his sword raised high over his head and a shrill battle cry flowing free from his throat; his white head wrap doing nothing to muffle the high pitched noise.

As the blade descended, Syandro stepped back; letting the blade harmlessly drop, before a new strike could be made, Syandro lashed out with practiced precision with his dagger and stabbed through his attacker's eye. The blade was withdrawn quickly as the man's body collapsed into the dirt; it shuddered and convulsed as death moved through his newly punctured brain removing his life by degrees. With a glance over his shoulder, he watched Simone open a man's neck down to the bone, only to make a sharp turn on her heal and amputate another man's sword hand at the wrist. As he held up the bloody stump, she shoved her blade through his chest and kicked him away. A third man leaped into the fray, armed with two short axes which by their look belonged to the same continent the men's swords came from. Simone jumped back as her opponent tried to cut through her skull, and parried a blow meant to cut her stomach open. Simone lunged forward and closed the distance faster than her opponent thought possible. She reversed her grip on her blade, ducked and quickly drew it across his stomach; his gleaming white garments were now stained crimson from the wound on his stomach. Simone kept low and swept his feet out from under him. As he fell to the ground, she punched her blade through his chest. He gasped only a second before his head lolled lifelessly to the side. There was a clap of thunder as Franchesca brought her pistols to bear on two foes. Their heads flew back as brain, and bits of skull burst into a cloud behind them before they collapsed to the ground. Franchesca tucked the pistols into the holsters at her hips and tugged her cutlass free as a third charged her with a howl. She swatted his blade away before decapitating him. Franchesca stood there, trembling as blood from the freshly made corpse sprayed her. Her chest heaved, her heart pounded. Gods was it hot or was it just her? Her mouth felt dry as sand, and it felt as if she weren't within herself. She'd killed before, why was this so different? She stared at the blood staining her clothes and the steel of her blade with saucer–wide eyes.

Don't let them see weakness, she remembered. Franchesca forced herself to blink and take in a deep breath. The coppery scent of blood was thick in the air; most likely because it was splattered against her face so close to her nostrils she worried about snorting it into her nose. She'd killed before, but it never got any easier. Was that a good thing or a bad thing? It was a question she would have to ponder later. Franchesca slid her cutlass back into its sheath with a steel hiss and tried to will her heart to calm. This was too much—today too much had happened. She just wanted to lie down and sleep, to curl up and close her eyes for a week. What were the chances of that? She gazed at the headless body and shook her head trying to bring herself to a calmer state of mind. It had only been a matter of moments, but it felt as if it had been hours. They stared on helplessly as the flames continued to devour Ayzza's shack. There was a rustling of leaves and branches, Franchesca turned her head and watched as one of the assassins broke from cover trying to flee. She pulled a pistol free from a holster that hung just below her shoulder and took careful aim. As he leaped over a log, she squeezed the trigger. The man fell clutching his leg howling in pain. As the blue–tinged, gray smoke wafted from the pistol's mouth; Franchesca's heart began to race once more in an anxious rhythm. Would this day never end? She tucked the pistol back into the holster. The four of them made their way over to where they'd seen the man fall. They watched as the wounded would be assassin tried to crawl away. His hands caked in mud and his clothes streaked with blood and soil.

"Crawlin away, jus like tha snake he is." Simone pointed out as she stepped in front of him and held the tip of her blade inches from his masked head.

"I'd be wary of calling them snakes; it's praise where they come from, as snakes are sacred." Syandro said as he kept his Castellian rapier out and ready.

"Mercy please, I beg of you." The assassin's mask–muffled voice pleaded. Syandro placed a booted foot in the center of the man's back; eliciting a moan of pain as he bent forward and unraveled the wrappings that obscured the man's features. A thick black beard grew upon the man's face. His olive skin had been painted with ash, and lampblack to make his visible skin blend into the night. Beneath the metal skullcap, serving as head protection. The man's black hair had been shorn down to his scalp and intricate lines creating some sort of seal were etched in henna in a neat line upon the top of the man's scalp; including two, made upon either of his cheeks just below his eyes. Though Franchesca couldn't read the words, she knew the land that wrote in such a flowing serpentine script. It only served to add to her suspicions, if not confirm them as to who was behind this ill–fated attack.

"Saaladan sends his regards I take it?" Franchesca asked as she knelt down and flashed a cunning, serpent's, satisfied smile. Letting the assassin know she'd pieced together the puzzle. The assassin pressed his face into the dirt and extended his hands before him.

"I speak a thousand pardons to you—a thousand upon a thousand apologies, and to you and your ancestors." The man's said shakily, showing extreme pain and discomfort from his wound. "I was only told to obey my lords bidding." The assassin confessed. "As were my brothers; I... I can only offer you my services..."

"What services?" Syandro asked as he stepped on the man's injured leg, causing Saaladan's man to cry out in pain.

"Might I be so bold as to say you are of no value to anyone?" Syandro pointed out raising an eyebrow. Franchesca tapped her chin for a moment.

There had to be a way to use this situation to her advantage. It showed that Saaladan had a certain amount of fear towards her. It also showed a lack of respect for the rules set in place by the pirate lords; which all upon Tornusia seemed to abide by.

"Tell me—what would Saaladan do to you if he found out you failed?" Franchesca asked, crossing her arms over her chest.

"I... I cannot say—perhaps force me to join his crew by being made a eunuch, or executed." The failed assassin said in a shame and pain–laden voice. He winced as he gazed up at them, feelings of dread sloshing about his stomach. Did he have so much to lose by joining them? They certainly wouldn't take his balls... he hoped.

"You will help me ascend to the Throne of Tides, by making sure all know what Saaladan attempted. In exchange, I will show mercy; in fact, if I ascend to the throne, I will reward you generously with a position upon my counsel. Do I have your word and your loyalty?" The assassin nodded quickly reaching out for Franchesca's hand to plant a respectful kiss on her knuckles. As the man's lips pressed against her skin, Syandro felt a strange feeling surge through his spine. His hands clenched into fists so tight that the strain made the joints in his fingers ache. His feelings of tension receded once he watched Franchesca pull her hand from the vicinity of his face.

"Now let us get our new friend some needed medical attention." Franchesca said quietly, glancing back at them.

"I know of a cave nearby. I have stashed a few supplies there. We can take him there and bandage his wounds; it would take far too long to make the trek back into the city with him in such a condition." Ayzza nodded angrily.

"Come; let us be on our way." She ordered with a nod in the direction they were to go. Syandro and Simone helped the man up and placed his arms around their shoulders so they could support his weight. Syandro became alarmed at the sudden rush of anger upon seeing this wounded man, plant a kiss upon Franhcesca's knuckles. It appeared he hadn't entirely cleansed himself of his feelings for Franchesca. That was a turn; he hadn't quite expected. He glowered at the assassin as they helped him limp along in the direction Ayzza indicated. Syandro took a deep breath; he would have to try harder to smother those feelings.

Chapter 26

Saaladan paced around the chamber he claimed for himself at one of the brothels close to the docks. His linen robes flowed and danced about him as he twisted and turned. Women in various states of undress lay sprawled across the bed; some smiling and giggling as they kissed and caressed one another, others watched nervously as Saaladan paced. He walked over to a luxurious, thick padded chair and sank into it. It would be daybreak soon, and he expected news of his plans success hours ago. The counsel of his peers and he used the term of peers loosely; would pay for their slights. How dare anyone stand against him? He needed to sit upon the Throne of Tides; his future depended upon it; indeed his very life depended on it. If doing a little killing was what it took to see his success assured then he would hire as many men as were needed to complete the job. It was the mark of a leader, do what is necessary. Eliminate any and all threats to you; this was a threat to him. It was also a wound to his pride that he would not stand.

A woman would not rule over him; he would not take orders from such a lowly creature. They served their place, and that was precisely where Saaladan liked them—in their place, that place was not above—it was not giving him orders. He was a man; it was man's job; nay his duty to rule. One of the women from the bed sauntered over, clad in nothing but a trimmed flowing, green gossamer train; swaying her hips seductively as she lowered herself into his lap gingerly. The effect of the cut was to make it look as if she were clad in nothing but leaves; harkening back to the classical paintings of mythical scenes when mankind first learned to cover their nakedness out of shame. Though the fabric and style of these leaves had been just that, style; there was no shame to be seen. As her weight settled upon his legs, and she leaned forward and began kissing his lips, Saaladan began to return the kiss; but a hacking cough put an abrupt stop to his display of lust. He shoved the woman roughly from his lap and strode over towards a brass serving tray which was crowded with decanters; carafes, and cups. He hastily reached for a cup and considered the various liquids assembled before him on the tray. After picking up the carafe containing water, he hastily poured some into the cup clasped within his hand, all the while keeping another cough from overtaking him. With a quick gulp, Saaladan drank it down quickly—it didn't help. His fit of coughing turned into a wet, undignified, sputtering as the water burst through his lips with the spasming of his chest. Once the liquid had been expelled, he placed a hand to his lips daintily and sucked in a greedy breath; though it was shaky and unsteady. It was always worse at night, always worse when he engaged in any strenuous activity; though his illness had grown to include moderately strenuous activity only recently. His heart palpitated, and sweat began to bead upon his brow. He turned and glared at the women who simply stared at him. None of them knew what to do or say. Should they try to offer comfort to him, try to help him? As his coughing ceased and Saaladan righted himself, they received their answer.

"Get out! Out you soiled whores! Get out of my presence!" He hissed, despite the fact he wished nothing more than to roar it at the height of his voice; Saaladan knew that was impossible and would only aggravate his condition. A small trail of blood began to seep from his mouth and eyes. As the women stirred slowly, the rage built within him.

"Out you jackal birthed lepers!" Saaladan threw the brass cup at one of the walls, where it hit with a clatter just above one of woman's heads. He'd yelled, and he could feel the tightness within his chest threaten to take hold once more, but he fought against it. The naked women scurried away quickly upon seeing his rage. Saaladan staggered back over to the chair he had been sitting in only a handful of moments ago. His limbs felt shaky, and a wave of weakness settled over him. He brushed the back of his palm across his brow and tried to calm his nerves. A sharp pain drove its way through his head and down through his spine, he gritted his teeth. One of Saaladan's personal guards rushed into the room, moving through the press of women.

"Sir..." Saaladan waved the thickly bearded man away as he sank back into the chair. He reached over and took hold of a pipe that'd been prepared with lotus root and held it above a candle. As he inhaled slowly, the drug took effect. His mind calmed, and the vice–like grip constricting his chest seemed to ease. One by one, Saaladan felt his muscles relax, and his eyelids grow heavy. It'd been a long time since he obeyed any of the strictures of his religion, but indulging in the various mind–altering substances wasn't strictly forbidden— so long as one didn't become an addict. Though that was something Saaladan couldn't truthfully say he'd staved off; if he were honest—none save himself needed to know such things, however. Given his current situation, being an addict was the least of his worries. A blue–gray cloud of pleasant smelling smoke clouded above him as he exhaled. The stabbing pain that moments ago gripped his mind now seemed to ebb slowly into the recesses of memory.

"Shall I fetch the physicians?" The bearded man asked as he bowed. Saaladan waved his question away as if he were swatting at a meddlesome fly. For the moment all he wanted was for the guard to leave him be so that he might relax fully into the stupor of the lotus root.

"They know nothing of my affliction; if the physician's in Sahar cannot help then the sea water blessing, root grinding peddlers on this waterlogged rock will know less." Saaladan growled as he rubbed his head.

"Forgive my insolence my lord, but how will ascending to the throne help you overcome your sickness?" Saaladan chuckled as he took another drag from his pipe. As the smoke cloud grew above his head, he took in a breath. How he wished he would just go away.

"You are familiar with what is referred to as the lost compass?" He asked with a sigh. The guard brought over a fresh cup; filled with water. Saaladan sipped it, as his guard shook his head.

"It is a compass that is not bound to the poles of the earth, but to its owner's very will; some have speculated the possessors very soul. It points only to what you desire most in this world." Saaladan explained feeling the cool caress of water moisten his dry throat.

"And that would mean a cure for your sickness in your case, my lord." The guard finished with a nod of understanding.

"That fool Konrad never saw fit to place much stock in such magical trinkets. I, on the other hand, I have reliable sources that have told me such stories are quite true. I've also heard it said the damned sea witch guards these treasures, and might need to be persuaded to give them over to the one who should rightfully hold them." Saaladan pointed to an ornately decorated, teak wood box resting on the nightstand beside his bed.

"Only one who sits upon the Throne of Tides may open the chest. That damned bitch, Ayzza is the only one who can open it—and she'll not open it for anyone unless they sit upon the throne. I've also heard it said that within the box is a master key. A key which can open any lock; upon any chest, door or vault. Once I find the cure for this illness, I intend to make use of such treasures, Maamin." Saaladan smirked.

"But surely with such treasures, one would be invincible; why would they just be sitting within a box, cast aside and never used?" Maamin asked as he opened the window of Saaladan's room.

"We return again to Ayzza; she hasn't seen fit to open the chest in an age. Not since this pathetic patch of rock was settled. They were locked away under her guard, and she's only ever admitted they existed, but never shown them or their damned location to anyone." Saaladan replied.

"But she will show them to me. I swear upon the wrath of the holy chosen prophet Mazeem that bitch will lay the treasures at my feet, or she shall feel pain the likes of which she has never felt." Saaladan swore as he stormed over to the brass serving tray and poured a measure of wine. He downed the contents and turned to Maamin.

"I sent a number of men to deal with the obstacles of this so-called Captain Flint and her companions. I haven't received word. You, my loyal Maamin, will go and find them. Bring me their heads, and if my men have failed... bring me their tongues so I will not have to listen to excuses." That was one way to get rid of the man so that he could be alone with his feeling of sedation.

"It shall be as you say my master." Maamin bowed as he turned and strode from the room, leaving his master alone. Saaladan took a pull from his pipe, letting the drug continue its work of numbing his body. His pain ebbed to a dull ache, and the dry crackling within his lungs seemed to calm. I will not allow myself to succumb to such a malady, nor will I be made a fool by such a lowly woman; he scowled as he stood and poured himself another measure of wine. Saaladan walked over to the bed and reclined. It appeared he would not exercise his more amorous urges this evening, but he could not calm his mind enough to sleep; so Saaladan lay upon his bed as wave after wave of drug–induced numbness washed upon him. Perhaps he would sleep when Maamin returned with news of his plans success. A crooked smile crossed his lips as he prepared himself for that joyous news. Perhaps the bitch had killed his men but he could always find more willing to take gold in payment for committing unspeakable acts of violence. For the right price a man would sell his soul, something Saaladan took full advantage of from those who he paid to do his bidding. He chuckled to himself as his nostrils welcomed the fragrant aroma of burning lotus root. When those treasures are laid at my feet I'll finally be rid of this damned condition. His eyelids grew heavier at the thought. Saaladan didn't know what the cure would be or where it lay but with the compass he could find it. Long ago he heard tell of a spring that cured all ills; some said it granted eternal life. Many said it was only a story. Many said such things of the compass and the key as well. Saaladan doubted his eventual cure would be so grand a thing as to come from a fountain of myth and story; doubtless it would lead him to the correct churgeon or apothecary. He smiled as the floral scent of the lotus root tickled his nostrils. Destiny waited. The throne is as good as mine, he told himself as a fresh night breeze blew over him; taking him deeper into his waking lotus root, fueled dreams

* * *

Ayzza poured a soothing salve over the man's wound and tied a strip of linen over the bullet wound. The man let out a grunt of pain which was silenced when Ayzza glared at him with growing rage. Thanks to him and his companions, under the order of Saaladan, she no longer possessed her home. Her sanctuary was gone. The scent of burning, smoking wood still hung upon the air. She wished nothing more than to beat the man within an inch of his life; though she resisted carrying out the action. Her eyes met his with the coldest of glares. If her gaze could kill, then he would have been dead three times over. Franchesca sat atop a rock within the cave that Ayzz lead them to, and reloaded the last of her pistols. Syandro stood at the mouth of the cave to keep watch, while Simone sharpened her blade.

"Saaladan must be getting desperate to order us killed." Franchesca announced. Ayzza chuckled as she tugged on the bandages to make sure they were secured to the assassin's leg.

"Actually... th... the master only requested that we kill the three of you. He cannot kill the sea witch, but he knows he can intimidate." The wounded man said hastily as he propped himself up on his elbows.

"Why does he want us dead?" Franchesca asked, tucking her freshly reloaded pistol into its holster. She smiled down at him, her long wavy black hair falling from behind her shoulders to the front of her chest. The wounded assassin couldn't help but answer.

"He... he spoke of a treasure... guarded by the sea witch." he replied hesitantly. He'd remembered something about his master being furious when he found a box. Well, he hadn't started furious; at first, Saaladan had been overjoyed—right until he opened the box and found it empty. After that, he'd launched into a tirade the likes of which one had to see to believe.

"And that bastard thought if he burned down my cabin I would cave to his demands?" Ayzza bristled as she rose to her full height. She nodded, wiping her hands on her disheveled raggedy clothing. "I think it's time I show Saaladan once and for all that he will never be fit to sit on the Throne of Tides. A serpentine smile crossed Ayzza's face, and she nodded slowly." I think it's best we get some rest for the night. There is nothing more to be done tonight... and I am sure that we all could do with some sleep."

"I'll take the first watch." Syandro announced as he glanced over his shoulder with a grin. Franchesca smiled as everyone went about making themselves comfortable. Syandro watched from the mouth of the cave, letting his gaze fall upon Franchesca's lithe figure. His blood grew hot within his veins. Quickly he broke his gaze and peered out over the wilderness beyond the cave. Nightbirds took flight and tree branches rustled with the breeze, or due to the movement of various nocturnal creatures. He could feel that want crawling through his skin once more. A desire for her he thought gone; he hoped and prayed had gone away—now he wondered if it ever truly had—and if it hadn't would he ever be rid of his desire for her. He released a quiet breath through gritted teeth, placing his hand upon the handle of his blade. Its reassuring chill helped to bring his mind back to the task at hand. I should have stayed at the brothel and purged myself of every flesh filled desire I could manage, he thought to himself. He was a passionate man, and his passions ran deep; perhaps deeper than Syandro himself recognized. He glanced over his shoulder once more watching the slow rising and falling of her chest; wishing he could lay with her, to lace his fingers with hers, and place his palms upon her cheeks. There was a deep desire to look into her eyes and feel her lips against his, to have the taste of her linger upon his lips and within his memory until the end of his days. The desires were deep, but there was nothing he could do. Syandro took a step from the mouth of the cave and began walking through the wooded area surrounding it. It wasn't that the desires or the want to be with her and feel her flesh against his which hurt. It was the fact that she would never love him—not the way he loved her. What could he do?

Syandro tried to keep a level head; his father warned him many times that decision made due to strife and panic always came back to haunt you. He heard the rustle of branches and undergrowth behind him, snapping him back to his surroundings. Syandro tugged his blade free of its sheath and made ready for an attack that might come from any direction.

"Show yourself, you dog." He shouted. A woman walked out from behind a tree; clad in nothing but a smile. His guard immediately dropped, his mind suddenly forgetting about Franchesca. The woman held a narrow pipe within her hand and brought it to her pale lips, taking a pull from it before blowing out a cloud of smoke. Lotus root—Syandro had smelled the substance in every brothel he'd ever set foot in. He even allowed himself to partake in the substance on a few occasions.

"Tell me... do I look like a dog?" The woman asked. As she stepped closer, there was no denying that she bore a strange resemblance to Franchesca, now that his mind had been focused somewhat he could make such details out. She was roughly the same height and same build; her hair was the same shade of raven black, and her eyes held the same cunning glint.

"I guess you see something you care for; you haven't stopped staring." She smiled as she took another deep inhalation from her pipe; blowing the blue–gray smoke in his direction. The breeze caught it and shifted it, leaving only the faintest floral scent of the smoldering narcotic to tickle his nostrils.

"I don't often see naked women in the woods, at least not at night." Syandro replied as he tucked his blade back into its sheath. Was he trying to be witty?

"Have you gone looking for them then?" The woman smiled as she stepped forward; by the gods, this stranger, even possessed the same quick wit that danced off Franchesca's tongue! Syandro felt his blood race and fire burn within him. His mouth felt overly salivated.

"Care to follow me?" She asked with a smile as she proffered him the pipe. Syandro cracked a sly smile and took a pull from the pipe; letting the waves of calm offered by the lotus root, caress his mind. He knew he should ask more questions, perhaps even turn back; but a deeper part of him desired to follow her because he knew what he would be rewarded with. As he followed the woman, only one name raced through his lustful brain—Franchesca.

"What is your name?" Syandro asked as he stepped over a rotted log. She glanced back over her shoulder and smirked.

"Does it matter? I am who you want me to be." She replied in a seductive, husky whisper. They stopped in a glade filled with fragrant wildflowers, and the gentle trickle of water that flowed through a small stream. She walked over to him and placed her hands on his chest and seized a fist full of his shirt as a sneer came upon her face.

"I feel something within you—darkness." Syandro couldn't help but laugh. Of all the things he was sure she could feel at this moment, he would have thought darkness would be fairly close to the bottom. Given how close, and visible other evidence was becoming.

"Is that so? Tell me are you a fortune teller too?" He asked as she tore open his shirt and scratched at his chest; gently at first, then with greater, but not wholly unpleasant roughness.

"Perhaps that is what I am." She leaned in and kissed him deeply tangling her fingers within the shaggy hair atop his head. He returned the kiss with unhindered enthusiasm. As she gasped with delight, he felt her grin.

"You know you never told me who you wanted me to be." She pointed out as he moved his attention to her neck.

"Don't worry," Syandro panted "I know who I want you to be." His heart raced as he grasped at her smooth, supple flesh firmly. The scene unfolding was one he dreamt of countless times before. He pictured himself in this place before, admittedly Syandro fancied himself somewhat of a romantic. It seemed to be part of being Castellian. He'd imagined making love to Franchesca in a surrounding such as this; the scent of flowers caught in the breeze mingling with the sweat of their bodies. The sensations of grass and skin brushing against one another and the pale moonlight offering all the light the two of them could ever need to enjoy each other's naked flesh. He felt his heart race as she tore off his shirt and reached for his belt. A primal growl escaped his throat as she bit down on his bottom lip. They lay upon the cool grass. The woman straddled him and smiled down at him as the silver moonlight gifted her a faint halo. Syandro felt her nails rake across his chest, causing him to smile.

"Do I look like a dog now?" She asked with a wolfish grin that only hinted at the mischief that was to follow. She continued to straddle him–her naked form illuminated by the twin moons overhead. He eagerly awaited the coming sensations. The illumination haloing her going from pale silver to red, as if the moons themselves warred to claim her naked flesh. His eyes rolled back as he felt her place one supple hand upon the center of his chest; where she'd scratched him moments ago. There was a sharp cracking sound, a branch being broken by the trod of someone's foot. Syandro awoke with a start and hastily glanced about; no, not now. Not before this had a chance to end. He paused for a moment. Where was he—back at the cave? No. How could that be? It was all so real. He finally had her—not her he reminded himself, though the resemblance was uncanny. Syandro's heart began to race, and his mind reeled. He placed a hand upon his chest. His shirt was open, and there were scratches on his torso. What had happened? Standing above him face partially obscured by shadows stood Ayzza.

"What... what happened?" Ayzza took a step backward, her gaze cold and unflinching. She maintained her distance giving Syandro all the caution one might give to a dangerous or rabid beast.

"I sense much darkness in you." Her tone was low, filled with warning. She gazed into his eyes for a long awkward moment; then turned back and looked at Franchesca and Simone. Her nostrils flared before she turned back towards him. Ayzza drew herself close, and Syandro flinched slightly as she smelled the area about him, like a dog might sniff a patch of grass. The mere thought of the word dog took him back to that dream, but he couldn't get past how incredibly real it felt.

"What happened? What's going on?" Syandro asked as he rose to his feet. How did he get back? Did he ever really leave? Had the frenzy of passion simply taken place within his head as a wondrous dream? Could a dream be so vivid?

"I shall be watching you closely." Ayzza warned. She spoke no more and retreated back into the darkness of the cave. Syandro glanced down and touched the marks upon his chest; four distinct scratches marked his flesh. He saw her use four fingers as she raked them across his exposed flesh. As he touched them the hackles of his hair rose. There was a strange sensation he'd never felt before; these marks tinged with electricity and serenity and utterly indescribable to his mind. He turned on his heel and peered back into the cave. All were sleeping soundly; all save Ayzza. She stared at him as she sat atop a rock, her staff lying across her knees. Syandro surveyed the wilderness and felt a shudder travel through every fiber of muscle in his body. Something was wrong.

* * *

Ayzza clasped her staff tightly. She could smell the touch of Khaos upon the boy. She felt its all contaminating, and distorting presence. There was truth in her words; she would be watching him closely. She could sense darkness within him, great darkness that she hadn't noticed before now. It left her with a much larger problem, however. It meant some force of Khaos was free upon the island, and it was close enough and strong enough to begin to influencing people upon the island. It had laid claim—had marked Syandro. Our young captain is going to have a hard go of this, Ayzza thought. Let us hope she is resilient. I fear she will be losing something very precious when she comes to power.

* * *

Maamin gazed upon the remnants of the smoldering cabin. The area covered in ash and charred, black lumps of driftwood. Those jars that'd not been destroyed by the fire lay blackened and strewn about; pots littered the ground in no clear direction. His mind created a vague impression of what the cabin might have looked like before the blaze consumed it. He poked a pile of ash with the tip of his blade. He called to one of the eunuchs who accompanied him. He ordered the eunuchs to sift through the ash; telling them to look for anything that gave proof that Ayzza might have escaped, and where she might have fled. The likely hood of finding anything in such a pile of ash and charcoal was practically nonexistent, but he would not have Saaladan accuse him of allowing a stone remain unturned. Maamin punished enough men on Saaladan's behalf for such an oversight; he would not fall victim to such treatment himself. By the six holy champions of the prophet, he could not wait for his task of dealing with Saaladan to be over. His fingers toyed idly upon the pommel of his yataghan as he stood and watched members of the crew work. He would be done soon; he could feel it in his bones. The thought made him smile. One of the eunuchs gave a shout of pain and pulled his hand back. While sifting through a pile of ash, he found one of the assassin's blades. Every assassin had been killed; the fire that consumed the shack had blackened four of them, but by all appearances, it seemed as though they failed in their task. Of course, perhaps they succeeded. Maybe they struck a mortal wound, and though they escaped the burning hut, they fled into the surrounding area to die. It was highly unlikely; but it was better to be thorough than be dead, Maamin told himself. He called for one of the company to assist him in searching the wilderness around the cabins remains, while the others sifted through the rubble. It'd been hours, and the area around the cabin had been searched once and searched again. The only things that Maamin and the eunuchs found were the charred corpses of the assassins burned within the shack; or the dead men of their assassination squad that layout in the night air. Though one eunuch did find two strange sea–green orbs with polished slits of jet the fire hadn't damaged. Maamin ordered the party back; he would have to give word to Saaladan that he found no trace of his targets. His master would not be pleased. Maamin only hoped that Saaladan would not choose to unleash his anger upon him. It hadn't been Maamin's fault; but when Saaladan flew into a rage trivial things such as who actually failed him were not taken into consideration. He exercised his wrath on whoever was closest at hand. Perhaps the man's sickness would prevent him from summoning forth his unfettered anger. Maamin witnessed Saaladan fall into coughing fits more and more as of late, with more and more blood trickling from various facial orifices. There was no doubt that he'd become slack in his raiding. It'd been a great deal of time since Saaladan had paid any of his crew. Even Maamin who remained loyal throughout the many mutinies that plagued life aboard Saaladan's ship wondered how long his master had his loyalties. Especially because I seem to be doing more and more of his work, Maamin thought to himself. What was to keep him from cutting Saaladan's head from his shoulders after the treasure was brought forward? He knew the answer of course; it wasn't what the Sultan ordered of him, not explicitly. He sighed; a thought is different from an action, he reminded himself as he tugged on his beard. He made a silent vow to himself; if Saaladan's crew decided to mutiny once again, they would find a supporter in Maamin. It had been too long since Saaladan thought of any but himself. His cruelty, arrogance and short sided selfishness would bring about his downfall. Until that moment, Maamin would play the faithful servant. Perhaps a better opportunity would present itself to him, then Maamin could snuff out Saaladan's already flickering candle and rise to fill his position; he could do as the Sultan asked, even if he was too much of a coward to do it himself at that moment. Maamin nodded all is as it shall be permitted, with that thought in mind; he continued his trek back to relay the news of his find to his master.

Chapter
27

As Maamin predicted, Saaladan flew into a rage at the news of his plan's failure. His fury was interrupted by a coughing fit that saw great clots of blood expelled from his mouth. The wheezing in his chest could be heard faintly. Nothing more than a wounded animal showing its belly to a jackal, Maamin thought as he poured a glass of water for his temporary master. It wouldn't take much, he thought, a drop of poison in his water; or wine, perhaps lacing his nightly pipe of lotus root with some sort of poison. Saaladan took the glass with the gentleness of a kitten and sipped softly at the water within. He rubbed his fevered forehead. Maamin sighed; he couldn't bring himself to kill this man. He was weak, sick and pathetic. Saaladan would sew his own undoing; Maamin wouldn't need to dirty his own hands to hasten it. To kill someone in such a condition seemed to violate a sense of honor Maamin didn't know he possessed. Acting as a faithful son, Maamin walked over and readied Saaladan's pipe. He filled it with lotus root and brought it and a candle over to the bedside table. Saaladan accepted the pipe readily holding it above the flickering flame of the candle. As the smoke began to rise from the brass bowl, he took in a few deep puffs. Sometimes Maamin hated the Sultan for sending him out to keep eyes on Saaladan.

"You are certain you didn't find them?" Saaladan asked. His voice dry and scratchy ravaged from the fit of coughing that seized him moments ago. Maamin sighed. This was truly a desperate man; it was actually pathetic and growing more pathetic with every protracted moment he spent in his company.

"I only found the bodies of your hired assassin's. It is a possibility they are dead. Perhaps they retreated deeper into the forests. I just do not think it likely." Maamin acknowledged quietly. Saaladan managed a raspy sigh, before taking another puff from his pipe. He paused to blow out a long stream of wispy smoke.

"I will just have to hope I am so lucky." A smirk slid across his face as he put the pipe back to his lips. He didn't take a pull; not right away. His eyes became glassy, and his gaze became distant. "Perhaps we can settle our disputes ourselves." Saaladan sneered.

"You mean to demand a fight to the death?" Maamin asked.

"Death; first blood—anything as long as that upstart bitch is stopped." Saaladan growled. "Though admittedly, death would be the preferred choice. She would be out of our path forever, but I will settle for whatever I can get." Saaladan nodded as he took a drink from his water cup and set it down on the nightstand. He watched the curling tendrils of smoke rise from the wooden bowl of the pipe with a smirk.

"All is, as it willed." Maamin reminded with a humble bow upon quoting the line from the Sharraa, the holy book of their land. Saaladan merely smiled as he took in a deep breath and exhaled the smoke, he held within his mouth. The crackling sound that accompanied his breathing faded, as it always did when he smoked the narcotic lotus root. His chest felt looser, and his muscles felt pleasantly heavy and relaxed.

"I think sometimes we are required to show our own will. A will to survive, or a will to take what is laid before us—it is up to us to grasp hold of our desires; our destinies. If it is not laid easily in our path... we reach don't we?" Saaladan asked with a small smile. His humility seemed to be a thin vainer, Maamin sighed to himself.

"We must stop them." Saaladan continued before clearing his throat and taking a long sip of water. Maamin bowed at the waist, as the sky blue curtains of his room fluttered in the breeze.

"I will see to it that eyes are kept out in the streets for their return." Maamin said giving a polite bow.

"What do the people speak of? Who do they favor for the throne?" Saaladan asked as he blew out a stream of smoke." Surely they must know by now Konrad is dead. They must know that the process of finding a new ruler is underway." He paused once more to admire the dancing tendrils from the pipe's bowl with the sort of smile that told Maamin the man was only half within his own head at the moment. The fragrant odor of lotus root hung in the air, Maamin sighed. The people only spoke of Saaladan with contempt; especially the women of this island. Many of the brothel owners seemed to favor the Castellian Captain, Frabranzo. Their business boomed whenever he made port, as he indulged in his fleshy desires, and encouraged his crewmen to do likewise. Though Saaladan visited a brothel and took up residence during his stays, many of the women saw him as cruel; many vowing never to set foot in the same room as him ever again, after experiencing the displeasure of his company a single time. He paid his room and board, and paid for any woman he wanted; usually twice over and in a business where coin is everything, it spoke volumes that Saaladan was looked down upon as a plague worse than cock sores. Many of the working girls and madams feared that if he were to sit the Throne of Tides, he would bring his self–righteous, if not hypocritical ideals and outlaw the brothels. The women would then be out on the streets with no way to earn their keep, on Tornusia, everyone earned their keep; everyone pulled their weight and did their share, and no matter what it was they did. Since he'd become sick, and his attacks on ships had grown to a crawl, and his stream of coin dried into a trickle at best; he was now in danger of losing a place at even the sleaziest, most run–down of brothels. Such a thing could turn Saaladan's petty mind against everyone. If he couldn't enjoy the pleasures offered by the brothels, he would see that no one would be able to. He was that petty—and that cruel.

"It is hard to say with certainty. Many of the brothel and tavern owners show favor towards Fabranzo. Some, however, have heard of the events at the temple and how Ayzza favors the girl; as a result, many are thinking of casting their vote for her..."

"And myself?" Saaladan asked as he sipped his water. He needed to be careful and control his rage. If he lost control once more, he would lapse into another coughing fit. His chest and sides hurt from the one which he just came through. The last thing he wanted was to endure another on its heals; there was no telling how long it would last—or even if this would be the one that did not stop. His time was quickly running out; he needed that damned compass, that damned key. He needed his cure.

"I am afraid, sir—that you are not spoken of fondly." Maamin sighed as he rubbed his head. He sneered and clapped his hands together. "Good; then it will show my power when that petulant child is struck down. Once I claim the throne for myself, I will bring these slime covered peasants to heal; primitive ingrates one and all." Saaladan hissed as he took a drink and set his empty cup down. Maamin allowed a fake smile to creep from the corners of his mouth.

"It shall be as you say, my lord." Maamin bowed. May the eternal one have mercy upon them all if that is true, Maamin thought to himself as he rested his hand on the handle of his blade. Maamin had been in Saaladan's service for many years; and knew that the man was at heart, nothing more than a spoiled child. He was a hypocrite who wrapped himself in the veil of the strict religious beliefs of their land, but regularly broke any stricture that seemed to be the least bit inconvenient for him. He was a product of two starkly different worlds. His father was wealthy; and in a kingdom like that of Tehraiq that was dangerous for any not fortunate enough to hold such coin, which was the case for Saaladan's mother. She'd been young when his father, Sultan Rahsmin Tallieam Alkuur, bought Saaladan's mother from her parents to join his harem. Of course, law stated that Rashmin could only have one true wife; unfortunately for Saaladan that one true wife was not the woman who gave birth to him. He'd grown up as a bastard and had been reminded of that every day he spent in his father's company. Still, his father paid for tutors, and fighting lessons; insisting that no one who carried his blood within his veins would disgrace him with stupidity, cowardice, or ineptitude with a weapon. Rahsmin would not have any in his line become a slave to another house because he lost a duel or a fight on the battlefield. Despite the luxuries of such lessons, life was far from easy for Saaladan and his mother. He watched his father dote and pamper his half–brother; the only son who was born of Rahsmin Tallieam Alkuur's real wife. He watched with bitterness and resentment as his half–brother, Maseek, received the best of everything; while Saaladan and his mother were only given a pittance to survive on. For years he watched his father come into his mother's room at all hours of the day or night, he would have his way with her—and she would let him. Saaladan confronted his mother on one occasion. How could she let him touch her? After the way he treated her? After the way, he treated him, with such malice? That conversation was still crystalline clear within his mind. His mother simply smiled and sighed. It was her duty; she told him. Saaladan still turned her pathetic response over in his mind. It was her duty. Still, he knew it as the truth. What could she do? If she denied him, she would be lashed, or killed. Though she could do nothing, he was in a position to change things. Or so he thought. One day while praying, as his forehead touched the prayer mat an idea rushed to the forefront of his mind. So quickly had it come, and with such clarity that it must have come from almighty God himself.

He would challenge Maseek to a duel. When he won, he would demand that their father Rahsmin acknowledge him as a legitimate heir. Saaladan failed to realize however that the laws stated that no matter what he did, he couldn't be named as a legitimate child.

When he demanded the duel, his half–brother accepted eagerly. Each sibling saw a chance to make their father proud. For Saaladan's half–brother, it was a chance to remove a stain from the family. For Saaladan however, it was a chance to rise to something greater. Rahsmin had forbade his son's from their duel, but neither of them listened. They met at dusk, a league from the palace gates. Each one sought to make their father proud, but Saaladan also thought of his mother. She deserved better than a cramped chamber, hidden away in the palace where Rahsmin would stalk when the mood suited him. As they dueled the sound of galloping hooves drew their attention. It was their father, accompanied by a handful of guards; and Saaladan's mother.

"I forbade this! I forbade you both, and you defy me?! How dare you!" Rahsmin bellowed; his once proud black beard now a mixture of black, and silver that came with age. He laid a hand upon the hilt of the blade sheathed at his side.

"I cannot let our family's honor be called into question. I'll not allow him to call me a coward!" Maseek said as he met his half brother's eyes.

"I'll not sit idle whilst you treat my mother and me, like refuse!" Saaladan roared. He pounded his chest with his fist." I am your son! Me! I was your first born! You dare to cast me aside for another!" Saaladan declared.

"She is my wife!" Rahsmin shouted angrily. He looked deep into Saaladan's eyes, a glare set in stone—eyes that had stared down threats, and promises of vengeance and other violent acts for years. "Your mother is a maid of the harem—nothing more, nothing less." Rahsmin growled.

"I am your son!" Saaladan howled angrily." Born of your blood—"

"And diluted by your mothers." Rahsmin countered sternly. Saaladan watched as his mother hung her head. Rage flowed through him; every muscle taught ready for violence. Could he take on all of his attackers and survive? Saaladan turned on his heel and howled up at the sky in the direction of the setting pale, orange and pink sun. He turned his head and fixed his half–brother with the coldest of gazes. With a speed Saaladan himself was unaware he possessed; he charged and tackled his unsuspecting half–brother to the hot sands. Saaladan tore a curved dagger from a sheath at his waist and without hesitation or a second thought, without a single care for what happened next, he tore his half brother's throat open. Just like that, it was done. He had expected a great duel; a fight between himself and Maseek, but his fury—raw and powerful, stripped away any thought of nobility; any notion of honor and left him little more than a base animal. Maseek gazed up at him as death stole away his soul. Glassy orbs looked lazily up at the sibling who'd killed him; caught in the dying sun. Rahsmin howled as he charged forward and threw Saaladan from atop his dead son. Blood stained Saaladan's white thobe, and dripped from the blade he held in his hand. He gazed down at his half–

brother, his mind numb. His muscles still coiled and ready to defend himself. Rahsmin howled his lament to the darkening sky as the first faint stars sparkled to life in the growing dark. He wept; like a child, Saaladan thought to himself. Rahsmin's guards stormed forward and surrounded Saaladan. Their shields held close, and spears leveled as they circled him. Rahsmin rose slowly and passed through the circle of his guards, tears cutting tracks down his olive-skinned face. His men took a single step back; their blades still leveled at the man who killed the Sultan's son. Rahsmin stepped forward and backhanded Saaladan. His chainmail glove making a gentle rattle as it connected against Saaladan's face, sending him down to the sands.

"I will give you a ship, only to get you as far away from my lands, and my sight as possible. That is my mercy to you as your father." Rahsmin hissed. He clapped his hands and immediately Saaladan's mother was brought forward. She was forced to her knees before her son. She whispered only one final thing to him—Run. Rahsmin pulled his kilij from its sheath in one fluid motion and brought it down on the woman's neck; severing her head in one swift, effortless motion. Saaladan screamed as he rose to his knees and crawled to his mother's headless body as blood flowed in a great river from the stump to cover him. Rahsmin turned on his heel and strode back towards his horse and climbed back into his saddle.

"The ship will be ready for you at dawn... if you stay in these lands I will kill you for what you have done to my son. Once you board that ship, you will receive nothing from me, except my ill will. You will have no title because as of this moment you are nameless to me." Rahsmin spurred his horse into motion as his men broke their circle and climbed back on the backs of their own mounts. Two of them strode over to Maseek; the Sultan's fallen son, and gathered his body up in a respectful manner. They marched off; leaving him, and his mother's headless corpse upon the cooling sands as the sun dipped beneath the horizon.

"I am Saaladan! I am your son! I will show you! You'll regret choosing that bastard over me!" He roared as he stood as he drew his sword from its sheath and waved it above his head. His father would notice him. Indeed, he might even curse him; but he would curse himself more. Saaladan would be the son that Rahsmin Tallieam Alkuur always wanted. His father would rue the day he cast him out, and curse himself a fool for choosing the wrong son to dote over. I will show you, father, he vowed, I will show you. For a long time, it appeared as if Saaladan had done just that. He launched attacks on any vessel flying his father's colors and left no survivors. Yet he always found something of importance upon those sacked ships and sent it back to the man that had denied him. It was a strange thing, Saaladan supposed. After all, he hated Rahsmin for what he'd done to his mother. He supposed he owed the man nothing except a lifetime of pain and suffering; haunted memories where the ghost of his favored son might walk. He supposed it was his way of showing his father just how wrong he was to have chosen his brother over him. He could have made his father proud, if only he was afforded that chance. If only his father had acknowledged him; if only Rahsmin had respected his mistress. Things would be very different.

Maamin watched a wicked sneer come to life upon Saaladan's features. No doubt thinking about yet another way he would show his uncaring father how wrong he was to not have chosen him. Maamin supposed he could see why Saaladan was so angry, but it baffled him at how he hated his father so, yet committed many of the same sins. It was not a secret that Saaladan enjoyed sleeping in many different beds with as many different women as he could find willing—a deed he looked down upon his father for indulging in. Saaladan also had other's carry out his dirty work for him. Maamin heard the litany of crimes perpetrated by Saaladan's father, but it was always clear that his father carried out his own work. I wonder if that makes him worse or better than his son, Maamin thought. Maamin took a deep breath as he prepared to make his exit. Saaladan called out to him.

"I thank you for your service." Saaladan smiled at him. It was a weak smile, doing nothing to mask the obvious pain that Saaladan was feeling at this moment. Maamin arrived at a decision at that moment, when that smile crossed Saaladan's features. Captains were supposed to be leaders—strong and fearless even when facing their own death. To a good captain, the welfare of his crew was amongst the highest of priorities. Saaladan became lax upon such things. Once he was a selfless man—now his sickness changed him into a selfish self–centered hypocrite. Maamin knew where his loyalties lay. He just had to seek them out.

Chapter 28

Ayzza watched as Franchesca's and Simone's eyes flitted away the last vestiges of a hard-won nights sleep. She cast a sidelong glance towards the mouth of the cave where Syandro lay sprawled. Ever since Ayzza warned him she would be watching him, Syandro hadn't the heart to wake anyone else to take the next watch. In fact, he was frightened. He replayed Ayzza's warning over and over in his thoughts. He recalled the venom that dripped in her warning of the darkness she saw within him. Such thoughts kept him from sleeping; kept him from waking anyone to take the next watch. In the end, due to the exhausting power of fear, sleep had come for him; at some time he'd failed to reckon. Franchesca awoke with a groan; her muscles stiff, and knotted with tension after sleeping on the earthen floor of the cave. She rubbed her tattooed arm and rotated her shoulders until there was a satisfying pop. She craned her neck right crack and then left feeling the crack and pop, immediately feeling more comfortable than she'd been moments ago. Simone did the same with her back as she stood, stretching deeply before cracking her fingers and rubbing her aching thighs.

"Best night's sleep we've 'ad in a long while." She said, before cracking her neck. "Even with the stiffness." She added quietly. Their wounded captive still slept upon the stone floor. For a brief moment, Franchesca thought he might have passed away during the night, but the rising and falling of his chest proved otherwise. She couldn't tell if she was happy about that turn of events or not. A hobbled man could be your death; one way or another. There was a sharp pisst which split the waking silence as Ayzza rose to her feet. She waved Simone and Franchesca over to her. Franchesca's hand strayed to the butt of her pistol and Simone's hand fell to the hilt of her blade ready to pull it from its sheath. Ayzza produced two oilskin-wrapped parcels and handed one to Franchesca and the other to Simone.

"Saaladan is looking for these; they are very important, and powerful artifacts." A smile crossed her face. "But I'll not let him get his spindly hands on them." As if anticipating the questions that would be asked, she began to explain.

"One is a compass that points to your heart's deepest, and truest desire. The other is a key which can open any lock, any door. I give them to you because you will become the next lords of Tornusia... and I suspect you will need of them. A need no other lord has had in centuries; in truth, none has been worthy of in centuries." Ayzza whispered.

"Keep them close, and keep them safe. The magics used to create these artifacts are great and powerful, and I can think of none alive who could recreate them in this day and age." She pressed the oilcloth wrapped packages into Franchesca and Simone's hands. Franchesca held a stained and polished teakwood box inlaid with gold and silver designed as compass points. In its center was inlaid a large black pearl, surrounded by sunstones. Simone held an entirely different, and more morbid treasure. A long slender finger bone; ivory white, with just the faintest tinges of yellow set in around the knuckle joints. The top of the finger, where it would have joined to the hand was capped with silver and ringed with a mixture of gold and copper. Attached to the cap was a loop made of silver where the key could be attached to a length of chain, or cord.

"Never tought I would actally see a skeleton key," Simone said as she brought the object closer cautiously and studied it.

"I hope I am not intruding?" An accented voice called out. Franchesca spun on her heel and pulled two pistols free from her holsters. Simone drew her sword out of its sheath and took up a fighting stance; as she tucked the key into her trouser pocket. The wounded assassin awoke with a start and flinched upon seeing who stood at the mouth of the cave. Syandro awoke quickly and rolled back, pulling his sword and dagger from their resting places. He had the presence of mind to keep his blades unsheathed while on watch; which served him well now. The newcomer held up his hands and shook his head.

"Give me one reason why I shouldn't put a shot through your head." Franchesca demanded as she pulled the hammers back on her pistol. She kept her gaze level and stern on the Saharian. Based on her extremely short and deadly interactions thus far, she was rather jumpy around men of that particular continent—she could guess with reasonable certainty to whom this newcomer owed his loyalties.

"Because I mean you no harm." He replied. He reached down slowly and untied his sword belt, and tossed it to the sandy cave on the floor. There was a dull scraping clank as the pommel hit a small rock. Silence descended over them as Ayzza rose to her feet.

"I bring you words of warning; so that you might prepare yourselves." The man told them softly as he took a step in and bowed, his thick black beard touching the top of his chest as he lowered his head. "I am Maamin..."

"I saw you standing with Saaladan at the gathering." Franchesca growled, her aim steadied on him. He nodded, as she tracked his movements with the mouths of her pistols.

"Indeed I was... and for many years I have served him faithfully. As faithful as a man can serve another he is forced to that is. However... I find he no longer meets the qualities of captain." Maamin confessed.

"He never did." Ayzza growled, stepping up next to Simone and Franchesca and squaring her shoulders.

"I come to say he is preparing himself to cast away with the votes. He has decided he wants the vote between you and himself to be settled by duel." Maamin said quietly.

"And did you come to deliver this message to us on his order then?" Syandro asked. Maamin shook his head.

"No. Saaladan no longer warrants my loyalty. He will ask me to fight on his behalf, and I will refuse..." looks of surprise, darkened with suspicion their faces. He couldn't say he blamed them.

"Why would he ask you, he seems to want us dead bad enough to want the pleasure of killing us himself." Franchesca scoffed.

"He is sick—in fact, he is very sick." Maamin replied quickly. "It is worse in the evenings, but it is progressing, quite rapidly. I came to tell you that; as well as to tell you this—after you kill him, there will still be a vote; but it will be between you and the Castellian Frabranzo. I have come to swear my loyalty to you, and I only ask one thing in return." Maamin said meeting their gazes steadily. Franchesca cast a glance over at Simone and another towards Ayzza. Simone merely shrugged, but Ayzza remained stone–faced and ridged, as unreadable as a background statue in a classic work of art. By the gods a little help would be nice—if you're supposed to help and guide me, then do it, Franchesca thought. A wave of surprise washed over her; had she really just thought that? How she hoped Ayzza could not read her mind.

"And what is it you want?" Franchesca asked staring at him intensely. The hair on the nape of her neck stood on end. If she were honest, the hair upon her head felt as though it were standing at attention for military inspection. His information sounded good, that was the problem—it sounded too good. It's not as though I have many deals I can make she thought.

"I want Saaladan's ship. After he dies, it will be held in the harbor until the new lord sits upon the Throne of Tides, he then takes possession of the ship and can gift it to anyone he desires. I am asking that you allow me to have his ship." He said as he extended his arms out to the side and allowed himself a smile.

"And what will you do with his ship?" Franchesca asked as she looked into his light brown eyes. Maamin smiled and bowed his head. "I will go home. You may call on me anytime you wish, and I will obey, but I want to go home."

"Perhaps I will become a trader. If you like I will even take him with me when I depart." Maamin nodded to the wounded assassin. Franchesca ran her fingers through her hair and thought a moment. Things certainly were happening fast.

"How can I trust you?" Franchesca asked. She'd meant only to think it, but there it was; cast out into the world like a stone thrown into a pond, the ripples spreading. How can I be a good ruler if I can't even keep my own thoughts in my head, except for that one? Nothing for it now she decided; the question was asked—it was out there, she might as well live with it. Besides, it was a question worth asking; and worth knowing the answer to. Maamin sighed. "Truthfully you can't. You never know if your trust is misplaced. But I swear an oath upon my ancestors; my homeland, my life and my god." Maamin bowed deeply at the waist. Franchesca tucked her pistols back into the holsters on her waist before tapping her chin for a moment appearing to give the matter some thought. She didn't think she had much choice. If she denied him, the man might very well fight for Saaladan in this supposed upcoming duel provided; he wasn't lying. By the Heavenly Lady's grace, a misstep here could cost her everything, even her life. As much as she hated to admit it, he was right. You never know if you can trust anyone, there is only one way to find out if your trust is misplaced.

"Very well, but if you betray me, you will die. I don't know how, and I don't know if it will be by my hand, but you will die." Franchesca warned. The steel in her voice was so cold, so sharp—his eyes widened ever so slightly. That momentary reaction told Franchesca something very important about this man, he believed her.

"Of that, I have no doubt." Maamin nodded as he bent to collect his sword and began to secure it back about his waist. "You might also be interested to know, the people of Tornusia are giving the deepest consideration to casting their votes for you. I suppose having the voice of the sea speak in your favor carries a certain weight." He said. As Maamin turned to leave, Ayzza called out to him.

"How did you find this place; and how did you know we would be here?" She demanded. Maamin paused glancing back and forth between the four of them.

"I didn't know if you would be here. Saaladan ordered me to see if his attack had been successful. I awoke early to follow his instructions. Though I do not relish the thought of letting him know he was completely unsuccessful—I will take some delight in watching him fall. If he sits upon that throne, he will be worse than Konrad by a hundredfold." Maamin replied.

"Tell Saaladan, that I personally accepted his offer to duel." Franchesca nodded. Maamin bowed politely. Franchesca had grown up in a world of bowing and could read the subtle language. His bow was one of acknowledgment and understanding; not one of submission or service. It was simply the sign of someone who understood what they'd been told; rather than one accepting a new station in life. He was not her servant, and he was not Saaladan's—that made him dangerous.

"You're quite brave, for such a young one. Unless I have missed my guess, I would place your age at only around seventeen, or eighteen summers. I only hope you are crafty enough to see the deed done—and ruthless enough to carry it out." A look of confident menace slithered across Franchesca's features. Fierce determination thundered within her chest.

"Don't worry about me; I'll be just fine." She said coldly. There was such confidence in her tone it made him nod with approval, and respect. A self-assuredness brought on not by arrogance, but by determination. Franchesca would never admit she was afraid, not to this man; but after the fight aboard Konrad's ship, she felt she could survive a duel against a single man; especially if that man was a man like Saaladan. Her mind traveled back to the behemoth of a man she'd faced in the holds on her way up to the deck of the Mange. She remembered the blow of a ham like fist slamming against her face, and being thrown around. Saaladan wasn't particularly large, and she doubted he could even lift her, especially if what Maamin said were true; but she didn't know how much of it was. Maamin might have seen him as weak, but that mean he was. Perspective was a funny thing. For all, she knew Saaladan was putting on an act to bait his crew into making a move against him. Perhaps she was being paranoid, but when her life was on the line, she wasn't willing to call that a bad thing. Franchesca could use her speed, and quick mind to her advantage and make it a contest of endurance; if Saaladan were sick, there would be no way he could last as long as she could.

"Tell him I look forward to seeing him tonight." Franchesca nodded. Maamin smiled a serpent's malicious smile and bowed as he strode away from the cave. Syandro took a step forward and watched as he walked down through the wilderness and headed back towards the city streets.

"You truly mean to fight Salaadan?" Syandro asked as he slid his blades back into their sheaths.

"Franchesca ya can't... ya shouldn't." Simone chimed in. "Let me..." Franchesca shook her head and kissed Simone on the cheek interrupting her. Her lips scarcely grazing the soft flesh of her face, but it was enough to get her attention.

"I can't. I can't let anyone else do this. These people expect a leader, a fighter; someone of bravery, and action. The crew expects the very same. If I let one of you do it, I will play right into Saaladan's hands even if I lose. I don't want people looking down their noses at me. They expect a stiff-backed leader; I'll give them one." Franchesca told them.

"I'm not afraid." She lied; with a smile that only attempted to fortify her courage. Her stomach knotted, and her throat felt dry, but she would not back down. The men of her ship would no doubt be watching her; she wanted to make them proud. Franchesca felt she had something to prove, and she was going to do just that.

Chapter 29

To say he was angry would have been a drastic understatement. When Maamin delivered the news Franchesca, and her companions still lived, it caused talons of black indescribable rage to course through his heart and brain. The only solace came when he heard Franchesca accepted the challenge of trial by combat. A challenge he had no intention of meeting himself. Maamin would prove enough of an adversary that he wouldn't have to risk life and limb. Saaladan smiled, even though he was quite sure that he could prove more than a match for his opponent. After all—she was a girl; only a child of eighteen or so summers. Perhaps then, child was the wrong word; if things had been different he might have even allowed her to live; provided she became a wife. Saaladan stood by the side of the dock, his retinue standing behind him as he toyed with the pommel of his blade absentmindedly. His bejeweled rings made dull clanking sounds against one another as he rubbed his fingers together. He glanced up at the sky; judging by the position of the sun it was late evening, despite the scowl on his face part of him was happy with the more recent turn of events. If Franchesca failed to show up for the trial by combat, then he would win by default. Her reputation would be ruined, and all would see her as a coward. Saaladan turned and regarded the assembled gathering. He held up his hands and chuckled.

"Tell me, how long must I wait? She has failed to show herself. The woman is a coward." Saaladan remarked with a dismissive wave of his hand. He turned to the weathered–looking old man and held up his arms. "How long must we wait." The old man held up a pale, wrinkled hand.

"The day is not out. You know the rules. Anyone challenged must meet at the docks; the battle must take place aboard a ship, and both parties are given until sundown." The elderly man replied as the bright and exotic plumes decorating his hat swayed in the gentle breeze.

"She is a coward Alfaido. What business does a child have in such things anyway?" Saaladan asked with growing irritation. Why did everyone stand in his way? Why was it none would stand up and denounce this girl as a leader. It was improper; she would turn the island into a laughing stock.

"One could ask that of you; if we were all being honest." The old man shot back. Age had done nothing to dull his wit or the sharpness of his tongue. Those edges were as keen and razor–sharp as they'd ever been; perhaps more so.

"I tell you now Alfaido; we are wasting our time. The girl is..." The crowd stirred, and murmurs that began in groups of ones and two's grew and spread until all began to clamor, twisting and turning to see what was happening. Saaladan felt his heart sink—he'd been so close.

"If you call me a coward one more time, I'll gut you where you stand." A sharp and confident voice shot back. Franchesca's thick–soled boots thumped against the wooden planks of the dock as her coat fluttered in the gentle breeze. Saaladan turned and observed the unfolding scene. Two of her companions carried a litter with the maimed body of one of his assassins; while Ayzza watched from Franchesca's side. Saaladan growled. He'd come so close.

"My apologies for being late; it takes a while to get through the streets with a man who can't walk." Franchesca announced, her stormy gray–blue eyes locking with Saaladan's hate–filled brown orbs.

"Why then did you bring him, child?" Alfaido asked as he took a limping step forward, propping himself up on his silver–topped cane. "He's now in my service. I spared his life after Saaladan attempted to have me killed." Franchesca scowled as her eyes met the Saharian's own. There was a murmur of disgust that rippled through the assembled crowd. Many turned their head to glare hatefully at Saaladan and his retinue.

As voices rose and arguments began Alfaido thumped his cane against the timbers of the dock. The shouting stopped, and the crowd was subdued and silent once more; although far more tension hung in the air than there had been only five seconds ago. The ancient looking man turned and glared at

Saaladan with scorn, much like the look an angered father might show his child after he'd been caught doing something shameful and scandalously wrong. Saaladan didn't flinch from the gaze as the sun cast its fleeting rays over his robed frame. He simply held out his hands and offered an unapologetic shrug.

"He also burned down my hut in the attempt." Ayzza growled angrily. This time there was such a commotion and energy of anger that members of the crowd actually reached out and shoved Saaladan and members of his retinue. Ayzza was right, the people of Tornusia, be they sailor, merchant, or merely a citizen, were a superstitious lot. Burning down the hut of one they considered the voice of the sea was a crime many thought Saaladan should be strung up for. He rolled his eyes and scoffed. He spat upon the dock as he watched Franchesca. Their eyes met, and there was an unspoken fury which crackled between them. Alfaido thumped his cane once more ordering silence. He cleared his throat and let out a sigh.

"Captain..." Alfaido allowed his sentence to taper off into a question as he allowed one eye to grow wide in his study of her. They'd met yesterday, but given his age, it was clear that some things didn't stick within his mind right away—her name evidently was one of those things.

"Flint, please, if you would be so kind sir." Franchesca interrupted with a polite bow as she took a step forward. Her guts felt as though some giant was squeezing. This was really happening. In a matter of moments, she was going to fight another pirate captain... with no help—she would be all on her own. She could do it—couldn't she?

"Very well, Captain Flint you've been challenged to a trial of combat by one named Sultan Saaladan. This is to be a duel to first blood..."

"No." Saaladan interrupted. "To the death." His self–satisfied smirk was evidence of the truth of Maamin's words. Evidently, he believed he possessed the upper hand; of course from the little she'd seen of his attitude, that could be believed at any time. Still, she didn't like that change. A duel of first blood that might not have been so bad. Death was bad; no matter how you stared it in the face. Maamin might have told Franchesca Saaladan was sick, but what if he was just strong enough to kill her. First blood was just a scratch—or a punch. Heavenly Lady, what have I agreed to?

"It is so amended. This is to be a duel to the death. The rules of the duel are simple. You will each have your blades; pistols are forfeit to a third party as are any ranged weapons. Poisoned blades are not permitted. The battle will be fought aboard The Crimson Tide. Any weapons aboard such as harpoons, boarding axes, belaying pins, pistols empty of shot and extra swords will be scattered about the deck; should you be disarmed or have your weapon break. Should all weapons be broken, then you will fight bare–knuckled until one of you should expire. Do you accept the terms of the duel Captain Flint?" Alfaido asked as he gazed into Franchesca's eyes. The elderly man held a look in his eyes which seemed to silently beg Franchesca to reconsider the duel; if not refuse to take any part in it at all—a silent plea which remained silent and ignored when Franchesca opened her mouth.

"I accept." She said calmly, as she shrugged off her long coat and unfastened the leather belt hanging at her hips containing two of her pistols. She unfastened the leather strap across her chest which secured a third, and handed them to Ayzza with a smile.

"Saaladan, do you accept the terms as I have laid them out?" The old men asked angrily; his face a mask of disappointment, and disapproval.

"Indeed." Saaladan smirked. "I now use my right to nominate a fighter to fight in my stead." Saaladan nodded.

"It is your right should you wish—much as it pains me to admit. You receive one nomination, only one as I am sure you know already." Alfaido growled. He looked the man up and down with contempt.

"I choose my humble bodyguard Maamin Al Kulm." Saaladan said proudly. Franchesca watched as Maamin stepped forward and approached her. He glanced back over his shoulder before turning and smiling at Franchesca. He sank to one knee and bowed his head. Saaladan's heart froze; his blood boiled with seething rage.

"I am afraid my captain that my loyalties have sailed elsewhere." Franchesca glanced up and smirked.

"You filthy son of a swine mounted whore! I'll..." Saaladan allowed his voice, and rant to fall silent but kept the fire within his eyes. As he spoke, he could feel his chest begin to tighten; the more fire stoking his fury, the tighter it became. His hands clenched to white–knuckled balls so tight it hurt.

"You have nominated a fighter, and the fighter has declined." Alfaido nodded, a smile coming easily to his lips. "With your one nomination done, we now turn to Captain Flint. Do you wish to nominate one to fight on your behalf?" Alfaido asked, his gaze fell upon her; now there came a critical moment where he placed her on a scale. She briefly wondered how she would fair upon Alfaido's scale of judgment. She'd seen the way he glowered at Saaladan when he'd elected to nominate someone to fight in his place. It was disapproval, harsh and deep–rooted disapproval. Could she risk it, dare she? Franchesca glanced back over her shoulder at Syandro and Simone. Each of them seemed to plead without saying a word. They didn't want her to go through with this; they didn't want her to risk herself. She knew that, had known it all along. But they wouldn't stop her, no matter how much they wished to; they knew there were something's one had to prove on their own. She loved them for it.

"I am no coward; I'll fight." She smiled. Saaladan scowled as the crowd laughed, entertained by her jibe; many crying out mocking him and branding him a coward. Men began to board The Crimson Tide, each murmuring with excitement and wonder. Franchesca felt a firm grip on her shoulder and turned.

"Be careful." Simone whispered, doing her best to keep her worry, and fear hidden as a single tear rolled down her cheek. She knew it sounded stupid. How could you be careful when you agree to a fight to the death; Simone wondered as Franchesca reached out and wiped the tear away. Her guts were in knots, and she wanted to vomit, but she'd eaten nothing. She wanted to pace, but what would that do? No, the truth was Simone wanted to be down there with her, wanted to protect her. Simone had lost too many people; she couldn't lose her too—not if there was something she could have done to help. Franchesca winked at her, and a smile pulled at the corners of her mouth; a nervous smile, but it was a smile. Simone let out a sigh as she watched Franchesca continue up the gangplank. Simone hurried after her moving to the quarterdeck and taking a position in the front of the packed crowd. The duel itself was to take place upon the main deck, with all spectators looking down at those fighting from somewhat elevated platforms such as the quarterdeck or the forecastle. Some climbed the rigging to gaze down on the spectacle that was about to unfold. Like sharks circling when they smelled blood, this would be a feeding frenzy of an entirely different kind. It was equal parts entertainment, and equal parts democracy for those assembled. Franchesca descended the steps that led to the main deck. The layout of The Crimson Tide was such that the poop deck, quarterdeck, and forecastle stood high above the upper deck; it was as if the builder had inadvertently created a large fighting arena. This ship's decks were more elevated than most she'd seen. Perhaps it was not so inadvertent maybe this ship was a floating fighting pit. She saw Syandro standing next to Simone, concern, and worry written across his normally calm features too. She did her best to flash him a reassuring smirk, though she could sense it did little in the way of being effective. Cannonballs lined a narrow wooden track, each held in place by the one beside it. Franchesca gazed about looking at the numerous weapons scattered around. Axes, clubs—some banded with iron, others spiked through with nails. Harpoons were tied to the rails; swords were jammed into the walls or left in the handrails of the ship where someone had sliced down and left the blade. Daggers were stuck into the deck; all around her were instruments of death. Each one arms reach away, each object ready to spill blood or take a life. She watched as Saaladan descended the steps down to the main deck to meet her. Many booed, others cheered; it made Franchesca feel a little better to know that the booing far outweighed the cries of celebration.

"I'll not forget your betrayal Maamin!" Saaladan shouted. "Once I am through with her, I'll claim your balls then your head!" Maamin looked down and smirked.

"We will have to wait to see whom fate, and god favors." Maamin replied as he placed his fingertips to his forehead and made a polite bow.

"When you hear the pistol shot you may begin!" Alfaido announced. Saaladan pulled a steeply curved blade from the sheath that hung at his side. Franchesca tugged her cutlass free and took a few practice swings to loosen her muscles to become familiar with its weight. What was she doing, she asked herself as doubt began to creep into her mind and veins? This was insanity. Her thoughts were cut short by the peal of thunder, as the pistol shot broke the nervous silence. Saaladan howled as he rushed forward. He stopped short and unleashed a flurry of downward strokes and furious slashes. His blade came from as many different angles as the human brain, and body would allow one to think of, and execute without harm to one's self. Fear gripped Franchesca tightly, as the song of clanging steel assaulted her ears. This was a mistake, she told herself. Her blade danced around just as quickly as Saaladan's; though her arm was quickly becoming numb from the reverberations moving through it after the impact and repeated assault from Saaladan's blade against her own. His footwork was as quick as his strikes pushing her back two steps at any given moment. This is what Maamin considered a sick man?

Franchesca watched for an opening, hoping with the fall of every swing there might be a gap in Saaladan's viper–like movements, large enough for her to exploit. With a wild shout and a curse—he lunged forward hoping to take Franchesca off guard as she batted away his previous strike. She spun and watched as he stumbled past her. He'd overextended himself, and left himself wide open. Now Franchesca's time had arrived. She began her own series of attacks. Swings meant to disembowel and blows intended to cleave and sever limbs. Their blades locked and Franchesca found herself inches away from Saaladan's snarling features. Her arms were so tired. Her muscles burned and ached from the sheer number of bone–jarring impacts. His speed was impressive, Franchesca would give him that much. Despite the rage, she could see fear deep behind his eyes. His strength was fading. Now that she was scant inches from his face, and the clatter of steel against steel had stopped, she could hear him begin to wheeze. She listened as he cleared his throat, and let out a small cough.

"It doesn't have to be like this." Franchesca hissed. "I already know you're dying. We could work together..." as the words left her mouth his expression darkened. Apparently, it was the wrong thing to say; perhaps the wrong thing to say out loud in front of all the spectators.

"Silence, you blasphemous whore!" Saaladan snapped. With a show of strength, he broke the lock and pulled her in by the collar of her shirt and rammed his knee into her stomach. The blow was hard enough to begin a fit of coughing as she sank to her knees. There was a collective shout of displeasure and even a few gasps as Saaladan stepped around her. Franchesca cradled her stomach in one arm as Saaladan came up behind her. Her eyes blurred, and she struggled to refill her lungs. He placed his blade at her throat; and though her back was to him, she could feel his sneer. He repositioned himself and the blade. It wouldn't do to cut her throat by pulling his sword towards him; with as sharp as it was he would most likely disembowel himself. Franchesca could see tears rolling down Simone's cheeks. She could see Syandro's grip tighten reflexively upon his blade, Maamin's jaw was clenched tightly at the unfolding scene. Gods it must look as grim as it feels Franchesca, thought. As he drew the blade up to strike her head from her shoulders, Franchesca quickly dropped down and rolled onto her back; fighting to bring air into her lungs—by the Heavenly Lady they burned so much. Her saving grace had been that Saaladan wanted to make sure everyone watching the fight saw him remove her head. He'd pulled his blade back too far—he exaggerated his backswing and which gave her time for the desperate. Survival instinct raged like an unattended fire and overwhelmed the pain she felt. As she rolled onto her back, she threw a hasty kick that caught Saaladan square in the groin. Her lungs burned as she sucked in air, but she pushed the pain to the back of her mind. With a muffled grunt, he doubled over dropping his blade. Franchesca rolled to her feet as Saaladan fought to keep himself upright. With both hands cradling the caressing pain from his groin, Franchesca had an opening. She booted him in the knee, and as he howled and sank back down, she kicked him in the face; stepping back cautiously. She peered up at the assembled crowd as they cheered, each one relishing the duel between two iron wills.

Franchesca spotted Simone, Syandro, Almin, and Cornando—each watching apprehensively. Almin and Cornando must have moved their way through the crowd to get a better view of what was going on. Almin appeared only slightly better than he had, but he was here; and by the Heavenly Lady's grace, he didn't look well at all. Surely watching this was playing upon his nerves. Maamin watched and waited for the killing blow that would see Saaladan's property become forfeit; which would see him free from his bond to that bastard. The only set of eyes that seemed to watch her without a trace of fear belonged to Ayzza. Franchesca watched her nod approvingly. She didn't know how Ayzza could watch without fear, but Franchesca supposed it was a good thing. Saaladan pushed himself to his feet and hissed angrily.

"I'm going to enjoy killing you." He said as he limped towards her, favoring the leg Franchesca had kicked.

"So you've said." Franchesca panted, as she watched him pick up his blade. As he charged her, Franchesca dropped down at the very last moment and placed her feet into his stomach and flipped him over, using his charge against him. His back hit the deck of the ship with a thud. Timbers rattled, and the weapons laying strewn in every direction clanked with the impact. The crowd roared its approval as she pushed herself up. Her muscles ached, and her sword arm felt numb. She could see Syandro grit his teeth and shake his head slowly. She knew that he hoped such a gesture would go unnoticed. Franchesca also knew that Syandro could pick up on her signs of fatigue; being a far more experienced swordsman. From the distance he stood, he could read the tired numbness of her sword arm. For a split moment, Franchesca could almost feel him trying to will feeling and vigor back into her numbed muscles. Try as she might to will herself to maintain the grip on the blade's handle, it became looser and looser in her grasp.

She turned just in time to watch Saaladan pick up one of the solid, three-pound iron cannon balls. The cannonballs were meant to be used in the swivel guns to end human lives as well as do damage to a ship if it missed its fleshy target. His fingers wrapped around the metal ball holding it with a grim determination to end Franchesca's life. He howled as he threw the ball towards her. Her blade clattered to the deck as the need to survive took hold. Franchesca dropped to the timbers and threw her arms over her head. The metal projectile clattered loudly against the wooden door that led below deck. With a howl of rage, Saaladan picked up another of the cannonballs and threw it at her prone form. Franchesca rolled for her life and felt the breeze of the thrown projectile as it narrowly missed her. The cracking sound it made when it hit the deck was almost deafening given its proximity to her ears. The three-pound shot rolled back towards her, and she scooped it up in her slender fingers. She pushed herself up as Saaladan ran towards her, blade in hand ready to kill. Franchesca gritted her teeth in grim determination; she had to wait for the opportune moment. She couldn't bend down to pluck her blade or any other weapon from the deck. To do so would be death. This was going to come down to timing and luck. Then when he was almost upon her—as he swung his blade to open her throat, Franchesca fell to one knee, ducking beneath the swing. In a swift, fluid motion with no hesitation, she swung a punch with the hand that held the ball of iron. The metal sphere connected with Saaladan's kneecap, with a gut-wrenching crack. He crumpled to his good knee, screaming in anguish. As his weapon fell from his hand, Franchesca rose and swung once more. This time the iron ball connected with Saaladan's face. He fell to the deck of the ship—arms wrapped around his bloodied head. An eerie silence fell over the assembled spectators as Franchesca strode towards him. She rolled him over using the toe of her boot. She gazed down at his bloody and ruined face. His eyes were closed, but his chest still rose and fell steadily. Saaladan's eyes suddenly flew open, and his hand produced a dagger. He swung it desperately and struck a wound upon Franchesca's leg. She took one step back before throwing herself upon Saaladan's maimed body. As he brought his arm up to stab at her once more, she grabbed his wrist. After a brief struggle, the knife was lost somewhere between the two of them. Hearts in the crowd sank—and breath was held in lungs as they waited for what was to happen next. None had ever seen a fight so fierce. Franchesca reared her head back and struck Saaladan's nose with her forehead. He cried out in pain and then seemed to go rigid. Franchesca sat up—her legs to either side of Saaladan's narrow chest as she straddled his bloody form. She reached out and picked up the solid iron shot and brought it up over her head. With a savage cry, she brought the solid iron sphere down once—twice—three times, before her ears finally heard the sickening crunch. Blood splattered her skin and covered the hand that gripped the cannon shot in a death grip. Franchesca screamed; not a scream of joy, not a scream of victory—but the broken hollow sound of a wounded soul. Her arms went slack. Her hands relaxed. The cannonball clattered dully against the wood of the deck as her hand released its murderous weight. It rolled away with a sound that could only be thought of as a dry breath caught in a throat; leaving a bloody trail as it fled away from her. Before Franchesca knew it, Simone had rushed over to her. She knelt next to Franchesca and pulled her in close. Simone held Franchesca tightly against her trying to soothe away the aches and pains, and the vivid nightmare images of the face she'd just caved in with her own hands. The crowd remained silent, but she felt the gaze of every set of assembled eyes burning through her.

"It's alright; it's over now." Simone whispered reassuringly as she rubbed Franchesca's back and helped her to rise. As she began to turn her head towards the man she'd just killed—Simone turned Franchesca away from Saaladan's ruined body and led her back towards Ayzza and Alfaido. The crowd began to disperse heading down the gangplank in numbers of one or two until the deck was all but empty. Alfaido bowed his head. Each of them whispered in somber and hushed tones about what they'd witnessed. Franchesca could still smell the coppery rich blood that clung to her. She could still feel the crunch of bone as the cannonball she had held in her hand cracked it like an egg. Gods—how long would her nightmares about this last?

"A fine and well fought duel. How I wish it had not come to that." Alfaido's firm voice mentioned mournfully as one of his heavily armored guards stepped behind him. "I believe business will progress more smoothly now."

"She has my vote." A silky, heavily accented Castellian voice announced from behind her. Standing with a roguish smile was captain Frabranzo.

"I thought you..." her mind swirled with confusion. It was difficult to grasp onto what was happening.

"I only added my name so that if no one voted for you, it would not default to that swine. Now that the pig is dead—it seems to me that the best choice is you, my dear." Frabranzo bowed politely at the waist. "You might be young—but you are a true leader; brave and bold. I look forward to what you will write as law, and what you will do with our humble little island. The last thing I would wish to do is get on your bad side—as you have so freshly shown. Besides all of that leading would get in the way of my... activities." Frabranzo smiled as he took up her less bloodied hand, and pressed his soft lips to her knuckles respectfully. "If you will excuse me—I have some... business to indulge myself in." He grinned as he retreated down the gangplank. "The ladies of this island love me, my dear, If I am ever land bound, and you find yourself lonely please do not hesitate to seek me out. Ask around—you will find me." Frabranzo called out tipping his hat at a jaunty angle before turning to walk away. Alfaido cleared his throat as he stood next to Franchesca.

"Other than captain Frabranso's offer—rather anti–climatic is it not?" The old man asked with a gap–toothed grin. "I do hope you will rule well." He nodded politely as he began his descent down the gangplank, the tip of his cane creating a dull *clack—click—clack*, with every measured movement. Franchesca sank to her knees, partly due to exhaustion—mostly due to shock.

She'd killed before but never like that. There was something terrifying, and haunting clawing at her, and she could hardly bear it. The crack of a skull, the feeling of it deforming beneath her hand. Franchesca still felt as if she were outside herself; watching everything around her take place. Ayzza glanced down and grinned as she sank down next to Franchesca.

"Why don't we stay for a while, then we'll go and get you cleaned up. We'll get you ready to grace the throne by sunup tomorrow." Ayyza assured quietly. Franchesca didn't answer. She just gazed at the pastel colors which began to darken into the shades of the night sky. The last rays of pleasantly warm sun caressed her skin. The faintest whisper of a breeze seemed to stroke her hair reassuringly as she gazed out in silence.

Simone sat beside her; her hand rested on Franchesca's blood–soaked extremity. It was gentle, reaffirming; but most of all it was loving and supportive. Franchesca fancied she could feel a weight of pride from Simone's hand. Simone seemed to be the only one she knew who could say all she needed to hear without saying a word. Franchesca turned and smiled tender smile at her—the skin of her face feeling tight and pinched from where the blood dried.

"I did it." She had to say it out loud. She couldn't believe. She was still alive; and now she was the ruler of a pirate—what exactly? An island kingdom? What exactly did one call her new position?

"I told ya dat ya could." Simone smiled as she kissed Franchesca's unbloodied cheek. "I jus wished ya did't—I mean, I wish ya'd let me do it. I was worried about you Chesca." Simone whispered. Franchesca noticed that she'd said the last part without her customary accent. It was one way she always knew when Simone was worried, or taking something incredibly seriously. Moreover, it told Franchesca when Simone was scared, and she knew; and Franchesca had known she was, she could see it in her face. She couldn't imagine watching that sort of thing. Franchesca glanced up at her with a smirk—which no doubt made her look half insane; covered in blood as she was.

"And if you'd done it I would've been worried about you." Franchesca replied gently. "Why don't we try to never—ever do this again." She added rubbing her head. Simone nodded with a smile of her own and took a breath.

Franchesca glanced down at herself and sighed. "I need a bath—a very long, and very hot one." Simone and Ayzza chuckled. It was one luxury they could all do with. For Franchesca however, the sooner she could scrub the sticky crimson off, the better she would feel on the inside. For at least then she would not be coated in a constant reminder of the brutal way she had ended a man's life.

"Come with me then Captain Flint." Ayzza said looking at them proudly. Franchesca pushed herself up and followed Ayzza down the gangplank into the city. She felt more excited at the prospect of the soothing, heated water lapping against her skin than she did about becoming the newest leader of Tornusia. Perhaps it would dawn on her while she lost herself in the warm waters of the tub. The only thought that her mind could grab on to at the moment was the question of what to do next. Gods help me, she thought with a sigh. I have no idea she told herself silently.

* * *

Syandro walked through the twisting streets. The narrow alleyways were home to various gambling dens and other buildings where one could pursue any number of desires wholesome or otherwise. Taverns with men and women shouting bawdy songs lined one side of the road; while on the other side, simple, modest apartments stood. Candlelight flickered in the open windows. On one ledge he noticed a rag doll propped up and smiled. Syandro watched as drunks stumbled down the streets, and while ladies of the evening practiced their lustful techniques in plain sight. Against buildings, or in doorways, it didn't seem to matter where the parties were. As he passed the building with the ragdoll propped up in the window, a voice called out to him. Silky and seductive, laced with the same undertone, of course, unpolished roughness of street talking whores who surrounded the area.

"Fancy a tumble?" The woman asked with a wink and a flick of her tongue. "I'll show ya a night ya won't soon forget." Syandro sighed as he stared at her. His eyes strayed up to the window. He watched as a little girl stepped to the opening and peered out into the evening; her innocent eyes glancing down and gazed at her mother. Syandro reached in and pulled out a gold coin and handed it to her.

"Here; feed yourselves. No services required." He nodded as he pressed the coin into her dirty palm and walked away. Listening to the sound of lewd calls as other women lured their men off, and shouts of encouragement from their drunken fellows.

"We don't need your bleedin' charity!" The woman howled back. "Ya think I ain't a good mother! I take care of my own! I do what I gotta do since her da left me with her in my belly an' no ways of makin ends meet! Ya wanna do it yerself, enjoy yer hand; or the fuckin bottle! Maybe ya farm the other field ya little shite!" Despite her rants, and shouts of insult—Syandro never heard her throw the coin to the stony street. He hoped Franchesca could do something for these people. Franchesca, the thought hit his brain like a hammer. Syandro stopped in his tracks and sighed. He glanced up and found a tavern. With a heavy heart and a knotted stomach, he strode inside. Fortunately, there was always one way to subdue one's thoughts. A few stiff glasses and all would be right with the world again. Syandro approached the bar and slapped down a silver coin.

"Bring me a cup and keep it filled." The barman chuckled as he picked up a cup and filled it with the pungent smelling drink. Syandro took a sip. It felt as if he was drinking hot sand. It burned and scratched his throat on the way down; causing him to cough weakly and clear his throat.

"New to the island rum?" The barman grinned leaning forward on pudgy arms. The barman possessed notable paunch and was bald except for a stubborn tuft clinging desperately to the top of his head.

"So it would appear." Syandro replied as he took another sip. Every time he took a drink from the cup he became more and more accustomed to its strong taste. Shortly after his last gulp, Syandro felt the familiar numbness and the faint tingling that came with a growing state of inebriation. The wound his pride suffered seemed at best a dull ache now, and after a few more drinks it would be healed entirely. I'll win her over one day; he chuckled to himself. Hope springs eternal after all, he reminded himself. As the barmen placed another cup before him, Syandro reached out and welcomed the cup into his eager hands. As he drank, he found his mind drifting to a calmer place; free of thoughts of Franchesca and his desire, he felt himself become increasingly free—or increasingly empty of feeling. Perhaps his not being able to tell was the work of the rum; if so he was thankful for it.

As Syandro gazed into the amber contents of his glass, he found himself thinking about his father. How had he faired? Where was he? Perhaps he had returned to Castella, or maybe he had sailed back to the ports of Forn to flaunt his success at Franchesca's parents. It wasn't until that moment Syandro realized how much he missed his father. He missed his advice, and the wisdom his father instilled in him. The talks of adventure, and freedom, if there was one man who could lift Syandro's mood it was his father. I hope your adventures are fairing better than my own, Syandro though as he finished his drink.

Chapter 30

It had been hours after her bath; and though her body still ached, what she saw before her silenced the protesting of her muscles. After she'd a chance to soak in the warm water and scrub away the muck, grime and the caked on gore; Alfaido came calling for her. He claimed there was something he wished to show her; though she was bone weary, she agreed. Best not to appear weak, she thought. How right she'd been. The sight before her was more revitalizing—more rejuvenating than she ever thought possible. Franchesca gazed upon the throne that stood before her. It was truly unlike anything she'd ever seen before, and for all of its chaotic features competing for the attention of one's eye—it was indeed a thing of strange beauty. The throne itself stood atop a dais built of a ship's quarterdeck. More accurately, according to Ayzza, and Alfaido—the dais was the deconstructed quarterdeck of the first occupant of the Throne of Tides. The captain known as Jaggo Blacktooth, had his ship, The Mad Black, taken apart only to have its quarterdeck be rebuilt inside the building. Where the ship's wheel once stood—there was now a seat crafted of iron and well–worn wood. Its legs made of old swivel guns, its back made of harpoons jutting towards the ceiling. The arms of the throne had been crafted from the ship's railing; ending in basket sword guards, which had been affixed where one could wrap their hands around them. Ayzza and Alfaido explained every captain that ever sat upon the Throne of Tides, since Jaggo Blacktooth, left his mark upon it; in some way. Bandannas of every color and material were tied around multiple harpoons; or even upon the arms of the chair. Cargo nets were draped across the back, taking the place of fine fabrics such as silk or velvet. Some captains even skewered their hats upon the barbed harpoon tips, while others carved out scrimshaw designs where ever they saw fit. A cluster of swords had been affixed to run horizontal to the harpoons; creating a steel back to the chair. Wound about and tied to the handles of those blades, making a puddle of fabric upon the floor, was a collection of satin sashes in a host of different colors and patterns; as well and a set of pistols crossed at the top of the throne. Adding to it in its ever–expanding lineage of modification, there were of course—two sashes tied to the barrels of the pistols. It was amazing—ostentatious, and gaudy, but amazing none the less.

"Now I believe that one day you will make your own mark upon the throne." Alfaido nodded as she ascended the steps leading to the throne. So awestruck was she that she'd not noticed that the rhythm of his cane had ceased; as he stood in place below. She ran a finger over its weathered surfaces, her youthful and slender fingers feeling every grove, notch and scar of the wood; and every dent within the iron. The harpoons appeared razor sharp and ready for use. Even the sword blades kept their edges keen. Franchesca was sure that if she were to squeeze one of the triggers of the guns, she would find the mechanisms in working order, though perhaps in need of a good cleaning. Coins from around the world were plastered about; some hung from strips of silk tied to the legs or arms, others were bound to straps of cotton which were lashed to the hafts of the harpoons baring various coins. It was hard to believe a band of murdering, marauding pirates, whom many believed only skilled in the art of bloodletting; could create such a wondrous thing. Pennants and flags of past captains hung from the ceiling, some beneath a blanket of dust and cobwebs—so long had they been up upon the wall. The familiar sound of Alfaido cane making its *click–clack*—clicking, rhythm began anew as he moved forward and ascended the first two steps of the dais. He watched as Franchesca circled the throne gazing upon it with a sort of reverence which he'd seen few hold in their eyes.

"Is—there a crown... or any ceremony I need to be aware of?" Franchesca asked as she turned and gazed at him. There was a moment of silence, and she took a step back. "Gods I'm not going to have to fight anyone else am I?" Alfaido smirked as he held up a hand and eased tension.

"There is no true or formal crowning ceremony to speak of; indeed there is no actual crown—though many a pirate has held a crown of their own word or design." The old man chuckled as he peered up at her from the step upon which he stood.

"When do I actually become the ruler, then?" She asked as she continued to study the room in wide-eyed awe. Feelings indescribable struggled within her. How could one truly appreciate the sights before them unless they gazed upon them with their own eyes? The rest of the wide world saw the folk of Tornusia as bloodthirsty and uneducated. If they could see this—how everything would change.

"First, I would refrain from using the term ruler. Pirates don't tend to take kindly to being ruled over; it's why many of them are here in the first place. Every man and woman is their own here." Alfaido corrected with a gentle smile as he took out a small silk handkerchief and wiped his wrinkled brow.

"What am I defined as then?" Franchesca asked curiously.

"You are a leader and guide... a sort of captain of captains if you will." Alfaido nodded. "A captain can give an order, but the order can be voted on by members of the crew, or vetoed by the first mate. If you think of it—picture yourself as the captain of a large ship, and think of everyone else below you filling a position. On a ship, if someone disagrees with the captain, the whole crew can put it to a vote. I've heard from your crew; you gave them a vote on if they wished to sail here. Everything here tends to work exactly like that." He explained. When put that way it actually did make her role easier to picture. She was a ruler, but she was a ruler who could pick and choose her battles. The island seemed to run itself smoothly already if she saw how then she would only need to make minor changes. *Perhaps it won't be as difficult as I thought* she mused almost optimistically.

"We're a bunch that likes to have someone watching out for us; to make sure we don't get our necks stretched on the end of a noose—or various other methods of killing. But we also like to have a say; and if we think we know better then, just it's the way the dice roll. The point is—just because you want something done doesn't mean you get it." Alfaido told her as he cleared his throat. "Especially if you're a bad captain—something Konrad and Saaladan never quite seemed to get through their heads."

"Yet people obeyed them." Franchesca replied as she turned and peered down at him running a hand through her raven locks.

"Out of fear. There were many mutinies against them; but when you kill or torture someone to death, it tends to send a potent message." Alfaido nodded.

"The pair of them have killed more than their share of their own crew and terrorized more than they should have of the people upon the island. They were hated—and they were feared—thus they were obeyed, unfortunately." The elderly man gazed up and smiled at Franchesca, a smile of surprising warmth and youth which seemed well beyond the man's years to give. "I don't think you will have such trouble. From what I've seen, your crew cares greatly, and you are quite loved by them—brave, courageous, fair in judgment and decisive in action—all markings of a good leader." Alfaido assured. "You will make mistakes, but I also assume you to be wise enough to learn from them. Something those shit brains never truly did. By that measure, you're wise beyond your years' captain." Alfaido said with a grin as he leaned against his cane.

"What then is my duty? Surely it is not to sit upon here and look pretty and give orders that might not be obeyed." She asked as she strode back down the steps.

"First, might I say that your job is to look after the people of Tornusia—as any leader or ruler would." He smiled.

"But without using the term ruler." Franchesca smiled as she glanced at him. Alfaido nodded in agreement returning the grin as he leaned upon his cane.

"Very good; you learn quickly. You are... well; you are simply asked to be a leader. Look out for the people; look out for any willing to sail under your command. In a sense, do as your heart desires. If you seek to go treasure hunting, raiding—do as you must; but know that in all you do a cut is expected for your crew, as well as those at home." Alfaido explained with a fatherly smile. A sort of expression she'd often seen grace her own father's face, yet his smiles never possessed the warmth of Alfaido's. Franchesca let out a deep sigh.

"I plan on changing things here..." her voice trailed off as she took in the sights. She'd planned on saying more; on filling him in just as she had Ayzza but looking at the chamber had thrown her, more than she'd believed possible. Alfaido held up his hand and nodded." Ayzza told me you plan to change a great deal. Though it is a noble goal do not expect everyone will follow; don't let that dissuade you. Change can take time to get used to." Alfaido assured.

"What if I should fail?" Franchesca asked. He smiled at her again warmly. This elderly man reminded her of a grandfather. He was warm and genuine. Franchesca guessed there was more strength to him than met the eye; and more to him than he allowed other's to glimpse. It was hard to believe this old man who could be a grandfather; a great–grandfather was a pirate—or had been. He seemed a wise sage, a scholar who'd harvested the choicest bits of knowledge from life's tree; and now shared his bounty with her.

"Then you fail, you pick up the pieces, amend your plan and try once more." Alfaido replied as he patted her on the shoulder. "Change your course, captain. Don't fight the sea; don't fight the island—and don't fight yourself."

"You are a wise one..." said Franchesca as she studied him. His warmth reminded her of Claude—reminded her of how much she missed him. His smirk reminded her of Simone's own playful, and mischievous grin. Gods above this man could very well be Simone's grandfather or great grandfather, couldn't he? She put the idea out of her head. There was no resemblance, except in the smirk.

"It comes included with the aches and pains of age." Alfaido nodded while his walking stick made a dull clack, as he walked the length of the chamber. "Stick to your guns as they say, and you'll be fine." Alfaido smirked. "As for when you officially take hold, I believe tomorrow will be the day. There will be a rather large amount of pomp, and circumstance tomorrow; ready yourself for that." Alfaido said. Franchesca watched Alfaido step towards the door where one of his heavily armored bodyguards pushed the portal open. He turned regarding her with one final smile before exiting. Franchesca peered up at the throne—she suddenly felt overwhelmed; the full weight settling on her now that she stood in the room that would be her seat of power. It finally dawned on her just how real her situation had become. It was no longer a what if. No more obstacles to overcome, or foes to fight to gain the seat. Now the throne was hers. Now she had people she was in charge of—citizens, pirates—a gods' damned economy. For the thousandth time, she asked herself why she'd agreed to fight for the Throne of Tides. For what felt like the millionth time she asked herself if there was a way out of what she'd gotten herself into.

* * *

The day finally arrived, the day when Franchesca would sit atop the Throne of Tides and become the next official Captain of Tornusia. She and a party consisting of Syandro, Simone, Ayzza, and Alfaido; made their way through the streets. There was more pomp and circumstance than Franchesca thought possible, at least for an island nation founded on pirating and looking like it was just scraping by. Her first scan of the buildings had been somewhat misleading. Though the buildings were in good repair; or good enough that they could call any nation their home, its citizens appeared to be having a rougher time. If she'd not seen it before, she would never have known by the look of things now. Crowds cheered wildly as they watched from windows, or doorways as the small procession went by. Franchesca smiled and waved; she even stopped when a crowd of children ran up to her and handed her a small bouquet of plucked wildflowers. She grinned and laughed; before kneeling and giving them each a brief hug, or tussle of the hair.

"She is exactly what this island needs." Ayzza whispered to Alfaido as she watched Franchesca interact with the children. Alfaido nodded and leaned on the silver griffon's head of his cane as he waited for the procession to begin once more. Franchesca rose, and the procession began again. They strode through the streets towards the building serving as Tornusia's palace; where the strangely, wondrous throne stood. The building itself was more like a fortified manse rather than a true palace. Everything upon Tornusia seemed to straddle the line between ornamental, and functional practicality. It somehow seemed right that their seat of power should be situated in a place designed in such a way as well.

It was all happening so fast; Franchesca thought as petals from flowers drifted down in a gentle shower. Drums banged and clattered—the music was a strange cacophony of different regions, different voices, and styles; somehow it all seemed to go together, Franchesca basked within the sounds. It was the sound of Tornusia. It was the heartbeat of its people; their music, their voice, their call of joy and celebration. She only hoped she could live up to their expectations. I hope I don't let them down, she told herself—I can't afford to, she added silently as the boots thumped against the paving stones. Syandro shifted his gaze; his hand resting on the hilt of his blade—his insides feeling as though all had been thrown into fire, and chaos. When the celebration began, he felt happy for Franchesca. After all, she was his friend; and the woman he loved, deeply. However, that changed as they paraded through the winding streets. He found himself wondering why it was she deserved this honor more than he did. How was this fair? Bile gripped his stomach tightly; feeling like the gnashing, chomping teeth of some beast chewing its way through his insides. Part of him wanted to challenge her to a duel; to prove he could beat her. She was a crack shot with a pistol, but he was better with a blade, and he knew it. Part of him wanted to, but only out of anger and frustration. The other part of him—the larger part, couldn't stand the thought. For that part dreamt of her; longed for her, and believed she shouldn't be here. For the first time since he was a child, Syandro wanted something he couldn't have; and that only made him want it more. He'd written his feelings in verse, but never bothered to show them to her. It would do no good, and besides, he thought as he smiled partly to himself—partly to the beautiful girl he'd paused to wave to as she stood on the side of the street. Why rub salt in the wound and pack it with dirt, he asked himself? There was no point in opening himself up even more. No point in showing her the wounds upon his heart, the bruises that had

been struck against his pride; not when they would gain him nothing. I'm not a
poet, not a true one; he told himself as he smiled at the cheering people.
Waiting for her hurt him deeply, but it was all he could do. He'd tried to
showcase himself, and attempted to show he was a capable leader and a fighter.
He did well; but clearly not well enough. His wounded pride recalled those
times Franchesca and Simone saved him. How it galled him to be so weak. Yes,
Syandro would wait; he would wait until he could think of another, more
strategic way to show himself better than Simone; better than any that dared to
challenge him. Franchesca would swoon over him then, or so he hoped.
Syandro felt a chill travel up his spine before the tingle traveled through his
arms. He glanced over and noticed Ayzza staring at him. Her gaze made him
feel uneasy. Every time he felt his eyes on her, Syandro could not help but
remember those dark words dripping with warning.

"I sense a great darkness in you." Syandro just smiled and bowed his head;
though Ayzza never removed her eyes from their glaring path. He wanted to
shout for her to look away but refrained from doing so. Was she right? Syandro
wondered. What could she possibly see within him that filled her with such a
feeling of dread? Syandro remembered it'd not always been so. Ayzza didn't
always fear him; or think him dark and evil or, whatever it was she thought of
him now. It was after that night in the cave. After that strange dream with the
woman who looked like Franchesca.

Though his head was foggy about much of that dream, he remembered the
beginning. He heard a noise in the woods and found a woman that appeared
eerily similar to Franchesca. Yes, he found her then, yes then they kissed; but
then what happened? Syandro asked himself. He'd woken up, only to find
Ayzza glaring at him, along with curious scratches that marred his chest. What
in the name of all the gods was going on, Syandro thought? What has
happened? Syandro sighed as he lifted his hand once more and waved, giving
small salutes to no one in particular. He watched as a few women, women he
knew from the local brothels, wink at him. He smiled a tiger's smile and bowed
politely—taking each of their hands and planting a small kiss upon their

knuckles. He would have to see them later; such activities always seemed to distract him from his maelstrom of unrelenting thoughts. There was perhaps no better night than this, for such amorous activities, he mused. Syandro watched as Franchesca ascended the curving marble steps of what served as the palace or to most, the lavish domicile upon the island. Two of Alfaido's armored guards pulled open the thick oak doors and held them as the small procession ascended the steps. Two more of the heavily armored guards lead the small group down a long hallway. The corridor was draped in finery; curtains of rich, wine-red hung over the windows. Paintings in all manner of styles dotted the passage. Portraits and landscapes, famous sights and prominent rulers—none of whom were from Tornusia—Syandro knew because he saw a portrait of a long-deceased member of the Castellian royal family, hanging next to beautifully painted meadows, or rivers. Some were made in the classical style; others portrayed the immerging, Austinean abstract, impressionist style. Quite the collection of fine treasures for an island filled with homes looking like they would topple over in a stiff breeze, Syandro thought. Unlike Franchesca, he'd not been impressed with the architecture; or the repair of the buildings. He worked hard to contain a scoff when she spoke with such enthusiasm about the sights when they had been together. At least she found a silver lining—Syandro supposed that there were more taverns and brothels here than he ever remembered seeing in one place, so he chose to allow that to be a positive for him. The last set of doors were tugged open then the small procession stood before the faithfully, and meticulously recreated quarterdeck of The Mad Black. The Throne of Tides stood atop it awaiting her, while the remaining crew of The Quest, watched her with smiles and radiating joy. Out of the corner of her eye, Franchesca watched as Almin and Cornando smiled and gave small salutes.

"You may sit if you wish captain." Alfaido nodded towards the Throne of Tides. Franchesca took a deep breath. Her legs felt as though the bones had been removed and the meat would simply dissolve into a puddle—yet she moved, one foot before the other; with as much grace and authority as she could manage. She hoped she looked graceful and authoritative at any rate. The soles of her boots thumped hollowly against the wood of the steps set up to climb to the quarterdeck. Every footfall was like a boom of thunder in time with her beating, racing heart. I hope I don't pass out—that would be the worst thing in the world—well that or my clothes falling away Franchesca thought to herself as she stood before the throne. Before her thoughts could race anymore, she turned and studied the gathered crowd and fought off a smirk, as she looked at them. She maintained a look of confidence and assurance she still hadn't completely nailed in place yet—as she lowered herself down slowly. She was amazed at how much control she was able to maintain during her decent. The numerous ribbons and swatches of fabric upon the throne gave a quiet rustle, and the wood issued a gentle creak as she settled herself in.

"All hail the Captain of Captains, the Captain of all Tornusia! Captain Flint!" One of the heavily armored guards bellowed. His voice, strangely unmuffled by his full face helmet. For a moment Franchesca felt herself wanting to jump. He saluted by holding forth his halberd and stamping the pole into the marble floor. The other guards did likewise, causing Franchesca to give a small flinch of surprise from the cacophony. From somewhere outside a trumpet blew a long single note before breaking into a handful of others. Joining the sound of the lone trumpet was the sound of a grand harbor bell chiming four times; the crowd outside erupted into even louder cries of celebratory joy. Those gathered within the chamber cheered, some removing their hats or bandannas and waving them over their heads. Franchesca watched those gathered celebrate, her heart pounding all the while. To say she was shocked was an understatement; perhaps the biggest understatement of her entire life. Simone gazed up at her and grinned as she clapped. Franchesca rose from her feet and held up her hands with a mischievous smirk.

"And what is your first order of business Captain Flint?" Alfaido asked with a broad smile, his back straitening as he gazed at her.

"I want a second throne built, one to sit beside this one." Franchesca nodded, her eyes regarded the crowd before locking on Simone.

"For I've chosen a companion, one whom I love, and wish beside me in all things." The crowd glanced at one another; murmurs passing between one another and whispers rising before they turned their attention back to her.

"I take this time to announce—I plan to share this responsibility, to share rule of this island with Si... Captain Steel—that is if she will assist me." Franchesca smiled. Simone gaped up at the throne; her doe-eyed emerald orbs, moist with tears. Simone tucked a lock of hair behind her ear and bowed.

"I accept the responsibility; happily." Simone nodded as she ran forward. Franchesca rose from her seat and caught Simone as she rushed into her arms. The two embraced, tears streaming down each of their cheeks as they let out chuckles and laughed as they held one another. The few murmurs from moments ago were drowned out by applause. Tornusia was a place where men and women were free—at least more so than most places. What better place for Franchesca to fully blossom into the person she wished to be—with the person she wanted to stand next to. Alfaido held up his hands and nodded.

"It shall be done as you say, Captain Flint." Alfaido nodded bowing his head politely.

"I think now, however, is a time for celebration and feasting." He said with a broad beaming smile.

"Here, here!" Franchesca shouted as she and Simone stepped forward and held up their hands, as they descended the steps of the dais.

"Everyone to the feasting hall," she ordered cheerfully. As she threw open the doors to the dining hall, she was taken aback at the sight before her.

"A new captain! Yes, yes; a new captain sits upon the throne now." The lanky man's alarming voice cackled. Simone's hand dropped to the handle of her blade; likewise, Franchesca tugged one of her pistols free from its dark leather holster.

"Who are you?" Franchesca asked the greasy, lanky man bowed at the waist—the remnants of his oily, stringy hair falling in front of his face. The stranger flashed a grin made of decaying, discolored teeth.

"My name... yes; yes my name." The man chuckled madly. As he glanced back and forth at all around him. A broad deaths–head grin stretching across his features.

"My name is Phizemann. That is my name, yes. I come to bring greetings to our new captain. To wish her well, yes; yes—well wishes, and prosperity." The madman broke into a laughing fit and doubled over clutching his hands tightly to his narrow chest. As suddenly as the laughing fit came about he stopped and reached out and plucked a leg from a roasted chicken. His rotting discolored teeth tore a chunk of flesh from the meat. Franchesca couldn't help but watch as he chewed; his teeth gnashing and twisting every which way. Manners were apparently a thing the madman had given up upon long ago—or had just never heard of. She thought more towards the latter given the spectacle of the way he chewed. She hoped the sight might be over once the meat was sucked from the bone, but watched in horror as the madman began to gnaw and chew on the chicken bone. Her stomach lurched once she heard the muffled crack of it giving way beneath his ruined teeth.

"Are you quite finished?" Franchesca asked; doing her best not to retch. Everything from his appearance to the odor which drifted off of him in waves; made her skin crawl and made her feel like submerging in a hot bath while chewing a fist full of mint leaves. The man turned his head quickly to look her up and down, like a predator that wasn't quite sure if he could bring her down.

"With your well wishes, I mean." Franchesca added in an attempt to break the uncomfortable gaze he held her with. A disturbing smile cracked Phizemann's face as he swallowed the bit of bone he'd been chewing on. She felt her gorge rise. The contents of her stomach were so close now. That sight, the oily smell of rot and unwashed clothing—musty flesh clinging to him like a blanket, made her want to shoot him. Perhaps the scent of blood would be a more appealing smell.

"Yes, yes—all finished. All finished with my greetings." He babbled as he scratched his greasy head with an even filthier hand.

"You've announced yourself Phizemann; you've shown yourself off to the new captain, and now I think it's time for you to go." Ayzza growled. If possible, the madman glared at her with a gaze even more disturbing, hateful, and predatory than the one he studied Franchesca with. Two of Alfaido's heavily armored guards stepped forward and flanked the lanky man. Alfaido likewise glared at Phizemann with as much disgust as Franchesca and the others. The lanky madman burst into lunatic laughter and nodded.

"Yes, yes—must be going. Much work to be done—much to do; many to see." Phizemann cackled as he strode towards the door at the opposite end of the chamber, seeing himself out.

"My apologies Captain Flint; Phizemann is our..." Alfaido paused as if unsure exactly how to proceed.

"Resident madman?" She finished Alfaido's statement for him as she tucked her pistol back into its holster.

"That is certainly one way of putting it. Perhaps the most polite and diplomatic way I've ever heard it put. He has his moments of brilliance... but those are few and far between. For the most part, he keeps to himself—locked away in one of his workshops; but every once in a while he's spotted out and about." Alfaido admitted. Franchesca just nodded and let out a sigh. She waved the assembled crowd into a room, and their feast and celebration began.

"Come, he is gone now, and we should be celebrating!" Franchesca announced with a smile as she waved them all into the feasting hall.

* * *

Hours passed, and more celebrants joined the growing throng, with offerings of food and kegs of ale or other assorted drinks they obtained. Franchesca nodded and raised a glass to the dwarf captain, Obman Ironbrow; he hoisted his large stein in salute. She bowed her head politely to the elf captain; she'd heard referred to as Ailmyrth; he regarded her with a faint smile and an almost imperceivable bow of his head. Franchesca found herself sagging in her chair. She'd grown tired with all of the excitement of the day's events, not to mention the copious amounts of heavy food and strong drink she'd consumed. She felt a firm hand on her shoulder and glanced up to find Simone smiling at her.

"Did ya really mean it? Do ya really want me at your side?" Simone asked, sinking down into the chair beside her. The chamber had been so loud she hadn't even heard Simone approach, but by the Heavenly Lady was she glad to see her.

"I wouldn't have said it otherwise." Franchesca nodded with the slightest of bit of red beginning to color her cheeks. She suddenly felt very warm, positively hot even; and she wasn't sure it was because of the drink she'd consumed. "It's because of you I'm even here. It's because of you I even had the courage to take this chance. I've been rewarded, and I feel you should share it with me. I want you to share it with me; I want to share it with you; all of this. I... love you Simone, truly; deeply." Franchesca told her gently as she caressed Simone's face softly. Gods what was she thinking; blurting it out in the throne room—in front of everyone? It should have been done in private—it should have been a moment between just the two of them. What if Simone wasn't ready? It could be very hard to say no, I don't really want to help you govern an island with a room full of armed people surrounding you on all sides.

"I... I understand I sprung it on you. And maybe you couldn't think about it because there was a crowd in the room. If you need time to think it over or..."

Simone cut her off by leaning in and kissing her deeply. It didn't matter to her that there were eyes everywhere. None were watching them. Even if they were, it didn't matter if they did—Franchesca returned the kiss, feeling joy surge through her very being; and nothing would have stopped her. It was as if every nerve, every piece of skin, felt joy of its own; felt love its own, and now it surged, burning with this acceptance, this love of a woman who only saw her.

"Dat's my anser." Simone smirked, as she pressed her forehead against Franchesca's. "But if ya need tha words... then yes." Simone whispered with a smile that couldn't be any broader or brighter if she tried.

* * *

Syandro stood in a corner and couldn't help but overhear what Franchesca said. It was because of Simone? The thought soured his stomach. A lie, if there ever was one; he told himself angrily as he gulped back the rest of the wine in his cup. It was because of him. Franchesca was here because of him. He was the one who told her to seek out and seize adventure. He spoke to her of the freedoms of being your own person—not Simone. That back ally slut was out picking pockets while he walked with Franchesca; telling her of how he admired her spirit and desire for more than she had. It was he—Syandro De Madonia, who told her to reach out and grab the life she desired. Now Franchesca was giving the credit of her success to Simone? He took a deep breath and shuffled his way through the crowd seeking to escape, and get some fresh air. He had to do something. He needed to get Simone away from her. Or perhaps there was another way. Syandro plucked up another glass of wine from a serving tray and downed its contents in two large gulps. Yes, that was the way—the best way he grinned to himself as he set the empty glass down and strode out into the night to wander the streets.

* * *

"Yes, yes; that is him. That must be the one." Phizemann babbled to the three men clad in thick black oilskin coats.

"Clear a space; yes clear a space." Phizemann droned to himself as he hopped into the flat–bedded wagon and began clearing a space. As he moved a small keg and a metal lockbox; the three men nudged the fresh mound of soil with the tips of their boots.

"Ya, sure we need ta do this?" One of them asked as he glanced back at the wagon. As if in reply, Phizemann threw three shovels from the cart and leaped off with the nimbleness of a man half his age. He ran his twitching fingers through his stringy wisps of hair and laughed evilly; his rotten teeth showing in the dim light of the lantern he held out before him.

"Find a use for everything, yes indeed. Phizemann finds a use for everything. Someone is very interested in our deceased friend here. Very interested yes." He cackled as he slapped his bony knees.

"Just doesn't seem right is all." Another of the black–clad men mumbled as he wiped a meaty hand across his forehead. Phizemann reached into one of the many folds of his dirty rags and pulled a pistol. He leveled it at the man, as his look of lunacy faded into a glare that was far colder; and more lucid.

"Does it seem right now?" Phizemann hissed; pulling the hammer back for emphasis. Without further word of protest, the men sank their shovels into the recently turned earth. Foot by foot they dug until they reached their morbid prize—a simple box, slightly larger than a man. Its lid nailed shut with a few loose coins placed atop the wood. Phizemann tossed down a prybar and pranced in circles around the open pit. There was the sound of iron nails squealing as his men pried the wooden box open. Finally, there was a loud, satisfying crack. Phizemann sank to his knees and peered over the edge of the pit holding the lantern out before him. His rotten grin gleamed wildly as he gazed at them.

"The buyer will be most pleased. Yes, yes; most pleased indeed." Phizemann nodded.

"Come now; I've much to do. Get him out on to the wagon." Phizemann clapped cheerfully. There was a collective groan as the men reached down and grabbed the cloth shrouded body. There were moments of awkwardness as the three men lifted the dead weight shoving their prize back up towards the wagon. Once the body was out, two of the men began to fill in the hole they'd dug; while the third loaded the body onto the back of the cart in the space, Phizemann cleared. The boards rattled as the corpse thumped against it. Phizemann slammed the tailgate and nodded.

The third man groaned and went about filling in the hole with his companions. Phizemann walked over and inspected their work; striding over the freshly turned soil. He gave a few stomps of his feet and nodded before throwing up his hood.

"Let's go, quickly now." Phizemann ordered as he waved his hand. The men threw their shovels into the wagon and clamored aboard; Phizemann climbed to the driver's bench next to one of the bulky men and nodded as the other two perched themselves on the sides. The cart rattled along for an hour. The only light breaking the darkness belonged to the lantern hanging on a pole beside the driver of the cart. Phizemann tittered as the cart rounded a corner, marked by a weathered road sign.

"What's so funny?" The driver asked in an unnerved voice. Phizemann pointed to a figure up ahead; clad in black and holding a forward curving blade. The driver stopped the cart quickly; there was a brief moment of fear when he thought the cart might tip. But his sigh of relief at the diverted accident was only temporary. The cloaked figure didn't appear the least bit concerned, didn't so much as sway, or twitch.

"Oh and this…" Phizemann said in the utterly calm relaxed fashion of a soul in the grip of mania—as he pulled the trigger of the pistol which suddenly appeared in his hand. There was a loud clap of thunder, and a cloud of twisting powder smoke as the brains in driver's head exploded outward. The two men in the back gawped on wide-eyed; one drew a large dagger but felt a flare of pain and an eerie, wet warmth. He stared at his upraised hand as he was bringing his dagger down, only to notice he no longer possessed a hand. Blood sprayed from the stump—showing Phizemann in its crimson. As his life force oozed and trickled from his arm, he caught a glance of the shadow-clad stranger's blade as it descended to bisect his head.

The third man lifted a shovel and thrust it like a spear towards the figure. The shape dodged it with such ease and skill; it was hard to see his movements. His blade came down on the haft of the shovel, severing its metal head. Far from being deterred, the thug swung his stave back up towards his attacker's head; only to watch as he ducked. The gleaming steel of the man's curved blade lashed out like a viper's tongue and slashed open his stomach. He dropped the wooden stave and clutched at his gut trying to keep his insides from slipping through the opening. The shadow figure kicked him off the wagon and climbed into the driver's bench beside Phizemann. As the man fell to the dirt the wind was knocked from his lungs. His vision growing darker and his hands growing slicker and warmer as his life's blood poured from the wound. The last sound he heard was of the wagon wheels clattering off into the night; accompanied by Phizemann's maniac laughter. The coach arrived at Phizemann's hut as the first gray rays of morning crept into the sky. The shadow–clad figure rose and unbound the layers of fabric which concealed his face. Maamin stepped down from the driver's bench and opened the tailgate of the wagon. He tugged the cloth wrapped body down. With a dull thud, the corpse fell to the dirt. Maamin pulled free a knife and cut the fabric covering the face and grinned. He gave a small nod of satisfaction.

"All is to your liking, yes?" Phizemann asked as he rubbed his greasy hands together stepping behind Maamin.

"Sultan Rahsmin Tallieam Alkuur will be most pleased." Maamin fished out a pouch of gold coins, and gems from a fold in his clothes and handed it to Phizemann.

"His excellence has wished to see his son for a long while—wished to see him dead even longer." Maamin nodded as he draped a length of fabric over the ruined face that was once Saaladan. Maamin had been employed by Saaladan's father a great many years ago. The elderly Sultan told Maamin even if he couldn't kill Saaladan; he wished his body returned after its final demise. Maamin didn't know the reason's why; nor did he wish to ask. Two men dressed in similar garb to Maamin stepped from the cabin and gathered up the cloth wrapped remains of Saaladan's broken body. Damn him for making me a babysitter to this spoiled fruit of his loins, he thought.

"You have a way of preserving him?" Maamin asked. Phizemann nodded as he rubbed the back of one greasy hand over his lank sunken face. He waved

Maamin and his men back into the cabin where he would set about his ghoulish work. "While you see to that, I must collect a debt." Maamin smiled as he bowed. "I shall return." He glanced at the two men standing next to the crazed Phizemann, as his hands grasped around a spacious container. The men nodded, knowing that without saying a word, Maamin asked the two of them to watch him. Maamin had one stop to make before he went to see the woman he'd helped ascend to claim right to sit atop the Throne of Tides. After all, he couldn't enter with his assassin's garb; especially bloodied as it was.

* * *

Franchesca gazed out the window of the chamber that served as the throne room. Despite the drinking she engaged in last night, fate seemed to smile on her as she'd not woken with a throbbing head or the lead like limbs which affected many others. Ayzza sat upon the steps leading to the dais upon which the throne stood. Simone still slumbered in the grand bedroom; she shared with Franchesca, doing what she could to sleep off the effects of overindulgence from the night before. Franchesca hadn't seen or heard from Syandro since the beginning of the festivities and felt a bit concerned for him. Ayzza peered at Franchesca as she watched the gentle light dance across the marble floor. The weight of realization fully perched upon Franchesca's shoulders now—and never before had she felt so afraid. She'd fought for her life—been aboard ships firing cannons, and crossed paths with men who could take her life in the blink of an eye by squeezing a trigger. It would have been easy miss a parry, or overextend—a shift in someone's position could have seen a pistol shot take her. Somehow all of that seemed easy now; the past always did, she reminded herself silently; watching the early rays of the sun dance upon the floor. What by the Heavenly Lady's eight paths did she know about running a kingdom?

"Don't worry." Franchesca heard Ayzza say softly. She glanced back and regarded the youthful figure of Ayzza—the being who was far older than she was. Franchesca sighed as she toyed with her father's signet ring; suspended upon the cord that graced her neck.

"I will guide you, as will Alfaido—any will help you if you ask."

"That's what I'm afraid of. Will they be helping me; or helping themselves?" Franchesca scratched her head thoughtfully. Somehow she couldn't shake the feelings that came to her when she laid eyes upon Ayzza. She couldn't help but think there was something about this visage—a deeper message perhaps? This woman was older than the settlement—and here she appeared younger than Franchesca herself—what did that mean? Maybe she was overthinking, she did that a lot, but one thing she couldn't deny was something called to her when she looked at Ayzza. The woman mentioned something about believing in a forgotten great purpose, and she believed Franchesca would help her to achieve it. Was that what she was feeling herself? A page walked over to Franchesca and gave a polite bow.

"There is someone to see you, Captain Flint. He says his name is Maamin. He told me to tell you; you would know what his call entailed." The man brought his hands behind his back. Franchesca nodded as she rubbed her forehead with her thumb and forefinger.

"Show him in. I'm as ready for his visit as I'll ever be." She sighed as she walked over to the throne and took her seat. Ayzza stood beside her, leaning upon her gnarled driftwood staff. Franchesca caught sight of a smile showing upon Ayzza's features. No doubt she was anxious to see how Franchesca would conduct herself; as this would most likely be her first test. How appropriate that it should be her very first meeting. Maamin's lean muscled frame entered the throne room, and he bowed deeply at the waist.

"Greetings and congratulations to you, Captain Flint; I wish you good fortune, and blessings." His thick beard bobbed as he spoke. Franchesca nodded allowing a slight bow of her head.

"Thank you, I'm sure. But let us be honest; you didn't come here to congratulate me." She replied. It was abrupt, and unladylike—in short, it was the most piratical and authoritative reply she could think of.

"Spoken like a pirate lord, already." Maamin grinned brightly with a slight bow of his head acknowledging the truth of the matter. "Yes, I have come to collect upon what is owed."

"Yes, you wish me to release Saaladan's ship to you to sail home." Franchesca tapped her chin. For a moment Maamin became concerned, it appeared as if Franchesca would retract her word. "What must I do to release it to you? Are there papers I need to sign, or can you simply sail it based upon my word?" Franchesca asked glancing between Ayzza and Maamin. This was a test of her devising. She would see who would answer first; and who would give an answer that seemed most in character with what a ruler might need to do. If Maamin aimed to cheat her and make her appear a fool, he would say her word was good enough; doubtless, for men with a reputation like Konrad, his word had been law. Franchesca expected there was more to it than a command, however. Think of myself in command of a large ship she reminded herself. If I give an order to distribute something, it surely must be recorded in a ledger she thought—after all one has to keep track.

"Alfaido will bring forth the ledger where you will make the necessary notations. Something you will come to learn is that very detailed records are kept here upon Tornusia." Ayzza said, as she patted Franchesca on the shoulder. At first she thought it a joke; but she was shocked at just how serious Ayzza had been. She doubted such detailed records could be kept, even by her father's ledger men. Everything from the number of crew, to the color the ship's accenting color trim had been recorded. Page after page of notes, the numerous scrawling lines of script seemed to be giving Franchesca a headache. There were lines noting how many died on one voyage, as well as their names. Crew sign up sheets recorded detailed heights, scars, builds, eye color; tattoos, and things of a nature Franchesca wasn't sure needed to be noted. One page of notations didn't make sense to her at first. It was a page of numbers; but all the columns started the same. The number two followed by another number, usually not very large; then another number slightly larger made beside it. Franchesca felt her cheeks color and her throat go dry when she realized what the measurements were. Evidently they did keep very detailed records. Heavenly Lady please let it be I don't have to measure or note such thing's myself she prayed silently. A page at the back kept track of injuries and the severity; and whether reimbursement was made to surviving family members or the crewmember himself. Other pages contained tables within the book for time and efficiency. There was also a table as to what injuries were worth, and how much each particular one was to pay the crewmember who'd suffered it. She'd come to find out that the ledgers were sorted by letter of the captain's name, as well as the name of the ship, and where the ship came from originally. In the terms of Tornusia—that meant the nation, or port, where the ship had been stolen from. She'd also been shocked to see so many ledger books in one place. Franchesca doubted even the royal library in Forn could lay claim to so many records.

After a few minutes of looking in the section she'd been directed to, she finally found the pages she was searching for. She made a note next to Saaladan's name; which simply said Slain in duel—she added her name, and how she'd killed him. It sent a shiver down her spine, and through the hand which did the deed, as she made the final mark in the sentence. She wrote out a new page; listing Maamin as the new captain, and that Saaladan's ship now belonged to him—the ownership being transferred over by her direct and uncoerced order. Franchesca blew on the page gently to help the ink dry quicker. She closed the leather cover with a pinch of her fingers. The book made a crisp snapping sound, and she placed the ledger back upon the shelf. She'd only just put it back when Alfaido handed her another piece of paper which required her signature. Once it'd been signed, Alfaido folded it, and dabbed a bead of indigo wax, pressing his signet ring into its cooling liquid which sealed the two ends. Alfaido passed the note to Maamin and nodded.

"All is in order. Sail when you please." Alfaido announced. Maamin bowed as he accepted the parchment and turned on his heel; more eager to sail back to the grand kingdom of Tehraiq—back upon the continent Sahar; to deliver his cargo—a cargo more precious than any in that room could ever understand. A step closer to home, Maamin grinned as he passed the page and stuck the sealed note into a pocket between his short–sleeved thobe and his chest. Franchesca slouched in the seat and sighed. She rubbed the back of her neck and peered back at Alfaido and Ayzza.

"I guess I'm waist deep in this occupation now; aren't I?" She asked. It was only the first hours of her first day.

"That you are girl... that you are." Alfaido nodded with a grin, as he and Ayzza exited the room, leaving Franchesca with her thoughts.

* * *

Simone stood next to Franchesca watching the ship that had once been Saaladan's, sail towards the vast expanse of ocean under the command of Maamin. Simone laced her fingers with Franchesca as the gentle rays of the sun danced upon their skin.

"He's still out there somewhere you know." Franchesca whispered as the white sails shrank in the distance.

"Who is?" Simone asked as she gazed at Franchesca, the light of the midday sun shimmering on the glossy raven waves of her hair.

"Quentin..." Franchesca trailed off quietly. Her heart slowed, and she could feel a pulsing throb within her ears at the mention of his name. How she hated him.

"Bah. fergit em. What's he gonna do now eh? Yer in charge of tings 'round dese parts, ya can ave em strung up from a tree or a mast." Simone chuckled. "Seems ta me he won't show his tail round 'ere if he's a smartun." Simone smirked; Franchesca could only manage a shrug. There was a truth to Simone's words, the only thing bothering her was Quentin was many things; a smart man wasn't necessarily one of them. An opportunist—lucky having found himself at the right place at the right time more often than not, but not what Franchesca would call smart. There was also the chance her parents were still investing coin in attempting to find her. Perhaps, that wouldn't be so bad; she thought as the sun warmed her locks. She closed her eyes and took a deep breath of the fresh sea air before opening her eyes and looking at her surroundings.

Ships were docking and unloading—children scurrying through the streets—others helping their parents drag in fishing nets. Perhaps if they found her now, they would understand. She doubted it, but it was always a possibility; even if a faint one. Franchesca glanced about and smiled. There was work to be done, a lot of work and she would be the one to help get everything done. She would be the one to better the lives of so many.

"I'll show everyone what I'm made of." Franchesca whispered.

"Aye, ya will; an yer a lot more dan a pertty face." Simone grinned. They pulled each other close and kissed one another intensely as the sea breeze swirled around them. They stayed for a moment lost in the breeze and the churning and fall of the waves; enjoying one another, and the tasks and challenges that lay before them.

* * *

Syandro stroked the naked flesh of the woman who lay next to him. He closed his eyes and took in the smoothness and the gentle warmth flowing beneath his palm from her flesh. He paused for a moment at her hips; allowing his fingers to trace out small circles before continuing down to her thighs. As he lay there, his mind began to wander. What is it he could do? What advice would his father give to him? His father would probably laugh and shrug; tell his son if he was unattached, he was free to enjoy any woman that would enjoy him. The only problem with that was Syandro didn't want just any woman. He wanted her, he wanted Franchesca. He'd wanted her from the first moment they spoke honestly with one another on that fateful walk through the garden. He was obsessing again; but he couldn't help it, perhaps part of him wanted to.

He explored the flesh of the giggling woman beside him with a smile; but with a mind far away in thought. Perhaps there was a way. He thought of his plan. Was it a plan—could waiting truly be called a plan? Or was there another way? Should he board a ship bound for Castella and cut his losses? Being here was so painful, seeing Franchesca with Simone made him want to pluck his eyes from his skull. It was like he was being bled dry. He could leave her behind— eventually the memory of her would fade; the wounds would heal—they would scab and after a time it would be as if they had never been. Though that could take years; and Syandro wondered if his father possessed enough coin to pay for all the drinks, nights in brothels; and copious amounts of lotus root or other substances it would take to erase the memory of Franchesca from his mind. Even then there would always be the "what if?" that made a domicile in his mind. What if he had her, what if Franchesca and Simone grew to hate each other—or perhaps just simply grew apart. What if Simone died; and what if she needed him—what if she wanted him afterwards? Syandro couldn't risk that. The woman beside him rolled over and stared into his eyes and reached out and took a hold of his manhood. His eyebrows rose as he felt her grip below the blankets.

"You are far too good at such things, are you sure you don't have any secrets?" The woman's eyes lit with a blazing and curious hunger.

"Just simply enjoy what you're doing." Syandro replied with a wolfish smirk. The woman leaned in and kissed; retreating after she bit his bottom lip before straddling him.

"I have a secret; I think it is one you would enjoy." She grinned as she allowed her hands to play over his chest.

"I can sense a desire in your heart—a deeply rooted one. A desire for something you desperately want but cannot have." She grinned. It was a feral grin like a predator, showing off a mouth full of white teeth as a warning. Syandro should have risen then and made his exit, but he was far too intrigued. She'd spoken far too many truths about him for him to turn away.

"What if I were to tell you there is a way to get everything you want? What if I told you," she leaned close and placed her finger gently upon his philtrum and gazed into his eyes hungrily "you can get Franchesca?" Syandro's heart pounded wildly. What was happening? The woman grinned as she placed her palms upon Syandro's chest and leaned back seductively. She pinned him to the bed straddling him; arching her back making a full show of her lithe figure.

"What are you playing at?" Syandro asked; though he tried to hide it—he guessed more than a little fear clung to his voice and more than a little anger within him as well.

"There are a few of us upon this island. A few secret followers..." she began in a seductive whisper.

"Followers of what?" Syandro asked; thinking about how he might reach the dagger he kept hidden beneath one of the pillows. For a moment he wondered if he really wanted to or if that was just a reaction born of panic and fear; of embarrassment and anger.

"Followers of The Decadent One. The Great Prince in the Darkness; divine, terrible, powerful and graceful; a granter of desires, dark and obscene. A giver of joys—which you fear to give name to." She smiled.

Syandro now realized the designs the woman was tracing upon his naked chest with her fingers—the mark of the forbidden dark god of indulgence, and excess. He dare not—he had to reach his dagger. He had to let Franchesca know of this threat. A Khaos cult upon the island could ruin everything for her. The thought shot through him like a spasm. Did he? Was that thought his own—Franchesca; Syandro thought again. He felt her name ebb from his thoughts as he stared at the woman's naked supple curves. He gazed up into her eyes, they were intense; hungry and drinking him in.

"Give yourself to him—follow his ways, and she will be yours. For how could she not. You can have her Syandro... you can have her and any you choose. All will be shown to you—if you follow and observe." She mused as she traced the blasphemous sigil upon his flesh with her fingernail. Over and over—faster and faster... Franchesca... he wanted her to be safe, yes; he wanted Franchesca to be safe. He... wanted—Franchesca.

"Tell me." He groaned as she pressed her hands upon his pectoral muscles and smiled down at him, grinding her pelvis against his.

"All shall be made clear." She purred as she leaned down and kissed his naked flesh.

"For now, I think it's time for we enjoy ourselves; and bask in the wondrous bounty of pleasure and rapture that Salaazz has allowed us to partake in." The woman purred with a lascivious grin. Franchesca would be his, but for now, he would enjoy her.

Epilogue

Her heart pounded excitedly as she strode down the gangplank onto the busy docks of Cannet's great harbor. The smells that caught the breeze seemed so familiar; yet so strange. She noticed a few new structures, and took note of a few new signs hanging over warehouses and dockside shops; some, however, Franchesca remembered seeing when she departed from this harbor three years ago. Had it really been that long? Franchesca smiled to herself as she breathed in the familiar air of her homeland. She heard a shout and glanced over her shoulder; she watched a dockworker embrace what she assumed was a friend. Her nerves were still raw with the anxiety of being recognized by her parents; or by some acquaintance of her parents—who would try and force her to accompany them—a task they would fail at. She didn't intend to go anywhere unless she chose to. Was she still being searched for? Franchesca gave a small laugh; it was possible she supposed. Her father was a man of certainties. If she hadn't been found, he most likely still had people looking for some sign of her or keeping their ears perked for word of her. If she were alive, he would never stop looking; not until he found her—if she was dead, he wouldn't rest until he received proof. She took a deep breath and smiled to herself beneath the brim of her tricorn hat. Even if her father was still looking for her, there was no way of knowing what she looked like now. Three years changed a person. They certainly changed Franchesca.

There was a glint of experience and knowledge in her eyes; which only being out in the world could impart in ones gaze. A self–assurance that stiffened her spine and squared her shoulders; confidence from facing challenges, hardships and coming through them—even if not always victorious. Not to mention the numerous nautical themed tattoos which now decorated her right arm, surely her parents wouldn't have suspected such a thing from their good and properly raised, noble daughter. She broke free of her father's name and shadow; laying down a legacy of her very own, and it felt liberating. It had taken years to set into motion, but she was on her way.

Tornusia was once a lawless island scrounging up an existence from whatever spoils pirates liberated, and redistributed to the markets, along with whatever coin could be split between the crew and the citizens. Though crops were planted and harvested it was a meager yield—most barely grew enough to feed their own families. Franchesca succeeded where so many others hadn't bothered to look; both Ayzza and Alfaido praised her for it. She organized those captains who docked at the island's ports into bands of mercenary sailors. Now experienced pirate crews rented their services and swords to nations with sparse naval powers; and served as escorts for dignitaries and ships, carrying other valuable cargo—and always for a rich cut. In the end, it'd taken very little convincing on the part of the other nations of the world. Having pirate allies was far better than having pirate enemy's. As a result, the economy of Tornusia began to blossom and grow, as did the economy of those within the wider world; who took her up on her offer. There were still those who refused to follow the rule's Franchesca stated. It was of no real concern, for she issued warrants for any who defied her. It gave her followers' free reign to do with them as they would; as well as their ships. Their cargo would be divided among the crew, with Tornusia receiving a cut upon their return. She'd changed the way of things; just as she said she would. Just as she told Cornando she would, he watched her follow through on her word with an outward showing of pride before he departed her company. It was only a few months ago that Cornando sailed back to Castella, along with what remained of those who accompanied him—they'd set out upon the newly repaired Quest. He'd told Franchesca that when asked about his excursion he could say the new lord of Tornusia is an honorable one. He also said that he would recommend taking them up on their offers. She was thankful she'd have someone speak so favorably for her in the Castellian court.

"Well, would ya look at dat." Simone said, interrupting Franchesca's thoughts as she pointed towards a familiar stone structure; which now sported a new sign above its weathered door—the Rusty Harpoon. Franchesca's heart leaped with joy at the sudden rush of memories which came forth. Her mind rushed back to the past. There she was sitting with Simone—drinking her first beer, remembering the lines of the bawdy songs the crowd sang that night. It was where things truly changed their course.

"I wonder if we'll see a friendly face." Franchesca chuckled as she took in the sight of the dockside tavern. The building brought back memories of sneaking out; secret meetings which made her heart race with fear of being discovered by her parents. Those experiences were exhilarating. Though she missed them, she was happier now than she thought possible. It seemed those thrilling experiences were added to a list that grew every day she was out from beneath her father's shadow; and the weight of her family's name. In the life she built for herself—the de Maret name, possessed the same weight as anyone else's; it was only through the sweat of her own brow, and strength of her own back that she was able to give it prominence and authority. It was an accomplishment she reveled in. Franchesca glanced at Simone and smiled.

"How about we stop in for a pull and see if old Fabrice is still willing to give us a discount." Franchesca joked. Simone smirked and patted her on the shoulder as she knelt down to hoist an open crate filled with tools and scrap materials.

"E'll take one look at tha way we're dressed an' make us pay double." Simone laughed as she walked up the gangplank to place the tools back aboard the ship.

"Which I'd be more dan happy ta do, now dat I can." Simone shouted as she dropped the crate which made a heavy rattle and clack. The sun began to set as the crew finished unloading the lower holds. Franchesca bartered with a few merchants, and tradesmen shortly after she ascended to the Throne of Tides, and was hoping to work out a trade with the goods she had aboard while in port, to procure a few supplies Tornusia was in need of. Some—of course, were luxury items requested and, paid for in part by those who possessed the coin. It was all part of Franchesca's plan to build a relationship with the nations of the world, both large and powerful; the small and growing nations of the world—as well as merchants reputable, and not so reputable. She'd not wanted to make such deals with any underworld figures when she'd first come to power, but after a talk with Simone and Ayzza—Franchesca learned that something's only men of a certain reputation could provide; sometimes even at a bargain. She hadn't liked the idea, but it had paid off and proven useful at times. She'd arranged merchant escorts through dangerous waters, had talked a few of the once fierce pirate captains, into training a few navies of smaller less powerful nations. There'd even been arrangements for vessels under her command to transport important and prominent lords and ladies.

So far her plan to change the reputation of pirates and the island nation of Tornusia had been going well. Slowly she was helping to grow the island into a power of its own. Perhaps not a great one, but the tide had shifted. When she'd laid down her plan and set her laws upon ascending to the most prominent position she could obtain—a few of the pirate lords in the council cut their ties to Tornusia in a defiant refusal to take orders from her or obey her laws. Franchesca knew such an event would happen, but she knew who she would lose and who would remain loyal. A few loose tethers to tie up; she thought with an imagined shrug, so what. They would be dealt with; she made that very clear once they spat upon her proposals and laws—it was proving to be more difficult than she previously thought, however. As the sky darkened with the aging hours, the crystal blues darkened to rich lavenders striped with the pale, golden–yellow and the fiery orange's and reds of the weary sun, Franchesca gave a sharp whistle. The cargo had been unloaded and then loaded onto the backs of flatbed carts or wagons with canvas roofs. The men stopped and stared at her.

"Alright lads, get those shipments to the warehouse and get back double time. Tonight drinks are on me; I'll buy a keg and a bottle of the finest spirits at the Rusty Harpoon—and tonight you can drink your fill!" Her announcement was met with wild cheers and whoops from the men, both aboard the ship and those who were overseeing the transportation of the goods to the various warehouses. Wagons rattled off into the distance, and the sound of horses hooves clattered off the paving stones, Franchesca smiled as Simone clapped her on the shoulder. "Anything get's broken, and I'll take it out of your pay!" She shouted. The men chuckled and shouted their understanding.

"Come on; let's see if ol' Fabrice is still mannin his nest." Simone smiled as she and Franchesca walked towards the Rusty Harpoon. The tap room was as rowdy as ever. Men laughed and swayed as they toasted each other or played games of dice and darts. Franchesca watched as one man leaned back too far in a chair and fell; the wooden chair clattered loudly, and the drunk and his friends erupted into laughter as he ordered another drink to replace the one he now wore like cheap cologne.

Franchesca and Simone looked over to the bar and noticed the familiar form they'd left behind three years prior. Moving behind the bar, a little heavier, and looking a little older, was the man Simone said was more like a father to her than her birth father. They moved closer as mugs clacked against one another and boasts were made by men who'd long ago lost the ability to control the volume of their voices.

Simone leaned against the bar and slapped it with an open palm and hooted.

"Why ya old salt, ya look busier dan ever; what did ya do, start given drink away?" She smiled as Fabrice turned and blinked. He rubbed his eyes with his palms in disbelief.

"Why slap my ass and call me Sam, don't tell me I'm dreamin." He said joyously. Simone leaned over the bar and pulled him towards her and gave him an affectionate kiss on his plump rounded cheeks.

"You are certainly a sight welcomed by these old eyes." Fabrice exclaimed as he pulled two glasses from beneath the bar and placed them in front of him. He laughed as Franchesca came and sat next to Simone before him himself leaned over the bar and pulled them both close and planted a kiss upon each of their cheeks. He pulled a third glass for himself and told one of the barmaids to bring around a keg of his reserved dwarf brew. "If ever there was an occasion to drink the fine stuff, now would be that time." Fabrice smiled. "Where did you lasses disappear to?"

"We traveled to Castella; then one thing led to another—and we landed on Tornusia." Franchesca smiled as she shrugged off her coat and laid it across her lap, revealing her heavily tattooed arm.

"Been hearin talk about them new lines of work, those pirates are taken up; hear they got themselves a new king an everything. Flint and Steel they call em—have ya met them in yer stay on Tonrusia?" He asked as he drew a measure of dwarf beer and passed it to Franchesca then to Simone. The two of them laughed as they brought their mugs together with Fabrice's.

"In a manner of speaking... you could say we have. Guess word of mouth leaves things out though." Franchesca replied as she took a drink. Fabrice studied them curiously before shrugging.

"Then fill in the gaps; after all, you were there." Fabrice encouraged with an excited wave of his hands; before taking a pull from his mug.

"Oh, aye we were dere." Simone assured. "Musta left out dose parts bout it bein a queen and not a king." Simone chuckled.

"And it certainly looks like they left out the part where it was two queens." Franchesca added.

"Who?" Fabrice asked, still not making the connection. Simone and Franchesca simply eyed one another before pulling themselves close and placing an arm around one another and extending their free hands.

"Flint." Franchesca said.

"And Steel," Simone added; raising their mugs to him in salute.

"Pleased to meet you," They both said in unison. Fabrice went wide–eyed and slapped the table with a wild laugh. He leaped from his stool and scooped the two girls up in his large arms and jumped about with them.

"Ah, I always told ya that ya were made for great things girl; didn't I?!" Fabrice asked as he took a long drink from his mug, before slamming it down on the bar with a hollow clap. He refilled it and shouted above the din.

"Oi—you lot! Join me in raising a glass ta Flint and Steel—new lords of the seas." Without needing any further prompting or another reason to celebrate, the assembled drinkers hoisted their glasses and shouted a toast happily, before taking drinks. Franchesca laughed as she watched a number of them set back into their stools or chairs. As they sat, she saw a sight which made her heart pause; only to then make it thunder like a galloping herd of horses. Through the clouds of pipe smoke and the jostling of flow of bodies, she saw a figure sitting in a corner. His attention wasn't on the happenings of the tavern but on a stack of papers and a leather–bound ledger beneath his nose. A dull light cast from the candle on his table. Franchesca took one final drink from her glass before setting it upon the bar.

"I... I'll... be right back." She told Simone and Fabrice, with an air shocked nervous awe. Could it be? The hair was a little shaggier—still tied into a polite, yet noble ponytail with a leather cord; still blonde though streaked in a few places by silver–gray strands which only helped add a look of experience and wisdom to his polite noble features. Leather gloves sat upon the table, in a neat pile one atop another and placed off to the side. His crystalline blue eyes were still sharp and keenly observant; though the faintest telling of crow's feet lined the area around them. The man must have heard the thump of her thick–soled boots against the wood because he blinked, and turned from his papers. Franchesca's heart pounded, so loudly; she feared he could hear it too. For the first time in years, she felt nervous—she felt shaky. Was it really him?

"As I live and breathe—Franchesca? Is it truly you? Can it be?" He rose from his chair and gawked at her in the dim candlelight. He placed his hands on her shoulders and held her at a distance as if studying her face and her frame. Then he saw the gold coin and the ring hanging upon the cord around her neck. Tears came to her eyes and began their journey down her cheek. It was him—and he remembered her.

"C... Claude..." at the sound of his name he brought her close and the two of them embraced tighter than Franchesca could ever remember. Locked away within his arms everything faded to silence; the only thing she could hear was the sound of his breathing—the smell of his clothes and the delicately perfumed oil he used filled her nose. An all–encompassing feeling of safety and protection washed over her—a feeling she couldn't achieve herself no matter how well she fought; nor could anyone else impart to her, other than him. After a moment he began to laugh gently—a sound of joy, though mingled with tears. He held her at arm's length once more and smiled with tears now streaming down his face.

"I... I'd always hoped I would see you again—but... I... I could never have imagined..." she cut him off by burrowing her head into his chest and wrapping her arms around him once again, this time sobbing as she embraced him. Just as so many times before; she felt his calming hand upon her head before he began to stroke her hair to soothe her. Simone wasn't the only one to reunite with a man she considered more her father than the one who bore her own blood, this night. She always hoped she would see Claude once again, and she dreamed of it often; but when she woke to discover it'd been a dream, it cut deeper than any knife. Simone and Fabrice watched from the bar, each of them smiling as they watched Franchesca reunite with the one man who'd always allowed her to be who she wished to be; and accepted her no matter what path she chose to travel. Simone watched as they sat down at the table and nodded.

"Gods above how you've grown." Claude said with a smile as he gazed at her. "You've grown from a beautiful girl, into a breathtaking woman." He added as he reached across the table and brushed a stray strand of hair from her face and tucked it behind her ear, gently noticing how her face reddened. The comment made her smile and blush slightly. "How long has it been?" He asked as he stopped to think.

"Three years—three long years." Franchesca answered with a sigh. She paused for a moment; thinking about the question that weighed heavily upon her mind.

"Claude... what happened to you after I left?" A relaxed smile crossed his noble features before he shrugged and let out a sigh.

"Well, after a few days, which didn't result in your return; as well as a search that came up with no leads—your father was understandably..." Claude paused considering the most polite way to proceed. It was a question of her parents after all, and everyone possessed very peculiar lines others were or were not allowed cross with regard to family. True Franchesca had been angry at them—was she still?

"Furious." Franchesca smirked. Claude nodded as he squeezed her hand gently, fighting off his own grin. Apparently, she was still mad at them—though perhaps not as angered as she had been those years ago.

"He dismissed me... which made sense. After all, my job was to see to your protection and well being. I only hoped you were safe." He told her with a shrug and a deep breath.

"I am so sorry Claude; for the trouble, I put you through—the trouble I've always put you through." Franchesca began. Claude's grip on her hands tightened slightly. His hands taking on the quality of a father about to halt a child's bout of self–pity before it could truly get started.

"That's enough of that, Miss Franchesca. You did no such thing—ever." Claude smiled warmly, laying his hand upon Franchesca's, in what he hoped was a calming fashion. He took a deep breath. "After your father released me from my duties, I started my own mercenary company. The Red Thorns, my own endeavors prove to be working quite well." Claude smiled with a bow of the head.

"It is quite fun being the rogue, making your own decisions. Fighting for your own interests or causes you believe in. Of course, we've been doing many escorts of caravans and serving as bodyguards for the time being." He studied her tattooed arm and smiled. "It appears you've become somewhat of a rogue yourself." Franchesca shrugged with a soft chuckle.

"You could say that." She told him bashfully as she glanced at the floor.

"I suppose you could, Captain Flint." He winked. A smirk grew on his face as he picked up his drink and took a sip from his tankard.

"You knew?" Franchesca exclaimed; as she gawped at him with widened eyes.

"Only because Fabrice shouted to everyone—I've been coming here for months on end, having a drink and a little dinner while I look over contracts and my payroll. This is about the first celebratory mood, I've ever seen him in;

now I know today was unlike any other day in the past months." Claude placed his hand upon Francesca's gently, before squeezing it affectionately.

"Tell me how does Syandro fare, or has he parted your company?" Claude asked as he took a drink. Franchesca shrugged; in truth, she wasn't sure how to answer the question. On occasion, Syandro seemed much like the charming, wonderfully spirited young man she began her adventures with. On other occasions, he appeared distant and surly. Sometimes it seemed as if she could feel his eyes upon her; sizing her up like a wolf might observe a sheep. She noticed he developed a tendency to over drink, and overindulge in a few other substances she couldn't name—if the largeness and redness of his eyes could be any indication. Something appeared most unnerving within him; and more than once, Franchesca wondered if she was actually safe in his company. With a sigh, she smiled.

"I left him in charge of affairs while I sailed here with Simone to attend to some business. I think he... well... I'm not entirely sure." She admitted. Franchesca tapped her fingers on the table nervously; a million questions raced through her head. Thousands of voices seemed to shout at her from within her mind; but besides Simone, Franchesca knew Claude was the one person she could speak to about anything.

"Do... you know how..."

"Your mother and father are fairing?" Claude interrupted, with a lopsided grin. He sighed as he rubbed his forehead. "I suppose there's no easy way to say it... they're all but destitute. Only by their name and family ties has the queen allowed them to stay upon their lands—but they are in decline. Your father paid a great deal of coin to find, and return you home. I also heard Quentin borrowed quite a bit of coin from them; of course naturally, he told them he would be joining in the search for you. He kept dangling leads in front of them so they wouldn't turn him down. In truth, the man who holds most of your father's fortune now is Quentin." Franchesca clenched her hands; anger seized her insides in a fiery grip.

"Do you know what ship he sails, or what flag he sails under?" Franchesca asked eagerly... perhaps too eagerly. Claude saw the flash of rage in her eyes as well for he pulled back slightly. It was a hunger within her. Hunger to destroy Quentin, and take her revenge on him.

"I'm afraid I do not. Quentin is a man of secrets and tight lips." Claude sighed. "Why do you ask?" Claude inquired, though he knew. Sometimes the best, and quickest way to guide someone from an unpleasant path was to ask a question related to it.

"I had to flee because of him... I think I owe him a bit of an unannounced visit." Franchesca growled. Simone came over and joined Claude and Franchesca with a grin. She placed Franchesca's mug in front of her; and laid a hand upon her shoulder.

"Catchin up on old times?" She asked as she squeezed Francesca's shoulder gently. The rage ebbed away slightly. Perhaps it wasn't so bad she had to run. At least she was able to run away with Simone. That had been the most important thing to her, but she would still see Quentin pay for screwing her over.

"Something to that effect," Franchesca nodded as she took a long drink from her cup—letting the ale do its best to wash away what remained of her anger. It didn't really help; but as she lowered the mug and saw Claude sitting before her, with an easy smile upon his lips and a glint of joy in his eye, her anger felt contained.

"How long are you going to be in the city?" Claude asked as he set his glass down and leaned back in his chair.

"Just for a night, then we sail back to Tornusia." Franchesca replied sadly. If she'd known she would find Claude, she would have said their voyage would be a long one; so that she could spend time with him.

"We usually get pretty busy wit escort requests just bafore tha winter sets in. One last push fer evryone ta get deir cargo where dey want." Simone said, tapping the side of her glass. Franchesca's eyes went wide and her head shot up faster than a mouse who hears a cat.

"Come with us." Franchesca blurted out as she eyed Claude. He allowed a shocked and bewildered expression to cross his features at the thought. She pushed her ale out of the way. With as excited as she was at the prospect, she was worried she might knock it to the floor. That wasn't something she wanted to do—it was shameful to waste good dwarf ale.

"Miss Franchesca I know nothing of sailing..." Claude began. It was a weak protest; perhaps he wanted it to be a weak objection. Was there truly a good reason to refuse?

"Neither did I, neither did Simone. Come with us." Franchesca replied as she squeezed his hand. It occurred to her just how childish she must appear, but Franchesca didn't care. She thought of Claude as her father; if not in blood than in bond, and in action. She never truly realized how much she missed him until she'd docked in the city once again—the city where Claude had taken her out when her mother and father were away. The city where he showed her a sausage from a street vendor could be just as delicious as anything the cooks in her parent's kitchen could prepare. Claude was her friend; protector, and partner in juvenile delinquency from time to time. The man who'd been her father more often than her own true blood bound father. He'd run with her in the countryside; been her shoulder to cry on when she was melancholy, or angry at her parents. She had missed him, and not until she saw him sitting in the corner of the Rusty Harpoon did she know how badly she needed to be in his company once again. Not until she gazed at him did she think what it feel like to have him ripped out of her life once more.

"I—I don't know miss..." Claude began as he began to chew his lower lip. She'd forgotten how she missed his scratchy voice; how it soothed her. As she sat with him now, she'd forgotten just how calming his presence could be. How reassuring it was simply being in his company. If ever there was a time in her life where she needed him—needed the solidness of him, it was now.

"Don't call me Miss Franchesca. I am Franchesca, your friend... your daughter." She choked out as she met his gaze. "If not your daughter by blood, then by everything you were there to teach me; and with every comfort, you ever tried to show me. Come with us." She pleaded as tears cut tracks down her cheeks. "I'll pay your men... I can give them work... I can give you work... please." Claude peered into Franchesca's eyes moistening with tears and closed his own. He took a deep breath; for a moment Franchesca thought he would deny her request—but he didn't.

"Alright, I will go with you." He smiled at her. Franchesca leaped from the table almost knocking over the glasses and the table itself, as she wrapped her arms around him and squeezed so hard she wondered how he could stand it. Claude laughed, as he embraced her and patted her on the back as she laid her head on his chest. Franchesca breathed in his familiar, comforting scent and smiled contentedly. She stepped back and placed her hand on his shoulders.

"Let's go get a Pikshaff and talk over the details." She smirked. She could imagine how she must sound; how she must look. Equal parts child, equal parts pirate captain, perhaps that was just how she thought she must look. Perhaps in Claude's eyes, she would always be the same child he'd always known.

"You still remember Pikshaff?" Claude asked with a laugh as he leaned back and crossed his arms.

"Aye, and I've missed it terribly—but not as much as I've missed you." Franchesca nodded as they finished their drinks and continued talking about all they'd missed.

* * *

Ayzza peaked into the room where Syandro scribbled on pieces of parchment. She watched him carefully since Franchesca's departure. Every day that passed a greater unease nestled within the pit of her stomach. She stepped back from the door and walked through the hallways of the manse which served as the palace, and pressed into an alcove. Ayzza could feel something. Something dark hung above Tornusia. For a moment Ayzza thought she heard a faint ethereal whisper creep into her ears from behind. She turned on her heel; her breath escaping her. No one was there—how could they be since she'd pressed her back against the wall. She turned again her heart pounding. Ayzza sensed she would have many rituals to undertake very soon. The sound of feminine laughter seemed to surround her.

Something was wrong as she stormed through the hallways—Ayzza needed to reach her hut—the hut Franchesca ordered rebuilt for her on the outskirts of the town. There was work that needed to be done. Ayzza whispered a silent prayer to the gods above and the gods of the seas. Bring her back swiftly; before this shadow settles upon all of Tornusia, for the sake of all bring her back.

* * *

Fridricht heard the whispers still. His brother thought locking him away and torturing him would be the death of him—would be the death of his cult. What a short-sighted and ignorant fool he was. To a true follower of the dark prince of pleasures, even such things as pain brought their own delights. Fridricht felt the pain throb through him; move through him like his blood, like a living breathing thing of its own. How glorious it was. Konrad had been cruel, and yes by the lord of forbidden ecstasies, it hurt but he still lived. The whispers within him told him he would not be stopped; he would rise—had risen, within his divine master's favor. When that pain had been forced upon him, he remembered a figure standing before him. He'd thought he was in the grips of delirium—he wasn't. A demon lord of his master's court stood before him and made him an offer.

"Would you like to live? Would you like to continue your service—your worship at the altar of Salaazz?" The voice sounded like a writhing mass of snakes hissing their demands; dripping with the opium-laced call of a siren who promised all the pleasures and pains of the flesh.

"I do; I live to serve at his command, to do his bidding." Fridricht remembered how the demon's divine and seductive face grinned.

"Do you open your flesh to me mortal—your soul?" The voice crooned seductively; all honey and lacerating roses.

"My soul and body; I offer them to my dark patron—such as they are. If he has seen fit to ask you to come to me, I'll not deny him."

"Excellent." The brutality Konrad inflicted upon him was as nothing compared to what surged through him when Ionuu entered the domain of his flesh—every feeling, every nerve, magnified a thousandfold. His body and soul were being ripped apart; devoured bite–sized morsel, by bite–sized morsel as his new patron entered him. Fridricht screamed until his lungs felt raw, and bloody—until he believed his throat would hemorrhage and he would choke upon his own blood. Even though the pain, and the blinding maddening torment, waves of gratification, of desire and passion, washed over him from a depth which was fathomless. A place he didn't know existed. It was as if it didn't come from within him—but from some hidden direction; some unknown place outside. It was madness and splendor at once. He screamed at the height of his voice; none were around him—none were being held down here. This was a special hell his brother created just for him; a place of privacy, where Konrad could take his time. Gradually his suffering began to ebb. It left his nerves alight and sensitive, and when his brother came back to finish his masterwork Fridricht smirked; he laughed madly as his brother hacked and carved at his flesh.

"I give you my strength to survive mortal; do not tempt your brother to stride further into the realm of blood madness that holds sway over his mind." Ionuu's voice said from within the bone cage of Fridricht's skull. He found he could feel snakes writhe and shift beneath his skin in the still darkness. "The dark prince has need of you alive. He has spoken to the twins of madness, and they have agreed to humor his path, his plan. Do not make the dark lords regret it." Ionuu hissed.

"What do you know?" Fridricht's response was met with silence. "Please, tell me." He begged. It was remarkable, though he couldn't see the demon; Fridricht had the distinct vision within his mind's eye of Ionuu sneering at him as he begged. It was as if he could see glimpses of the demon within his mind.

He supposed he shouldn't be surprised; after all, he could hear Ionuu, why should the beast also not reveal himself in glimpses as well.

"You are to be free, in time. Such plans move in the time of gods; not of men." Ionuu relented. Fridricht couldn't help but believe—no, couldn't help but feel, Ionuu's terrible smile from within the confines of his own body. "You're to open a doorway for the dark lord of ecstasy. He will enter this world, and all will tremble at his magnificence. He will then open a door for his brother gods, for such is the way of his mercy." Ionuu crooned seductively. Fridricht couldn't help but smile in his darkened cell. He would be free. The prospect sounded too good to be true; like the cruel taunt of a murderer, trying to squeeze and ring every drop of hope for his own pleasure from his victim. He had done such things with those he'd laid upon the altar, to his god. As his cult tortured them and indulged in every dark whim that came to them. Then they watched the hope drain from their eyes in the shedding of all the tears a soul could shed; as their life was snuffed out. Was that what was happening now? Was he being played for a fool; would his lord and divine master savor the last dregs of his dying hope, as his body sank into death? As he wondered day in and day out—Konrad never returned. His brother hadn't returned for—gods how long had it been now? He couldn't recall; not truly. Though Konrad hadn't returned, he hadn't been freed as Ionuu said he would. He was delirious, wrapped in thirst; his stomach had given up protesting a desire for food long ago. Fridricht knew the only reason he lived was because Ionuu sustained him—revitalized him with his demonic powers, enough to keep him alive, and on the cusp of awareness. What was that he heard? Boots; unless his mind was playing a cruel joke upon him, which was entirely possible.

"Is that you Brother?" By Salaazz's dark visage Konrad was back. His thirsty and addled mind worked at what such a thing meant.

"It is him, swiftly. Get him out." A voice called. Fridricht's eyes fluttered weakly.

"Wake, vessel—your freedom is at hand." Ionuu hissed. Fridricht felt a surge of power shoot through him as Ionuu spoke. The spark was enough to bring clarity to his eyes, enough to give him the mental capacity to begin to think once more. Fridricht glanced up weakly at the small group that stood before him.

"Brother Dusk, it is you." A voice said in wonderment as he knelt next to him. Fridricht thought the voice was familiar, but he couldn't place it right now. He didn't care enough to try either.

"How... did you find me? How... long..." Fridricht wheezed his parched throat and cracked lips making speaking painful. One of the men in the cell passed forward a wineskin and pressed it to his lips. The nectar was sweet and crisp upon his tongue. As he drank, he was able to open his eyes. After a moment he pulled back from the wineskin and held up a hand; not just wine, poppywine with steeped blue lotus petals. Ionuu—Fridricht said within himself; ask Salaazz to bestow gifts upon these men, especially the one who thought it fit to bring poppywine with steeped blue lotus. He could feel Ionuu grin within him, and it sent an electric chill through his being.

"We've a new member that wishes to join. Your brother is dead; killed by the new captain of Tornusia. Once we learned of his death, we began searching for you. It wasn't until this new captain placed her friend in charge of ledgers that we found where Konrad had been keeping you. As I said he wishes to join; and hopes this will be proof of his devotion." The man said as awareness began to settle upon Fridricht's mind and a lantern was turned up—he found himself recalling this man before him.

"Jerrivo, if you can get me out of here, tell them I'll meet with him in a week; in our fall back meeting place. I would imagine my dear brother has burned our main gathering place to the ground."

"We didn't give up on you Brother—didn't give up upon our desires, and didn't turn our backs upon Salaazz. We spread his name and his truths where possible." Jerrivo acknowledged, as he slipped an iron key from a pocket and unlocked the shackles which kept Fridricht's arms chained to the wall.

"You will be rewarded." Fridricht announced as the chains fell away from him. He stepped forward into the light, cast by the lantern and beheld their terrified looks.

"Salaazz's flesh what happened to you!?" They gasped as their gaze fell on his scarred and ruined form. Fridricht studied them and smiled at their shock—at their horror.

"In the crucible of my brother's ministrations, Salaazz saw fit to forge me anew. Now tell me the name of this new hopeful." Jerrivo stepped forward and extended a folded robe of rich, dark purple silk he pulled from a pack.

"His name is Syandro, Brother." At the mention of the name, Ionuu writhed with joy in his fleshy prison.

"Excellent." Fridricht smiled.

* * *

Cyrillio De Madonia considered the ruins of his ship. Three years ago, it'd been a luxurious vessel; a show of power, bravado, and wealth. Now it lay broken, little more than a collection of timbers. He found the Black Isle, had glimpsed the Tower of Burning Shadows; in fact the very island itself swallowed his ship. Perhaps swallowed was the wrong word. More accurately, one moment there was sea deep enough to dock; moments later a terrible trembling—followed by the disappearance of the water he and his men previously weighed anchor in. Before he or his crew could comprehend what happened, an immense rock blossomed under the ship with such force it split the vessel in two. None would believe him; if he could tell them what'd happened, especially given the way he appeared now; the way his men looked now, filthy with disheveled hair—while dirt and gore caked their skin. Cyrillio was well aware he and his men looked as if they should be locked away in an asylum—gods help him maybe they should be. He'd glimpsed the tower of Burning Shadows through the twisting motes of mist, and fog that heralded every new morning. Try as he may, neither he nor his men could draw any closer to it. Every day it seemed to be farther and farther off. Cyrillio gazed at

471

the menacing tower from where he stood within the clearing which had formed around the hull of the shattered ship. This place was a predator; it was going to kill them all. Ten of his men had gone mad within their first few months stranded upon the isle. Each man that he was forced to kill narrowed his own window of survival, of escape; narrowed it for everyone. There was a sort of safety in numbers within this cursed place. In their first trek towards the tower they'd been attacked by twisted creatures, which loped out of the trees to charge them. His men fought bravely, and managed to kill a few of the beasts— but not before the creatures reaped a terrible toll.

"I think it is time we admit to ourselves that this place is our home now; or shall be for a long time—perhaps until my son or the royal family decides to send a party in search of us." Cyrillio admitted as he slumped against a large rock. There was a collective groan and shouts of protest from those that remained alive. He tugged on the thick unkempt beard that'd grown upon his chin and regarded them.

"Do any of you have any plans?" He asked angrily as he pushed himself away. The heat and humidity were near unbearable on this forsaken rock, and it tested the limits of his patience and understanding. True his men might've been upset, but he was just as despondent—perhaps more so than they were.

"This is your damned fault; your damned son's fault!" One of the men shouted angrily as he leveled a sweat covered, trembling arm at Cyrillio. His chest heaved and his gazes appearing to be far off as if his mind were in another place. There were shouts of agreement and rustling anger spread through them like rats in a refuse pile. The sailor stepped forward boarding axe in hand and leveled it at him. Cyrillio remembered putting his hands up to show he was not a threat. Cyrillio blinked as sweat dripped into his eyes, snapping him from his thoughts. No. No that hadn't been what happened—not quite he remembered as he peered into the dancing flames of the small fire pit he'd created. He remembered the man stepping forward—he remembered killing him before turning to the others. Blood spattered his arm and face from where his blade had sliced through the sailor's arm, before opening his neck. Cyrillio put a hand on his forehead; as what few tears he could shed came rolling down his cheeks. It'd all gone terribly wrong. After he'd killed him—the others merely became quiet. They seemed resigned to their fates. One by one they succumbed to the cruel machinations of the Black Isle until he was the only one left. He cursed himself a fool and cursed the day he learned of the Black Lamp locked away within this hidden tower. The Tower of Burning Shadows! He cursed the name over and over within his mind as the sun continued its descent. He threw his hands to the side of his head and let loose a scream of anger, pain, and madness. Why did he think to sail here to take the lamp; did he truly need to show the world his importance? Did he need to show that girls pompous father, how much better he was? Cyrillio glanced around as he heard a rustling from within the woods. He grasped his sword and held it in a ready grip. Would he eat this night—or would his stomach continue its protest? He peered out past the fire into the darkness of the forest; over the crackling flames, he swore he heard laughing. Cyrillio realized as he noticed the shaking blade in his hand that he was laughing. His crew was dead; he was the only one left—and had been for some time now. He was going mad, perhaps already was.

"Syandro my boy..." the sound of his own voice startled him, "I hope you're out there. I hope you haven't forgotten me. I need you lad." He said to the darkness. It'd been his prayer; his only request, whispered into the night sky, his secret between the trees and the twin moons hanging overhead; and whatever beasts that might be listening to his voice. Cyrillio looked into the fire and closed his eyes, faced with the stark, bitter realization he was going to be stuck on this island until the end of his days. He stared up at the pinpricks of stars and allowed himself a weak smile as the heaviness in his heart grew.

"I love you boy... I miss you. Perhaps we'll meet on the other side." Cyrillio felt he needed to speak the words, even with none around to hear them but his own ears. His eyes closed and before he knew it, he was asleep. As the first rays of the sun's warmth settled upon his skin; his eyes fluttered open—and he wept.

Glossary

Aged One The: One of the eight aspects of the Heavenly Lady. The aspect which represents wisdom. See also Hag The.

Ahalak: God of the continent of Sahar.

Apsu: Also known as the Tomblands. An Ancient cursed and fallen kingdom lost in the deserts of the continent of Sahar.

Austinea The Empire of: The largest empire of men, and the most powerful and technologically advanced of all the realms of men.

Austinean Imperial Gunnery Division: Regarded as the best artillerymen in the mortal world, outside of dwarves.

Brass Shilling: Smallest denomination of coin in Forn.

Bride The: Aspect of the Heavenly Lady representing love, fellowship, and union with others, especially a follower's significant other.

Black Heart Jellyfish: A jellyfish, black in appearance with a bruised color heart upon its top. Its sting never heals, and often drives its victim's mad, or drives them to kill themselves. It's said the pain is like being locked in a forge and holding your flesh over the fire.

Black Ivy: A plant used to calm nerves, and often to treat pain, though it is highly toxic if prepared improperly.

Blue Lotus Petals: A highly narcotic plant, and addictive plant; when paired with other substances it amplifies their effect.

Bushbur apple: A mildly tart apple that is very widely consumed.

Calldun: Often called the Great Isle. A kingdom famous for its fierce warriors, rolling and rolling green hills, a shroud of mist keeps most away from its shores, as they are fiercely protective of their homes: and distrustful of outsiders. See also Great Isle.

Castel: The language of Castella; the Castellian language.

Castella: World power. Known as a land of passion, and equality and tremendous freedoms.

Castellian Blade Dancers: Highly trained swordsmen, mostly in the style of the
Castellian Rapier the form involves many turns and spins which lead many to compare it to dancing.

Castellian Rapier: A rapier which is slightly shorter than normal rapiers, but is also broader making it just as capable of cutting off a limb or disemboweling as normal broadswords.

Cher: The Lassinian slang for Cheritte.

Cheritte: Fornish for sweetheart.

Churtzzie: A spicy cured Castellian sausage made from pork, garlic and a powdered chiles, often bright red in color.

Chuhuay: A land often referred to by its main export and trade good rather than its name, as some find it difficult to pronounce. See also Silk Lands.

Copper Penny: The second smallest denomination of coin in Forn, equals 15 Brass Shillings.

Conquistadoro: A group of troops in the Castellian military known as explorers, and conquers. Usually used to explore new lands and protect new settlements.

Counsel of the Black Flag: A gathering of pirate captains, usually called by the occupant of the Throne of Tides.

Crescent Empire: See Sahar.

Crescent Kingdom: See Sahar.

Darkwater: A mysterious oily black substance, which appears to be sentient in some capacity.

Dea: A nation of the east. Known for its many gods, and rigidly strict caste system.

Doktor: The Austinean spelling of physician, the most common way of spelling it through the world.

Doting Mother The: One of the eight aspects of the Heavenly Lady which represents healing, hope, life, and protection. See also Mother The.

Emaziai and Caszall: Castellian myths and legends say they were wife and husband, it is said that they were fierce warriors and lovers. They gave birth to the first peoples of the land and helped guide them to found the kingdom that grew to be Castella. It is believed they gave the people of the nation a portion of their passion, and it has persisted in every generation since the founding. They are the colossal statues at the entrance to the great harbor of Castella. Most students in history, however, believe they were simply heads of a clan of warriors who united the country into one kingdom, thus claiming that the folk of the land were their people. See also Giants of Castella.

Eland: The neighbor of Forn, it also shares a border with the Empire of Austinea. Though it is far less advanced than Forn, and Austinea. Preferring to hold to the old ways of chivalry and serfdom. Eland and Forn were once a single nation long ago, but after a civil war erupted, they were split into two separate nations.

Fishwife The: An aspect of the Heavenly Lady, representing prosperity and good fortune, and hard work.

Forn: One of the largest empires of man. It shares a border with The Empire of Austinea.

Fornish Gambling Wheel: A wheel made of red and black squares and a single blue square with double zeros, even numbers painted on red and odds painted on black.

Giants of Castella The: See Emaziai and Caszall.

Great Isle The: See Calldun.

Guest The: The eighth aspect of the Heavenly Lady which represents death. See also Wanderer The.

Gutterfoot: A Colloquial term among the people of Forn for the poor of the cities. This is in reference to their usual lack of shoes, as well as their supposed lax attention about where they walk, as many of the wealthy view them as too stupid not to walk in the gutters of the city.

Gypsy The: Aspect of the Heavenly Lady representing youth, joy, and adventure.

Hag The: Alternate name for the aspect of the Aged One.

Haraht: Term from Sahar meaning, harlot, or whore, essentially woman of ill repute.

Heavenly Matron: Another name for the Heavenly Lady.

Heavenly Lady The: The chief deity of Forn. Though it is one deity, it is often thought of and represented in eight aspects. Meant to represent not only the life of a woman but all life.

High–necks: A slur used in reference to the wealthy or nobility of Forn, the joke being that they never bother to look or see the people below them.

I'm going to toss/ I want to Toss: I'm going to/ want to throw up/ vomit. Though other variations exist.

Kaffra: Known as the continent of the wilds. Its people are tribal, and it is known for its many deserts, savannahs, jungles, and beasts.

Keeper of the Code: One in charge of maintaining the laws of pirates as passed down from the first pirate lord of Tornusia, as well as recording the law of Tornusia.

Khaos: The dark gods of disorder, opposition, and darkness within the world.

Lassin: A small region sitting on the border between Forn and Eland. Having a particular accent and way of pronunciation.

Lost Compass The: A compass crafted long ago, which points to its owners deepest desire.

Marienndet: Austinean sea goddess, patron of sailors and merchants.

Marcilona: Capital city of Castella.

Mazeem: First prophet chosen by Ahalak.

Mother The: See Doting Mother.

Ojin: A island nation of the east, and one of the most isolated. Known for its fiercely prideful warrior caste.

Pikshaff: A sausage made from goose livers, and sheep tongues, coming from Austinea.

Pilaas: Silver coin second highest denomination in Castella.

Pistoleros: A group of Castellian troops skilled in black powder weapons. Including being crack shots upon horseback as well as being able to reload on horseback.

Poppyhoney: A substance made by mixing a special tincture of poppy with special honey. It staves off infection and helps to numb a wounded area. It can also be given to children as a less bitter pain medication than Poppyspirts, and also less potent.

Poppyspirts: A fast–acting painkiller. A tincture of poppy and drab of alcohol in order to make it more palatable.

Poppywine: Similar to poppyspirits though often preferred by the nobles.

Red Thorns The: Claude's mercenary company.

Sahar: Sometimes known as the Crescent Empire, or the Crescent Kingdom. A land of deserts. Its people are often thought of as extremely devout followers of their god, of whom the Crescent moon is one of his holy symbols.

Sharraa: Holy book written by the prophet Mazeem containing not only the word of Ahalak but the story of Mazeem's life and his philosophies.

Salaazz: One of the Khaos gods. The patron of excess and all forbidden delights.

Seahemlock: A poisonous seaweed, if it makes breathing, and swallowing hard as well as making the joints stiffen and seize. In a high enough dose, it causes joints to calcify.

Seamstress The: One of the aspects of the Heavenly Lady, said to represent crafting and creativeness.

Seawidow: A crab–like creature which secretes a poisonous slime beneath its shell. Its poison can cause wounds to bleed continuously, as well as cause veins within the body to rot and decay swiftly.

Shield Maiden The: One of the Heavenly Lady's eight aspects representing, courage, strength, warriors, especially strength through trials and all hardships of life.

Silk Lands The: See Chuhuay.

Silver Quents: Currency in Forn, it takes one hundred¬–fifty Copper Penny's to equal one silver Quent.

Stromboze: The God of storms and pirates, and a dark mirror to Austinean sea goddess.

Tehraiq: A Kingdom in Sahar.

Throne of Tides: The seat of power of the lord of all pirates rules.

Tomblands The: See Apsu.

Tornusia: An independent island nation governed by pirates.

Twins of Madness The: An alternate name for the Khaos gods of magic, fate, lies, and trickery.

Wanderer The: Alternate name for the eighth aspect of the Heavenly Lady. See also Guest The.

Wine Parlors: Establishments in Forn which cater to the upper echelons. They specialize in high–class high price imported liquors and are often staffed by well–trained cooks.

Meet the Author

J. P McMahon lives in sunny southern California, Riverside to be specific. When he's not making up stories he spends time with friends, family and his dog. In addition to a love of writing he has a love for things nerdy, and heavy metal.

Comming Soon

Cyrus & Kalic Oathtaker

The Adventures of Flint & Steel Tides of Betrayal

Extra

Sample

The Adventures of Flint & Steel

Tides of Betrayal

Franchesca parried the oncoming blow and took a single step back to adjust her footing. A gust blew her wavy raven locks, and her keen stormy blue eyes studied Claude for a clue to his next move. Once properly adjusted, she took two quick steps forward. Steel rang against steel as she took step after step, and made attack after attack. She'd made great leaps in her swordsmanship since Claude agreed to accompany her back to Tornusia. Even by her own admission, however, Franchesca tended to feel more comfortable using pistols rather than swords. She was nowhere near the talent with a blade Claude or Simone was. Claude told her she was proving quite a worthy opponent with a blade. That was his way- reassuring, gentle and father like way of saying she still needed work. Such a thing when phrased like that grew her confidence. Claude was the father she'd never had; he was the father she always wanted. As she blocked and parried Claude's incoming strikes, she reflected on the drastic turn her life had taken those short years ago, though they seemed long. She'd only been seventeen when she fled her home and left her former life behind. Once she belonged to a powerful family in Forn, a distant relation to the queen, wealthy and with a good measure of power and influence. She gave that up, and many thought her crazy for such a thing. Claude did not; he knew why she left such supposed comforts behind. It was not comfort to live continually bowing to the whims and desires of others. She deserted her former life, of lace and social confinements, for freedom. It sounded so silly when placed into one single word. Freedom, It sounded ridiculous, but it wasn't. Franchesca wanted a chance to live her own life, to make her own decisions. She wanted to think for herself; she wanted something beyond what the weight of her birth name afforded her—indeed she wanted to succeed on her own. Most importantly

Franchesca left so that she could live and love with the person she'd fallen in love with. Simone, her beautiful and wonderful Simone.

   Her father and mother forbade her from seeing, or even so much as speaking to Simone, once Franchesca admitted her feelings, and once they realized Simone had hardly so much as a piece of clothing to her name, and the fact she was a woman, It appeared it would not be fitting, or proper. They feared the scandal and thus were content to tell their daughter that for the good of her family, she must ignore her feelings, even if it meant being unhappy and empty for the rest of her life. They truly expected her to obey and live in such a hollow, sorrowful state. That moment made her realize her parents did not truly expect her to be happy, or indeed live a life with her name. Those events only proved to her that she pawn in her parents' games. She was a tool of leverage, part of a business contract. It was a life Franchesca didn't want, so she fled, the very night they'd told her never to see Simone again.

   She left the money of her family. She left the titles, the lands, the gowns, and comfort and fled with Simone. By luck, or perhaps by fate, her friendship with Syandro De Madonia, who had at one time been a suitor, and who was now a good friend of hers, agreed to help Simone and herself to sail hidden away in the ship bound for Castella. The beginning of that journey had been uncomfortable. There'd been many moments in the last six years that had been uncomfortable. They'd come under attack by the former lord of Tornusia, Konrad The Mad Dog Kursz. Franchesca herself had also battled against a contender for the Throne of Tides by the name of Saaladan. A man she found most vile and disgusting. She killed him in a duel when it appeared that Franchesca would receive more votes than him. He'd challenged her to a duel to save face and make his own ascension that much quicker. His plan failed when Franchesca caved his skull in with an iron cannonball. Still, despite the blood, the death and the difficulties that she'd overcome, it hadn't been all bad. After, all she was with Simone, and the two of them were perfect for one another. They both made many loyal friends, many who journeyed with them to Tornusia from when she and Simone worked the docks while in Castella. They'd made many more when they sailed in their hunt for Konrad. Six years,

485

Franchesca thought as she blocked the next strike and stepped forward, elbowing Claude's stomach before pulling out an unloaded pistol. She pulled the trigger and let the hammer strike the empty pan. There came a *click* as the metal struck and she smiled.

"I win again."

"You live again," Claude corrected "best not to think of fights as games. They're not always going to be simple, bare-knuckle wrestling contests." Claude smiled as he sheathed his sword and enveloped her in a great crushing hug.

"You certainly do me proud. If I'm going to lose to anyone I'm glad it's you." He grinned before releasing her.

"My apologies highness, I should have asked your permission before becoming so familiar," Claude said as he stepped back and gave a formal court bow.

"Don't start with me." Franchesca grinned as she gave Claude a teasing push of the shoulder. "I hope you'll be there today when Simone and I hold court." Franchesca sighed as she tucked her empty pistol back into its leather holster.

"Of course, if you truly wish me to, I shall do as asked," Claude replied with a slight bow of his head.

Franchesca nodded, as Claude knew she would. He was one of her most trusted advisers, more than that he was her most faithful friend. Claude knew Franchesca even better than she knew herself, at times. She could count on Claude to always tell her the truth, even if that truth might hurt. He might use words which stung less, but even if the truth of his words pained her, he would soothe away the hurt with a smile, a hug and an apology, which always made her feel better.

"Will Syandro be there? I have noticed the last few times court has been held he's been absent." Claude inquired. Franchesca simply sighed and shrugged.

"I can't place my finger on it, but something seems odd about him recently." Claude confessed quietly. Franchesca put her tattooed arm through the blue sleeve of her weathered captains' coat and shrugged into it until it rested comfortably upon her slender shoulders. She did her best to ignore what Claude said, Syandro was a close friend after all. At one time she thought of marrying him, she didn't like—didn't want to think ill of him. He had changed, they all had in one regard or another. Still, it made her uncomfortable to think that Syandro might have changed for the worst.

"Franchesca..." Claude spoke again. She paused and reluctantly met his gaze. Claude walked in front of her and looked into her eyes.

"You know what I'm speaking of." Claude told her softly before placing a gentle hand upon her shoulder.

"He's grown arrogant, and foppish, though admittedly he's always had a streak of arrogance within him, as do we all." Claude told her gently. He was trying to ease her into the worst of his observations, as he'd always done. Claude was always sweet, gentle and caring, ever the guardian looking out for her in every way that he could.

"I don't think you should trust him as much as you do." Claude's words hung between them for a long silent moment.

Follow Me On Social Media

Come visit my very own little slice of the internet at my webise:
https://jpmcmahonwrites.wordpress.com/

Follow my adventures on, Instagram:
https://www.instagram.com/jpmcmahon1188

If you liked the book, please consider leaving a review it would really help me out.

I look Forward to hearing from you.